**Maureen & Edward Burns**

Married 1933

Dublin

| | |
|---|---|
| **Daughter & Son-in-Law**<br>Pamela & Sir Clive Mornington Hunt | **Daughter & Son-in-Law**<br>Iris & Archie Hartley |
| Married 1956 | Married 1957 |
| Paris | Co. Sligo, Ireland |
| **Son & Daughter-in-Law**<br>Crispin and Adaline | **Son**<br>Mark |
| Married 1978 | Died in infancy |
| Paris – Dublin | Paris |
| **Daughter**<br>Kate | |
| Born 1980 | |
| Dublin – London – Co. Sligo, Ireland | |

# Secrets
# We Keep

FAITH lives in the west of Ireland with her
husband, four children and two very fussy
cats. She has an Hons Degree in English
Literature and Psychology, has worked
as a fashion model and in the intellectual
disability and mental health sector.

Also by Faith Hogan

*My Husband's Wives*
*The Girl I Used to Know*

# Secrets We Keep

# faith hogan

First published in 2017 by Aria, an imprint of Head of Zeus Ltd

This edition first published in 2018 by Aria

9 7 5 3 1 2 4 6 8

A catalogue record for this book is available from
the British Library.

ISBN (TPBO ): 9781788542043
ISBN (E): 9781784977184

Typeset by Divaddict Publishing Solutions Ltd.

Printed and bound in Great Britain by
CPI Group (UK) Ltd, Croydon CR0 4YY

Head of Zeus Ltd
First Floor East
5–8 Hardwick Street
London ECIR 4RG

WWW.HEADOFZEUS.COM

*This book is dedicated to you, James Hogan – always.*
*It turns out, 'what if?' is even better than we could*
*have ever wished for.*

# Prologue
## Dublin – 1988

It was Kate's most vivid memory from childhood, maybe her happiest. Her father, coming home, rain on his coat, the smell of cold from him, and in a small box he left by the fire, a dog already named: Patch. 'For you,' he said and she ran to look inside.

In the background, she could hear her mother's voice, low and gin-tainted: 'It is nowhere for a dog.' Kate did not care. Her very own puppy, a black and brown sheepdog. 'He's too big for the city,' the words were whispered on the far side of the kitchen. Kate stroked his shivering woolly-haired coat and brown eyes stared vulnerable and watery at her. His nose was wet, his tongue was soft and warm against her face. For a moment, Kate was oblivious to the conversation at her back. 'Typical, you just never think, Crispin, that's what's got us into the mess we're in. Thanks to your gambling, we can hardly afford food for the table, and you bring home every waif and stray you come across.' Her red lips turned down and Kate often thought how lovely her mother would be if only they turned up instead.

'Adaline, please. Not now.' Her father stood wearily at the table, Kate heard him unscrew the gin that sat there. 'What's done is done. I've brought you here, to this house, away from the debt collectors, let me be.'

'Yes, this house,' Adaline's words were spiteful jabs, 'living off your grandmother, even your own family don't want to know us now.' She sipped her gin noiselessly, she wore her bitterness close to her, malice spiked every interaction. 'You're a bad lot, that's what they produced; however they managed it between them.'

The smell of damp and faded wallpaper, ornaments her mother wouldn't choose and a pervading silence that both muffled and incised at once, this was Kate's childhood. They lived in St Kiernan's, a faded Georgian pile on the wrong side of Dublin city; it was all they had. Bequeathed in a long forgotten will that the great-grandmother they didn't know had written. She had bypassed her daughters, Pamela and Iris – perhaps she knew that he'd need it more than them; she left the lot to her only grandchild, Crispin. They moved, Kate and her parents, to St Kiernan's when she was five. It was for the best: they were on the brink of divorce and financial ruin. They hoped Dublin was far enough away from where her father's gambling debts might find them. It was not far enough to mend the damage done. Her home was silent, the time for words had passed, and mostly, apart from that final night, with the dog her new companion, she spent her time alone. An only child. A lonely child. At the time, they thought it for the best. 'Not in front of the child,' her mother said more often than anything. 'Kate, go to your room.'

She held the puppy close as she padded up the stairs, the

world better now than it was before. Beneath her, the sounds of their voices, vicious and low, rose as she ascended each step, until she closed the door of her room. They argued for hours, but the thick Georgian walls drowned them out so Kate did not hear their final words. Instead, she snuggled her face close to the soft coat in her hands and felt the comforting warmth of him in her arms. This was a night she'd remember for many years – the arrival of that little dog gave her something to love that would love her in return, unconditionally.

It was a starless night, the night her father left them. Before he went, he kissed her on her nose. She remembered that still, how it felt, warm and soft and light. She remembered the sweetened scent of brandy and green Irish tweed, as he stayed before her eyes for just one second. Perhaps he knew this was goodbye forever. There had never been a bond, not really. Not the way you expect with your father. Perhaps that's why she remembered him leaving so vividly, it was because he kissed her goodbye and it was something he'd never done before or since. He didn't kiss her mother. She slammed the door behind him and volleyed up the thick-carpeted steps of the house on Parnell Square. A second door slammed and Kate watched her father get into a Dublin cab in the street far below from the silent house.

# I

## Iris, 1956

It was a sunny spring morning in 1956 when their worlds would take an unexpected turn. Iris was making her way down O'Connell Street to buy a pound of imported coffee from Bewley's for the guesthouse. The city was heaving with its own self-conscious weight and, occasionally, Iris caught a glimpse of her purposeful movement in the shop windows. She was a young woman, tall and well-proportioned, her auburn hair caught flecks of sunshine in its glossy length, so its shine was more than arresting against her ivory skin. She cut a striking figure in her powder blue skirt and the matching coat Mrs Muldoon had made for her Christmas gift. Black fur, taken from a pelt long forgotten in the attic of St Kiernan's, hugged her neck. Warm and soft, it collared the simple wool coat. She felt like a movie star and perhaps there was a passing resemblance to a precocious Lauren Bacall.

It seemed that with each passing day, the grey of Dublin was fading from sight. Fast receding was the importance of the war. 'If Dublin were not bombed it was only because it was hardly worth the effort,' her mother often said. It was still a mixed honour to have a father who died for the King of England. He had not returned from the war. He died a hero, in Sicily, which was meant to be something for them all to hold onto. The new Dublin, the city of this bright morning, was one of showbands, awkward liberals and pulpits vying for domination. It was a place of opportunity and a growing optimism that there must surely be good times ahead.

Iris stopped for a moment at Cleary's, examining the latest styles that were far beyond the few shillings her mother gave her each week for her work in the guesthouse. She couldn't stand for long, but it was hard to pull herself away. The shop fascinated her with the constant stream of people milling through its doors. Cleary's was the countryman's store. They came from all over Ireland to shop here. It had a reputation for quality and that did not compromise the style she admired in its huge gleaming windows.

Overhead, the clock ticked unapologetically towards lunch. Iris turned away quickly only to be bowled over by a young man with piercing blue eyes. Even as she fell backwards, she found it hard to wrestle her attention from their depths. She landed in an undignified heap on the path; her abuser quickly stood and held a hand out to help her straighten herself.

'Forgive me, it's not every day I fall for a good-looking girl so literally.' His eyes danced and it seemed to Iris they animated his whole character.

'You should be looking where you're going; you're not on a rugby pitch now,' Iris said crossly as she tried to unhook her coat from the man's jacket. Indignity made her defensive. Somehow, they were stuck together by virtue of one loose hook and a flapping grey lapel on the sports jacket the man wore.

'I'm so sorry,' the young man said, his accent slightly clipped. 'I didn't see you, we were rushing to...' His long tapered hands hovered over the hook for a moment. 'Here, let me.' His fingers slid gently across the hook, unfastened it with an experienced slip.

When Iris looked up into his face, she thought she never saw eyes that held so much danger in their depths. Suddenly her temper subsided, overwhelmed by something new, something she'd never felt before. She felt her cheeks redden and stepped back from the man as quickly as she could.

'Oh, it's...' Iris did not finish her sentence because, when she looked to his side, there stood Sir Clive Mornington-Hunt, surly and sour and condescending. 'It's okay, I'm fine.' She shook out her skirt, picked up her purse from the path. 'It's my fault, I wasn't looking. Sir Clive,' she saluted him.

'Au contraire, it was my fault, entirely.' The man held out his hand, his voice more confident now they had locked eyes. 'William Keynes, at your service.' He clicked his heels and bowed elegantly and then looked to his companion. 'Are you going to introduce us, Clive?'

'Of course, this is Pamela's sister,' Clive looked away and, for a moment, Iris wondered if he knew her name. He had been staying in room five at St Kiernan's, her mother's guesthouse on Parnell Square, for weeks now, but he had never once made conversation with her beyond his requests in terms of his accommodation.

'I'm Iris Burns,' she felt bold saying it and holding out her hand, but when William kissed the back of her glove, she felt giddy with a kind of excitement that she thought only happened in books from the library.

'Enchanted, I'm sure.' He looked deep into her eyes, seemed to move indecently close to her and said, 'I can see why Clive is so fond of your sister, if she's anything like you...'

'Oh, I'm afraid we're not alike, Pamela is so much more...'

'I don't believe it, not a word of it; she couldn't be lovelier than you.'

'In the name of all that's decent, Willie, can't you see, she's just a child.' Clive sounded petulant, as though he wanted to be somewhere else, and Iris suspected anywhere else would do. 'Come on, we have to make it back to Wynn's Hotel in less than an hour.'

'Ah, well. Duty calls, Miss Burns.' William did a little bow, and somehow it seemed to suit him, as though only someone as handsome and charming as William Keynes could get away with it. 'I have no doubt we will meet again, Miss Burns, and I will look forward to it.'

And so Iris made her way to Bewley's; her imagination filled with thoughts of William Keynes and no real expectations beyond maybe dipping into her five shillings for a Dracula ice cream on the way home.

*

Iris's mother described the trade as 'mainly commercial'. St Kiernan's, a grand Georgian red-brick had belonged to an aunt of her mother's, it was too large to be a family home and Mrs Burns had turned it into a respectable guesthouse while her husband had gone off to save them all from Hitler. It was true, their little guesthouse was home to a handful of 'permanents' – a few retired professionals who wanted to live out their days in domestic comfort without having to take on the running of a house alone. For as long as Iris could remember, Miss Peabody and Miss Chester had shared the large ground floor bedroom, facing onto Parnell Square. The two women were treated like elderly aunts. They had become part of an extended, disjointed family that shared all of the major events in the Burns family calendar. Mostly it was down to Iris to look after the permanents. Her older, more glamorous sister Pamela was front of house, booking in and dealing with 'the commercials'. What Maureen Burns wanted more than anything was a good husband for Pamela. Not just any of the weekly commercials, but Maureen had her heart set on a professional man, a doctor or a solicitor perhaps. When Sir Clive Mornington-Hunt booked in, neither Maureen nor Pamela could believe their luck.

When Iris caught a glimpse of Sir Clive, she couldn't quite believe Pamela was setting her cap at him. The second son of the Earl of Mayo, he was hardly five foot two and his words stuttered from him in a fury of bashful smiles and spitting consonants. The only respite seemed to be when he was engaged in discussing the finer points of rugby or the state of Europe and how things might be remedied. Unbelievably, it seemed Pamela was smitten. Maybe not as she had been by the handsome English medical rep who'd brought her to the cinema four times last year. He had made her smile for weeks after, but then cry like her heart might break. Iris heard her sob in the little single bed opposite her own. Iris had a feeling Clive would never make Pamela cry; she had a feeling he'd never make her smile in the same way the medical rep had either. Clive was enchanted immediately, most men were. Quite apart from Pamela's silver-blonde long hair, she was blessed with eyes as bright as the Pacific Ocean and skin so smooth a baby might be envious. She managed to be demure and witty, all at once. Their mother had long ago drilled into both girls the importance of being a lady first and everything else long after.

Before very long, Clive was taking Pamela to all the major events in the city of interest to the great, the good and the seriously connected. 'We'll have an announcement very soon,' her mother whispered one morning as she double-checked the dining room was set out perfectly. They announced their engagement at Christmas. Now, Pamela was furiously planning a spring wedding in Clive's family seat in Mayo. Iris found herself promoted to the front of house; the hostess role that Pamela had once filled. Her mother was in no rush to find her a husband, she was after all not yet twenty, compared to Pamela's twenty-two. They secured a girl to come in each day to look after the permanents, tend the fires and take on some of the heavier tasks that had once been Iris's domain. And so it was that Iris found herself serving breakfast one early morning to William Keynes. She had thought about him often, since that day on O'Connell Street. Once or twice, she'd asked Pamela about him; her sister supplied information sparingly. 'Clive says he's bad news, really, Iris, you don't want to waste your time thinking about him.'

'I'm certainly not thinking about him or anyone else for that matter,' Iris snapped.

'Good, because you could do much better than the likes of Willie Keynes. Clive says that he's from bad stock and you know what mother says.'

'The apple doesn't fall far from the tree?' Iris shook her head. It was typical of Clive to think that just because William was not a chinless pudding like himself, he must be trouble. She would put him from her mind. After all, they had only met that once and it was unlikely he'd thought of

6

her since. An emergency at the embassy changed that, when Willie Keynes could not catch his usual tram home, Clive booked him in to St Kiernan's late one night.

Iris's hand shook as she poured his tea. She only realized how nervous he made her when she returned to the kitchen with a hot breakfast for Miss Chester.

'You need to be minding your business,' the old lady said as she prodded her poached egg meaningfully when Iris laid the plate before her. Iris wondered if old Miss Chester's heart had ever flipped over because a young man was nearby.

'Don't be minding her; sure can't we all be a bit forgetful now and then.' It seemed to Iris that William stood unnervingly close to her, but somehow it wasn't unpleasant. He liked her, she just knew it. She felt him watch her as she made her way around the tables earlier and she caught his eye too often not to know he felt the same. 'Come on, we should make plans for a date,' he said as he was leaving. It was the first time they were alone and Iris felt intoxicated by the challenge in his eyes.

'Oh, my mother would never let me go on a date, I'm much too...' Immediately, Iris regretted the words falling from her lips. At nineteen, other girls her age were getting married, but more often these days her mother spoke as though Iris would be staying put. Perhaps Maureen thought she'd never find another Earl or maybe that Iris would one day care for her as she had for the permanents.

'Well, then, we better not let her know, I suppose.' He put a finger to her lip and Iris thought she might explode with excitement. 'What time is bedtime here?'

'I...' The hall was empty apart from themselves. Even still, just talking to William felt illicit, never mind that he thought she might sneak out to meet him.

'Say, ten o'clock? I'll meet you at the entrance to the square?' He winked at her as he made his way out the door. 'Don't leave me waiting too long.' He was gone before she could set him straight.

Iris spent the morning floating through tasks that normally took half the time. Their conversation going over and back in her head. She couldn't possibly sneak out of the guesthouse without her mother knowing. Well, perhaps technically, she could. After all, her mother settled into her room just after eight. A decade of early mornings had set their routine in stone. The Burns household rose early and slept soundly.

She could not leave him standing in the square all night, could she? After all, he was a colleague of Sir Clive's. What would they think of her if she left him out in the cold for the night? She tossed every scenario over in her thoughts, but she knew, more than anything, she wanted to meet him.

By eight o'clock, she had made up her mind. She would go to the gate and tell him she couldn't possibly go on a date with him. She painted her lips in the ruby lipstick Pamela had cast aside in favour of a timid pink and changed into her best clothes; just because she wasn't going dancing, didn't mean she couldn't look her best. Creeping down each step, she cursed as they groaned in loud creeks beneath her stockinged feet, she didn't dare make a sound, so she hugged her shoes tight to her chest. She would be coy and evasive. Perhaps, he would fall madly in love with her and wait until her mother could be as thrilled for her as she was for Pamela.

'I'm freezing, but you were worth the wait,' William pulled her close before she could say a word. But then she knew, she had wanted to come, really, even if she told herself she wouldn't. He hadn't needed to convince her. Then they were stalking down O'Connell Street, his arm tight about her, his pace fast and words sparse. He smelled of tobacco and beer; it seemed to Iris the most sophisticated aroma. From his coat, there was the tang of aftershave, or perhaps, a perfume worn by some woman, brushed too close to him before they met. She matched his purposeful strides; feeling like they owned the city, youth and beauty and illicit love. He did not say much until they turned into the basement steps of a hotel she never noticed before somewhere well past Trinity.

'You're with me, right. If anyone asks your age, just say nothing.' He bent and kissed her full on the lips. It was strong and sweet and it felt to Iris like he might have sucked her soul from her. Her whole body emptied for a moment. When she floated back to ground, she just knew she was in love with William Keynes.

# 2

## Kate, Present

Sometimes crossroads appear in the last place you expect them. Kate Hunt knew, as the Atlantic winter air dug hungrily into her bones, that she was standing at one now. The beach was empty, save for an occasional reluctant dog walker; certainly, she was the only holidaymaker. Was she a holidaymaker? She was staying with her great-aunt Iris and her husband Archie in their quaint hotel as far away from her real life in London as it was possible to get. Even if it was only an hour by plane to the west of Ireland, Kate felt like she was in a different world. Iris was her only real family now, unless you counted her mother and, well, she and Adaline had never been close.

Ballytokeep did not get many tourists outside the summer months; none at all at the end of December. Kate booked the break on Christmas night. It was a whim, she needed to get away, to jump off the treadmill her life had become, just to breathe. Since they met at Pamela's funeral, Iris sent a Christmas card each year. Just a card. *'Hope you're well, thinking of you, love if you had time to pop across,'* it was the kind of thing people said. Probably, you never took them up, but Kate saw it as a sign, a lighthouse in a vast ocean – maybe a place, or people, to call her own. Alone in her London flat, it felt like the whole world was sharing the holidays without her. The city outside twinkled with festive cheer. She convinced herself for so long that it didn't matter. It was a time for drunks, rows and disappointments and, for almost a decade, she managed to ignore the silly cheerfulness around her. This year, she'd cracked open a bottle of champagne, a gift from work, had it made her maudlin? Rumour had it her boss, Lyndon Tansey, had just bought a winery in South Africa. He brought in a crate of white and red for their Christmas drinks and they'd all got nicely sozzled. Maybe, Kate thought that Christmas night, as she eyed the half-finished bottle of champagne, maybe that was what had made her feel restless, as though she was missing something. While other people were buying vineyards, she was wading through divorce papers for the rich and famous.

She booked it on a whim. Now, she was pleased she'd come here to this antiquated little place that was too big to be a village, too small to be a town. Ballytokeep, for all the desertion of the summer trade, was a place like no other she had ever been to. It was built on a stony hill, a picture postcard of gaudily painted shopfronts and houses looking down to where the powerful ocean swept up to the weathered promenade. The sea, with its rolling surf whispering slowly and determinedly up the golden sand, seemed to promise the cleaning rejuvenation she so badly craved. Far off in the distance, the towers of a Norman castle keep rose high into the skyline and Kate knew she would visit here again to sit beneath its stoic turret. She loved the little hotel; her room the only one with a guest, peeped out of the centre of the Victorian building. The view was spectacular, small blue and white fishing boats bobbed on the icy waves that beat against the old harbour.

In London they'd call Hartley's Guesthouse boutique, shabby-chic or maybe bohemian. If the place was a little faded, its chintz too threadbare to be fashionable, its varnishes dulled with age, it was no less charming for all of that. Here, it was what it was; there was no pretension about the Victorian building with all its original features and impressive views.

On New Year's Eve they stood looking out across the harbour, just the three of them and toasted the year ahead.

'To family,' Archie said and Kate knew she had done the right thing in coming here. The night air was fresh, it seemed that every lighthouse in the distance might wink across the blue-black ocean waves. If Kate could wish for anything, it was that she could have these people close forever.

Iris and Archie were genuinely delighted to have someone to fuss over in the off-peak season, even more so because it was Kate. They made sure there was a dancing fire in the cast-iron grate for her every day and a hefty basket of turf that never seemed to empty. They offered hearty full Irish breakfasts and seemed relieved when she told them she was happy to muddle along with them and she did not want them going to any trouble. Even so, the aroma of freshly baked scones, a medley of fruit, cinnamon and malt seemed to waft through the hotel every day. Iris had a light touch and her warm scones tasted like heaven when Kate was ravenous after the fresh sea air.

'We can't have you fading away with all that walking you're doing, can we?' Iris said as she dropped a laden tray on the writing desk that filled the bay window. Here, they were facing the long promenade that kept the sea mostly at bay.

'There's no danger of that with you and uncle Archie about.' Kate knew she looked gaunt and pale compared to the locals in Ballytokeep. She'd spent a decade in London, working, sleeping, and going through the motions: lonely. She could admit that here. In London, surrounded by people she knew, surrounded by millions of people and possibilities, she was lonely. Here, she walked across empty beaches with only the curlews for company and she was quite content. It was time for her to move on. The only problem was, Kate was not certain there was anywhere for her to move on to. 'I'll go back to London refreshed with the sea air and two stones heavier thanks to your breakfasts and baking, Aunt Iris.'

'You should think about coming here in the summertime, it really is quite beautiful.' Iris's eyes were wistful as she looked out at the promenade. There was a high tide and it energized Kate, as though it vibrated within some part of her she never knew existed before.

'Oh, I don't know, I like having it all to myself. I'm not sure I want to share it with crowds of noisy holidaymakers and ice-cream vans and loud music blaring from every pub and shop along the promenade.' Part of her didn't want to impose, but deep down she was longing to return.

'I think you'd love it. Actually, I think it would do you the world of good. The tourists we get here aren't the kind you get in your usual Brighton or Bangor. Most of our visitors have been coming here for years, some first came with their parents.'

'Well, I can certainly see why they come back.' Kate leant forward to give the little fire a shake with the thin poker that looked as old, if not older, than Archie. The turf moved and fell into a shaky pyramid with a satisfying hail of sparks and peaty smoke before she covered it over with another layer of fuel.

'Oh, Ballytokeep is like that. People always come back – that's the one's that actually leave.'

'How do you mean?' Kate found it hard to keep the smile from her voice, she liked talking to Iris, even about mundane things. It felt like she was catching up on conversations that should have filled her childhood. Her great-aunt was a queer old thing, but there was genuine warmth to her mixed with a familiar emptiness that Kate couldn't have missed even if she tried.

'Well, look at me. I came here, just like you. I was meant to wait for a few weeks. I was making plans, just back from Paris and my life before me, who knows where I'd have ended up? And then I met Archie and well...'

'The rest is history?'

'Don't say it like that, you make me feel old.' Iris smiled and then straightened the little posy of snowdrops picked earlier in the day. 'But, I suppose that's what it is now, history.' She sighed and, for a moment, a terrible silence descended on the room, as though the very fabric of the place was waiting for her to admit something. 'It's all a long time ago now.' She looked at Kate, just for a moment, as though confirming that she was there and then she said goodnight.

There was no sign of Iris the following morning. Perhaps it was all too much for them; this place was a huge responsibility for anyone. She guessed they closed for the winter months as much to catch breath as to conserve profit. The Hartleys were in their seventies, if not their eighties and this was a big place to keep up and running.

'Oh, in the summertime, we couldn't do it on our own.
We get help in. But, you dear, you're no bother to keep. It's a
treat to have you here, you're family,' Archie assured her the
next day. 'You'll have to make your way over to the castle
before you leave. Well, I suppose, you probably wouldn't call
it a castle now, it's an old keep – almost a thousand years old.
It really is very beautiful.'

'Of course, I've seen it, from my room and when I'm
walking along the beach. I thought maybe when the sun was
shining…'

'We had a bathhouse there on the purple rocks. Well, my
brother had at any rate, for a while. Robert was very popular
with the girls, maybe too much so in the end.' His eyes
stretched their gaze into the distance and she had a feeling
that he was very far away. 'Sometimes, if you're lucky, the
porpoises will come right up. Of course, it's all down to tides
and weather and heaven knows how many other factors, but
even without those scallywags, it's worth a visit.'

'A bathhouse?'

'Of course, you probably wouldn't get too many of them
in London.' When he smiled his eyes creased even further,
but Kate could see he must have been very handsome when
he was young. Even now, he stood tall and straight and his
features had a distinct masculinity to them that made you
think of dashing Hollywood leading men who might have
been around when he was in his prime. 'Bathhouses, like the
one here, were all the go at one stage. Apparently, they're
making a bit of a comeback now. It's the seaweed, you see.
It's full of all sorts of minerals and what we believed years
ago was that it could cure anything from TB to gout and
people came from miles around to bathe in it.'

'In a pool?'

'Oh, dear no. Nothing as fancy as what you'd have now, with your spa this and your therma that. No, the seaweed was harvested and we would fill copper baths with it mixed with hot seawater. You could move over and back between the bath and a steam press. It took out all the impurities and put back every vitamin you could name.' He smiled at her. 'Sounds a bit daft now, but we sweated out the bad and absorbed the good – they're doing it again down in Strandhill. It's running all the year through, with people coming from miles around.' He shook his head. 'Funny, when you get to my age, the number of things that go out of fashion only to come back again.'

'I've heard of the purple rock, but I just thought it was the name of the amusement arcade?' It was an unsightly place, boarded up now; Kate wondered if it would open for the summer months.

'Oh, that place. No, they called *that* after the purple rock – and even that's not going to be around soon, it's been bought by a developer, making it into fancy flats, or whatever they're called these days.' Resignation gripped Archie's eyes in a way that only comes with age. 'Probably do the same to this place, when we're gone.'

'No, they'd never knock down somewhere so beautiful.' Kate tried to soothe. 'And you're not *going* anywhere for a long time.'

'Wouldn't they? They went mad to get their hands on the bathhouse and it's a little gem.'

'Is it still running?' Kate would have loved a real seaweed bath, now she'd heard about them. 'The bathhouse?'

'I'm sorry to say, it hasn't been properly run in sixty years. We took it over for a while, but there comes a time when you know what you're able for. Pity though, we closed the doors on it at the end of the season, so everything in it is just as Robert planned it.' Archie began to clear some imagined crumbs from the table. 'He died. Tragically, young. I'm afraid that the heart went out of the both of us at that stage.' Archie shook his head sadly. 'Will I make you a nice fresh pot of that tea now?' he said, placing his time-worn hands on the pot and finding it still warm.

'Ah no thanks, Archie, like I said to Aunt Iris, you'll be responsible for ruining my figure if I don't call a halt somewhere.'

*

It was nine o'clock before Kate set off walking towards the keep. It was hard to believe she had spent one precious week here already. Lyndon Tansey told her to take as long as she needed. Maybe he knew, maybe they all knew. Maybe everything she bottled up for the last decade had been blatantly obvious to the people around her while she remained blind to it. She had her heart broken long enough ago for her to have moved on. The public humiliation was harder to shake. Bad enough to be jilted at the last minute. It seemed to Kate that being reminded of it each time her ex-fiancé's love life featured in the celebrity gossip columns made it into an ongoing nightmare from which there was no escape. Other people unfriended their exes on Facebook and cut their photos in half. That was not so easy when your ex was in the national newspaper every other week.

'The important thing is that you come back safe and sound, old girl,' Lyndon had said, patting her hand with sincerity. He had taken the helm of the law firm when he was almost fifty. He was old enough to have learned from the mistakes of others and he knew when someone was worth holding onto. Kate had raked in millions over the last decade for the practice. She had represented the spouses of rock stars, royalty and the ridiculously rich and managed to pull hefty and healthy settlements every time. People knew her in the divorce courts by reputation, and if they did not fear her exactly, they advised their clients that she was particularly adept in aspects of family law.

She looked around her now. This place with its vastness and intimacy cuckolded into the cold of the climate mixed with the warmth of the people, it was just what she needed. It was a five-mile round trip to the bathhouse and the keep, which would bring her along a track kept clean by a scurrilous pack of sheep and goats. She drank in the clean air greedily; the only sound here was the crashing of water to her right and the call of the gulls across the empty strand to her left. She walked slowly, surveying from her high middle ground the austere beauty of the place at this time of year. She stopped and sat on a rock that seemed to have moulded into her shape long before she ever knew she would be coming here. She knew now that she would come here again, it was as sure as the air she breathed. Perhaps this was the first step on that crossroads.

In the distance, she watched as a middle-aged woman made her way across the strand. Even from here, she recognized her. She saw her many times walk through the town, always with a shopping bag in her hand, sometimes wheeling one behind her. Today, she was making her way energetically with a yapping dog in her wake. Her face was puce despite the cold that must surely be biting into her. She rounded towards the ridge where Kate sat and stopped short as she neared her, surprised to see anyone out on such a cold day.

'Hi.' Kate did her best to smile, remembering that she was not in London now. It was okay to make eye contact; people here wanted you to talk to them.

'Hi yourself.' The woman panted and seemed to take the greeting as an invitation to join Kate on her rock. 'I'm wrecked,' she said and she plopped her considerable weight down awkwardly. 'Hot flushes,' she said and she fanned herself with gloved hands. 'Phew, who knew, hah?'

'Your dog doesn't seem to mind,' Kate watched as the little black and white terrier skipped out after the tide and then scudded back towards them as each new wave arrived. He was yapping happily, enjoying the chase of something he'd never catch.

'Ah, Barry. Yes, I got him from the rescue – best thing I ever did. I wanted one for years, but you know, you need to put the time into a dog and my Duncan is allergic to anything with a coat, so...' the woman smiled enigmatically as if his discomfort might actually please her in some odd way. The dog, as though he heard his mistress, came running across the beach towards them, digging up sand as he came.

'You're a super little fella,' Kate said and she rubbed his head affectionately as Barry licked her fingers and danced a greeting frenzy up around them.

'You're lucky, he likes you,' the woman said, reaching out to the little dog. 'Not everyone he takes to, he's nipped my Duncan more than once when he's not expecting it. He had to have a tetanus jab, the works, didn't he Barry?' She nuzzled into the dog's neck. 'You're such a good boy.' She looked across at Kate. 'You can't beat a terrier to judge character, no fooling our Barry.'

'No, I suppose not,' Kate said, thinking of the unfortunate allergic husband upon whom he'd been foisted.

She turned to study Kate now. 'You're not from around here?'

'No. I'm just... taking a little break.'

'Funny time of the year for it.' She dug into her rain jacket, pulled out a pack of mints, flipped the lid in a practised move and popped two on her hand then offered some to Kate. 'Smoking, I figured the mints were better than the fags.' The words were philosophical. 'I'm Rita, by the way. Rita Delaney.' She stuck out a short-fingered chubby hand.

'Kate Hunt.' Kate shook hands with a lot more warmth than she used when she was in London. 'I've seen you about,' she nodded back towards Ballytokeep.

'Well, you would, wouldn't you?' Rita looked out towards the ocean. 'I'm always knocking about the town, retired, you see. Last year. It's why I got Barry,' she nodded towards the terrier. She blew out, as though that somehow explained everything in life. 'It's a nice spot here, isn't it? I mean, you could sit here for the day with your thoughts,' she looked at Kate, 'not that too much thinking is good for you.' There was the hint of warning in her voice, as though she was scolding a child.

'I like it. It makes a change. Normally I don't get much time to think.' Kate smiled; this woman was easy to talk to.

'London?'

'How did you guess?' Her accent gave her away straight off. In London, they all thought she was Irish, here they thought she was English. The truth was she was a bit of both.

'It's a gift.' They both laughed. They sat for a while:

strangers in companionable silence. 'It's a good place to lose yourself,' Rita's voice was hardly a whisper. 'If you need to.'

'Doesn't everyone at some point?'

'Does everyone? I don't know. I know that it's easy to lose your footing and feel that life is moving away from you.' Rita sighed. 'I think that's what I feel now I've retired.'

'Was it tough?'

'Two years.' She said it with the finality of death. 'Next June, it's two years.'

'Early days so.'

'You're trying to make me feel better.'

'Is that a bad thing?' Kate would love someone to come along and make her feel better.

'No, but I suppose it's that whole losing yourself thing. I need to get... something.' She looked out into the ocean, as though it might provide the answer. 'It feels like I've lost something and even if I can't have it back again, I'm sure there's something else out there for me to find.'

'That makes sense to me.'

'Yes, it does, doesn't it? It sounds simple too.' They both laughed at that.

'Come on.' Kate stood and shook the sand from her windcheater. 'I'm going to the old bathhouse; the walk will do us both good.'

'Right,' Rita called the little dog. He was playing at the water's edge and then ran obediently towards her. His coat was soaked and filled with sand, but his eyes shone bright with happiness at this unexpected excursion from their normal route.

\*

'I've never seen anything like it,' Kate said. It was her first thought as they turned down the cove and saw the bathhouse snuggled into the cliff face. It was a turreted, stocky grown-ups sandcastle. 'It could have been emptied from a child's bucket,' was her first reaction. It had been painted, white with a light blue trim once, then the waves and the spray had all but washed that away. It still sat proudly, if shabbily, on a huge flat rock, that upturned in a lip over the sea. It was a plate, large enough for any giant.

'Genesis Rock – it's a metamorphic rock, probably over a thousand million years old,' Rita said. 'Sorry, did I mention I taught geography and home economics, once upon a time.'

'No, but I probably should have guessed.'

'I don't remember the bathhouse even being open. I could imagine that I'd have spent all my days here if I had.' Rita looked at the washed white walls that reached high into the cliff face.

'Well, Archie said they ran it for a few years, but he didn't say when it shut.' This place probably held sadness for Archie, if his brother died here. Kate couldn't feel it. Instead, it made her feel energized, as though the sea was spraying something like an invitation deep into her lungs. It made her heart pound with an expectation she hadn't felt in years. Even the deserted castle keep that loomed up in grey stone at the tip of the headland seemed to carry a hopeful secret in its towers.

'It must have been lovely once. Even now, you can see.' Rita rested her hands on the thick window ledge, her nose pressed firmly to the cold glass of the windows. 'It looks like they just closed up one evening and never came back.'

Kate walked to the back of the bathhouse; it dug into the cliff face, as though the construction of one depended on the other. Alongside the building, a small narrow road clung to the cliff for a couple of hundred yards before it feathered off onto what counted as a main road in these parts. Far below, the waves lapped serenely against the stone. It was low tide now; Kate wondered how close the water actually came to the rock. 'I'd love to get a look inside.' Rita followed her round to the front of the bathhouse. They peered through a sea sprayed window for a few minutes. Inside, Kate could see there were tables and chairs, a small stove and an old-fashioned counter where once someone had taken orders for afternoon tea. 'It's a little café, wouldn't it be lovely if it was open for coffee?' Kate mused, it was so much more than just a bathhouse.

'I was thinking the same thing. Wonder if they left a key about.'

'Wishful thinking, I'm afraid.' Kate settled herself on one of the giant window ledges that ran along the front of the building. She could imagine this place in summer, flower planters leaden with colours, the sun reflecting off the white and blue of the rounded walls and the gleaming window glass casting sparks of sunlight across the ocean.

'Wishful thinking, is it?' Rita smiled, she held a key she'd found tucked deep in one of the huge cast-iron planters standing sentry at the arched front door. The key was sturdy, blackened and ancient. When Rita slipped it into the lock, it turned as if it had been waiting for them all this time. 'Oh, my...' It was as much as either of them could manage. 'Oh, my...' Rita uttered the words again.

'It's beautiful,' Kate said and she felt it as much as she saw it. The place had something. It was a real Edwardian tearoom. The cake stands on the counter stood dusty but still upright to attention, the china cups and saucers cobwebbed but delicate and lovely. 'It's such a shame. That it was just left, like this. It feels as if...'

'It's waiting for something or someone to come back for it?'

'Yes, maybe.' It was exactly what Kate thought. This place, it was like herself, and as she walked about the cast-iron tables, she had a strange feeling. It sent ripples through her. This was happiness; she knew it, remembered it from before. As the sea breeze dashed through the little room, so too it seemed to rush into her heart, breathing in something close to hope.

'I should probably be getting back.' Rita looked at her watch, but her expression said she would prefer to stay. 'Dinners to be cooked, husband to be fed and all that jazz.' She lingered for a moment, lightly grazing her fingers across one of the wicker chairs. 'It really is beautiful, such a shame.'

'Yes, such a shame,' Kate said absently.

'Perhaps I'll see you again,' Rita said as she handed the key to Kate. 'You will lock up properly, won't you.' She cast a reflective eye about the place.

'I live in London,' Kate said, 'I double-lock everything.' It was true, she lived in London, but now she was wondering, did she actually belong there anymore.

# 3

# Todd

Todd was not sure what the blonde-haired woman's name was, but she was out cold and it looked like they had had a good time. He was wasted; the big venues did that to him. It was as much a product of adrenalin as it was the booze. He needed one to get through the other, that was the truth of it. The other guys in the band figured it was age. They had all settled down years ago – not that it stopped them much. 'You should consider it,' Jeb had said late one night as they drank whiskey in another characterless bar, in another anonymous city. 'A wife keeps you fit and young, regular meals, early nights, healthy lifestyle for eight to ten months of the year – you can't put a price on that, mate.' Jeb had gone through several wives – they got younger each time – and, at last count, he had eight kids – Todd did not want to think about what Christmas was like in the drummer's household.

'Yeah, well, I'll take my chances,' he slapped Jeb's slightly wobbly middle. They'd started the Ace of Spades more than two decades ago. Back then they'd been too fired up on life to think about much past the next record. Then there had been no sagging bellies or scary wives. It was before a string of Grammies and the cover of *Rolling Stone*. They had been different people.

'That's relaxed muscle, that is,' Jeb had said; he was only half joking.

'Mate, that's been relaxed so long, it's comatose now.' Denny agreed with Jeb though; he married Meg over twenty years ago. They were a real couple, kids, fights, break-ups and make-ups.

Todd didn't see himself settling into that.

Now, he looked out at the white waves that drifted in and out rhythmically in the distance. Wondered for a moment if he should wake the girl up and ask her what city they were in. He had a feeling it was Atlantic City; it had to be. He'd been here before; when they were starting out. It was exciting then, different from London, unlike anywhere he'd ever been. The sea was light blue here, back in England, this time of year; he thought the sea was black. 'That's the drugs for you,' Denny had said wisely, though they both knew that Todd's drug of choice was whiskey; always had been; a man knew where he was with whiskey. Atlantic City meant they were at the halfway point. Two more weeks on the East Coast and then they took a break before heading out west. He looked back at the blonde again, slung his jacket over his shoulder; he needed coffee, strong coffee. Maybe she would take the hint and be gone before he got back.

The hotel was plush – 'best in the city', Denny had said. It was too fancy for Todd, but it was clean and he could have things as he wanted them and that was important. 'It was rock 'n' roll enough for Elvis when he stayed here, good enough for Aerosmith and the Foo Fighters,' Denny had shaken his head. The five-star restaurants would be fine by him.

Todd made his way out into the sunshine, cursed under his breath that he'd forgotten his shades – now that wasn't very rock 'n' roll. A little way away, he spotted a sign for Starbucks. A couple of years ago, it would have been enough to make his day, now of course, you could buy a cup of *Joe* at your local petrol station. What was the world coming to? It was a question Todd found himself asking more often these days. When he pushed the door open he was greeted by the smell of breakfast, only the heavy undertone of caffeine stopped him from heading back onto the street again.

He cast his eyes about the place first, it looked okay, ordered his coffee, took a corner pew. It'd be at least an hour before he was fully awake, ready for civilized conversation. In the meantime, he would nurse his hangover gently, to the sounds of some unheard of country singer, maybe pretend to read the local paper. The seediness of the city suited his mood perfectly. The glitzy nightlife cast a dark shadow on sunny days. This was a city where gambling was a religion and morality was long ago sacrificed at the altar of profit.

Todd caught a glimpse of his reflection in the plate glass window; he ducked his head down. He was unrecognizable from the publicity shots. Here, today, with his unshaven face, hair coloured too dark for his Belfast grey skin, he looked like a badly aging fifty-something-year-old. Claudia said it was the fags that wrecked his skin. Like he cared. The booze didn't help, but she knew better than to mention that. Anyway, he was in better shape than poor Dave. The Ace of Spades had started out as a five-piece. Todd, Dave, Jeb, Pete and Mike; they never replaced Dave when he overdosed. A thing like that – death – it should bring you closer. With them, it actually did the opposite. Now, whenever they sat in the same room, all they could see was the empty space.

Jeez, but he was maudlin today. He moved over on the bench seat an inch, better to avoid his depressing reflection in a mirror. Oh, yes, there was much to be said for Photoshop. Not that he was vain – he never considered himself vain – it was the suddenness of it all. One minute he was swanning about London with the world's hottest model, the next he was sitting in Starbucks feeling and looking old enough to be her father.

Claudia.

He fancied Claudia from the word go, problem was, like everything else, he wanted her most when he thought he couldn't have her. She made him work for it, and for a while, it had been worth the effort. They had fun. It was good while it lasted, but now, well it was a big world out there and Claudia wasn't getting any younger, was she? She was thirty on her last birthday; he threw her a big bash in her favourite fancy restaurant, all the usual faces turned up and then some, because they were London's golden couple. Everyone worth knowing had been there. Thirty – that was when, in Todd's experience, women started to get broody.

He sighed. He was glad of the row. Not when it happened. Not that he'd actually engineered it, well not much. A year ago, he would have done what he could to avoid a fight, but now? Well, if Claudia didn't ring him, it wasn't something that was going to keep him awake at night; it would be a relief more than anything.

Denny said all along that Claudia was too good for him. It annoyed him a little that as usual Denny was probably right. At least he could take the moral high ground and claim he was doing her a favour. Not that any of the guys would believe for a minute that Todd was putting Claudia, or anyone else, before himself. That was the thing about being the lead singer; it gave you an absolute right to be a selfish bastard. They expected nothing less of him.

He drank his coffee in brooding silence. Accepted a refill, knew all the caffeine in the world would do bugger all to change his mood.

Down from where he sat he could see the Atlantic City Boardwalk Hall. They had, if he remembered correctly, two more nights here: Sell-out gigs. Lucky guy. So why didn't he feel so lucky anymore?

'Pancakes, sir?' the waitress smiled, but Todd knew that it was all about the tips here, she didn't recognize him. Her nasal twang was New Jersey through and through.

'No, I'm good thanks,' he tried to sound American, but there was no covering his Belfast brogue. The breakfasts here looked good, everything about the place looked clean, but it was too early for food. Todd did not like to look at anything solid, not before noon. His mother would be dismayed; she always started her day with a decade of the rosary and a bowl of porridge. He wasn't sure which of them kept her on the best side of the daisies for almost seven decades and still fresh-faced when she'd succumbed in the end. He pulled out a ten-dollar bill, placed it under his cup and drew the leather jacket closer to his neck. Even with the startling sun, there was a cool nip in the air. The Yanks had some sense of humour when it came to weather; it was seven degrees in spite of the sunshine. At least in Belfast you knew where you were; it was rain or more rain. Todd made his way back to the hotel.

'So, you came back?' The blonde had not taken the hint;

she was still here, parading about in the complimentary bathrobe.

'It is my room. I thought you would be gone by now.' Blunt honesty was one of his greatest weapons in clearing out what he didn't want from the night before.

'It's Daniella by the way,' the blonde said; she looked older in the glaring sunlight. Older and harder than she looked when he was drunk. Was this what he was coming to? Pulling women who were almost as old as himself and bolshie too? 'I get the feeling you don't remember much?'

'If it was worth memorizing, I'd have managed.'

'You're a real piece of work, do you know that?'

'I try,' he said, taking out his cigarettes. Normally he didn't smoke in hotel rooms, he'd set off too many alarms, but he had a feeling the nicotine would do him good. He could feel a headache coming on, the fag hitting him straight made him a little dizzy.

'And tell me this, will you try to remember when I publish the interview you gave me last night and you cried like a baby about that girl you left standing at the altar all those years ago?'

'I said nothing of the sort.' The dizziness made him sway.

'Oh, yes. And Claudia Dey, I think what you said was Claudia Who?' When she smiled, he thought there was something oddly familiar about her, but he was too busy trying to catch his breath to focus much on it.

He backed away from her, fell into one of the designer chrome and leather sofas that liberally littered the suite. He pulled open his jacket; suddenly the room seemed too confining. It perched too high over the incessant waves, crashing white and frothy on the shore too many storeys below his penthouse room. The ceiling was moving towards him oppressively. The plate glass windows restraining him from real oxygen, his lungs felt like they were filling with something that might suffocate him. The blonde was looking at him, assessing him, she was speaking but he could not focus on her words. He watched as she moved towards him, then bent over him, as though examining him. She was taking his pulse, shouting now, running towards the phone. 'Oh my God,' he heard the blonde shout, 'he's having a heart attack.' There was nothing he could do. The world as he knew it was disappearing into a grey mirage, and when he closed his eyes, he began to feel like maybe it was all fading fast away from him.

# 4

## Iris, 1956

She would marry William Keynes. He had seduced her, it was the only way she could put it. Taken her, as she never dreamed it was possible to be with a man, and she was glad. She was a woman now. Afterwards, he pulled up his pants and roughly spit in the handbasin. He said they would have to leave the little room that had been theirs for almost five hours. She felt like she could stay here forever, although it was grubby and other people's clothes hung from hooks on the wall. She loved being in his arms. It was time to go back to serving breakfasts and settling accounts with travelling salesmen for another day. Already, her mother would be shuffling about her own room. She would be applying rouge to her sunken cheeks and pinning her pewter-coloured hair high, selecting clips carefully from the dish they rested in at night. She'd thought of her mother last night. Guilt, that was what had pushed her mother to the front of her mind. Mrs Burns expected more of her daughters than this. She had let her down, let them all down. But then, she reasoned, she couldn't help herself. The attraction to Willie Keynes had been too strong, she'd never felt anything like it in her life. Had Mrs Burns ever felt like this? Had she felt like this for Iris's father? Iris pushed the thoughts out as quickly as she could.

William was walking ahead of her as they rushed up O'Connell Street. The early morning traders beginning to open up their businesses mostly ignored them. She wondered if anyone would guess the change that had occurred overnight. He was silent now, walking fast towards the waiting day ahead. Occasionally, she would catch him up but he was preoccupied, she could tell.

'The embassy,' he told her the previous evening when he'd taken her to The Forty-Seven Club. The venue sounded rather glamorous. Inside, it was a seedy bar with tables laid out for cards and dice games. William was familiar with many of the people there. But as much as they welcomed him, they'd mostly ignored her. He'd squeezed his arm about her tighter. It loosened lazily when some of the more attractive women came over to talk to him. Iris was not sure quite what to do when he'd stood whispering with a tall redhead called Clarissa and caressed her back while she stood silently by. Perhaps he brought a different girl here every week, she'd thought, he was very handsome after all. Then she'd reminded herself that he had asked her here, not Clarissa. 'It's complete nepotism, of course. If you haven't got a family connection, you may as well forget about it. Clive is well in, obviously.' He'd shaken his head, three thin lines digging into his pale forehead. 'Not much good to me though, is it? I mean, he'll be heading off for Paris once he's married...'

'Paris?'

'Yes, lucky bugger. He is going to the consulate there, only a matter of time before he's appointed Ambassador. Why wouldn't he? His father owns half of Connaught?'

'Oh right.' Iris hadn't known that Pamela and Clive would be living in Paris. Had Pamela any idea that she would be leaving Dublin? She was quite sure it would come as news to her mother also. 'When do they leave?'

'Oh, it's not official yet, but I've seen how these things work. Clive will get married and then it will be announced like a wedding present, he has the posting. Honeymoon in Paris, isn't that romantic?' His voice had rasped and Iris had a feeling he smoked too many Players. 'There's them and then there's us, Iris,' he'd said and she hardly heard the words, they swept so quietly from his lips.

'Sure, there's more to life than the Embassy,' Iris had said lightly.

'Maybe there is if you come from a family that can support you, but a man who's going to have to support himself needs to make his way any way he can.'

'So, you'll be still trying to get a better post?'

'Every way I can, pet, every way I can.'

He bent down to kiss her at the steps of St Kiernan's. Iris pulled away quickly, anxious that they might be seen, she dreaded going in the front door. Her mother would have a conniption if she thought she was out all night with Willie Keynes. If she knew what had taken place she would probably drop stone dead on the cold floor.

Iris opened the door quietly and ran lightly up the three flights of stairs to her room in the eaves. For once, she was thankful that Pamela was in Mayo on wedding preparation duties.

As she was stepping out of her dress, she realized that

William had not arranged to meet again. She laughed then, sure, he would make another date with her soon. It had been the night of her young life. If perhaps it was a night that should not have happened, then she didn't realize that until much later.

It turned out to be longer than she had expected before she laid eyes on William Keynes again. She tried to find out where he was from Pamela and even from Clive, but either she wasn't direct enough, or they were being purposefully evasive. All she could glean was that he was busy with some new diplomatic business.

It took two months and a lot of worrying on her behalf, but it was inevitable they would meet at the wedding in Mayo.

The problem was she was late. Two months late, by the time it came to Pamela's wedding. Although she knew what that meant; she had no idea what it would really mean for all of them. She had to tell William, knew that was her only hope. She would meet William at the wedding. He would tell her where he had been. She would tell him that she was carrying his child and he would say that he loved her and they must marry immediately. At least, that was what she expected would happen.

\*

It seemed everyone they knew was invited to Pamela's wedding. All of the permanents travelled down from Dublin on the train with them. Her mother made a big affair of closing the guesthouse for three whole days.

Sir Clive's home was impressive and stately, and Iris had never actually seen anywhere quite so grand before. Her mother pronounced they did not go to town on the dusting front, but they were welcomed with the kind of warmth that her mother aspired to for the guesthouse. They all spoke like Sir Clive, as though they just stepped out of the House of Lords in London. Their biggest redeeming quality was a shared sense of humour and an easy-going approach to everyone they met. Iris figured that Sir Clive was probably the haughtiest of the bunch. Pamela corrected her swiftly if she ever hinted at that: 'He's just shy, Iris, you really should give him more of a chance.' But Iris had far greater worries than giving Clive a chance.

'I haven't seen William Keynes, so far.' She tried to make her voice sound offhand as she pinned up a lose tendril of Pamela's hair. It was two hours to the wedding. They were sitting in their finery in the large room that had become her sister's over the last few weeks. Their mother stood silently at the nearby window, perhaps contemplating the loss of her daughter. Iris knew that any sadness was diminished by a sense of relief and blessing at having married Pamela off so successfully, even if Clive was taking her sister to Paris. They'd announced it just before the wedding. Pamela looked beautiful; she wore a white gown that came all the way from London. Iris thought she looked like a real princess. 'Your father would be so proud,' her mother had sniffed. Of course, this was a society wedding and most society brides these days wore white dresses. Pamela would be the toast of Dublin when her photograph appeared in the Irish Press and Iris was delighted for her sister.

'Well, you can count your blessings on that score, can't you?' Pamela sounded suddenly cross.

'Oh look,' her mother said from across the room. 'Speak of the devil and he'll surely appear.'

'Really, Mother, not you as well,' Iris said. It wasn't like her mother to sound so cynical about anyone.

Her mother walked from the window. Iris took over her lookout position, her eyes fixed on William as he made his way jauntily towards the house. She waved, but perhaps he couldn't see her – probably because he just looked away, as though they had never met.

'It looks like Clive was right about him, all along.'

'What do you mean?' Iris turned quickly. There was something they weren't telling her and she suddenly had a feeling that it was not good news for her.

'You should tell her really. It cannot do any harm Iris knowing today. I mean, let the whole country talk about it in a week's time, but for today, it's only the family that need to know.' Maureen Burns placed a gentle hand on Pamela's shoulder.

'I should have mentioned it sooner, but Iris, it never seemed like the right time and then I had a feeling that you were a little soft on him, so...' she sighed and a small nerve knotted in her forehead. Pamela never liked giving bad news. 'He's been carrying on with Clive's sister.'

'Who?' Of course Iris knew who, they were talking about her William. 'I mean, which sister?' Clive had four to choose from after all.

'Clarissa.' Pamela shook her head, as though there had been a death in the family. 'And, I'm afraid they are getting married. They *have* to get married,' she stressed the words, slowly, perhaps assuming that Iris would not understand her meaning.

'He's not marrying her.' Iris shook her head vehemently. 'He can't marry her. He has to marry me.' Suddenly she felt quite faint, felt herself lose balance and managed to flop down on the large eiderdown before she fell down.

'He is marrying her, Iris. I'm sorry. They are having a very small wedding here, next week. Family only are to attend. Clive's mother is beside herself with shame, but there you have it.' She let her hands fall to her sides and threw herself down beside Iris. 'I'm so sorry, I know you liked him, but I did try to tell you…'

'He can't marry Clarissa. He can't…' Iris felt her breath slip away from her. Without warning, the room seemed stifling. Her dress was suddenly too tight. Her body boiled with a kind of heat that made her feel like she might explode. 'He can't marry her, Pamela.' For the first time since she realized she was pregnant, Iris felt panic hold her in its grip. Later, she would look back and realize how naïve she was. Wandering through the days, knowing she was pregnant, believing that William Keynes would propose to her. Seconds disappeared into minutes as she sat on that bed, Pamela with her arms tightly about her. They might have been swallowed up into days and weeks had it not been for the fact that Pamela was marrying Clive at three o'clock. Iris had to dry her eyes and somehow stand beside her.

\*

Pamela got married to Clive in the small family church that was tucked beneath the castle, which would, it looked like, be Pamela's home one day. Iris got through most of the ceremony with very little attention to what was the biggest moment in her sister's life. She knew from the moment she saw William and Clarissa with her fiery red hair and fine features, so different to her brother, that she could not tell her mother that she was pregnant. William Keynes would certainly not marry her. In Clarissa, he had everything he could want: beauty, sophistication and, most importantly probably to William, connections. Why would he bother with someone as unworldly as Iris? She was an artless child who threw herself at the first man who looked at her. Someone who ultimately was not quite as good as Pamela or, it seemed, Clarissa. She remembered them, that night, Clarissa and William, whispering while she stood on the sidelines; she was just part of his game. William Keynes had used her and discarded her and she meant nothing to him. The understanding, when it finally hit, made her feel numb. The sadness, fear and humiliation somehow slid from her awareness and it was replaced with chilling detachment that rallied her for the ceremony so she acted her part perfectly.

After the service, guests were invited to have tea on the lawn. Music floated over the sounds of animated conversation from a nearby pavilion where a band played low but lively. It all passed in a daze for Iris. The ramifications of being pregnant, of what it meant for the rest of her life, were just settling on her. In 1956, Ireland considered itself quite cosmopolitan, but there was no question of who ran the country. The politics of the day still bowed to the stronger deeply held conservative beliefs of the Catholic Church. In holy Ireland, Iris knew too well, there was no room for unmarried mothers or their illegitimate children. She knew there were only two options for her. The first was the mothers and babies home, but the shame of going there would kill her mother and disgrace her sister. She couldn't do that to either of them. The second, the kinder thing to do, was to end it all as soon as possible.

Clive's mother and Pamela had organized the meal. Iris sat through most of it, with Miss Chester on one side of her and her mother on the other. She did not taste a morsel and if she actually ate anything, she didn't notice. The previous evening she'd walked around the grounds. There was a small river, some way down at the back of the house and it rushed into a lake that Clive said was too dangerous for swimming. It seemed now like a lifetime since Iris had stood over it. Then, the evening sun faded far down into the mountains and she romanticized her blissful future with William and their baby. Today, here in the grand banqueting hall in this beautiful home, she looked across at William and Clarissa. He had not as much as said hello to Iris. She very much doubted Clarissa even remembered her from that night in The Forty-Seven Club.

By the time she was setting off for the lake, she was glad that William hadn't acknowledged her. Her mind and her body felt oddly empty. It was as if the guts were rattled from her and a hand much more powerful than her own will was guiding her. She believed that suicide was her only path to right the wrong she had committed on that night with William Keynes. She had brought shame on herself and on her family. The sooner that she was dead and forgotten, the better off they would all be.

*

She walked slowly but deliberately to the back of the castle, leaving the gay noise of the gathered guests far behind inside its sturdy thick walls. The night air was soft for the time of year. They say that the west is wetter and colder than any other corner of Ireland. These were the thoughts that she allowed free rein through her mind as she walked down towards the little jetty overhanging the rippled lake. There was no one else about that she could see. Just as well. She had said goodbye to her mother and to Pamela in her own way earlier in the day. Told them both she loved them, but maybe not enough. She put aside thoughts of the child she would bring into the cold water with her or what might become of her as she sank into the dark icy depths. The night air was heavy with the smell of honeysuckle, as though someone had run the path before her and beaten every tree.

She stood, for just a second on the jetty, felt a prayer fall from her lips, although she knew it would not save her. She offered it up for the child. Somehow, she felt responsible for the baby, but of course, there was nothing else for it. At least, this way, they would be together. She walked to the end of the timber slats; one more step and it would all be over. She placed her foot above the water. *Forgive me*; she thought as she felt gravity take over and the water swallowed her greedily.

# 5

## Kate, Present

It was dark by the time Kate got back to the hotel. Apart from the ship's lamp that cast light about the steps like a net, there was no sign that anyone was about. Inside the heavy door, the hall welcomed her with the dim glow of table lamps and she paused for a moment to unwrap a fine cobweb from her wet hair. Her normally sleek blonde hair was blown out wild and loose so it fell untidily to her shoulders. Her pale cheeks had colour and her blue eyes danced with an excitement she hadn't felt in a long time. She peered a little closer; in London she had noticed the beginning of feathery lines just around her eyes, here the skin crinkled because her smile was real and the lines didn't matter so much in her happiness. She should be hungry, she hadn't eaten since breakfast and she didn't want to count the hours in between. The bathhouse had entranced her, stolen the whole day from her and she had loved it. Every second, it felt like it was soothing her soul, it felt like in some strange way, she'd come home. By the time the pale winter sun sunk behind the evening darkness, it felt like she'd spent a lifetime here and it was where she belonged.

She was glad of the supplies left out by Iris when she got to her room. The fire danced to life when she patted it into place with the poker that lay always across the cast-iron fender.

When Kate finally climbed into bed that night, she knew something in her world had shifted. She slept for almost fourteen hours, woken only by the call of the ocean and a lost guillemot, which perched in the eaves above her window. Her first thought on waking was the bathhouse. She had to go back there again.

'It's very lovely.'

'Yes, it's a special place,' Iris replied, 'Archie's brother owned it, but it dates back much further than that. In the end, well, Archie probably mentioned that Robert died there, it'll be sixty years, this summer. A terrible tragedy.'

'Yes, Archie mentioned Robert. I expected the place to be a little melancholic, after he told me, but it's the opposite. It's as though the place has a spirit of its own, but I felt it was a happy place, welcoming almost.'

'I'm glad to hear that. Robert is never far from my mind. It's good to think he's at rest and what he's left behind is the joy of his life and not the sorrow of its end.' Her smile did not quite reach her eyes, as though some part of her still remembered the sadness of losing someone who had been special to both her and Archie. 'Of course, it needs a lot of work now...' Iris sat with her once she finished her breakfast and poured tea from a gleaming silver pot. 'It's been waiting for someone, all this time. I have said so to Archie, many times over the years. You know, we've had offers?' Her smile held the wisdom that Kate figured only came with time.

'Yes, Archie mentioned that. Developers?'

'Oh, they wanted to buy everything in town, given half a chance, they'd have had this place too,' she shook her head. 'It was all nonsense of course, the bubble burst in the end and we were glad we held firm. What would we have done with ourselves, eh?' She nodded towards Archie. He was repairing a cracked tile on the fireplace in the main reception. 'And the bathhouse – as you say, it is very special. So you were inside?' Iris sounded almost wistful.

'Yes, I met a woman from the village, Rita Delaney? We walked every inch of the ground floor.' They had, and Rita had explained how people still travelled to the far side of Connaught to avail of seaweed baths throughout the year. A brand new bathhouse had opened up fifty miles along the coast and they were doing a roaring trade. Their popularity and benefits had not diminished just because there was no longer a bathhouse in Ballytokeep. 'People paid to bathe in fresh seaweed and hot water?' She still couldn't quite believe that it was so popular.

'Oh, yes. Even still, people come into the hotel here and talk about travelling over to Strandhill for the baths there. Good for the...' she thought for a moment, perhaps there were many health benefits, but she settled on, 'skin. It's meant to be good for the skin.'

'And for clearing you out,' Archie shouted from the hall, although Kate couldn't imagine how he'd heard them.

'Detoxifying?' Kate supplied. She knew from London that many women were looking to detox; whether it was tea or men, it was all the same. It was still, as Archie said, a process of clearing out.

'Yes, that's what one of the women was telling me recently. Of course, some believe that the actual seaweed is good for all sorts, from asthma to eczema, though I'm not sure the doctors would agree.'

'So, these baths they go to now...'

'Oh, they're quite a trek away, but if you want to go, you're welcome to our little run-around,' Iris said. 'Really, though, compared to the bathhouse, well – it has a lot of charm. Did you say you had someone with you?'

'Yes, I met Rita Delaney and her dog?' He really was the cutest little terrier. It was hard to imagine how anyone could object to him, but maybe that was the point for Rita. Kate had dealt with too many acrimonious couples to be surprised at how women managed to exact their little pleasures in married life.

'Ah, yes, her husband wanted to buy the place, of course, they are cut of different cloth those two.' Iris smiled, touched her soft grey hair, her eyes were vivid green for someone so old, but they held in them the sharpness of one who's mind was still as nimble as ever.

'Well, she seems very nice, anyway. We met on the beach and walked across. She found the key so we had a little look inside.'

'What's it like now? It's years since I've been down there,' she sniffed a little, 'too many memories for me, I'm afraid.'

'It's...' Kate looked out into the ocean opposite. 'It's probably the same as it was when you left. Of course, there is no electricity, so it's a little dark, but everything is there, it's like...'

'We just closed the doors on it at the end of the season?' Iris shook her head. 'That's exactly what happened.'

'You could have leased it, I'm sure you'd have had plenty of takers.'

'Maybe, but we never felt the right person came along.

The last thing we wanted was to see it turned into a... What do they call that place in Coolmara, a surfing shack?'

'Well, that would be a shame.' Surfers liked things laid-back and biodegradable and they were not into having afternoon tea from china cups.

'You'll go back again?' Iris did not quite meet her eyes.

'If you don't mind?'

'Spend as much time as you like there, the views are lovely and when the tide is high, on a summer's evening, it's quite spectacular.'

'Do you know, I really was happy there yesterday, it was like...?'

'A different world?'

'Hmm.' Kate thought about it. It was like a different world. 'I think I could spend my days there, just drinking in the views.' There was something more pulling her back to the place, but she couldn't put it into words, so instead she helped Iris clear away the breakfast and then kissed her gently on her cheek before putting on her coat.

She headed out into the crisp sunlight just after eleven walking past the newspapers that Iris kept on the hall table. She hadn't read a newspaper or heard the news in two days. It was a record of sorts. She ambled towards the pier, forcing herself away from the tall castle, but her feet moved slowly, begrudgingly in the opposite direction, so eventually she gave in and turned north towards the bathhouse. She had planned a little better today, and brought a flask and a couple of buttered fruit scones. Maybe she would take one of the chairs from the back of the tearooms out onto the rock, sit in the cool sunlight with her coffee and scone, and let the place soothe her soul.

An elderly wicker chair, sat among ornate cast-iron dining

carvers, proved heavier than it looked, but she hauled it out of the front door of the little tearooms. At the back, she wandered about through the various rooms containing a small bakery, kitchen, baths and steam presses. The pale sunlight bathed the south- and east-facing rooms in a buttery glow, so the heavy copper baths and tiles looked dull against the black of the slate floors. Everything about the rooms felt like she had just walked on to the set of a movie. It was as though she was stepping back in history, but somewhere, out of sight, someone would shout *time* on this fragile space.

'Hey, who's there?' The roar when it penetrated to the rear of the building almost took her breath. Kate peered around a door to see who the voice belonged to.

'Hi,' she said more confidently than she felt. The doorway was filled with the frame of a man who looked as though he'd been running. His breath was a warm blast on the icy air. 'I'm Kate Hunt; I'm staying with the Hartleys. They said I could look around here.'

'Did they now?' He made no move towards or away from her and, for a moment, his presence sent a small shiver of fear through her. She could not make out his face, but they stood opposite each other, he with the advantage of the light at his back. He let out a long sigh. 'I haven't been in here since I was a child.' He moved towards her now, his body relaxing somewhat. 'Colin Lyons,' he held out his hand to her. 'I live just up there,' he pointed his thumb to the right. She presumed he meant the cottage that overlooked the sea from high above the shaven rock. 'On the mountain. You'll have met my sheep along the way. They roam all about here. Sorry if I scared you.'

'I probably gave you a bit of a fright too.' It must have given him a start to see the front door open.

'This place, it hasn't been open in years. Everyone thought the Hartleys would sell it, when times were good. No chance that's going to happen now though, is there?' He was almost enquiring. 'It would be good though, to see the baths up and running, bring a bit of life to the town.'

'What about your sheep? Wouldn't it upset them?' Kate smiled, couldn't help it, it was this place.

'Do them the world of good, I'd say.' He stood at the counter where someone must have stood for many hours, years earlier. 'My father used to supply the Hartley's with the seaweed – back in the day. He reckoned that Robert Hartley was sitting on a gold mine here, if only he'd...'

'He died young.'

'Tragically, they say.'

'It doesn't feel like a very tragic place, does it?'

'It doesn't at the moment, anyway.' Colin Lyons smiled at her and she felt a small smile quiver on her own lips. He was tall and broad and his dark hair hung in waves about his tanned face. 'I'd love to see the rest of it,' he smiled at her now and she knew she was smiling too.

'Sure,' she said and she led him through the tearooms and into the large area at the rear where the baths and storage took up most space. 'I know it's covered in dust and years of neglect, but you can imagine how charming it must have been.'

'That must be the flat?' he said when they came to the narrow spiralling staircase at the furthest end of the corridor.

'I haven't been up there, I assumed it was just storage,' she said.

'Come on, this is like being a kid again. It's like exploring,' he said, taking the steps two at a time.

She followed him up, a little trepidation floating about her stomach. She faltered at the top of the stairs, entering the flat felt like there might be no turning back from this place.

The door was arched, oak and dark brown. It hung low so Colin had to dip down to pass through it. Kate noticed the walls in the entrance were almost two foot thick. It made her wonder what this place had started out as. Colin pulled open the shutters that faced out onto the Atlantic. The rooms stretched for the entire length of the bathhouse. There was a generous living room, a grand affair – more suited to a hotel drawing room. At the one side of this were similar arched doors to two small bedrooms. At the other end, matching doors led to an antiquated bathroom and a galley kitchen.

'Opening the windows here would make all the difference,' Colin wrenched open a living room window. The cool fresh drift was bracing, as though it might wipe out any ghosts that remained.

'It's not what I expected,' Kate said.

'What had you expected?'

'I'm not sure; I suppose I expected something much more basic.'

'Old Robert was quite the ladies' man, according to my dad; he did a lot of – entertaining.'

'Well, he certainly did it in style.'

'It's unbelievably dry and cosy, isn't it?' Colin was running his hand along the wall. 'You're not from here, but let me tell you, that's no small thing. Winters here, well they're not always as mild as this.' He picked up a newspaper, yellow, faded and dusty. 'Not that I'd want to put you off,' he said setting it down again.

'Put me off what?'

'Well, buying the place, of course,' he said simply, flopping into a deep leather reading chair positioned beside the long-dead fire. 'You are thinking about it, aren't you?'

'I... don't know.' Kate realized that, actually, she didn't know. Maybe this was exactly what she needed, but she was on holiday and people didn't just go on holidays and buy bathhouses, did they? Then a small voice whispered in her ear, *but people do go on holiday and buy wineries, is that any more absurd?* She looked across at Colin Lyons, 'Maybe, I hadn't really thought about it.' She sank into the sofa opposite him. 'But, yes, maybe.'

'You have a bit of thinking to do; I'll leave you to it,' he said, stretching himself out of the chair. He stood for a moment looking out at the sea, chopping blue and white for as far as the eye could see. 'You really should consider it, that's if the Hartleys would sell it to you.' He stood for another moment in silence, and then walked towards the door. 'It suits you, you know, this place,' he smiled again, a twitch of lips that was playful, 'and of course, it'd mean we'd be neighbours.'

After that, it hadn't taken long. It wasn't the idea of having Colin Lyons as a neighbour that swung it for her in the end. Kate had lived too long in London not to know that if a man was still single into his late thirties there was bound to be something amiss about him. No, in the end, it was the sea and the thoughts of having to return to a soulless existence in London, and maybe Iris too. Kate had family here, the kind of family she had always craved. Iris was warm and loving and she wanted Kate around – she was everything that Adaline could never be. Kate sat for hours, a small chair pulled into the casement window, letting the sea soothe away pain she had carried for almost a decade. Then, out of nowhere, one of her colleagues sent her a text. Nothing urgent, just hoping she was enjoying her holidays. She was not missing much in London. In a flash, Kate knew that she didn't want that lonely life anymore. Sure, she was making good money, she had a career people would kill for, but she was adrift. As she looked out into the determined waves, she knew, she'd wasted a decade of her life and all she had for it was a flat and a hefty bank balance. 'I'll make them an offer; if they won't sell, perhaps they'll lease the place to me,' she said the words aloud, startled herself with them. She pulled her jacket closer to her, firmed up the shutters on the windows and pulled the door of the bathhouse closed tight behind her. If Iris and Archie said yes, she'd begin immediately.

# 6

## Todd

Todd wasn't sure that he actually loved Claudia before his heart attack, but that was then. When he thought about it now, they got on well, and she was a fantastic looking girl. She was successful, maybe in her way more so than he was. She was wealthy and any man would give an elbow to have someone like her on his arm. What harm was there in asking her to hang around for a few days? It'd be good for both of them in terms of the press coverage. He could imagine her now, immaculately turned out, dark glasses in place and fending off the photographers outside the hospital; then, posing with him, looking up at his face adoringly when they discharged him. This could launch her on this side of the Atlantic. She should be thanking him, he was actually handing her the press opportunity of a lifetime. Did he love her? He must love her, hadn't she stayed around longer than just about anyone else? What was love anyway, sure all those years ago, hadn't Denny said it was all about timing?

As he drifted off to sleep, he thought of the long journey,

from a filthy corner on the Shankhill Road to Wembley Stadium in London. That had been the pinnacle, for him and the lads – playing Wembley when the kids at home were still standing in the dole queue. Maybe it was all the sweeter with where he had come from. His family were poor, hardworking, if they got a chance, but it seemed unlikely to anyone in his street that they'd live anything but lives of poverty. His dad died a couple of years back, but Todd made sure he was looked after. Pickled liver killed him in the end; Todd could put a lot of the bad stuff down to that. He managed to get them both looked after. The best money could buy – that is what they said in the leaflet for Four Oaks, and it cost too. It was worth it, he hadn't made it to his father's funeral. It upset his mum at the time, but he figured she understood. What would it have been anyway, but a week on the beer and a row at the finish? He was smashed in a hotel room in Korea of all places, but he paid for everything, only the best for his mum. His mum. He went home for her funeral. A two day affair that made the newspapers; probably a good thing, if it had not been he wouldn't remember being there. He'd been blotto for the whole thing. He bawled like a baby at her grave, the rain pelting down upon the gathered white-faced group. His mother oblivious in her coffin, they filled in the grave while he looked on, heavy stones and clumps of damp soil thudding unmercifully off the oak. When he flew out of Belfast that day, he knew he was finished with the place. Even now, a decade later, he refused to play there with the band. It was the past, and he did not want to go back there again. He did his duty, more than his share when you thought about the rest of them. He had paid his dues. Now it just left a feeling of emptiness and sure wasn't that to be expected?

God, but he hated hospitals; he hated the germs and the smell of disinfectant that reminded him that they were still lingering about the place. He hated the noise too: it didn't wake him, but didn't let him sleep properly either. It was after five the next morning when his eyes flickered open reluctantly. It seemed everything was brighter in the states than at home. Well, you don't get much grimmer than Belfast. Here, it was either very bright, or never quite pitch black. He missed that. He missed the black of night in Ireland. It seemed to him that he had not seen a night sky, not properly in nearly thirty years. Suddenly, it was all he wanted to do, to sit beneath the stars and hear the wind on the waves. Maybe have a mug of good old-fashioned builder's tea – there must have been some truth in what that old quack had said.

'You'll find yourself re-evaluating everything,' she looked over narrow glasses that seemed to float delicately in the middle of her generous features.

'I have a feeling there's some things I'll never like,' he said as he drank down the glass of prune juice they gave him.

'Like they say, some things are an acquired taste.' She wrinkled her nose and he suspected she was an opera lover. 'Anyway, don't be too surprised if you find yourself hankering after things you'd long forgotten.' She smiled at him, 'You're lucky to be here Mr Riggs, I suggest you go back to your life and make the very most of it.'

The first thing he noticed was the smell of coffee. Good old fashioned American Joe, he loved the stuff, always had. It drifted along the corridors in front of Denny and when his manager planted two paper beakers of the strongest stuff he could find in front of Todd, he actually thought he might throw up. Was this what she meant by re-evaluating?

'Jesus, take that stuff away, what are you trying to do, kill me?'

'They didn't say anything about coffee,' Denny poured the offending liquid down the sink. 'No, I'm pretty sure that they said fags and booze and, of course, any recreational drugs you might dabble in, but no – coffee is still good.' He plopped into the chair that had become his own in this bizarre little world they were sharing. He dug deep inside his leather jacket, pulled out his phone. He always had it switched on, always had it near. Family was everything to Denny and he spoke to his wife a dozen times a day, more when he was on tour.

'You sound like an old woman,' Todd felt a prickle of resentment flash through him; suddenly he did not want to be here. He wanted to be up and walking about the place. 'Come on, let's get out of here,' he inched towards the side of the bed, immediately fell back down, his head spinning hostilely. 'Bloody hell, that's some stuff to knock you out.'

'You can't just decide you're getting out of bed, mate. It doesn't work like that here. Do they even know you're awake, have you had a bite to eat?'

'Call some of them; tell them I want to get out of here.' Todd searched about the bed for a call button, found it and pressed it hard and long. His reward was a nurse who might have been older than his mother and four times the size of her.

'Now, Sir, you know that I can't discharge you without a doctor takin' a look-see, make sure you're fine.' She masterfully tucked him in to the bed. 'Doctor will be doing rounds in about an hour. You wanna get outta here? You better start eatin' some breakfast, start gettin' your strength back.' Five minutes later, she arrived back with a breakfast tray and a smile. 'You English guys, all skin and bone.' She tutted as she made her way back to the nurses' station.

Todd began to tuck in. He couldn't remember the last time he ate a proper breakfast. He cleared the lot.

'I suppose, you haven't eaten in days, not properly anyway.' Denny said as he sipped his own coffee.

It was the dreams that were the worst. Todd didn't know who to say it to, maybe it was normal. He'd never been a dreamer. All he needed was a couple of stiff drinks before he went to bed and he was out cold. The last few days though, bloody hell; it felt like he was dreaming for Spielberg. They were full on, wake you up in the middle of the night dreams, technicolour and surround sound and starring a cast of long-forgotten faces from his past. Was he surprised that he dreamed of the love he lost? He had made some bad decisions, some that kept him awake at night now he didn't have whiskey to knock the edges off his nightmares. Guilt was a terrible curse when you had a near death experience.

The doctors looked like teenagers to Todd. The surgeon spoke with a light inflection in his voice, as though it was his personal duty to bring happiness to each patient.

'It went very well. Of course, there was a lot of damage there, but you understand, that with your lifestyle.' He looked down at his notes, 'You were very lucky.'

'When can I go home?'

'That very much depends on where home is, Mr Riggs. I can let you out of here in about twenty-four hours; we just need to make sure that there are no complications, bleeds or reactions. Don't worry, it is very rare.' He looked now at Todd closely, 'But flying would be out of the question yet. You're from Ireland?'

'Yes, originally.'

'Ah, I love Ireland,' the surgeon turned to a young red haired doctor, 'I spent a year there as part of my training,' he smiled. 'Yes, I can see how your arteries might get blocked up very easily in Ireland.' He laughed a gentle sound of reminiscence for happy times past. 'But, no, Ireland would be out of the question, for at least a week.'

'A week?' Denny echoed. Todd looked at his manager; it was as devastating for him as it was for Todd.

'Yes, you see flying, well, a long haul flight like that, there would be too many risks.' Then he looked again at the red haired girl beside him. 'Thrombosis, lowered immune system – it opens up the possibility for all sorts of infection.'

'So?'

'Well, we can discharge you from here, the day after next, all going well, but I would prefer if you didn't fly, for at least a week.' Then he turned towards the door: busy man and Todd Riggs was just one more patient on his list.

'Thank you, doctor.' The words were out before Todd realized it, and it took him a minute to realize what he was thanking the guy for. After all, he'd just grounded him for over a week. He watched as the doctor turned and looked him in the eye. 'Thanks for, you know, doing the operation and all that. Ye've all looked after me really well.' Todd felt tears well up behind his eyes, he managed to lower his gaze from the faces that stood transfixed in the door way before he started to cry like a baby.

'You're welcome, Mr Riggs,' and then he was gone.

'Don't you say a bloody word Denny, not a bloody word.' Todd couldn't make eye contact with his manager, had a feeling that his emotions would certainly get the better of him.

Claudia Dey arrived at about eleven. Denny rang her.

Maybe he had suggested she come, but most likely he outlined the possibilities in terms of the press coverage she could harvest in the US. Their relationship was hanging on the brink, but for today, that seemed to be irrelevant to Claudia. She looked well; the flight had done her good. She always slept when travelling, made the most of her time with hydrating creams and sleeping pills. She was wearing a white suit, her hair smelled of coconut when she brushed her lips on his forehead and her hands had the smoothness of one who has spent some time getting them just right. She was ready for all eventualities; the press had managed to get a few words from her on her way to the foyer. She confirmed Todd's surgery had gone well and he was doing fine. She cancelled any work she'd lined up for the next week and even if she wasn't exactly delighted about it, Todd was genuinely grateful.

'You look good,' she said, but he knew she was lying. He had caught a glimpse of himself earlier, his face dragged, his eyes bloodshot, the bags beneath them beginning to droop. He'd aged by at least ten years since he'd come here. He felt like an old man, his hair standing shocked on top of his head, his slowly rounding trunk giving only a hint of the decades of abuse he'd put his body through. Before the heart attack, he thought, if he could still sing, then what was the problem? He hadn't figured on the rest of him giving up first. Of course, he'd convinced himself that he was still young. Claudia was part of the fairy-tale.

'What day is it?' he asked her as the sun cast shadows of deep orange about his room.

'Sunday,' she said absently, she was checking emails on her phone. 'They've run that piece I did for Guinness.' Her manager had sent her copy of a shoot she'd done for the drinks company at a castle on the furthest west coast of Ireland. 'Of course, it's even bigger news now that you're in the headlines.' Her voice sounded like it had lost its glint. Maybe she was tired. She hadn't mentioned the blonde and there hadn't been any interview anywhere that was anything like he expected. Maybe the shock of it all made her think again, or maybe it didn't matter to her as much as he would have expected it to.

'Can I see it?' he said holding his hand out for the phone.

'Since when did you care about fashion shoots?' she laughed passing him the phone.

'They're great Claudia, really great.' He said and he actually meant it. There was something about them, they made her look... otherworldly, the light and the sea and the way they'd done her up. 'Can I take a look through them?'

'Sure, I'm going to get myself some diet coke; can I get you something?'

'No thanks,' he said, but he hardly noticed her leaving, was relieved if anything. He couldn't talk to Claudia, not really. Not about important things, he stared now at a long splintering crack in the plaster opposite him. His life was changing, changing whether he wanted it to or not, but oddly, he felt on some levels he was ready for change. It felt like he'd outgrown some parts of his life. What he had to do now was figure out which parts, London, the band, the booze or Claudia? He felt an arrow of pain shoot across his forehead, knew it was too much to figure out here, in this room, right now. He needed time, that's what he needed more than anything and he would take time. He would learn to live a different life, one that contented him and made him feel like it was worth something.

He began to read about Ballytokeep, a little village on the

far west coast of Ireland, and the Norman castle that didn't look much like a castle to Todd. It was more like a square tower, built on an outcrop of rock. It stood tall and strong on the ragged coastline, long windows winking out at the Atlantic Ocean. He read about the little fishing village that filled with family holiday makers for the summer and about how much Claudia loved the place. 'The most magical place in the world,' she called it. He had to borrow Denny's glasses as he made his way down through the piece. The voice in the piece was Claudia's, but it wasn't a Claudia he knew. Todd felt himself re-evaluating her. All he'd ever seen, all he'd ever wanted to see, was a glamour girl on his arm. He'd never really wondered about what might lurk beneath the surface. He'd been to her flat in London, often enough to know that homemaking wasn't one of her skills, but here she was talking about this forgotten castle as though it were her soulmate. As he read deeper into the article, he became more entranced with the place. It was a stocky Norman keep – didn't Jeremy Irons have one of those in Ireland somewhere too? The doctor had said he needed to simplify his life, to make time to smell the roses, practise a little mindfulness or yoga. Todd had laughed, but it was a laugh that sounded hollow, because at the moment his emotions were all over the place. He could cry or laugh really; the truth was, he was as scared as it was possible to be. He'd try anything to get away from that feeling. He needed to make changes and as he held the images of Claudia at the base of that windswept fortress a plan began to formulate in his mind. A plan that felt right for him now. A plan that didn't involve picking up strange women who just wanted to sleep with him and sell their story. It was a plan that would bring him home. A plan that might even make him happy.

# 7

## Iris, Present

It was hardly a surprise, when Kate asked to meet with them both that night. Her face, a few soft lines about the eyes, had a flushed look to it, as though she'd just opened the Christmas gift of her dreams. The eagerness was a striking contrast to her manner since she arrived. Iris had seen the change in her since Archie had sent the girl off in search of the bathhouse. Iris had not been as enthusiastic as Archie about the possibility of Kate finding solace in Ballytokeep. The place was little more than a village, and a dead one at that for half the year.

In the years since Robert's death, they had never considered selling the bathhouse, but the last few months had set her thinking. There were many little things, but they all boiled down to one thing, she knew that she and Archie could not go on forever. It seemed to Iris that within the space of a few months, she could see Archie moving away from her. It was in the way she caught him, too often now, she knew he was back in that time. He forgot things; things that he shouldn't forget. Sometimes, he looked at her and she had a feeling he was working things out, maybe figuring out what he was meant to be doing. She knew, knew for certain, that twice now, he didn't know who she was. His eyes held a kind of trembling fear, for just a fraction of a second, and then the recognition came back, but she was losing him, just as they had lost his father. She only hoped that she could keep him a little longer.

When Kate returned from her visit to the bathhouse, Iris was in the kitchen, far behind the front reception, past the little snug bar they closed up long ago. She was baking, up to her elbows in flour and reluctant to leave the job at hand. Still she found the rhythm of kneading and sieving relaxing. Memories of busy and blithe times flooded her thoughts as bread took shape.

'Sit there, dear, Archie will be back in a moment, he's just gone to get more fuel.' Iris pointed to a large kitchen chair. It had been her mother-in-law's. She had sat in it when she was too old to make her way about the kitchen usefully, too interested in the goings-on not to be included, too wise not to be involved.

'It's really cosy here,' Kate said and she leaned her hands towards the old stove.

'Ah, you can't beat the Aga, can you? It heats all of our living areas and I can bake and cook on it, the only down-side is poor Archie spends his time filling it with turf.' Iris smiled now at Kate. 'You look much happier than you did, my dear.'

'Thank you.' Kate smiled, her eyes gleaming like one who hasn't known simple happiness in some time. 'I feel much happier. It's this place and the people. It's very... special.'

'Yes, you need to watch it all right; it can get under your

skin a bit.' Iris knew what she was talking about. 'Anyway, if it does you good…' Iris turned out the flour.

'Ah, you're back. Nice walk?' Archie shook off the old jacket from across his shoulders. 'I was just getting the…' he looked down helplessly at the basket of turf, 'the stuff we put in the fires.' He shook his head. 'Tea, dear?' he asked, making his way towards the kettle. His mother had instilled in him many years ago that anyone visiting needed tea. It was like the remedy to all ills, the cure for all tribulations. He pulled the old steam kettle onto the hot plate and, before long; he was heating the pot and setting the world to rights with a couple of spoons of tea leaves. He placed the pot at the end of the long scrubbed baking table. 'There's something on your mind?' He beckoned Kate to move her chair nearer while he pulled one out for himself.

'It's that obvious?'

'Everything is obvious once you reach my age, dear, it's the Lord's way of saving you valuable time trying to work things out. It has to do with the bathhouse?'

'Yes.' She smiled at him now. 'I'd like to buy it from you.' She let out a deep breath, as though saying the words caused surprise in her own mind. 'Or at least take it over, start up the baths again.'

'I thought you might. You know we've had offers before, people who looked at it and thought…'

'I don't want to pull it apart, I want to keep it exactly as it is. I'd like to move here and run it as it should be run.'

'And, forgive me, dear, but you could afford to do that, to throw up your life in England and move back here?' Iris glanced at Kate before making her way to the oven.

'I think what my wife is trying to say is that, well you can see for yourself, you won't be making a lot of money here for a good part of the year.'

'Maybe not on the tearooms, but I'd say there's a good business in the baths. If I bring in a therapist or two, maybe look at developing the seaweed business again.'

'Aye. True enough, that wasn't something we ever really followed up. Truth be told, there was probably a whole business there, but we just didn't have the time.'

'No, nor the heart.' Iris looked at Archie, but he hardly met her eyes. She sat down at the table beside them. At the window, she saw a large black cat snake past in the shadows. The wind was beginning to brew again and the chimney echoed its lonely howl. 'I hadn't expected this,' she whispered, 'the bathhouse opened up again.' She smiled, a small swell of pleasure rippling down her back. 'It is a good time, Archie, it'll be sixty years this year, time to let it go.'

'I've known that for a long time, Iris,' he placed a hand across hers. It was aged, speckled and shaking, but it was still strong and comforting. He still made her feel safe and cherished. 'It was just waiting for the right person to come along.'

'Kate, I think he's saying that you are that person.' Iris met Archie's eyes, they were still brown and kind, but they seemed always on the edge of tears now. His smile let one escape so it ran unchecked down his cheek. 'It's right, isn't it?'

'It's right.' They drank their tea in celebration and some of the loneliness of their past lifted from them that evening.

*

They sorted out the details quickly. At this stage, making a profit came far down on Iris's list. It had never really figured for Archie. They would have handed it over to her gladly, just to know she would look after it. After all, she was family; but she was a solicitor too and she insisted on having it all above board.

'We should go down and say our goodbyes,' Archie said a few weeks later when they were getting ready to sign the papers. 'It will be Kate's tomorrow.' His voice petered off. Of course, in many ways, although they owned it, it had never been truly theirs. How can you accept something that comes with such a high price tag?

'Better if I wait until it's cleaned up and fresh.' What Iris did not say was that the decay of the place could kill her. It was silly of course. Robert was long gone and it made no difference to him now. That was half the problem though; she had never let him go.

# 1957

Iris did not hear Clive call her and she hadn't thought about the possibility that anyone would rescue her. By the time Clive took her from the water, she was almost dead. They brought her back to the castle, and there she lay for four days. On the brink of pneumonia, it seemed like Iris would die if not of one thing, then of another. Feverish and incoherent, the story of her predicament came from her without her even realizing it.

Before she woke, it was settled.

Clive's mother was probably more upset than Mrs Burns was.

'Well, she's stuck with him as a son-in-law, isn't she?' her mother said coldly. 'At least, well, we'll be all right.'

'You'll come to Paris with me,' Pamela said flatly. It was just days since she had married, but already she seemed to have the assurance that came with being Lady Pamela. 'No one need ever know. The child can as easily be put up for adoption there as here.'

'I cannot just go to Paris with you and Clive.'

'Of course you can, it's for the best, mother agrees.' Pamela looked across at their mother. It was done.

'It's better than the alternative you were thinking of.' Maureen Burns would be hard-pushed to choose which was the bigger sin, sex or suicide. Iris knew that she was just relieved that she was alive. 'Pamela is right. It's the best thing to do.'

'When is William getting married?' Iris despised how weak and feeble she sounded.

'They married this morning, just family as witnesses. We won't be seeing them for a very long time. The Consulate offered him a junior position in the embassy in Boston. Clive's mother is devastated, but then Clarissa was always a bit wild.'

'It will be fine, Iris, you'll see. You will head off to Paris. Pamela will look after you until you have the baby. Sure, wouldn't any girl your age be delighted to be seeing a glamorous city like Paris. Who knows, you might be coming home to me a proper lady, speaking French and everything.' Her mother was trying to make the most of things, but they both knew this had to be heart-breaking for her. Iris thought she would die of shame for the way she had behaved. She almost wished Clive had left her where she was, at the bottom of that cold lake.

*

Paris was not at all that Iris or Pamela had expected. Their mother waved them off at Dublin Airport. If it weren't for what lay ahead of her, Iris might have been excited at the idea of her first flight and her first time leaving Irish soil.

The embassy supplied Clive and Pamela with an apartment in a smart part of the city – from what Iris could see, most of Paris was smart, but then she didn't venture too far in the early days. They had a maid called Marianne and a little car that none of them drove. Iris was not sure where Marianne had come from, but Pamela explained that the Earl's wife always had help. Her mother-in-law had secured Marianne and she would cook, clean and generally take on tasks that were considered beneath Pamela now. Iris liked Marianne from the start and they spent many evenings in her little flat admiring the fashion magazines that Marianne adored. It was Marianne who took the girls to the best dressmakers in Paris. She showed Iris how to give her drab Irish clothes some *je ne sais quoi*!

'I can't sit around here all day waiting for the baby to arrive,' she said one day to Pamela, and it was true. The apartment was quite small and it did not take long for the two girls to feel cramped and bored.

'Perhaps you could get a little job?' Clive said that night as they sat down to dinner. Clive, for his part, had been very nice. Everyone had been very nice. Iris was all too aware that what she deserved was a good telling-off and to be thrown into a convent in the back end of nowhere and forgotten about. Instead, Clive made her feel like she was a valued guest.

'I don't even speak French, how could I get a job?' With Marianne, her French was improving each day, but she was nowhere near ready to call herself proficient.

'Well, neither of you are going to learn just sitting here all day,' he said, laughing, as he tucked into dinner. 'Why not take a walk about the hotels and guest houses and see if they need an English-speaking receptionist?'

So, that was what they did. After a week or so, with very

tired legs and a growing French vocabulary Iris managed to get a job in a nearby cookery school. Initially, she set about clearing up after the men who were learning to become great chefs. Soon she managed to secure a position that meant she could spend her time assisting in the classes and she enjoyed watching the lessons and improving her French.

Pamela wasn't successful in securing any employment, but they both knew that was probably a relief to Clive anyway. The following week, she realized that she too was pregnant. A honeymoon baby. Clive was over the moon and Iris was more delighted for them than she was worried for herself.

Each night Iris would lie in her little single bed and try to figure ways she could hold onto this baby a little longer. She tried hard to make peace with having to give it away to strangers. She fell asleep tired but content with the days she had spent learning far more than she expected to. Clive and Pamela were the initial beneficiaries of her new unofficial education. She regaled them with stories and kept a journal of each recipe she assisted with at the school. She was full of energy, while Pamela had a terrible time between morning sickness, cramps and heartburn. They were polar opposites when it came to being pregnant. Iris bloomed, while Pamela wilted. Iris dreaded her baby arriving because she knew that she would have to give it up, while Pamela couldn't wait for her child to arrive.

'You could get a job at the Ritz at this rate,' Pamela said one night, but of course, they both knew she couldn't. There were only chefs, no *chefettes* in Paris. The Ritz and any of the other big hotels wanted a real chef, not a cook from a guest house on the wrong side of the river Liffey. They would never want someone who brought such terrible shame on herself, even if her family had managed to keep it secret.

*

It was late on a Sunday evening when Iris felt the first gnawing pain at the base of her spine. She ignored it for an hour or two. She knew she would have to tell Pamela. She and Clive were attending a reception to celebrate a West German visit to mark their World Cup win a few months earlier. By the time Pamela arrived, Iris was in the throes of labour. There was just time to get the local midwife, an English woman called Henrietta who had delivered babies in the blitz. She was neither a soother nor an ally. Instead, she was a no-nonsense woman with limited time and even less patience. They were all glad to see her leave.

Iris held her baby boy close to her for as long as they would let her. She marvelled at his dark hair and eyes. He was his father's son – a real heartbreaker from the start. Iris thought he was the most beautiful baby she had ever seen. If there were any choice, they would not give him up.

'I've had an idea, but I'm not sure how you'll feel about it,' Pamela sat on the side of Iris's bed. The baby, Mark, was just two days old and Iris knew her heart would break when she had to say goodbye to him. 'Clive has agreed and…' she cleared her throat and Iris had a feeling that this was something that she had been thinking about for a while. 'If you let us, we will adopt Mark from you. It would all be completely legal, all above board.' Pamela reached her hand out and placed it gently on Mark's head. 'The truth is, I love him too much to let him go, Iris. We could say I had twins, look at me, sure there's only going to be a matter of weeks between them and in a year's time you won't even see that.'

'I…' Iris did not know what to say. Surely anything was better than never seeing Mark again? It was, probably, an ideal solution, better than any she dared to dream. But how would they go through life and keep this secret? How would she manage to see him and not reach out and pull him close to her? How could she give him away to anyone? Then she realized, it was her best option. If he were put up for adoption here, in this city that she had grown to love, but that she would soon leave, she would never see him again. This was the best chance for both of them. He would be loved; he'd have a good life, every opportunity. Perhaps it was far more than she deserved for him, but she had to take the offer. 'Oh, Pamela, I don't know what to say. Yes. Yes. I couldn't ask for a better home for him.' It was true. This was best for everyone. His blood relations would surround him and there would be no scandal.

Clive had come later and explained that she could stay until Pamela's baby was born, but then she would have to go home. They would be a family, a real family, with twin babies and she would return to Dublin and make the best life she could for herself. 'You're still young and lovely, you'll meet someone decent,' Clive said. She had a feeling he wasn't just saying it to console her. He actually believed that the boys would be lining up for her back in Parnell Square.

The days that followed had a surreal quality to them. Sometimes, Iris would hold Mark close and dream that there was some way she could keep him. Sometimes, when she closed her eyes at night, she couldn't believe how lucky she was that he would have such a good home. In those days, her heart grew in heaviness; it was the weight of love, more than guilt. She knew her purity was gone on every level. She had experienced love in all its forms, sadness too, and knew they both had many layers. She knew instinctively that her heart would never be the same again. A big part of it was parcelled up in her perfect lovely son, her emptiness the price she gladly paid for his future.

When Pamela's baby arrived, he was nothing like Mark. He was small and fair and, it seemed to Iris, already far more bad-tempered – perhaps that came from his blue blood. The midwife took one look and pronounced, 'colicky,' as though that would explain the huge gulf of difference between two children who were destined to be brothers. It made no matter, Clive set about organizing his family and made it clear that Iris had to go. He was pushing her out, but only because he thought it would be easier for everyone – maybe even for Iris.

'Do not worry, I will take special care of Mark for you,' Marianne whispered in her ear as they embraced before she headed for the airport. 'I will write and tell you all about him.'

'Promise?'

'It is my word.' Marianne hugged her tight and Iris had to pull hard to walk away from that little apartment.

*

It was a cold and wet April day when she arrived back at Dublin airport. She left behind not just her sister with her lovely 'twin boys', but her heart too in that beautiful city far away. Her 'whole life stretched before her', as Clive put it, and she supposed this was true. But the ache in her heart for her Mark had emptied her soul. It felt like she stood on the precipice of a very deep canyon into which she might fall endlessly for as long as she was away from him.

She resumed her duties at the guest house, but now she ghosted about the old house like a lost soul in search of

an anchor. Maureen Burns did not quite know what to do
with her.

'I'm worried about you, Iris. You only work. You spend
your time in your room. From what I can see you are pining
your life away, looking out that bedroom window for
something that you can't possibly find.'

The letters from Paris told of a happy family, growing
quickly and seamlessly closer each day. Clive made it clear
that there was no going back. All the same, when Marianne
wrote, in her curling stylish hand, Iris could almost imagine
that she was right beside Mark. Marianne's letters told her
all the things that Clive and Pamela left out. In trying to be
kind, they managed to cut her off. She knew from Marianne
that Mark was growing fast and his hair was dark. He liked
peas and pears, but sometimes he refused everything unless
he was sitting on Marianne's lap. He was growing into a
little boy, intent with purpose. He was not as jovial as his
younger brother, Crispin, but very charming all the same.
He was the burlier of the two. By comparison, Crispin was
the paler, less vigorous version. Iris sometimes thought, they
both took after their fathers, but then she would push all
thoughts of Willie Keynes from her mind. Oddly, she found
herself praying that Mark would grow up to be the decent
kind of man that Clive had turned out to be.

'Perhaps a change of scenery,' her mother said as they
cleared away the breakfasts. There was a distant cousin of
Miss Chester's in County Sligo, far enough removed from life
as Iris knew it to make a new start. 'A summer in that little
seaside hotel with the Atlantic air to brighten your cheeks
and she has two sons...' her mother said lightly. Iris had no
interest in the sons. She had met Archie Hartley a couple of
years before. True enough, he seemed keen on her then, but

they were only children. Then, they spent more time racing bicycles about the square than they did anything else. This time she was nineteen going on forty-nine. She was jaded and cynical after her brush with William Keynes. Sometimes she thought of him, living in a country so far away, oblivious to the birth of his first child. Iris thought about Mark all the time, it seemed odd that William didn't even know about him. No doubt, Clarissa would have already presented him with a lovely baby by now. Iris pushed their situation from her mind as hard as she could.

'I'll go.' She had nothing to lose; perhaps she might make something of it. 'I will go as a cook, tell them I have trained at one of the best schools in Paris.' She said the words with far more determination than she felt about anything since before that night when she'd headed off with William Keynes to The Forty-Seven Club.

# 8

## Kate

It didn't take Kate long to get everything sorted. Ten days in London and she'd put her flat on the market. She drew up the papers for the purchase of the bathhouse and arranged for her belongings to go into storage. It was an unexpected relief to be rid of most it; even the wedding dress that she had stored so faithfully for the last decade. It was Dior. Even if she wasn't one for labels much, she still caught her breath at the exquisiteness of the gown. It was more than she could have dreamed for in a wedding dress; a silk sheath that fell across her body like a white morning rose. It was empire line, soft and ivory, with akoya pearls encircling like tender stars around the bodice.

'Pearls are for tears, you know that?' her would-be bridesmaid had said. She got married the following year to an accountant from Bristol and they had hardly spoken since. Kate did not look at the dress in years. It hid in a heavy travel bag at the Narnia end of her wardrobe.

The temptation was too much when she pulled it out, it

still fitted perfectly and she glided about the flat for almost an hour, the sadness somehow quelled now. She stood before the full-length mirror that hung on the back of her bathroom door, took in the full effect. When she knotted her fair hair on top of her head, she could almost be the same person she was then. On closer inspection, a tinkering of fine lines danced now at the corners of her blue eyes. Shadows beneath them spoke of the long hours she worked because there seemed little point in much else. But the vibrancy in her eyes was returning and this made her smile as though she had a secret that was bubbling up inside her. The bathhouse was igniting something in her, calling her to something that had eluded her for at least a decade, she suspected maybe longer. In the end, she hung the dress back in the bag and left for the Oxfam shop; someone was in for a very pleasant surprise. She wished its next owner well.

Lyndon Tansey pushed the boat out for her farewell party. They spent an afternoon knocking back champagne while every other barrister in Britain was vying for a piece of the forthcoming divorce of a young Royal and a playboy. Instead, the workforce at Newbury, Crocket and Tansey Lawyers feasted on sushi and spoke maudlin words on the passing of time and the loss of good friends.

'You know that if it doesn't work out, your place is always waiting for you,' her boss said to her many times over those last few days.

'I know that, and I'm grateful, but I've a good feeling about this, I need to do it, I feel like it's where my future lies,' she smiled at him, 'if that doesn't sound too clichéd.'

'No. You need a change, I can see that. I think we've all seen that these last few years and I'm glad you're getting the chance, it's just...'

'You'll miss me?'

'Don't be so big-headed!' he joked. 'It'll be hard to find anyone as good as you; we won't replace you, you know that.'

'Thanks for that.' She sipped her champagne, looked about the foyer that she passed through every day of her working life. 'I promise not to set up in competition, if that makes you feel any better.'

'Of course it does, I would hate to be facing you across a courtroom. For all our melancholy, I'm sure there'll be plenty of divorcing wealthy spouses who will breathe a sigh of relief.' They both laughed at this and Kate realized she would feel a little sad leaving this place.

*

As it turned out, there wasn't much time for sadness. Packing up the flat, saying her goodbyes, ten days flew by maybe more quickly than she wished before she was walking along that deserted beach.

Her mother thought she was mad. But then, she'd lived her whole life in city suburbs, perhaps the idea of all that space scared her.

'It sounds like a real adventure,' her mother said drily when she rang to tell her of her plans. Adaline had always believed her daughter was a jolly hockey sticks, secret seven sort of girl. That was probably down to boarding school. 'You're really sure about this?' she asked her. Of course she'd never met Iris or Archie and she'd probably never understand the beauty of Ballytokeep. 'Crispin,' his name sounded strange when she said it, 'your father, he never mentioned this Aunt Iris?'

'She's nothing like him, Adaline.' Adaline made no secret of the fact that Crispin had been a bad lot, maybe Kate couldn't blame her, after all he was a drinker, a gambler and, by all accounts, a terrible womanizer. 'She's nothing like my grandmother either.' That was true, Lady Pamela was just that, a lady. Sir Clive made all the decisions and the only part he wanted to play in his grand-daughter's upbringing was to pay for her education in a school that kept her well away from any of them. Maybe it was the pain of losing their son in a car crash – but their distance was hard to take, after all, she had lost her father too. 'I feel there's a real connection here.' She knew Adaline wouldn't get it in a million years, she'd think she was mad for throwing in her career for a run-down old bathhouse. 'I know I need to do this, I'm as sure as I've ever been about anything.'

'I've often wondered about you, you know after...'

'Yes, it's been the defining part of me, hasn't it?' Everyone in England knew Kate as the girl Todd Riggs ditched at the altar before heading off to Copenhagen with a Russian bimbo.

'You mustn't think that, Kate. You've had a stellar career, the kind of stuff most girls only dream about.' Adaline never had a career. Kate assumed she'd never wanted one. She played a secondary role to her second husband's corporate career; in many ways, that was her career.

'I suppose I want more now. Time's moving on and I've made as much money as I need to set me up and keep me afloat for a few years.'

'You could always go back, set up on your own, if you wanted.' Adaline really thought she had a choice. But then it was a long time since they'd actually spoken about much more than Adaline's holiday plans.

'I need to get my life sorted all round, before it's too late.' It was true, the open sea air, the rushing tides, the sand slipping beneath her feet had all reminded Kate of the passing of time.

She invited Adaline to stay for summer holidays and maybe someday she'd genuinely hope to see her. Their relationship had never been easy. Adaline married young and her family thought well. It turned out she married a playboy who didn't understand loyalty and knew even less about responsibility. He spent his life chasing the next horizon and died long after he left them, but much too soon for a man who seemed always to have somewhere else to be. Kate's memories of him were scarce. Those of their times together as a family, made her feel nervy. These days, she put that down to the uneasiness she felt with her mother. It was obvious to Kate, even from a very young age that she would never quite measure up to her father's family's expectations. She doubted her father did either. So, once she hit her teenage years, she just stopped trying. She attended her grandfather's funeral alone, surrounded by a couple of faded hangers-on who meant nothing to her and probably less to her father. Kate told her mother that Iris was nothing like her sister – Lady Pamela, but Adaline just laughed. 'Oh, Kate, you're just too naïve.'

\*

Her final morning in London dawned bright and crisp. The flat was fully packed up with only the sheets on her bed and the clothes for the journey left to be sorted. She had not as much as a pint of milk in the fridge for coffee. She ambled down to the little bakery a couple of streets away for breakfast. There were a few hours to kill before her flight, so a leisurely breakfast and the morning papers were just the ticket. She picked up a broadsheet without noticing the headlines.

She ordered muesli and a pot of breakfast tea and settled into a chair in the morning sun. By the time the tea arrived, she'd lost her appetite. The front page had a third of its headlines given over to the sudden heart attack of one of Britain's most famous rock stars. Kate couldn't help herself, not this once. Normally, she made herself put down anything written about Todd. She knew, from bitter experience, that most of it wasn't true anyway, so she reasoned there wasn't much point. The other thing was that it still depressed her, knowing that he had gone on to live a happy and successful life. She knew, she should be able to wish him well, but it still seemed unfair. There he was with his young supermodel girlfriend, still doing just as he pleased. She, meanwhile, had spent a decade nursing a broken heart, a fragile ego and a contemptuously public humiliation.

But she was soon absorbed in the story. Todd's heart attack happened the day after he played one of the best gigs of the tour to date. On pages four and five, various doctors explained his cardiac event, as they called it, from a medical point of view. Kate didn't need to be an expert to read between the lines; he was lucky to be alive. She read the story three times, from start to finish. At least, she told herself, the *Times* was as reliable as you got. There was a picture of Todd and Claudia Dey, his current squeeze, leaving a nightclub, before he had his heart attack. He looked tired; he looked much more than his age, while Claudia looked glowing and glamourous. As usual, she was dressed in white, an ethereal vision of timeless beauty. He looked crumpled and unshaven in black leather, with hair that was a shade too black against his greying stubble.

Throughout the article, there were several photos of him over the years with the band. He seemed more familiar to Kate in these, as though she might reach out and touch him and he would still be the same as all those years ago. As usual, they alluded to his bachelor status and that he had almost got married a long time ago. Kate was delighted to see that this time they did not slip her name into the article. That was an improvement. Sometimes it felt like she went through most of her adult life with a byline beneath her name: *Jilted at the altar by Todd Riggs.*

Perhaps it was the report of Todd's heart attack, or maybe the decision to move to Ballytokeep, but it felt as though something fundamental had changed. She had spent ten years feeling her stomach flip over when she saw even a photograph of Todd. She supposed it meant she still loved him, in spite of all the therapy and self-help books. Today, with the sun shining and the promise of a new life before her though, Kate felt something in her heart close to pity for Todd Riggs. At the end, what had he? Sure, he had a supermodel on his arm and millions in the bank, bully for him. But his eyes gave away the secret to the familiar emptiness from before.

For the first time in a decade, Kate pitied him and it felt good. She folded up her newspaper, left a tip for the waiter and walked towards her new life with a determination and optimism she had never experienced before. She said goodbye to London. She was saying goodbye to Todd too. Leaving her flat, her job, her friends behind, she knew she was becoming invisible to him. He could not come back to find her now, even if he wanted to. After ten years of waiting, Kate Hunt had finally moved on.

# 9

## Todd

Todd never believed he'd be so delighted to get back to puddle-soaked pavements and cheeky cabbies. Touching down in Heathrow, he could have kissed Denny for organizing a jet to get them home. The oddest thing though, when he got into London he was filled with that sensation once more. Everything was the very same, but nothing was quite as he left it. Like the smell of coffee, it was no different but now he craved a cup of tea instead. London left him cold, it no longer fitted, like a jacket he grew out of and it stretched uncomfortably across his senses.

It would take little more than an afternoon. Todd booked a plane and flew out while Claudia was getting her nails painted, or some other part of her anatomy pampered. The pilot flew him across the Irish Sea and over the patchwork of green fields in less than an hour and a half.

The Norman keep was the most prominent structure in Ballytokeep. He found himself constantly looking at images of the place on his phone; it was almost a thousand years old and ran across four floors. It sat on a tip of rock just beyond the town, jutting dramatically over the sea. Todd didn't care that it might need a new roof or indeed that the place might soak up millions before it could even be habitable, wasn't he only going to look at the place? The town itself was cheerful enough, certainly prettier than any part of Belfast he had ever known. The shops that lined the bottom of the village were painted in various pastel shades. The town stretched out high above him to the top of the rocky hill where a grey church loomed over the village goings on. He could imagine in summertime, the promenade filled with tourists and ice cream vans. It was the sort of place he would have loved to visit as a child. It had narrow streets, what looked like an old arcade in need of repair, tennis courts and shops that sold buckets and spades, ice creams and sodas, old-fashioned fish and chips. This time of year, almost everything was closed, except the estate agents.

'Rock Castle?' the girl said, trying to place him. She was no more than twenty, too young to be a fan. Since the heart attack, he was not kidding himself anymore.

'Yes, it's for sale, isn't it?' Todd said, sinking into his default flirting state – of course it didn't work so well when people didn't realize who you were, but it was hard to change the habit of a lifetime.

'Everything is for sale,' a middle-aged man made his way from a back office. 'I'm Mick Skeffington' – he nodded to the sign over the door – 'and, you're Todd Riggs?' he smiled, smelling the money in a town that had struggled for the last decade.

'That's right.' Todd still liked being recognized. Enjoy it while it lasts, he figured now. Amazing what the previous few weeks had taught him. 'Is it for sale?'

'It was. I'm not sure if the owners are still interested in offloading it. Didn't you hear, it seems that the property market is taking off again?' He wasn't fooling either of them, but it was probably second nature to give the sales spiel. 'I'll see if I have keys for it, will I?' He was doubling back to his office, slow day in the real estate business obviously. 'I haven't been up there in a while, but...' He was back in a second. 'Here we are,' he held an ordinary-looking Yale key in his hand. Not very impressive; but there was no commitment on either side yet. 'Rebecca, I'm taking Mr Riggs to look at some property, any calls you can take a message.' He fiddled with his phone for a moment, switching it off and smiling. This was getting his full attention for as long as it took.

The castle was as imposing up close as it was from the chopper. It was less so inside.

'Of course, it's years since it's been lived in. You can look at that either way. I'd prefer to think it gives you plenty of scope for putting your own stamp on the place.'

'Aren't there restrictions, I mean; is it listed or whatever?'

'Well, as you can see, it's just a shell. You couldn't be expected to live here without some alterations.' Skeffington laughed, a hollow sound; he didn't really take Todd for stupid. 'A good designer, all mod cons, it will need a new roof of course, damp coursing, repointing, but to a man like yourself,' he almost bowed. He pulled back one of the window sashes; they were facing out to sea. The only thing before them was water and sky. The effect was breathtaking. 'Most of these have been snapped up by people like you...'

'People like me?' Todd rounded on him.

'Discerning buyers,' Skeffington said smoothly. 'Rock stars with taste. You know how it is, some of you guys just never get old, you can think of a few I'm sure. But, here in Ireland, anyone who's anyone, with a bit of levity as well as success, well, they have a castle, don't they?'

'Do they?' Todd had decided he was not going to fall for the banter, but the man had a point. He had grown out of living in a hotel for the rest of his days. Who did that anyway? Even the Rolling Stones had big houses in London and out in the Cotswolds, and let's face it they were the ultimate rock stars.

Todd walked from the bottom to the top of the tower. The place was much bigger inside than he imagined.

'With a good interior designer, you could live like a king, and there are the outbuildings.' A couple of low-roofed stone buildings hunched along the back of the tower. 'Perfect for guest accommodation, maybe a recording studio, a games room or a cinema.'

They were making their way back down to the ground floor when he spotted a castellated white building standing on an outcrop of maroon-coloured rock. 'There's another sign of optimism in the area,' Skeffington was saying. 'That old place was recently sold. Of course, that was a private sale, never thought I'd see that place change hands, but there you go.'

'What is it?' Even to a cynic like Todd, it had a romantic look to it. He couldn't help but feel that its location, and the way the owner had painted it up with touches of French navy in places, was far more welcoming than this draughty old keep.

'It was a bathhouse, back in the day; closed before I can remember. They came from all round to the place though. Seaweed baths and the like. Course it's all the rage again now with ladies who lunch. It's like a mini spa on your doorstep.

I think I heard that they're opening up the old tearooms as well, so that's good for the village.'

'Hmm, I suppose.' Todd wasn't particularly bothered about what was good or bad for the village, but somehow he felt drawn to the peculiar building in the distance. Then he remembered the odd little feelings that had been welling up inside him since his heart attack. It was normal, the doctors said. Wasn't it why he was here? He never considered buying a place like this before the heart attack.

He hadn't told anyone he was thinking of buying the place. Wasn't sure how he'd broach it with Claudia or Denny. He knew why he didn't tell them. They'd have tried to put him off, called it a whim, maybe he was afraid they'd talk him out of it and this was too important to risk that. Perhaps he should have told Claudia. After all, weren't they—? He wasn't sure what they were anymore. Hadn't he wanted to finish with her on that morning, the morning of his heart attack? Now the idea of all that just made him sick. What was he thinking, wasn't she the best thing in his life now? The only constant of the last few years, if you didn't count Denny and Meg – and let's face it, he couldn't marry Denny. He pulled himself up for a moment – had he said marry? Did he want to marry Claudia? Maybe he did. He was here, wasn't he? Buying what was little more than a shell of stone in a godforsaken corner of Ireland. This was the nearest he'd come to putting down roots – with Claudia at least.

'So, its sale's agreed?' he said to Skeffington when they locked the gate.

'I'll have to put it to the owners, but I'd say they'll sell. They might quibble about the price. It reflects downturn

figures, more than the new inflated optimism of the last year.'
He could hardly make eye contact with Todd.

'Look, Skeffington, I'm not stupid. These places are a dime
a dozen all around the coast. I just happened to pick this one,
but we both know that having me as a neighbour here will
help put this place on the map.' He had no intention of being
made to look like a fool by some yokel. 'I'll give you my
contact number, if they want to accept my offer they'll need
to get back to me quickly, I'm looking at other places this
week on the East coast.' He stalked back towards the village.

'Don't you want a lift?' Skeffington called after him, some
of the wind taken from his sails.

'No, the walk will do me good.'

Todd phoned the pilot who was having coffee in the local
hotel and they set off for London as quickly as they had
arrived.

*

It seemed to Todd that Claudia was a bit off with him when
he arrived back at the hotel.

'You sick of it here, babe?' he asked her as he poured
himself a small glass of red wine. Of course, what he meant
was, are you sick of me? He could see the way she looked
at him had changed. In the beginning he felt she was angry
with him, angry for getting sick and for making her miss out
on work. The last day or so, it felt like things had changed.
Now she looked at him with something else in her eyes and
he was afraid to figure out what it might be. Pity? Practised
tolerance or disappointment? It wasn't lust, anyway, he was
sure of that.

Todd didn't need to be a genius to feel that Claudia was slipping away from him. These days, it was as if she was on a different planet. Denny reckoned that she needed more. Meg shrugged her shoulders, unusually silent.

'Claudia, do you ever think about the future?'

'Course I do, doesn't everyone? I mean why do you think I work so hard – someday, when I lose my looks I don't want to be cleaning toilets for a living,' she laughed at him.

'There's no fear.' He wanted to say so much more, but they never had those conversations and now maybe it was too late. 'It's just, with things, you know, the last few weeks...'

'Your near-death experience,' she said drily as though it was yesterday's news and, even then, not very relevant.

'Yeah, with the heart attack, it gets you thinking.' He closed his eyes for a moment, imagined himself sitting on the damp wall that overlooked crashing waves and that cute old white and blue-trimmed building beneath. 'It got me thinking.' He lowered his voice, so it was almost guttural, making her stop and turn towards him. 'About what's important to me. About where I'm going in life.'

'I thought we were going to dinner,' she laughed at him.

'Seriously, Claudia, can't you talk to me about this?'

'About what, Todd? I get that everything has been thrown up in the air for you and that maybe you're feeling your age, but...' her voice faded, distracted by the ping of her phone. Damn Twitter.

'I've bought a castle,' he said the words quietly, as though he was confessing, but her head shot up immediately.

'You've bought a what?'

'I bought Rock Castle, where you had your picture taken in Ireland.'

'Why in the name of Prada would you want to do that?'

she sounded like a teenager with attitude to Todd and he wondered if they had always been this different.

'Babes, like I said, things are changing for me now. London just gives me a headache, I need a little space.'

'From me?' she asked and Todd wasn't sure if her voice was tinged with disappointment or the faintest echo of relief.

'No, not from you, doll. I need space from everything: this city, the press, the band...' That was it, for the first time in his life, London was hemming him in, his life here was stifling him. 'I need to get my head straight, sort out a few things. I need something to distract me, it's just a... project.'

'Oh.' Claudia's eyes drifted back to her phone. Perhaps she was slighted. The fashion people called her precocious, these days Todd found it hard to know where he was with her. 'So you decide to buy your first home in a different country and that's your project? Todd, people build model airplanes for projects or they take up golf – they don't go out buying castles in the middle of nowhere.'

'I need this, Claudia – I can't go on living in a hotel for the rest of my days.' He kept his voice low, he wasn't arguing about this with her. It was a done deal and he was over the moon to get it at a good price, he was actually excited about getting the work started.

'And what about the band? You're in the middle of a world tour or had you forgotten? Denny has only postponed the dates, Todd – fans have bought tickets, the Ace of Spades have been your life, are you just turning your back on them too – on a fancy?'

'No, of course not.' She made him sound like a petulant child. 'I haven't forgotten my responsibilities, but I'm not going to be touring for months, you heard what the doctors said.' Todd couldn't think about the tour or the band. Like everything else, the thoughts of that life just made him feel sick and uncomfortable within himself. Maybe he just wanted to run away from it all, for a while. Maybe it was what he needed – a complete change of scene and then he'd feel differently again.

'I swear, Todd, you've just hit the far side of crazy with this, I'm having nothing to do with it.' She looked down at her phone again, thumbed the screen over and closed her eyes for a second as though he was keeping her from some very important social media engagement.

'Don't be like that, I'd like you to come and see it. Give me your advice, we both know you have a great eye,' he was coaxing her. He couldn't face an argument, not now. Claudia believed the world missed out on the fact that she could be more than 'just a model'. She was waiting for the chance to team up with a designer to put her name on fashion, housewear, sportswear, anything that made her feel she was more than the world perceived her as now.

'I've seen it already remember, it's a dump.'

'You said in that interview that you loved it?'

'Of course I didn't say that, Todd. My publicist said that. Do you know how many big brands are coming out of Ireland now? I want a slice of that pie.'

'Well, you didn't see inside it, and you didn't see it with the sun shining on it. Come on Claud, just come for a few days, I've bought it now.'

'I suppose, it could be a great party house.' Her mind was working in a completely different direction to Todd's. She would think differently when she saw the place through his eyes, yes, Todd was sure of that.

## 10

## Robert, 1957

Robert had spotted the girl before she set foot on the pavement of the hotel. She was petite and slim and wore sensible tweeds that might have made another woman invisible. They only managed to heighten Iris Burns' beauty. And she was beautiful, Robert could see that. She was beautiful in a way that struck you instantly. Her auburn hair glinted in the sunshine as though it might capture heaven in its depths; she had strong features that were delicate and defined all at once. She reminded him of Lauren Bacall, that same mix of sweetness and smarts, with a knockout figure that stretched her clothes in all the right places. She carried her bag with the ease of the young and healthy. Robert noticed there was only one, a battered case that looked as though it was travelling long before Iris was born. Perhaps she was not planning to stay for too long. A pity. He had a feeling that was something he should set about changing.

He scampered down from the top of the hotel, three steps at a time, to book her in. He would give her the best room in the house; his mother would complain, but it didn't matter. He stopped on the first floor, just for a second, checked his appearance in the sideboard that held only fresh flowers. He was an attractive man. It was impossible not to know it. For as long as he could remember, women had smiled and blushed at him at every turn. He was, he knew, quite the catch. His parents would sign over the bathhouse to him for his next birthday. Although it seemed like an unlikely gold mine, he was making a real go of it. It was the farming and sale of seaweed as a health food that really put the place in profit. People loved the big copper baths, filled with seaweed and hot running water – business flourished in bad weather and in the winter months there was plenty of that. The Carrageen Moss was a surprisingly profitable sideline. Boiled in milk and eaten for breakfast or supper as a pudding, he was selling tonnes of the stuff. Its qualities were extolled by the President of Ireland himself. People believed it was a remedy for ailments from asthma to skin rashes, even if the local doctor was sceptical, the Irish loved a natural 'cure'. Robert had seized on the opportunity and now, with a couple of the locals, they were flogging it in both the Irish and English markets. People had no idea how popular it was. He knew that Archie thought he was certifiable. 'Selling weeds? Whoever heard of anything so daft?'

Archie, poor Archie. There were only two years between them, but Archie still seemed a lot younger. Stuck here with his parents until the day he died. He had no get-up-and-go. That was the problem with Archie, as Robert saw it.

He sighed deeply, smoothed his oiled hair back from his face. He had a rakish look to him, and he strutted with the self-assurance of youth. It was the moustache, the even teeth and the dark eyes. Even if you did not know who he was, there was no mistaking the confidence success gave him. He plucked a small white rose from the urn in front of him and slipped it into the lapel of his sports jacket. Satisfied with his appearance, he turned quickly and headed towards the antique reception desk that Archie refused to get rid of.

'Good morning, how can I...' She was beautiful, no doubt, and Robert, if he could find the words, had a feeling that in the moment he laid eyes on her everything in his world managed to flip, just a little.

'Hello. I'm expected. My mother spoke to Mrs Hartley on the telephone. It was a terrible line, but she said she would set aside a single room.'

'Oh, I'm sure we can do better than that for you, Miss...' he smiled, dipped his head slightly, knowing that it gave the impression he was shy and unassuming.

'It's Miss Burns, actually, Robert.' Archie came along the hall, buoyed up with excitement. 'Iris, dearest, how did you manage to make such good time?'

'Oh Archie, it's lovely to see a familiar face.'

'Umm...' Robert stood and watched as his younger brother greeted Iris Burns and he couldn't help feeling that somehow he had missed a step.

'Robert, sorry. You haven't met Iris, have you?'

'No, but it's my pleasure to meet you now, Iris.' He swept up beside them and in a turn managed to stand between them. 'How do you do? I'm Robert Hartley.'

'Lovely to meet you, Archie has told me a little about you.'

'Told?' Robert really was feeling as though this was all too much. Archie had this adorable creature under wraps for how long exactly?

'Well, I've been writing mainly. Pen pals, sort of. We met that year, when you went to the spa place in England, you remember? Mother and I stayed in St Kiernan's Guest House in Dublin.' It was true, Robert had taken a couple of weeks to see how other people were making money in the bath business, he'd learned less than he'd spent on the trip. Now, as he looked at Iris Burns, he realized it may have been even more expensive than he thought. 'Iris has spent the last year in Paris at a top cookery school, am I right?'

'That's right. I got back a few weeks ago and my mother thought it would be good for me to spend some time in the country. Get the colour back in my cheeks after city living.'

'So the people of Ballytokeep are going to be eating cordon bleu?' Robert raised an eyebrow.

'Hardly, your mother said if I wanted to help out at the hotel for a few weeks I'd be welcome to come and stay, before I look for a post in one of the big hotels.'

'And, so you are. How long can you stay for?' Archie was like a cat with cream.

'I have no plans. I will have to find some sort of proper work, but for now, I can take it easy.'

'Well, we will have to show you the sights, introduce you to the best Ballytokeep has to offer.' Robert tried to sound suave, but his voice faltered with an unfamiliar nervousness. With Iris Burns, was he in real danger of being out of his depth?

He watched as Archie carried her bags and led her up to one of the smallest rooms in the hotel. From the foyer, he could hear their merry conversation and her light lilting laugh at whatever comment Archie made. Robert stood for a long while, looking after them, contemplating what had just happened and it made no sense to him.

She was just a girl after all. He'd had many girls; none of them had affected him like this. She wasn't just any girl though, was she? It looked like she was Archie's girl, or at least Archie thought so. He wondered if Iris agreed; and that thought made Robert want to die of despair.

Robert set his perfect jaw at an angle. It was simple. He would have to make her his.

# Iris, Present

I ris patted back her silver hair. These days it had taken on the white of the ocean. She wore it short now, short and curled, and sometimes she thought that maybe she was turning into her mother-in-law. Maureen Hartley had worn her silver-white hair in a halo of curls just about her face. It was not a bad thing. Iris loved her mother-in-law and she knew that the feeling was mutual. Iris had cared for her until she breathed her last. A short easy breath that sent with it a sigh of contentment as she left Ballytokeep and her life's work far behind. Iris hoped for the same peaceful passing for herself and Archie when the time came.

Archie. Even still when she thought about him, she smiled. It could so easily have all been so different. She had been lucky. It took decades for her to see it, of course.

She could hear him, deep down in the belly of the hotel, pottering about. Today he planned to sand down some of the garden chairs ready for varnishing before the summer visitors arrived. He and Oisín Armstrong had stored them carefully at the end of last season and yesterday Archie took each one and completed any repairs needed. 'Good as new,' he told her proudly after he bought sandpaper and varnish in the local hardware shop. 'There won't be a chair to match them this side of the Shannon when I'm finished with them.' Dear Archie, he said it every year. She wouldn't be surprised if his father had said it before him. Sometimes she wondered how they had ever run the hotel all through the year. Now it took all their time and energy in the winter months to prepare for the summer. Of course, they got help in each year. Oisín Armstrong doted on Iris and he called every other day since his son took over the fishing boat. Then there were the local women, who arrived behind the swallows and dusted, aired, hoovered and scrubbed so the little hotel sparkled as it had the first time she came here.

'Tea, dear.' Archie pushed the door in gently. He balanced a tray set with cups, pot and one of her home-made scones smothered over with preserve she bought from one of the ladies locally.

'Oh Archie, you really are too good to me,' she said and she touched his face lightly with her hand. To her, he looked the same now as he did all those years ago. He was the softer, gentler version of his handsome brother. His dark hair had faded like her own. His eyes shone less but reflected more and about his face fine lines dug in truculently. 'You should have called me earlier; I would have gotten breakfast ready for Kate.'

Iris sighed. Kate, what a lovely young woman she turned out to be. Pamela's grandchild, tall and striking as Iris's sister Lady Pamela had once been, but with the colouring of their mother. Kate was the last in the line. That made her even more precious and Iris couldn't fathom why there had been such a gulf between Kate and her grandparents. True, her father died tragically years before and perhaps that made it painful for Pamela. After all, Crispin was her only son – to lose him so tragically in a car crash must have left a terrible scar. They said he was a playboy – not at all like Clive, Iris hardly knew Crispin. When she saw him all those years ago she only had eyes for her own son. It would have been too much, seeing Crispin could only open up her pain again after her lovely Mark, so she kept her distance and her silence. Life had somehow slipped between them. Pamela was broken-hearted when Crispin died, of course, and even her grandchild didn't make up for it; perhaps it only made the pain sharper. Clive said she died of a broken heart in the end. Iris could understand that; after Mark, she always thought the living had been harder. 'Ah, mon dieu,' she still prayed for him in French; still, sixty odd years on, the words fell from her lips. Archie didn't even hear them anymore, they were just a way of life.

'You have me spoiled, you know,' she said as Archie folded his tall frame and crumpled clothes onto the bed beside her. All those years ago, she fell for Archie, maybe because of his kindness, but there had been warmth there too. His mother treated him with great care. '*Scarlet Fever,*' Mrs Hartley whispered as she lay dying. '*You'll take care of him for me, Scarlet fever when he was just a boy. I almost lost him. It leaves scars you don't see.*' And it did. Archie was not a weak man, quite the opposite. He was her strength, a tall quiet rock that never let her down and made her feel like she was standing in the sunshine when he was near. But the fever took its toll in other ways. Archie, it turned out, would never father a child. It was a disappointment. Iris hadn't been surprised, not really. She felt it was karma. She was atoning for Mark. Life had a funny way of taxing you for your sins. 'You do far too much.'

'All under control, my dear. Remember, I was making breakfasts before most of the lads around here make their communions.' He winked at her now and if he said the same line a hundred times before, it didn't matter to either of them. He sat beside her, looked out at the tide making its way towards them. 'I was at the bathhouse.' Archie whispered the words.

'Why on earth would you go there?' She looked at him now, a little perplexed.

'Well, you know Robert wouldn't think in a million years of having fuel for that stove.' For a moment, he seemed very far away. 'It's worth the walk, if only for the air and to see the sport, the porpoises were playing out in the water.'

'There won't be any dolphins there, not this time of year.' Mostly, these days, she could tell when his voice was dipping into the past; his eyes took on a look of utter concentration, only a quiver of perplexity in his brow let him down.

'Porpoises, dear, they're porpoises.' He smiled sadly, and she had a feeling he was coming back to her again. 'Do you remember all those summer evenings when we'd walk down to the castle? The world was full of possibility then.'

'We've been lucky, Archie; we've had a happy life.' He was a good man, her Archie, far wiser than she realized when she married him. That was how she'd best describe him. Now that he was getting older and forgetting himself occasionally, she could glimpse what a wise man she had married all those years ago. In many ways, she hadn't seen it when she met him at first. Oh, she'd seen that Robert was clever, but he was clever in an obvious way. Archie on the other hand – well, he was gentler in every way, even how he understood the world and the people around him. 'I hope that Kate is as happy here as we've been.'

'She's fallen in love with Ballytokeep; it's all she needs to start again,' Archie said; taking her spoon, he slipped it carelessly in his pocket. He made her tea just right. It was just hot enough, not too strong, and not too weak. He actually made it better than she did herself, although, even with sixty odd years of marriage behind them, she wasn't going to tell him that.

'Hmm, maybe.' Iris wasn't so sure, she had a feeling that if Kate stayed she might be running away from more than what she was running to. 'Maybe.' Along the corridor, a pipe rattled belligerently. It seemed to Iris that each year the hotel grew noisier in the emptiness. Too many ghosts here, she thought.

'Perhaps I'll take a look at those pipes today,' he said, but they both knew that there was no fixing old age.

'Weren't you going to ready some of the garden furniture?' she reminded him gently.

'Oh, was I?' he shook his head, smiled a thoughtful smile. 'I really can't remember. What was it I was going to do with that?'

'Well, you've bought enough sandpaper to clean the strand, so...' She laughed gently to hide the worry in her voice. 'Honestly, Archie, I might be as creaky as those pipes, but you're far more forgetful.' The summer season might do them both good, blow away some of the cobwebs.

## 11

# Kate

'It is truly returning to its former glory.' Colin Lyons was standing in the doorway. It seemed he filled the place more each time he arrived. It was more than just his tall muscular frame; it was his voice, his eyes, his smile. Colin Lyons was a big man, but he had a quiet ruggedness about him that gave him a presence far beyond his size.

'Well, if it is, I have you and Rita to thank for that.' Kate walked towards him. It was true, Colin, her new neighbour, had helped her drag out the cast-iron chairs and table so she could clean and polish them. He'd stayed late into the night to help her move dressers and paint walls that would never be seen by a paying customer. Most days when he was not busy with his own work he arrived to help with any jobs he could.

'Don't be so modest, it doesn't suit you,' he leant forward and pulled some dust from Kate's hair. The action was intimate, and he pulled himself back a little as though he realized, too late. 'Anyway, it would be still sitting here an empty shell but for you,' he said, dropping down the provisions he had picked up for her.

'Well, I'm very proud,' Kate said and she meant it, 'although, it is a real group effort.' Her chance encounter with Rita, a retired school teacher with time on her hands and a terrier who just wanted to chase the waves, had opened up a friendship that saw Rita pop in almost every other day and set the little bakery at the back of the tearooms to rights. They laughed as hard as they worked, with Rita regaling Kate with tales of her husband, Duncan, and the woes of married life.

'We call it a meitheal here. It's what people do for each other, everyone rowing in for his neighbour to get the hay saved or lending a tractor or whatever you might need.'

'Does it apply to sharing lunch?' Kate smiled at him.

'You can be sure, if a man was waiting for some kind of payment around here he'd die a pauper. I'll take the dinner when it's going.' He laughed now and nodded towards Rita who was filling the kettle. 'How's the menu coming along, Rita?' Lucky for Kate, it turned out Rita was quite the cook, as well as being a home economics teacher she had a lifelong love of baking and testing. Her talents ran from the sweetest of desserts to the wholesome end of the scale. When Kate offered her the job for as long as the season lasted, Rita jumped at the chance. She rolled up her sleeves and helped with getting not just the menus ready, but knocking the tearooms into shape as well.

'Good, we've settled on a simple fare of sandwiches and salads, quiches and baked potatoes.' She pointed towards Kate. 'Of course, herself thinks it'll be all cucumber sandwiches and apple slices.'

'Bless her,' Colin looked across. 'You'll soon learn.' He

pulled down three mugs, dropped tea bags into each one. 'A
day at the seaside here and people will be famished. It'll be
spuds, spuds and more spuds to keep them going. The fancy-
pants that come in for the baths, they will be your salad
customers, bottled water and a slice of lime, for sure. The
families who come here every year, they have been crying
out for somewhere like this to come to. I'd say if you had the
energy to put on a dinner menu, a little soft music, this could
be a romantic spot for couples in the evenings too.'

'Steady up there, Colin. People will think you're getting
notions,' Rita said as she cut up the rolls she'd made earlier
for them; she did not notice the colour rise to his cheeks.

'I'm just saying, that's all.' They sat in companionable
silence, at a table by the window so they could watch the
waves crash far out at sea.

Kate looked back at the coffee shop and a feeling of
pride bubbled through her, it was happening more often.
They would open for their first day's business in a few
weeks' time. It was the beginning of the season, the hotel
had bookings for the Easter holidays, just a few regulars,
just enough to road-test the menu if they dropped into the
bathhouse. Kate invited the whole village to come along
and join them on that first morning. When they were in full
swing, with bookings for the baths, Colin promised to help
too, organizing the fresh seaweed and taking away what
was used. Rita would bake and prepare the food. She found
Amy and Zoe, two youngsters who were delighted to wait
on tables and help with the baths after school and when
the holidays started. Kate was glad to have them. They
were bright, enthusiastic girls and she had a feeling that the
customers would love them. For her own part, she planned
to be front of house when things were busy and otherwise

she would spend her time overseeing and making sure that everything was running smoothly. She wanted to spend the next week making everything just right.

All of the major renovations were complete now. The builders had been and gone. In their wake, they left behind not just new plumbing, electrics, kitchen and damp proofing, but also a mess that in some ways represented more work than when they began. The curtain fitters had finished just this morning. Now she had blue and off-white ticking at the windows and on thick seat pads on each of the chairs and benches. When they looked in the stores, there was enough crockery to last a lifetime. Delicate china cups, saucers and side plates, all with a light blue wisteria pattern. On Rita's advice, Kate had gone out and purchased ten dozen white dinner plates, the best quality she could get. They would continue to use the heavy cutlery Zoe had spent almost two days shining back to its former glory.

Colin showed her how to build a fire and keep it going for the whole day using local turf. 'A moving-in present,' he told her as he unloaded a heaped trailer of the stuff into one of the sheds at the back of the bathhouse. 'Plenty more where that came from.'

Kate loved the smell of it, burning softly away in the big recessed chimney.

'I think we should have a fire every day,' she said to Rita.

'You might need to, even on the hottest days outside, you're going to be facing the ocean breezes coming through that door.'

So, it was the first thing Kate did each morning when she came into the bathhouse. She emptied the ashes from the previous day and built up a new fire for the day ahead. While it took off, she set up her first cup of coffee. It took nearly a week for them to become proficient in making proper coffee. They still weren't exactly baristas, but they were improving with every cup. Sitting by the fire, with the aroma of fresh coffee before her, she would then set about writing out her list of things to do for the day. It was the nicest part of her day. Sometimes, she just thanked whatever had sent her to this place; she was meant to be here, this she knew for sure.

*

Kate planned to move into the flat on the Friday before she opened the bathhouse for business. She'd miss staying in the hotel with Iris and Archie, but she was looking forward to getting settled all the same. She would see them every day, after all, they were a big part of why she loved it here. Finally, she felt like she had family around her and she knew it was as important to them as it was to her.

'Housewarming?' Colin said hopefully, but there was too much to do and, anyway, they were a week away from the official launch of the bathhouse. 'You'll have to mark it, somehow.' He gave her a huge bunch of wild flowers, tied with string bleached by years of sun. Then he helped her to assemble the sleigh bed, which had arrived to much local amusement, in a forty foot truck that had no way of making it down the narrow path to the bathhouse. It had taken Colin and a few of the local men half a day to transport it between two small trailers and manoeuvre the parts up the winding cast-iron stairs to her flat. 'We should at least head down to the Weaver's Knot for a nightcap before you stay your first night.'

'Okay.' She liked the Weaver's. It was the only pub in the village open the whole year through.

Although she'd only been here a couple of months, already she felt like a local. Her first few visits were greeted by the curious looks of the old men who kept the business afloat in the dead months. As the weeks had crept by, she noticed the place fill up a little more each time. Now, on Friday and Saturday nights there was live music and the pub was packed by nine o'clock in the evening. It was strictly a beer and crisps sort of place. Plenty of Guinness and a friendly welcome – just what she thought Irish pubs were supposed to be.

Colin signalled to the owner from the doorway. A pint and a glass of black stuff and Kate grabbed two high chairs along the bar. She was glad to sit, the bar was full of stools made from tractor seats perched on single steel uprights. They were surprisingly comfortable. The place was wedged. The music struggled over the loud voices and laughter of local drinkers and visitors sampling what the town had to offer. Rita never came out with them for these evening drinks.

'Someone has to look after my old Duncan,' she said. 'Barry has shoes to chew and an allergic reaction to aggravate.' Apparently, Duncan came out in a rash if Barry so much as looked at him and this seemed to give Rita more satisfaction than any sticky toffee pudding. Kate had a feeling that Rita headed home to an empty house and an evening spent in the company of her adored Barry and the television soaps. 'Anyway, you don't want me cramping your style,' Rita had said when Kate pressed her.

'Believe me, I don't have any style left to cramp,' Kate laughed, and it was true, everything was so much more laid-back here than in London.

'You could do worse, you know?' Rita had smiled conspiratorially. 'He's the best catch around these parts, easy on the eye and he's solvent. I wouldn't want to be putting you off Colin, just because I married a bit of a spare.' Kate had a feeling that she wasn't joking, in spite of the hammy winks. She also had a feeling that Rita was spot on, he was the most eligible man she'd seen in the village.

Colin handed her the glass of Guinness, rescuing her from her thoughts.

'Thanks for that,' she said, sipping it. She had a low tolerance for alcohol, no point pretending otherwise, any more than two of these and he would be carrying her home. He seemed happy with two pints as well and she never asked, but she assumed he had the same resistance to the stuff. She looked at him now; he was handsome, in a rugged sort of way. His face was slightly more weather-beaten than the men she met in London, but his eyes were alive in a way she had never seen. If they held some sadness, they did not linger in it. His voice lilted with the kind of infectious enthusiasm that made you feel like he would always find the good in life. Kate wasn't looking for love, or at least, she wasn't aware that it was something she was looking for. Colin Lyons threw something stark at her and it took her a while to fathom it. Colin was probably the nicest, most suitable man she had ever met. They never spoke about love or romance. They were strictly friends. He was a good friend. Kate felt that the more time she spent with him, the more she was aware of him. She watched when he stood waiting for their drinks; other women noticed him too. She wondered why he had never married. He was the only decent-looking man in town at his age. The rest of the men were either married or too fond of standing in the Weaver's Knot most nights. Part of her knew that if he was snapped up from under her nose she would be sorry. Sometimes, she wondered too if he wanted to be anything more than friends. Or indeed, if deep down she wanted to be anything more than friends.

'Colin, I owe you thanks for more than just the drink, you've been a great...' She wasn't quite sure what the right word was.

'Friend?' he smiled and her stomach did a little flip. 'It's what we do here, you're going to be my neighbour, and of course I'm going to help you when I can.' He sipped his pint now, looked at the crowd thronged about the bar. 'I'm glad to have you, to tell the truth. Sometimes living out there,' he nodded towards the sea, 'well, it can be a little...' He thought for a moment, 'Isolating.'

'Of anyone here, I'd say you never need to feel isolated, Colin.'

'Oh, you think?'

'Surely you've noticed how the women look at you; you should be married by now with a family. You wouldn't be isolated then?' She raised her glass, she had broached the subject bravely, but keeping eye contact might give her thoughts away.

'The same could be said for you,' he said, suddenly finding the contents of his pint glass very interesting.

'Oh, my story is very tragic,' Kate smiled. 'Dumped at the altar, so long ago it shouldn't matter anymore.' It was good to talk about Todd and not become emotional.

'God, I'm so sorry,' Colin looked at her now and she could see it in his eyes that he was.

'It's history now, but it was the only time I came close to anything that might lead to...' She smiled at him, 'Domestic contentment.'

'And there's been nobody else?'

'No one I'd settle down with. Basically, no one that lasted more than two weeks.' She leant over towards him, lowered her voice, 'I'm very fussy and London isn't exactly thronged with the kind of men I want to spend the rest of my days clearing up after.'

'Well, his loss,' Colin said and the light blue of his staring eyes held her in their trance for a second too long. 'My story is much more boring. I fell in love much too young, didn't realize how to handle it and I messed it up.'

'So?'

'She married someone else, they've left here now. The last I heard they were living in Baltimore; she works in computers and he's a big noise in the security business.'

'I'm sorry.' Kate knew she genuinely was.

'Ah, sure that's life, isn't it? It wouldn't have worked out anyway; I mean we grew into two very different people. I couldn't see her being happy to live on the side of a mountain with the sunset being the highlight of the day.'

'I suppose you've heard that there are plenty more fish in the sea.' Kate spotted a local girl, late twenties giving him the eye.

'Oh, I'm not a hermit, or anything like that. I've had my fun, but in a town like Ballytokeep, you can't knock about too much without there being expectations and I haven't met anyone that I'd share my sunsets with.'

'Hmm,' Kate said, suddenly not sure that she wanted to continue this conversation. She intended to live in Ballytokeep for a very long time and that meant that she needed to keep her neighbours as her friends. The last thing either of them needed was a failed love affair and all the baggage that might mean between them.

'I agree.' Colin covered her hand with his, reading her

thoughts, he lowered his voice, 'It's probably better if we stay friends, although, you know that I feel a great deal for you.'

'How do you manage to do that, it's like you're reading my mind half the time?' She smiled at him, was he letting her down gently? Perhaps, but she was glad in some ways that they had named what lurked between them. Maybe a little sad that they both knew it was better to carry on as friends.

\*

Colin walked her back to the bathhouse that night, kissed her lightly on her forehead before she ran inside and bolted the door. The flat was perfect. She kept the antique sideboard and the large dining table. Robert Hartley's papers had covered almost every available surface of the flat; for now she had moved them into the spare bedroom.

'Burn them,' Archie told her, when she brought back some of the old ledgers that he had recorded the day's takings in. 'It's of no use to any of us now,' he said. 'We should have cleared it all out years ago, but to be honest, I never had the nerve to do it and Iris wouldn't have the heart.' Maybe, Kate thought now as she flicked through a notebook that belonged to Robert Hartley, she didn't have the heart either.

She lit two Kinsale candles in the windows, luxuriated in the scent of heavy fragrant wax mixed with the turf smoke. In the open fireplace, she had set a fire earlier. It welcomed her now with an orange glow that warmed her face as she sat before it.

This was her first night in the bathhouse and as she lay in her familiar bed tucked beneath the arched window, she snuggled between the crisp sheets to the sound of the waves crashing on the rocks below. She was home.

# 12

# Todd

Denny just thought Todd would grow out of it. Todd knew it was why he drove him to the airfield and patted his back as though fortifying him. 'See you soon, mate.' Of course, he would, because if Todd didn't forget about this whole crazy plan, Denny would just move the tour forward. Todd was flying over there a couple of times a week now, but the place was nowhere near finished. Perhaps when it was Denny would understand, or maybe Todd believed he'd be ready to settle back into 'real life'. Meg wasn't so sure, she said it suited him. Denny said Todd wouldn't survive more than a week away from London. A night or two over there with the sea howling up at his door would surely be enough to bring Todd to his senses.

They were mates, first and last, and their business partnership was just a lucky coincidence that boosted their friendship. Denny had come across him when he was living in a squat in London. Denny put the band together, got them their first deal and shepherded their way through the last two and a half decades. It was Denny that put up his Christmas dinner every year. They both knew Todd had nowhere else to go and Meg knew just how to do things right. Todd would arrive, Christmas morning, a bottle in each hand. Perfume for Meg, whiskey for him and Denny. Meg. He loved Meg as if she was his own sister. Meg looked out for him too. Meg had fed him, sobered him and put him to bed, too many times over the years to count, and she was still there. She stood, staunchly in the background, with kids of her own, a home running on a constant supply of love and pots of tea and family dinners, but always looking out for Todd. Their kids were big now, with flats of their own and lives of their own. It struck Todd, one day as he was walking along the sea front in Ballytokeep, that it was time that he too struck out and made a life for himself.

Since the band made their first top ten hit, Todd had lived as he felt a rock star should. He moved from the squat into a hotel room and never moved out. The Embassy Rooms suited him. It was a faded nineteen seventies colossus, with an owner who liked to beat him at poker and a suite of rooms he now called home, whatever that was. The staff knew how he liked things done. They understood how important it was to him that things were just so: soap on the left, toothbrush on the right, no dust, no ribs, no germs. All the same, leaving for Ballytokeep, checking out after over twenty years, it would be liberating. He would not miss it. He wouldn't miss London either nor, and this surprised him, would he miss the guys in the band. They were all getting on with their own complicated lives. He'd miss Denny and Meg. Denny picked up the pieces of his heart attack. And Claudia. He'd miss Claudia, after all, they had been together for a while now. He was sure to miss her, wasn't he? As Denny said, he was lucky to have a girl like Claudia around, even if things were a bit strained since Atlantic City. It'd all sort itself out in the end, that's what Meg said, it was time he settled down now. Maybe, being out of London was the best thing he could do for all of them.

\*

Rock Castle was coming along quickly. He was pouring a barrel of cash into it, 'get it done fast and get it done right.' He might not have an expensive designer on board, but he knew what he wanted. Life for Todd needed to be simple; it needed to be clean and it needed to be organized. The guys in the band called him 'OCD Todd', but he'd much rather be called discerning. He put it down to his poverty-filled youth. This castle was going to be his home and he wanted to please himself; he was glad to be here on his own.

Ballytokeep was in off-season mode for now; each time he visited, he managed to go unnoticed. He wasn't sure whether to be relieved or depressed about that.

Skeffington had put him in the way of a couple of builders. They were working fast, with a sea of yellow high-vis vests, hammering and chiselling from early morning until late at night. Todd had a feeling they weren't the cheapest, but he also knew instinctively they were the best. The castle was taking shape, morphing from a dilapidated barbican into a space that could yet be welcoming. The finer points could hold off until he found someone who would do a tasteful job, maybe he would call Bono or Jeremy Irons – he had a place somewhere down south. Skeffington suggested a few names, but Todd had muttered something about having to think about it and then changed the subject. The truth was he just wanted to get into the place. He wanted to move in, and he knew that some crackpot ponce walking about with colour palettes and swatches would only drive him bananas.

Summer was tripping closer by the day. Todd knew one thing for sure; he wanted to spend it here, in the tower looking out onto the Atlantic Ocean. He had a feeling he'd be content with nothing more than a cup of strong Irish tea in his hand, the sun in his eyes and the wind on his face. He wanted to walk along that beach each morning before the world woke up and enjoy the sun disappearing over the horizon every evening. Maybe he would make his way down to that cute bathhouse for a look, or walk up to the quaint hotel for a glass of something small.

*

Denny landed at Knock airport at three o'clock, one very sunny May afternoon.

'A mad place altogether, whoever heard of an airport built on a fen?'

'Here, we call it the bog,' Todd said wryly, but he was delighted to see Denny.

'Very apt.' Denny started to laugh, 'Don't even get me started on the roads.' He scratched his head. 'Seriously, the lads are wondering when we're getting back on the road.' They both knew this was a lie. The lads were up to their necks in their own lives; apart from the band, there was a chasm between them. They didn't meet up these days unless there was a reason and that usually involved getting paid. Todd wasn't even sure they liked each other very much anymore.

'Oh, yeah, I got their flowers,' Todd looked at him. 'Come

on, Denny, it's all about alimony and college fees these days for them.'

'Naturally enough.' Denny smiled. 'I'm wondering when you're coming back, and so is Meg.'

'I don't know. Like I told you, I'm...'

'Having a break?' They had breaks before, only then it had been Todd itching to get back to work. This was different, Todd knew it was, and maybe Denny knew it was too. They walked in silence along the narrow track that led to the castle. Beneath them, the bathhouse baked in the afternoon sun, and below that, cool waves lapped hungrily at the giant purple rock that jutted out over the water.

'I suppose, I'll come round soon enough,' Todd said quietly.

'I'm sure you will.' Denny's voice didn't carry a whole lot of conviction. As a heron swooped low, London and the life Todd had lived there seemed very far away to both of them.

*

'It's a bit basic, mate, to be honest.' Denny looked towards the top of the tower, his eyes slits against the evening sun. Denny liked his home comforts and he missed Meg when he left London, as much now as when they first married.

'Don't just judge it from here.' Todd wanted Denny to like it. He wanted it to be a place that his friend would visit, where they could shoot the breeze. He hoped it could be a place Meg would visit too and then they'd sit and watch the evening waves lap about the rocks below.

'Whew,' Denny said, 'that's a lot of scaffolding.' It was true; it covered the tower like a futuristic defence layer, up to the natural slate roof. It would be coming down in the next day or two, Todd thought it made the place seem smaller, squatter. 'A bit different from a mews in Kensington.' Denny took out a cigar. Usually they never mentioned the one time that Todd had considered buying property. 'Who'd have thought back then you'd be doing the rock star thing and buying a place like this?' They had looked at it together. It was cool, but classy, in the right area. It wasn't exactly palatial in floor space, but it suited Kate and Todd perfectly when they were planning a life together that he managed to derail in one night.

'Different times, mate, different times.'

'You can say that again. This place is big enough for the whole band and all the relations.' Denny was just getting a sense of the space.

'Don't worry, I'll earmark a room for you and Meg.' Todd laughed. 'You'll be better able to check up on me here.'

'Who said I'd want to check up on you?'

'I saw you counting my tablets, Denny.' It was true. After Atlantic City, Denny phoned him twice a day reminding him to take blood thinners, steroids and cholesterol tablets. Once, Todd even caught him counting the contents of his medication press to make sure he was taking them properly. 'Seriously, mate, there's a lost Florence Nightingale in you.' Todd was touched, after all, no one else was checking up with him.

'You haven't fallen off the wagon anyway?' Denny said, perhaps a little disappointed. He had not kicked the cigars himself, but then, as Meg pointed out, he hadn't really tried.

'No. Not a fag since that day and at most two or three glasses of red wine on occasion. No whiskey.' That was the killer of course. Todd drank whiskey for breakfast, dinner and tea back in the day. The last few years, his stomach had protested to any before five in the evening. After five, he saw it as his personal mission to make up for lost time. Yes. He very much missed the whiskey. 'Amazing what a bit of heart surgery will do to your taste buds.' They were walking to the top of the tower. 'You'll see why I had to buy it when you look out here.' The view was spectacular.

'I'm sure it's lovely.' Denny panted, he was out of breath after two flights of stairs. 'You putting in a lift, are you?'

'Nah, sure I'm fit and healthy now, Denny.' Todd laughed, but it had winded him too in the beginning. He heard the builders give out all the time about the narrow stairs and the amount of uneven steps. 'Here, we'll take a breather, have a look out.' Todd pulled open the shutter, faced out towards the peculiar little bathhouse. Denny pulled up close.

'Jeez, that's lovely all right,' he wheezed. 'Who's the bird?' he said, nodding down towards a woman who was tending flowers at the bathhouse below. 'Another perk?'

Todd moved closer to the window. He looked down to where a woman was planting summer flowers in heavy cast-iron pots, somehow drawn to the sight of her. Todd thought there was something vaguely familiar about the woman. He brushed the thought aside quickly, damn these funny feelings that kept catching him off guard. Unexpectedly, an odd thought occurred to him. This was his future. It was no time for chasing ghosts. He shivered, as though something greater than himself whispered in his ear and pulled closed the shutter.

# 13

## Iris, 1957

Mark died without her knowing. They had not sent a letter to Iris; perhaps they could not face that either. Her mother wrote and told her what she could. Of course, there were no words. The telegram arrived at St Kiernan's just as Mrs Burns was readying the supper for the permanents. It had been brief and devastating. They woke to find the child dead. Iris's lovely baby, Mark, lying in his cot like an angel. His silken hair fallen in waves about his head. 'An angel,' her mother wrote. They buried Mark in Paris. She held the letter close.

'My nephew,' the lie tripped from her tongue as easily as Clive had hoped it would. 'He died in Paris,' she told Archie when he found her crying. 'I was there when he was born.' There was so much she wanted to say; so much, she never could.

She dreamt about him every night, cried herself to sleep now for a very different reason. She realized that her anger and sadness before were so unfounded. At least then, he was alive. At least then, she knew he would have a good life. In the stillness of her little sparse room, the waves crashing against the pier in the distance the guilt hit her. It was her fault. If only she could have been happy for them. If only things had somehow been different. If only...

She did not have the heart to contact Pamela. She couldn't take pen and paper and commit the thoughts that haunted her every waking hour. She wanted to go to Paris, to see his grave, to double-check; perhaps they had made a mistake.

And then, Archie found her crying. He put his arm around her and somehow made her feel safe. He did not want anything from her. Not like William or, she guessed, like Robert. He held her close and let her cry until she could cry no more. His simple act of humanity made her cry even more before she was done.

'You know, you can't live in the past, Iris,' he whispered the words in her ear. 'You can only live here and now and, wherever you end up, you have to learn that, or you will never have peace of mind.'

She pulled away from him, had he guessed her secret? The secret of her lovely son in Paris. Mark, buried in a grave she may never see. The secret of her shame for William Keynes and the way she had let herself down with him. When she looked into Archie Hartley's eyes, she saw only kindness. Maybe she knew then that it was all she would ever see there and she was not sure if that gave her comfort or filled her with deep shame. 'Of course, you're right.' What a luxury it must be to enjoy the life before you; simply and innocently. Would she ever taste that kind of freedom again? She did not deserve it, she knew that, but she longed for it.

It was with a heavy heart that she picked up the letter that arrived from Pamela and Clive a few weeks later. Archie was beside her in an instant. She couldn't open it, had to build herself up for that. She certainly couldn't open it in front of Archie or anyone else. She didn't trust herself not to say what was burning her up inside. She had lost a son, and even if Mark would never know he was hers, Iris would never forget him.

'I'll read it later. It's from my sister,' she said the words unnecessarily, tucked the letter into her pocket and burned it after she memorized every single detail of Mark's last few days.

## Present

It was the smell that brought her back there more than anything else. She said so to Archie too. As though it had lingered here all this time. They stood in the centre of the tearooms, surrounded by neighbours and friends. Archie, she thought, was as tall and handsome as any man in the room and he stood proudly by her side.

'It's that old stove, I told her she should send it off for scrap, but she was adamant,' Archie shook his head affectionately. 'I don't know, sentimental, that's what it is.'

'Maybe, but it's the candle wax and the sea breeze and...' It was everything. Everything about the bathhouse. It made her feel a little dizzy, as though she'd stepped out of her own time zone and into a reality lived long before by someone else.

'Do you really like it?' Kate didn't need her seal of approval, but Iris was flattered that she wanted it. Archie had spent hours down here with Kate, it had done them both good. Iris loved that they seemed to have developed such a bond, but then it was impossible not to love Archie – his eyes still twinkled and his sense of fun made his voice lilt, so he made you smile even just being near. Kate felt it too, she called it the 'Archie effect'.

'It's... Robert would have loved it.' And that was the truth of it. 'He'd have loved it all. You've managed to save so much and still, it looks so fresh. No one would believe these spoons were around when I was a girl.' She held a teaspoon in her hand; it seemed heavy now, but sixty years ago they were positively the most modern design.

'Robert brought them back from Sheffield, they were the talk of the hotel for a week at the time,' Archie said fondly. He was tapping his foot lightly to the sound of a three-piece band who started playing a medley of old ragtime and ballroom tunes. 'It'd bring you back, all right,' he said to no one in particular, but Iris caught the sadness in his eyes.

'You've got a great crowd,' Iris said and she wondered at all of the familiar faces and quite a number she didn't know from Adam. 'Are they all local?'

'Mostly, but I asked the builders as well and anyone that gave a hand getting the place up and running.' Oisín Armstrong was wiping spills from tables, still thankful to Robert for saving him so long ago. Oisín had grown into a lovely young man, although Iris suspected that a drop of guilt propelled him to their door throughout the years. After all, the whole village had celebrated on the day the Hartleys were plunged into mourning. That was Maureen Hartley for you, she insisted that the good work must go ahead and they mourned alone for that first night.

'I see Colin Lyons is keeping busy,' Archie winked at Kate. Iris had watched them earlier. They would make a striking couple, but there was no real chemistry between them, not the stuff that lasts, at least.

'He's not the only one,' Rita Delaney placed a side plate with sandwiches and tasty bits down before them. 'It's great, isn't it?' she said to all of them at once. 'She's done a great job of the place. Mind you...' She looked across at Archie and Iris, 'if you hadn't held firm when my Duncan wanted to buy the place, there'd have been nothing to rescue at all.' She shook her head and Iris was reminded again of how different Rita was to Duncan. It seemed some couples grew in opposite directions the longer they stayed together.

'Well, I suppose without the developers we'd have no progress,' Archie said mildly and Iris knew he was only trying to be diplomatic. Duncan Delaney was the worst kind of developer – the kind that gave all others a bad name. He was a small rat of a man, with too much hair, narrow birdlike eyes and the demeanour of a shark in a tuna tank.

'Oh, please, Mr Hartley,' Rita shook her head and bent in low, 'I can say this to you, because I know, you're not tittle-tattles, but I'm so glad Kate got this place and not Duncan.' Her eyes held a satisfied gleam and Iris knew she wouldn't like to get on the wrong side of Rita if she could help it. 'Our next job now is to sort out that husband of mine.'

'Happy thoughts, Rita, happy thoughts.' Kate patted her back and steered her towards more hungry guests. 'Least said and all that,' she said after her, then she looked across at Iris. 'Divorce lawyer one minute, marriage counsellor the next.' Kate laughed, but Iris had a feeling that it'd take more than counselling to sort out Duncan Delaney and she was sure Rita knew that too.

'I'm so very happy,' Iris said to Archie later when they

were back at the hotel. 'It's like we've settled something, don't you think?'

'What's that Iris,' Archie looked at her and she suspected the party might have been too much for him.

'Never mind, it was just a lovely afternoon,' she said and she knew that if she was losing Archie just a little, it still felt like the world held promise for them. It was an unexpected blessing, however oddly it had come about.

# Robert, 1957

R obert hit on the idea, just for the summer months. The baths were already proving popular with women of a certain age. What he wanted now was to get the younger set in. 'Tea dances,' he said, hardly able to keep the excitement from his voice. He had a new Victor record player and a collection of records to surpass anyone on the peninsula. 'So, will you do the baking?' he asked Iris. She was a lovely baker, her touch so light that they were travelling from two counties away just for her pastry. Word spread quickly that she had trained in Paris – that alone was enough to bring the locals flocking for a taste. It wasn't why Robert wanted her though.

'Oh, Robert, I don't know, your mother asked me to take on all the baking for the hotel. I'll be doing afternoon teas as well as breakfasts and deserts?'

'This would be different. It's just to test the waters, so to speak. See if it would work out, and all we'd be offering is a plate per person and a cup of tea. I can't see us getting a crowd initially. If it takes off – who knows, maybe I could get someone in full-time. Maybe I'll treat you to another week in Paris?' He held her eyes for a fraction longer than was decent, but there was no mistaking what he meant. She may have met Archie first; it did not mean that Robert couldn't want her.

'I'll have to talk to Archie, see if it suits,' she said, moving away from him. He liked that she hadn't just fallen for him. The other girls around here, they were too easy. Robert Hartley was the most eligible bachelor on the peninsula, probably in the whole county. The only one who came close to him was his brother, and Archie was never going to be a player. All of the other men who stayed around were farmers – muck savages, hoping to take over the miserable smallholdings their fathers still farmed. Robert was not looking for someone easy. He was looking for someone extraordinary; someone who was equal to him, someone who would interest him long after the chase ended. Was he looking for a wife? No, he definitely wasn't, but he wanted Iris and he wanted her like he had never wanted anything in his life. It was as if she was a prize above any other and Robert wasn't sure that having Archie in his way didn't add to her allure.

'You and he aren't...?' Robert leaned in a little closer to her, could smell the fresh scent of lilac.

'Aren't what?' She laughed at him now. Maybe she didn't realize that she was torturing him, but she seemed to enjoy the effect. 'Sweethearts?'

'Well, you're hardly that, not with Archie,' he scoffed, managed to make his voice sound more offhand than he felt.

'Why not?' Her voice had an evenness to it that surpassed

the joviality of her eyes. 'You think that because he doesn't drive a fancy car that...'

'I think that you and Archie are different people, that's all. I just can't see you settling for Hartley's Hotel for the rest of your days, and that's what it would be with Archie.' He took her hand, pulled her close to him, it was a bold move, but he was desperate for her. 'You could have so much more.' He could feel her breath deep and uneven in her body next to his. He bent his face next to hers, couldn't stop himself even if he wanted to.

'Don't,' she breathed and he felt a wave of excitement flash through him, he wanted her more than ever now. He could feel the length of her, warm and soft through her light cotton dress, it made him ache with desire. 'I can't do this...' She pulled away from him, leaving him feeling as if half of him had been hoven off. He watched as she walked back towards the hotel, somehow feeling bereft and joyful all at once. Was this love? He wasn't sure. He was sure though that she had felt something too; he could see it in her eyes, buried there behind the guilt. She might not admit it to herself, but Robert could see she was as attracted to him as he was to her.

In the end, he asked Mrs O'Neill to bake some tarts, shortbread and queen cakes. It wasn't exactly the fare of the Savoy, but it was good enough for Ballytokeep. He asked one of her sons to put up notices about the village. The first tea dance was on the May bank holiday Monday. That gave him just a week to get everything up and running and, what was there to do, except push back the tables and load up the plates?

'You should come, Archie; shouldn't he, mother?'

'Well, it is the start of our season.' His mother spoke under her breath, but Robert knew, she worried that Archie would never find a wife.

'You could bring Iris, it would do her good. You can't expect a girl like that to sit out every dance if she goes on her own, can you?' Robert had a feeling that if Archie didn't come to the tea dance, neither would Iris. Archie being there was not something Robert was going to worry about, so much as Iris not being there.

'I should probably ask her, shouldn't I?' Archie knew better than to address this question to either of them.

'Yes,' they both answered together.

The May bank holiday was as sunny and warm as any summer's day. From late on Friday afternoon the hotel began to fill steadily.

Robert had all the popular songs lined up. He had Frank Sinatra, Ruby Murray, Dickie Valentine and, at the bottom of the pile, he kept Doris Day. He was going to have his arms around Iris for 'Secret Love'.

He hung a huge banner at the front of the bathhouse. The day was hot and he pulled all of the tables outside onto the rock. Inside was room for the dancing and for Mrs O'Neill to get the tea and cakes distributed.

At three o'clock, cars, bicycles and carts began to arrive on the road just above the rock. By four, the party was in full swing. Robert could hardly move for the crowd – locals and plenty of tourists too. The atmosphere was merry, the dance floor packed and they quickly ran out of rhubarb tart and shortbread. It did not matter. Outside, the men looked out to the sea, girls at their sides. Everyone smoked rolled up tobacco and enjoyed the optimism of summer spool in off the waves. One girl took off her stockings and stood in the water up to her calves. Robert watched the sunlight making darting lights on her milky legs. He scanned the crowd for what seemed like the hundredth time that afternoon. There was still no sign of Iris and Archie. He decided to go inside again; change the record. He was nervy with anticipation and it was all about Iris. The last thing he wanted was 'Secret Love' going on before they even arrived.

Later in the afternoon, standing in the doorway; he spotted them ambling along the narrow road that trailed down from the village. They looked like they were in no particular hurry, just happy to be out of the hotel. The fresh air pushed the hair from their eyes. Archie walked tall and straight, his sleeves rolled down, a straw hat sitting jauntily on his head. He swiped happily alongside the stunning Iris. She, for her part, had pinned her hair in the fashion of the day. Her lips were scarlet, matching perfectly the dress that clung to her impressive curves. Her shoes, glamorous but not garish, gave her added inches. When they halted before Robert, it seemed that she looked him directly in the eye. And whether Archie knew it or not, Robert imagined he saw something of a challenge there.

'Come on, you two, I've got something special just for us.' He led them to the back of the tearooms, through the throngs of dancing couples. At the foot of the stairs to his flat, he left three glasses and a bottle of gin, with a small container of peppermint next to it. 'Bottoms up,' he said as he handed a large measure to Archie and Iris and poured himself something much more modest.

'Oh, my,' Iris said. Robert guessed correctly; she was not used to alcohol.

'We probably shouldn't have too much of this. After all, there's dinner for thirty people for this evening to be served up yet.' Archie was conscientious as usual.

'Oh, lighten up, Archie, it's a party. You have the next four months to make dinners and work like a slave. Iris needs to have some fun too.'

'Right,' Archie said, eyeing up Robert. He was, after all, the expert in affairs of the heart.

'Come on; let's get a dance or two in before it's over. One of those feisty Corcoran girls has been throwing me some very saucy looks all afternoon, what do you think? Should I make her day?' Robert had a plan. He'd been hatching it since before they arrived; it was either this or make a complete fool of himself.

'Not Jackie Corcoran's daughter? Robert, he's the church warden and there's none of them even out of school yet. They are hardly seventeen.' Archie was aghast.

'I'm just going to dance with her, Archie, that's all. Didn't you know, I'm a changed man?' He looked at Iris now, held her eyes for a second too long. 'I've fallen in love, properly fallen in love.'

'Oh?' Surprise or alcohol fired up Archie's eyes. 'When did this happen?'

'It's been brewing for a while. Do not tell mother though, will you. As luck would have it, the lucky girl already has a bloke, so she hardly knows I exist.' He smiled, didn't want to overplay it, but he had a feeling he had piqued her interest. 'Come on, it will be over before we get there.'

Iris drained her glass and gasped, she was no drinker. On their way to the dance floor, one of the local boys was taking photographs of the tables.

The Corcoran girl turned out to be a nifty dancer. She was just sixteen and built like Rita Hayworth. Robert figured in a few years' time she'd be a farmer's wife and hauling calves across ditches as if they were winter snowdrops. She rattled away into his ear, enjoying the daggers half the other girls in the room were giving her. He wasn't listening to a word of it. He made all the right facial expressions, leant in close occasionally and laughed when it was required. Robert was only interested in Iris. He watched as she swayed to the music initially, her face flushed from the gin. Then she and Archie took to the floor, a little nervously at first, but she could dance. She could dance well enough to make Archie look like he knew what he was doing. Then again, anyone would look good with Iris. After four energetic jives, he nodded to Mrs O'Neill's eldest son to slow things down a little. He made his excuses to Susan and walked over towards Archie and Iris.

'May I borrow her?' he said to Archie as he took her hand. 'It's just that Susan is only sixteen and I don't want the bishop closing me down before we even get going on these tea dances, old boy.' He smiled at Archie who was probably relieved not to have to attempt a waltz. Robert on the other hand was confident, smooth and elegant on the dance floor, just as he was with everything else in life. They danced the first dance in silence. He enjoyed having her in his arms, smelling her hairspray and the scent of ginger soap she used before she left the hotel.

The music broke before he held her away from him. They stood for a moment, looking at each other, not quite at arm's length, but with enough room for the Holy Spirit to make his way between them if necessary.

'So you're in love now, are you?' She arched an eyebrow in that way she had so he knew she was sceptical.

'You think that's strange?'

'Robert, I may seem like a country bumpkin to you, but remember, I've lived in Paris for a year. I've seen more of life than you might imagine.' Her eyes were a little glassy – the gin.

'I never said I thought you were a country girl,' he whispered as he pulled her in close. 'What I said was that I didn't think you should settle for someone like my brother. Anyway, what difference does it make what I might think of you?' It was a dare.

'I...' She searched the room for Archie. 'Of course, it makes no difference, I hope you and... whoever you are in love with are very happy together.' She made to move away from him.

'Why are you always angry with me?'

'I'm not angry with you. I don't feel anything at all for you, Robert.'

'It sounds like you're trying to convince yourself far more than you're trying to convince me.' He smiled at her. She had no answer to this, not immediately.

'I can feel it too. This thing between us; but it's nothing. There, that is what you want me to admit, isn't it?' She blew out a long breath of exasperation. 'I've felt it since the first time we've met, if you want to know the truth of it.'

'I knew you did, I just wasn't sure if you realized what it was.'

'Oh, I know what it is all right, Robert. But, it's toxic. You're the kind of man who uses people.' She was spitting the words and he had a feeling he was getting the brunt of her anger meant for someone else. 'You belittle Archie at every turn, but the truth is, he's decent and honourable, and even if he doesn't drive a sports car, that doesn't make him any less of a man.'

'If you two end up together, God – Iris, there's a real possibility you could die of boredom in that place.' Robert didn't dislike Archie, he just figured he was better than anyone else in the county, his brother included.

'I don't think so.' She pulled away from him, looked him square in the eye. 'Let that be an end of it now.'

Robert watched as she walked across towards Archie. Iris didn't see the Corcoran girls give her daggers for captivating the richest man in the village from under their noses. It made no difference to him, he knew that he was going to have her. He had no choice, it was already done, even if Iris didn't realize it, the attraction was too strong.

# Iris, Present

'A rock star?' Iris let the words float from her. If she wasn't so worried about Archie, it might be exciting or at least interesting. 'Never heard of him, sorry.' But the name was familiar, she knew exactly who he was. He broke Kate's heart, of course she knew who Todd Riggs was.

'Well, it seems he's quite the celebrity and he's going to be living in Rock Castle.' Annie Murphy loved to chat. She called every other week, dropped off a couple of magazines, drank some tea and then chatted away about whatever village gossip was currently doing the rounds. Iris suspected the church ladies set her upon them, or perhaps social services? They weren't getting any younger, even if they sometimes forgot it themselves. 'I'm sure Kate won't be very happy about it though,' she said now, sitting opposite her.

'I'm sure she's happy to have people like that about, it'll bring more business to her.'

'Apparently, she knew him, in London, quite well it seems. I don't think she'll be that keen.'

'Well, she's a good judge of character; I'd say if she didn't take to him there was good reason.' Iris wasn't going to put oil on the rumour mill. She placed the cover on the butter dish, her scones were still popular and she tried to bake a few times a week when the season was up and running. This year it seemed she was doing less in the hotel, with the local women taking over more of her duties. They were nice, she'd give them that. It was lovely to have a little female company in the kitchen while she set about her baking.

'Lorna Simons – you know, her mother had the wool shop for a while? She's certain that Kate and he – the singer were... you know...' Annie couldn't keep news to herself, never could. 'Engaged, only he left her at the altar.' For a Christian woman she really was a terrible newsbag, Iris thought to herself.

'Ah well, you know it's a good thing we never gossip,' Iris said, hoping it might stop the conversation short. It was all some crazy mix-up. The village yappers realized that Kate had been engaged to Todd Riggs and now the castle was being renovated by some celebrity. It was some of the locals putting two and two together and coming up with twenty two. She wouldn't even mention it to Kate – it would only worry her. Todd Riggs indeed!

'Well, it's not like she hasn't made up for it since she came here. She has Colin Lyons practically running after her like a pet lamb since she arrived and we all know what he's like...' Annie pulled herself up once she saw Iris's expression. Everyone knew Iris Hartley did not gossip.

After that, Iris found her gaze wandering often to the castle that overlooked the village. There had been a lot of speculation in the village as to what was going on up there

– this was probably just idle chatter to fuel the hunger of the village chinwags.

More and more her mind wandered back to the past now. She wondered sometimes what might have been. If she had stayed in Paris with Mark, if Robert had not died, if Archie did not have scarlet fever as a child – then she would realize how futile all these questions were. Iris supposed it was a feature of getting older. Archie still pottered about the place, the weeks had made him slower now than before, but as always, he marched to the sound of his own drum. If occasionally he forgot the beat of that, Iris reminded him quickly and glossed over the lost expression in his eyes. Neither age nor pace seemed to fracture his resolve. He went about the hotel, greeting guests and bringing pots of tea or baskets of turf with equal dedication. All of the women loved Archie. He was a gentle man with a proud bearing, charming and funny and welcoming people with genuine warmth.

Some days, for her part, Iris thought the memories would flood her whole world. Mark had shared her thoughts with Robert for so many years, they filled her with guilt and longing. It grew to a hunger that could never be satisfied; living with it was her only hope. She had promised her mother when the darkness of the water let her down. She didn't want to forget either of them, nor could she. She imagined she saw Robert walking along the pier one day, so vivid was he that she grabbed her coat to try to catch him up. Of course, when she reached the door, she knew she was too old to run along the promenade. It was all too long ago for Robert to be anything more than a ghost. She wondered sometimes if he watched her. She wondered if he taunted her by setting up home in her memories and never truly freeing her spirit for Archie. Archie, darling Archie. Many times over the years, she told herself she should never have married him. That night, that cruel, illicit, ferocious, wonderful night, she knew then that she would only be settling for Archie. Surely, he deserved more than that.

For years, she managed to push it from her memory. It tumbled out again, of course, rose up when she least expected it. Those hours, days and weeks of passion – they had stayed with her far longer than they had any right to haunt her. When she looked back, she knew, it was something she never experienced before or since in her life. It was heaven and hell; even more because she knew it could not last. It was all a heady emotional melange to digest.

'You're a million miles away, pet,' Archie said to her when he came into the kitchen late one evening.

'Oh, I'm just thinking,' she said, but she knew he saw her tears. He had been her very best option, all those years ago. There was nothing for her in Paris, and Robert, she knew, deep down was no better than William Keynes. 'Did you have a nice walk?' He had been gone for most of the afternoon.

'Oh, yes. I called into the bathhouse.' He shook his jacket off, hung it on the hook behind the kitchen door. Iris was glad that Kate was there now. In the past she worried about him going down there alone. 'Robert needs more turf; I told him I'd order an extra trailer from the Murphys, next time I see one of the lads in town.' His voice never changed and Iris didn't correct him anymore. It only made him anxious. Soon they would be talking about Kate, the present tense, safer ground. He would remember that Robert wasn't there anymore. Iris told herself that this was just a slip and everything was fine, really.

'Goodness, it's almost seven. Where did that go to?' It

was true. She had sat down at the kitchen table to prepare tomorrow's breakfasts and that was almost three hours ago. The oats remained untouched before her. Time was slipping from her, just as the memories were slipping past Archie, and it was slipping fast.

# 14

## Kate

Kate had the oddest feeling, as though she was being watched. She looked up towards the castle, her eyes drawn there against the evening sun. Unfinished business? That was the feeling. She saw the two people at the top window of the tower. Rumours were rife of course in the village, since the 'For Sale' sign came down, but she was not one for gossip. The tower was sold that was all she knew.

'Probably,' Archie said, 'to the fisheries, or the Department of the Marine. Who else would want a draughty old tower that hadn't a decent room in it to make a cup of tea?'

Colin thought it was all nonsense. No one had been near the tower in years and now some of the locals were getting a small fortune for a big clean-up job on it.

'You must be getting very wealthy neighbours,' he joked when he dropped in one morning.

'Well, let's hope they like pastries and seaweed baths, eh?' She laughed at him and playfully slapped his hand when he tried to help himself to an almond slice. Their relationship had settled into an easy friendship, only occasionally she felt an undercurrent of what might have passed between them.

When Kate closed up the bathhouse for the evening and sat outside to enjoy the view, she often felt like pinching herself. Life was so good, it could be just a dream. She had been lucky and less often now she thought about the life that might have been. The husband, children, public school, and stellar career – she was exactly where she was meant to be. She felt as though she had been rooted in this place long before she was born. Everything was ticking along perfectly.

'If this keeps up for the whole summer we'll have broken even by the year's end,' she said to Rita as they closed up shop one evening.

'If this keeps up I'll have baked the equivalent of K2 in fruit scones,' Rita said, laughing.

'Is it too much for you?' Kate worried about Rita. She seemed to have something on her mind all the time. She knew that things were not good at home. She had met Duncan once, hadn't warmed to him. He reminded her of an alligator with plastic hair. She had heard the village gossip that he was seeing some girl that was half his age and fond of his wallet. Rita confirmed it when she confided in her.

'Been at it for a while, but he's afraid to leave me in case it'll cost him too much.'

'It's not a reason to stay together, Rita.' They weren't a couple that Kate would have put together from word go.

'Ah, it's not so bad. I mean, Barry and I, we make the most of it. I couldn't imagine living anywhere else and, to be honest, I'm not even sure that I'd get to keep the house if we went alerting the taxman to half of Duncan's *business interests.*'

'I could help, you know, maybe with...' She meant everything, but she didn't want to say divorce. In all of her career,
she'd never encouraged anyone to break up their marriage,
even if she felt very strongly that it would be the best thing
they could do. Instead, she waved her hands about the place,
to cover any help she could give.

'Listen, Kate, no offence, but even when you make sandwiches it stresses me out. I hate to break it to you, boss, but
you're no natural in the kitchen.' Rita smiled, moving the
conversation away from Duncan – perhaps she was happy
exacting her own kind of payment out of him. A lifetime of
antihistamines and a trail of Barry's destruction to Duncan's
expensive shoes might be repayment enough for an unhappy
marriage.

'I know. I never realized how fast I'd have to move here.
I really thought it would just be an occasional toasty and a
pot of tea.' She looked around the tearooms. The girls were
putting the place to rights; another hectic day over. 'Not that
I'm complaining mind, I love when it's busy.'

'Your bank manager will love it too, I'm sure,' Rita said,
smiling. Kate hadn't told anyone that she was operating the
bathhouse out of her savings. She had a feeling that not too
many people in Ballytokeep would have a couple of hundred
thousand lying idle in a bank account.

*

They quickly settled into a routine of sorts. Kate rose when
the sun shone bright through her bedroom window. She
wandered down to the tearooms and set the ovens on, made
a morning cuppa and was just about to tuck into breakfast
most days when Colin arrived with the morning papers.

The ovens warmed up the bathhouse first thing, so by the time Rita arrived, it was just a question of popping the day's baking in and then waiting for the aroma to fill the place. Rita did some of her prep the evening before and while things were still busy, she spent most of the day churning out fresh bread, scones and cakes.

They soon became used to seeing activity up at the tower. Colin arrived one morning with news of the buyer and he was greeted with hardly a glance.

'Well that's okay if you don't want to know. Let me just say this; you're going to have a bona fide celebratory next door...' Colin poured tea from the pot before him. 'And, if you believe what the *Weekly Chronicle* has to say, you might have a full-blown celebrity wedding here by the end of the year.'

'I suppose it's some movie director shacking up with wife number six?' For one with thirty years of marriage under her belt, Rita cast a very cynical eye upon the institution, hardly unexpected though – she was married to Duncan.

'No, I think all the movie types are getting sense and heading to Lake Como and places with guaranteed sunshine,' Kate said absently. 'Mind you, it'd be good for Ballytokeep to have a bit of glamour; certainly the shopkeepers and the Hartleys would be glad of the extra business.' If they got any busier in the bathhouse she would have to take on more staff, and to be truthful, Kate liked things just as they were.

'Well, obviously rock stars are not casting their nets that far afield.' Colin's voice dipped now; perhaps he was bored because no one much wanted to play his guessing game. 'Give up?' He looked at them both and then opened the paper to show a grainy photograph of Rock Castle. 'It's Todd Riggs and that model he's going out with.' Colin didn't notice Kate's reaction.

'Oh, I always liked him, what did he sing again? "Thunderstorms" wasn't it, or something like that?' Rita started to hum the broken melody of one of Todd's biggest hits. 'He's around a while, a real jack the lad,' she said absently, popping a piece of fruit scone into her mouth.

'Can I see it?' Kate whispered, taking the paper in her hands. She felt as though she was operating from outside herself. It was as though, somehow, she'd left her body and floated to a place where her emotions were padded out. She felt a rising sickness in her stomach. She held the paper before her eyes, her hands shaking, so she placed it on the table to look at the article and there was Todd, a recent photo of him, walking on some street in London. The better part of London, perhaps Kensington? He looked older, tired and thinner than she ever saw him before. As though someone had come along and shaken the vitality from him overnight. His eyes no longer sparkled, his cheekbones jutted out, a little too starkly. His smile had softened, but his jaw was slack – he looked worn out and far more than the age she knew he was.

'Kate, are you all right, you look like you've seen a ghost?' Rita said softly.

'Oh, it's just…' She could tell Rita, of course she could. You couldn't keep something like this a secret for long in a place like Ballytokeep. She would tell her and Colin too, just not yet. 'I'm fine,' she said.

Kate scanned through some of the feature, drew out the pieces that were of interest. They could confirm that Todd Riggs had purchased the castle in Ballytokeep, a small village in the west of Ireland. There was a reference to Claudia Dey, who had fallen in love with the place, and a picture of her impossibly beautiful face staring coldly from a shoot taken earlier in the year. There was mention of Todd's heart attack, of Claudia's successful campaigns and finally whispers of wedding bells before the year was out for the happy couple. At first, Kate thought she might be sick. In quick succession, that feeling was replaced with something deeper: anger. How dare Todd Riggs come and spoil her lovely life? How dare he hijack her happiness now that she had finally found it? Maybe there was some resentment too. At the end of the day, she wasn't entirely sure that she could wish him well with Claudia. After all, she still had a broken heart to mend.

*

It took almost two weeks before she could face up to the fact that Todd Riggs could be arriving on her doorstep someday soon.

'You've been very quiet lately,' Colin said one evening; he called in as she was closing up for the day.

'Have I?' she said absently. Colin was her friend, and she could see in his eyes the genuine worry for her. 'I'm sorry. I don't mean to be, it's just that things have been so busy.' She was lying. It was a small white lie, but when she looked into Colin's face, it wasn't one she was comfortable with. 'Fancy joining me for a glass of wine?' she asked as she cleared away the last of the tables.

'Well, I do have a lot of sheep to count...' He smiled at her and reached behind the counter for two large red wine glasses. 'Outside?'

It was a lovely evening. The warm summer sun was still

full and orange in the evening sky. It basked the front of the bathhouse in a deep amber glow. Kate took two large cushions from the bench that ran along the walls of the tearooms and popped them down on the wrought-iron seats outside. Colin followed with the drinks. They sat in silence for a long while, staring out into the waves that flashed up foamy white in the evening sun.

'It's so beautiful,' Kate said finally, 'you know, when I sat here for the first time I thought I could live and die in this place.'

'I've always known that there's nowhere I'd rather be. Even when I was younger, I travelled, you know, to see the world!' He grimaced slightly. 'I knew I would come back here, wasn't sure when, but I knew that this place was always pulling me back to it. It's the silence, I think.'

'Maybe, but for me, it is the people too. Everything and everyone is so different to what I knew in London.'

'It is that, I'm sure all right.' Colin did not like cities. The image of Colin in London just didn't fit; he would be like Crocodile Dundee in New York. He just suited here. He fitted, just as Kate felt she fitted too. 'Something has changed for you? Here?'

'You could say that,' she smiled what she hoped was a smile, but behind it she could feel a huge ball of emotion pound steadily up through her.

'Can you tell me?' Colin leaned forward, covered her hand with his own. 'You're cold. Here.' He took his jacket off, placed it gently around her shoulders. She hadn't eaten properly in days, hadn't slept. Feeling cold was just one more thing now. 'Seriously, maybe there's something we can do to...'

'Make everything better?' She whispered the words and

looked into his eyes. Suddenly, she felt a huge tear roll from her own. 'Sorry, I'm just...'

'You're scaring me,' he said, trying to keep his voice light. 'I didn't know that legal people cried.' He moved nearer and put his arm around her. It felt nice, strange but nice. 'You have to tell me what's upset you, Kate, if I can help, you know I will.'

'I know that, Colin. But...' She wiped a tear from her eyes. 'There really isn't any helping this. It's all and nothing, and really, it's something I probably have to make peace with or just move on.'

'Well, you can't move on, you're making a life for yourself here, you're part of us now,' he whispered the words, but beneath them, she felt there was so much more.

'It's the castle,' she nodded up towards the huge structure that seemed to loom larger with every passing day. 'You know, Todd Riggs? Who has supposedly bought it?'

'Yeah, the singer?'

'The one and only. You haven't followed his career, I suppose?' Of course, he hadn't. Colin read the papers daily, but celebrity culture or trivia was his weakest subject in the local pub quiz.

'No. Should I?'

'No, but...' She searched for the words. 'I knew him, in London. Years ago now, we were...'

'Seeing each other?' Colin's eyes had grown a little wider now.

'We were engaged. Getting married.'

'Kate, it was him? You were the girl he left at the... He was your bloke?' He shook his head sadly. 'His bloody loss, that's what it was. I always knew he was a plonker, but what a rat?'

'You could say that. We had it all planned, down to the last detail. Then, on the morning of the wedding, Todd skips the country with some bimbo and calls the whole thing off. He left it to his manager to tell me. I never...'

'Got a chance to tell him he was a swine? Sorry.'

'That too. It was a nightmare. I've spent a decade, afraid to open a newspaper because I felt like half my life was a byline. It's hard to forgive and move on when you keep seeing your humiliation played out in the national press. Then I moved here and I thought I had closed that chapter for good.'

'You're not looking to have a reminder of that time on your doorstep?'

'Yeah, something like that. I...' Kate took a deep breath. 'I suppose, I never really got over it.' She felt new tears fill up her eyes. 'I never really got over him. My life in London was,' she searched for the word; there was only one, 'empty.'

'I'm so sorry, it must be terrible.' Colin sat back in his seat, pulled his heavy jumper up about his neck to shade off the chill that was creeping steadily into the evening, now the sun was fading.

'There's no need to be sorry. That's life, right?' She shrugged, knowing that she had genuinely felt like this when she arrived in Ballytokeep. It was just a bad hand of cards. Everyone gets something in life, and Todd Riggs was her joker in the pack. 'Anyway, I came here; fell in love with this place. Maybe it is the first time I have been in love since that time, who knows? It took a decade, but I felt I was healing, you know, finally.' She looked at him now and he was nodding, he understood. 'Then a few weeks ago I had the strangest feeling.'

'Go on.' Colin topped up their glasses needlessly.

'It was an evening like this, perhaps a little colder. I was planting the hydrangeas, when I happened to look up at the tower. I don't know why I looked up. There wasn't any reason to draw my eyes up there, but I looked and then I felt like I couldn't look away. In that moment, I felt like I was back there. Back in that time, before the hurt and the pain when there was so much to look forward to. Then I saw people up there.' She pointed towards the uppermost window that looked back across the beach. 'I couldn't tell you what happened in that moment, but I felt a sense of complete panic overtake me. As if I'd left a frying pan on full heat and it could explode at any moment.' She shook her head, still trying to comprehend the feeling. 'It was as though…'

'You have things to do – you're not over him yet, that's what it was telling you, Kate.' Colin's voice was cold, emotionless almost. For a moment, it felt like the sun had been swallowed by the sea, because the whole place seemed to grow dark.

'I didn't think that was what it was at the time, but then, when we found out that he'd bought the tower, I understood. There's half-finished history, and I guess the world, this place, has thrown us here to put a close to it.' Colin was right, she needed to tell Todd Riggs that he was a nasty brute and that what he'd done to her was unforgivable; then she could finally move on.

'Hmm.' Colin looked out to sea, sipped his drink thoughtfully, 'I hope so, Kate.' He looked at her now, his eyes steady. 'I hope so, because you deserve so much better than Todd Riggs.'

\*

It was a shock of course, but seeing Todd Riggs sitting in the bathhouse had not been nearly as awful as she had expected. She fled – obviously, fight or flight? It was a gut reaction. She ran upstairs, up to the large drawing room that looked out on the harsh sea beneath. Some might say the past surrounded her here. Robert Hartley gazed back at her from the silver frame she picked up off the writing desk. He was standing on the prow of a boat, the sun in his eyes, a Cary Grant expression on his face. He exuded masculine elegance that had not survived the decades. It was that, timeless, endless quality that was everything she loved about Ballytokeep that grounded her that day. She was part of something. It had taken a decade, but her life had moved on. She was not sitting in that London flat waiting for Todd to knock on her door. She wasn't spitting out spurned spouses so she could make a cynical living. Kate hugged the photo to her, not because she was in love with Robert Hartley, but rather because in some ways this place had pulled them together and if she wasn't a Hartley exactly, she certainly felt she belonged here. That day, the day Todd was sitting in the bathhouse – that day, this place had steadied her. The bathhouse and all of the connections she'd made around it made her feel the world would not subside. She was exactly where she was supposed to be. If Todd Riggs was supposed to be here too, well good for him.

\*

The following afternoon she noticed Rita looked a little peaky. The bathhouse was busy all morning, but Rita was normally in her element, the busier things were. She offered to bring her home earlier, but Rita had turned on her.

'That's her.' She nodded towards a corner table where a young couple were whispering conspiratorially, their heads close, their attraction unmistakable. 'That's Duncan's floozy, out here with some young fella, as if she hasn't a care in the world.' The girl was hardly twenty, a tanned skinny blonde with ripped jeans and a fresh face, her designer handbag sat in a heap on the floor at her Converse-clad feet.

'Perhaps it's all off with Duncan, I mean, for all we knew, it was all gossip anyway, who's to say there was ever anything in it,' Kate soothed; she didn't want Rita to have a meltdown here, not in front of this girl, so the whole village could talk about it. 'I'd say Duncan has been well and truly dumped, young love, eh?'

'Young love, my soda bread.' Rita huffed and she picked up her rolling pin.

'Whoa, hold on.' Kate guided her back towards the safety of the kitchen. 'What's the matter?'

'Sorry,' Rita dropped the rolling pin. 'It's a long story.' She turned to grab her coat. 'But taking the rolling pin to her,' she pulled the coat around her, 'that would be unforgivable. I'll go.'

'You'll do no such thing.' Kate knew a broken heart or at least a broken woman when she saw one. Generally, they were not carrying rolling pins with intent to use them for purposes other than baking, but they wore the same expression. 'Tell me, come on, we are friends, aren't we?'

'We are.' Rita sighed, as though the admission was almost too much. 'It's my Duncan, well; he's more like her Duncan now. He's been carrying on with that wan. I thought it didn't bother me. Then, in she walks and I'm mincemeat. I swear. I hardly know my backside from my elbow. It makes me so mad. And there she is, smirking at me, as if she knows something I don't. It makes me want to...' She took up the rolling pin to demonstrate, but there was really no need. 'In my head, I had a plan, you see.'

'I'm not sure I do see.' Kate flicked the kettle. Stories like these, whether they were in the middle of London or in the west of Ireland, required tea. Lots of tea. 'Do you still love him?'

'Hah.' Rita shook her head. That was an emphatic no. It did not come as a great surprise to Kate. 'My Duncan has always been a weasel. You know what they say, if it looks like one, acts like one and smells like one...'

'Indeed.' Kate had met plenty of cheating men in London; thankfully, they were filling her pockets, not breaking her heart. Once was enough for that. 'So he's been having this affair? Is it love or just...'

'I don't know, I assume so. I mean, have you seen the state of him. Of course, it'll be his money and that flash car he drives about in.'

'It generally is. Amazing how stupid they can be, isn't it?'

'I never thought he was, but there you go.' She nodded towards the coffee shop. If Duncan was cheating on her, there was no doubt he was being cheated on too. 'It's nearly worse that she thinks I'm doubly stupid. Not alone that I wouldn't know she's cheating with Duncan, but it's almost twice as insulting to think she'd trail her fancy piece in here before me. She must really think I'm thin on top.' Rita shook her head.

'Isn't that a good thing though?' Kate asked. 'I mean she obviously thinks you have no idea. You certainly have the element of surprise on your side.' Years of experience had taught Kate one thing and that was that nothing worked to your advantage in these things so well as having caught the cheater on the back foot. 'So your plan?' Kate loved a plan.

'I've set up a direct debit on his business account to go straight to the dog refuge, give some other poor blighters a chance,' Rita smiled, it was a little wobbly, but behind it Kate could see the triumph in her eyes. It seemed to Kate that the bathhouse had given Rita something too, she'd changed since that first time they met. Like Kate, she'd finally taken the steering wheel of her own life.

'It's very noble to give it to the rescue centre but don't you think it would be good to make sure that you're secure? You know, with the house and all that.'

'I didn't think I could do that, I mean, it would feel like stealing if I was taking money out just for myself.'

'No, most women, when this happens, it's not the first thing they think of. First off it's the hurt. Next up, it's revenge, or the kids. You have to hit rock bottom before you actually think about taking care of yourself and by then, unfortunately, it can be too late. The really smart women get a good lawyer in the beginning.'

'Well, we have a solicitor. She takes care of the business for Duncan, but,' she leaned conspiratorially towards Kate, 'I've always been the one who sends her cakes when she's not well, or when her kids are having birthdays, you know the little things. I'm pretty sure she thinks Duncan is a creep too.'

'That may be the case, but, Rita, if he's paying her bill she's going to be looking out for his interests.'

'So, I need to get someone else? I know a fella from school. He's in Galway now, I suppose I could...'

'Yes, you could, but will he be the best you can get?'

'I'm not sure.'

'Maybe I can help you there...' Kate put her arm around Rita. She was going to enjoy teaching Duncan Quinn a lesson.

*

If Kate enjoyed the hectic routine of the coffee shop each day, so different to the stuffy office in London, she enjoyed her free time even more. In Ballytokeep, she only had to walk out her front door and she was on permanent summer holidays. She wondered some days if that sensation would ever leave her. Even Castle Rock in the distance, seemed to shrink in the days after she had seen Todd. It no longer loomed above her, casting a cold and judgemental eye over what she had managed to eke out of life for herself. So, she hadn't married a super handsome barrister, nor had she managed to fill her home with the children that always seemed part of the deal. But she was happy, in this place, sharing her days with Rita and her nights with the wind whipping up the waves beneath the rocks. She had Iris, Archie and Colin. She walked through the village and there were people who were glad to see her. She had peace of mind and, for the first time in over a decade, she was not searching for something she could not name.

She enjoyed the ongoing work that was involved in running the bathhouse. The builders had sorted out the coffee shop, the baths and the steam presses. For this season, they were up and running. Perhaps, when winter loomed dark and cold she could look at making space for a therapist or two to offer massages or treatments. She spent her evenings sitting on the rock, watching the porpoises and dolphins play in the frothy waves. When the sky inked to darkness over her head, and the stars sparkled brighter than it seemed they had any right to, she dragged herself inside. The flat held its own attraction. She was still making her way through the papers and belongings of Robert Hartley.

Archie told her she should just dump them. They would be old and moth-eaten and hardly of any interest to anyone now. Perhaps he was right; certainly, Archie had no interest in anything of his brother's that she found.

'It's like going back there,' Iris whispered one day when Kate gave her Robert's watch. It was engraved, from some girl; Iris couldn't remember her. 'Robert had many girlfriends, I'm sure neither Archie nor I knew half of them.'

'It's a really good watch.' Kate held it up to the light. 'It's definitely gold and it still works, listen.' It was keeping perfect time. She wound it up the previous day and it hadn't lost a minute. 'I thought maybe Archie might like it?'

'I doubt it,' Iris took the watch in her hand, draped it across her crepe skin. 'He was so smart, so dapper,' she said the words softly, as though she forgot Kate was there. 'So well dressed, and then you would see him bring seaweed from the beach and you knew he was strong and full of life. Such life.' She shook her head.

'He was certainly handsome,' Kate said. It didn't capture the sense she had of him. 'Sometimes, I think I can feel him in the bathhouse. I am never lonely, because it feels like he is there, watching over the place. Does that sound a little mad?'

'Not at all, I could feel it too, when you opened the place up. I suppose it's just the fact that it's all the same as it was before, but of course it's not the same at all.' She lifted her head, smiled a wisp of a smile at Kate. 'Well, they were different times then. I'm not sure that things would have worked out the same if they happened now.' She looked out towards the sea, as though she might spot someone familiar on the soft waves. 'Anyway, it was all a long time ago.' She held the watch close to her for a second, listened to the soft murmur of its ticking. 'You keep it, Kate. It won't do Archie any good now.'

'I'd love to have met him,' Kate said as she took the watch back.

'Oh, yes, he was quite…' Iris smiled a small movement of her quivering lips. Then her eyes travelled towards the porch door where Archie was making his way in.

*

'I thought it was you that day at the bathhouse, but I couldn't believe it, I had to come back to see.' Todd was waiting for her on the narrow track that led down the back of the bathhouse.'

'Oh, yes, it's me alright, what were the chances, eh?' Kate said, but she smiled at him and felt much better than she ever imagined she might. Here, with the sea rolling toward her and the bathhouse glinting welcome, her years of anger seemed to dissipate as she met Todd for the second time in a decade. 'How are you, Todd?' There was nothing to be gained from crying or recriminating now, and it took standing here in this place to know that for sure.

'I suppose I'm well,' he said, joining her step and they walked side by side down the steep hill. 'Small world?'

'Well, chances are we would have met up eventually, somewhere.' She looked at him now. All that booze and probably drugs, she thought, his heart attack too probably had knocked a lot out of him. He was only in his forties, but he looked so much more. 'I hoped maybe I might have the pleasure of meeting you in court, actually.'

'So you did think about me?' His smile was still the same: rakish, raw, assured.

'Do you really want to go there?' She laughed at him now, fingered Robert Hartley's watch in her pocket. 'No, I thought maybe you would marry and you'd cheat and then...'

'Revenge?'

'It helped me sleep easier for a while.' She laughed. It was true. Somehow, it was cooler to laugh now than to scream and shout, as she'd always wanted to before. 'Anyway, I'm glad you met Claudia, she's very beautiful and you seem happy together?' It wasn't any of her business, but it was better to talk about him than have to tell him about herself.

'Yeah, me and Claudia, I suppose, we are...' He was distracted for a moment. From here, Rock Castle looked austere and isolated. 'This was going to be a new start.'

'I heard about your heart attack, I was sorry about that,' Kate said the words and meant them.

'Yeah, well what is it my protestant buddies say, what you sow you reap?' He shook his head. 'It was a long time coming. Lifestyle.' He looked at her now, studied her for a moment too long for either of them to pretend was polite. 'So, we're going to be neighbours?'

'You'll never stick Ballytokeep.' Kate laughed again.

'Why do you say that?'

'Because I know you and I've been here for the quiet season. Most of the pubs close and the days are short, miserable and cold. Let's just say, it's not Monte Carlo.'

'Maybe I'm not looking for Monte Carlo anymore?' He pitched a stone out towards the water. The rock was beautiful today, almost light pink, dried in the wind and baked warm by the sun.

'Oh, Todd, I think you're always going to be looking for Monte Carlo.'

'I get the feeling we're not talking about geography anymore.'

'Were we ever?' She turned towards the bathhouse and, in that instant, it looked the best she'd ever seen it. The sun cast orange radiance on the white rounded walls. The baskets and pots of hydrangeas were blooming hard against the salty sea air. 'It is nice to see you, by the way, Todd.'

'Can I...' He moved towards her, uncertain, his voice just rising over the cry of two homeward-bound gulls. 'Can I call down someday...' he was before her now, 'to talk?'

'Well, you know where I am, Todd,' she said, smiling. 'I'll be charging you for the coffee though.' Suddenly, he was too close. She heard her voice begin to wobble; he would not notice. She was elegant at covering nerves, had learned too many tricks in the courtroom to let Todd Riggs pull her down now.

'And if I knock on your door when the coffee shop is closed?' His confidence deserted him, she had a feeling he hadn't planned to speak like this.

'I'm not sure.' She stepped down from the doorway. 'Todd, I'm not sure.' Then she retreated to the safety of the bathhouse, banged the door and stood listening to her heartbeat keep perfect time with Robert Hartley's watch.

Things were changing. A year ago, Kate knew, she'd have handled Todd very differently. Was it just the effects of time? Of age? Perhaps, but Kate had a feeling that Ballytokeep was at the core of her new detachment. Time had taught her that love, loss and life were what you made of them. It had taken belonging in Ballytokeep to help her let go.

# 15

## Todd

Todd replayed that scene a million times over in his mind. He couldn't help it, couldn't get the whole thing from his mind, it was all too surreal.

Kate Hunt. He hadn't thought about her for years. Actually, that wasn't strictly true. He had thought about her a lot these last few weeks. Since his heart attack, he thought about her frequently. Another unexpected consequence of his recovery – his mother would have been rejoicing. He had located his conscience, finally. He just hadn't thought about her before that. If she did wander into his mind, he'd have assumed that she probably hated him, with good reason. He imagined her married to a boring barrister and producing legal sprogs in the depths of London suburbia. He'd been a complete rat to her. When he thought about her now, it was different. Not guilt – he knew guilt. That was the emotion his parents evoked all too readily. No this was different; when he thought of Kate Hunt, it was with an emotion that was new to Todd. Some people, people like Meg for example, would probably call what he felt regret. Not, he clarified for himself, that he regretted not marrying her. It wouldn't have worked, he wasn't ready to get married then. No, he regretted the way he'd done it. That, he knew, was unforgiveable.

Never in his wildest dreams would he have imagined her here. Face to face with him, a decade on, he wasn't sure what he expected. She was still beautiful, that was the second thing he noticed. The first was something else. Something he couldn't put his finger on, but it was warm. Kate Hunt hadn't wasted her time on anger or hatred or bitterness and that, he realised was a quality that only added to her attraction after all these years.

'How do you know her?' Claudia's interest had changed to concern when she saw his reaction. She was out of her depth here. She'd arrived for a visit, he was glad to see her, of course he was. He was relieved that it would be short. He was growing to like the solitary life. He realized it most when people came to stay. It was, he presumed, just a passing phase. Possibly, they'd be out clubbing again before the year was out?

'For God's sake, Todd, say something. Anything? You're as white as a sheet, are you all right? It's not your heart again, is it?' She was wittering on now and he stopped listening, tried to catch sight of where Kate had disappeared.

'I…' It was no good. There was an easy explanation for this. There was a reason that he bought a castle in the middle of nowhere, somewhere he had absolutely no connection with and it had thrown him straight into the face of Kate Hunt. He was only half aware of the words Claudia was whispering. They were empty, completely passing him by. He strained for sight of Kate again.

'It's Kate Hunt – the girl I almost married.' This wasn't fair on Claudia. He watched her now, maybe it was being out of London, but this place drained her.

'Are you sure? I mean, it's a long time since...' Claudia knew the story; everyone in England knew the story of how he dumped Kate Hunt. He winced now when he thought of it. He had been a complete shit back then.

'Claudia, you don't forget people like Kate. I mean, you move on, but...' He searched for the words. 'I was going to marry her, you know.'

'But you didn't,' Claudia sounded as though she was defending him, more than cross-examining him. Then again, that would be more up Kate's street, wouldn't it? 'Did you know? When you bought the tower, did you know?' There was an odd tremble in her voice, as though it might trip itself up.

'Of course not, how could I...' Todd shook his head.

'But?'

'It's a coincidence, that's all. Just one of those mad accidents – and we'll probably never see her again.' Well, that wasn't true, was it? He had hung about waiting for her. He had to. It wasn't fair on Claudia, he knew that. What was happening to him? These things would never have occurred to him before his heart attack. He turned now towards Claudia. He took her thin hands and smiled, pretended everything was normal. Todd had a feeling Claudia would not be in a hurry to have tea at the bathhouse, no matter how nice the food.

\*

'Kate Hunt, eh? There's a blast from the past.' Denny blew a circle of cigar smoke upwards. They were sitting outside the castle; sharing a bottle of red wine and watching the gulls chase home a small trawler in the hope of easy lunch. 'So what's she doing in Ballytokeep?'

'She's taken over the bathhouse and apparently it's doing a bomb.'

'She didn't move here for the money, Todd. You know that, she would have been making plenty in London, I can name five blokes she's fleeced in the name of the law in the last two years.' He circled another loop of cigar smoke into the air before them, the tobacco ring static for a second before drifting on the salty air. 'Is she married?'

'I don't know.' There was no wedding ring, Todd noticed that, not that he'd been looking; well, he couldn't help it could he? It was only natural to be curious, right?

'Not that it matters,' Denny's tone dipped. 'You have Claudia now – a supermodel, no one could compare to that.' He winked at Todd, 'Half the men in London would give a kidney to have someone like Claudia on their arm.'

'I suppose,' Todd said. He thought about this a lot recently. 'Me and Claudia, it's not…' He searched for the word. 'It's not the same, you know?'

'I bet it's not.' Denny chuckled, his dirty old man laugh that he kept just for times like this; it didn't really fit him anymore, but it was probably useful when he was making deals with some of the promoters.

'Not like that, I mean, it's not the same as it was with Kate.'

'Course it's not, you left Kate, remember?'

'Yeah, but maybe I was just being a shit?' He'd thought about this a lot since that day she walked into the bathhouse.

'You'll always be a shit, Todd. That's not going to change.' It was a matter of fact as far as Denny was concerned. 'But, Todd, you didn't marry her for a reason.'

'Yeah, but what if it wasn't the right reason? What if it just wasn't the right time? Or...' He was being stupid, but if he didn't say it to Denny, well who could he say it to. No one ever *got* him like Kate, down to how she packed his bags when he went on tour. She understood that he needed to be organized. She got that there was so much he couldn't do for himself. She got all that, and what had he given her back? Nothing. Denny was right. He'd always been a selfish bastard. It hadn't changed. The only difference was, now he could pay people to organize his life the way he wanted it. The problem was, it hadn't made him very happy.

'Would you listen to yourself, I swear, those tablets you're taking, they're making you soft in the head, not in the arteries.' Denny put down the cigar and cleared his throat to lessen the phlegm that coated his words. 'You listen to me now, Todd. You haven't seen Kate Hunt in ten years, and I'll wager that you haven't thought about her in just as long.' He put his hand up to stop any words Todd might add. 'Whatever kind of crap luck has thrown you two together on a god-forgotten stretch of rocky coastline; it doesn't mean anything more than that. You didn't love her enough to hang around a decade ago. You don't love her enough to screw things up with Claudia now. It's a phase, like going off coffee, like buying this place, don't throw away what you have for what you didn't want back then.'

'Right.' Todd agreed, because it was what he always did with Denny. Maybe he was right, maybe Denny was always right. Claudia had been good to him. Blast it, she'd been good for him too. They both knew that without her he would still be playing to audiences well past their sell-by date and in much smaller venues. Claudia gave the band a new lease of life, an entrée to a younger audience. She made them absurdly, unexpectedly cool. Now chart stars, writers and rappers that had been babies when Todd started out wanted to work with them. They were good for each other, a promoters dream. Todd knew it clouded all of their judgements when it came to Claudia.

'You stick with Claudia, forget about the lawyer, that's my advice to you, Todd.'

'Yeah, not many old blokes can pull a supermodel, right?' Todd agreed. Denny was right, he had nothing in common with Kate Hunt anymore. The only problem was, he couldn't stop thinking about her. She intrigued him. What had really brought her here? Was he meant to atone for his sins? God, he could hear his mother's voice sounding out the words. Was it a second chance? To reset his moral compass? Then he saw her in the distance, standing at the door of the bathhouse, and reality seemed to wash over him like the salty waves against the rocks. Too much had happened along the way. What was he thinking? His best bet would be to keep well out of her way.

*

The next time their paths crossed, Todd thought he'd be prepared. He stopped walking past the bathhouse. Instead, for the next week, he took his five-mile trek across country, delving into the marshy fields that strode away from the sea spray. Sometimes, he would find himself walking back towards the castle and knowing he would be using the track that passed by the large outcrop of rock, he would sit for a moment. He would consider the possibilities and then, carry on, taking a longer route to avoid meeting Kate.

Today, looking out at the blue sky, falling hazily onto the

shining rippling water, he thought she had every right to hate him. After all, she never had her say. He just disappeared. Not like people who disappear and they are never seen again. No. Nothing as classy as that. Todd had disappeared with a Russian stripper called – what was she called? He could not even remember her name. They were as hammered as each other. The papers had made enough out of it for him to concoct a few rancid memories. It had started on his stag night. Or what was meant to be a few drinks with the lads from the band. Some of them – they were all jokers – had organized strippers for the night. Then, maybe even now, Todd could not look a gift horse in the mouth. He still half remembered being bundled on the euro train, the darkness outside, the smell of alcohol and cheap perfume. They had lost days. Days when he should have been getting married, should have been going on honeymoon, should have been a decent human being.

Anyway, the point now was, Kate Hunt deserved to have her say. It had all been so agreeable last time, standing there in the summer sun. It was as though they hardly knew each other, as though they meant nothing to each other all those years ago, as though she had almost forgotten it and him. If they were going to move on, there was air to be cleared between them. The question was; what would he say? He had a feeling the truth wouldn't be enough. He found himself circling the large outcrop of flattened rock once more. There was no doubt, the bathhouse was quite beautiful. Not at all the kind of place he would have imagined Kate settling for. But then, he had never intended to buy a Norman fortress on the most western coast of Europe.

\*

It was great news, wasn't it? The best news, right? Meg had insisted on flying over for one night.

'Todd, I actually think you've managed to put on weight,' she said, throwing her arms around him and then holding him away to inspect that he was taking care of himself.

'It's the fresh air – I'm eating three square meals a day instead of throwing back two bottles before bedtime.' Todd laughed at this, but it was the truth. His skin had been grey and his body scrawny when he came here. Now, well, he actually felt himself getting stronger. Meg sent them walking on the beach while she cooked dinner – she had the makings of his favourite shepherd's pie in her giant handbag.

'It's bloody the weirdest thing,' Denny said. 'Flipping karma, according to my Meg. Ending up with your ex on your doorstep.' Denny had laughed when Todd told him the therapist had suggested he 'seek forgiveness for his past wrongs.' Denny breathed in the salty air and grimaced, he liked his oxygen more dioxided. He was a city boy; the seaside was for postcards.

'Fate, it's like the universe is throwing us together?' Todd shook his head. He had a feeling Kate forgave him. Certainly, he had not received the bashing he expected and knew he deserved. Perhaps, they *could* be neighbours. Maybe, they could even be friends.

'Maybe. The universe would have been better placed to give you that heart attack *after* the world flippin' tour.' Denny grunted. 'Let's face it, Todd, everything in life is all about you. Always has been, for as long as I've known you.'

'Well, not any more it seems.' He shook the sand out of his Birkenstocks. In the distance, the low barrelling bathhouse seemed so bright, airy and carefree. Sometimes, he couldn't believe Kate actually lived there. Like Todd, she seemed to be entrenched in London life, all those years ago when she'd been the hottest divorce lawyer in London. She had changed little. Perhaps she was thinner. Some fine lines had crept in around her eyes and lips. Her hair had brightened and her cheeks seemed a little hollower. In London, he had never noticed her cheekbones, but then his own skin fell more heavily around his eyes and cheeks too now. Too many of the people he knew in London resorted to surgeons, specialists, and they just looked weird. Kate had colour in her cheeks, life in her eyes and lightness in her step; she looked good. Todd hoped that Ballytokeep would do the same for him, give him that sense of belonging and happiness he craved since Atlantic City, maybe since before it.

'So, what's next?' Denny squinted at him; he was not a sunshine person. Todd had a feeling that he was allergic to the sand and, if he questioned before why he visited so regularly, now he knew. It was all about the tour, the album, and the lads. 'You're going to spend the rest of your days here, walking the beach and meditating on what some therapist told you in the cardiac recovery unit and that's it?' They both knew that Todd's attempts at meditation were dismal at best. He liked the idea that people might think he had enough depth to make a go of it.

'I can think of worse places to hang my hat at the end of the day.'

'And of course, there's nothing like the smell of fresh coffee to make a man look at his life choices.'

'What's that supposed to mean?' Todd kept his eyes closed, his voice even.

'I'm saying don't let you ending up next door to the only woman who came near to getting you to the altar be a reason to give up what you have in London.'

'Yeah, well nearly never made it first across the finish line, did it?

'It looks to me like Kate has a very eligible man on her door step night, noon and morning.' They had watched Kate and a tall bloke sit outside the bathhouse one evening, sharing a bottle of wine while the sun went down. Todd turned away from the window. Sometimes he felt crowded out with the oddest feelings, of course it was just getting over the heart attack, he'd never been jealous in his life before that.

'She certainly has that.' Todd smiled.

'You know damn well, I don't mean you, Todd.'

'Oh, really?'

'You've had your holiday; it's time to get back into the real world again. There's a big city waiting for you to get back to.' Denny wanted dates; he wanted the band back on stage. He'd said it at the beginning of this tour, they could sell more music this year than in their heyday. If only he could get them back on stage. 'If it's Kate Hunt that's holding you back, you better forget about her.'

'Why's that?' He had rightly screwed up things with Kate long ago, if they could be friends now, wouldn't that be enough for him?

'I hardly need to spell it out for you, Todd. You humiliated her beyond any girl's worst nightmare and she's no ordinary girl. We both know plenty who'll tell you that she's one smart lady.'

'Ah, yes, but she's not a divorce lawyer any more, is she?'

'It doesn't mean she isn't smart, Todd. And it doesn't mean she hasn't forgotten last time.'

'She's not like that.' Todd said the words low. Kate had plenty of reasons to hate him, but they were older and wiser now, and that counted for a lot.

*

A week later, early morning, when only a few surfers dotted the morning waves, he set off walking before the village woke. It had been a hot and sticky night and, in the end, he left his Caesar bed to take his measure of morning air. Most mornings he kept his head down, his iPod blasting rock anthems that were meant to keep his mind off his proximity to Kate Hunt. This morning, the bathhouse door was open. There seemed to be no one about and, like Goldilocks, curiosity got the better of Todd.

The bathhouse was empty, save for Kate, sitting exactly, it seemed to him, where she should be sitting.

'You're my first customer,' she smiled at him and raised her cup. 'Actually, I'm not even open yet, but would you like some coffee?' Her welcome was warmer than he deserved, but he felt himself relax in a way he hadn't for a very long time.

'I wouldn't want to put you to any bother,' the words did not sound like words he would ever say back in the day.

'I think, Todd, the days of you putting me to bother are well and truly behind us. Have a seat.' She went to the coffee machine and expertly set about making him what he truly thought was the best coffee he had ever tasted. It was his first cup, since Atlantic City and even if he hadn't liked it, he had a feeling he'd have drunk it anyway.

'Perhaps, it's the company,' she teased him when he told her so.

'Maybe. I haven't seen you about, these last few days, I was...'

'Worried?' She smiled at him, but he caught something else in her eyes. 'About me? Well, thank you, but I'm fine. I've just been burning the candle at both ends a bit, so I've been taking it easy.'

'I noticed you weren't tending the flowers.' He sounded nervous, knew she'd catch it too.

'Colin said he'd help me out. My hose is blocked and the water can is so heavy.' She smiled at him, their eyes locking for a moment too long, and then she turned away towards the kindling fire in the stove.

They made small talk for a while, the season was ending, and she was quite looking forward to it. 'Lots to be done,' she nodded towards the back of the coffee shop. 'Upstairs, I'm still clearing out things that are over half a century old.'

'You seem to be enjoying it.' It was true, she seemed happy, perhaps happier than he ever remembered her.

'I am. Who'd have thought I'd spend my free hours going through musty old letters and photographs.'

'Any big spiders?' She was afraid of spiders, he remembered that.

'No, I have them all under control.' She winked at him.

'Of course, you have Colin.' Colin Lyons, Todd had asked around, was in and out of here at all hours, hard to miss him, even if you didn't overlook the place.

'Colin?' she said his name as though it was new to her, still somewhat exotic perhaps. 'Yes, but I also have wonderful sonic devices I bought in the hardware shop. I have them everywhere, had to get something, can you imagine the size of spiders here? No, I'm a technology girl when it comes to spiders.'

'It suits you, here,' Todd said then; enough of spiders and Colin.

'I know. I am very happy here, Todd.' She looked at him for a moment, broke away again. 'I'm happier than I thought

I could ever be.' She lowered her voice, 'I wouldn't want anything to ruin it for me.'

'I wouldn't want that either, Kate.' He leant across and touched her hand, wanted her to know that he meant it too. Her skin was soft and familiar; it sent a tingling current through him. When she pulled away he felt a wrench that surprised him in its ferocity.

'Good.' She blushed and sipped her coffee, a small nerve in her lip giving away that she felt it too.

'It's probably a cheek, but do you think we could be friends?' It sounded clichéd, but he had a feeling it was what they both needed.

'That would be something, wouldn't it?' She smiled, traced her fingers about the rim of her coffee cup. 'Back then, you and I? It is all a very long time ago. That's where it should stay, too.' She took a deep breath. 'You have Claudia now. We are both lucky to have found happiness in the end.'

'I have to say something, we both know, it needs to be said.' He thought for a moment she let out a little gasp.

'Todd, really, there's no need to...'

'No.' His voice was soft and for a second he listened as her breath deepened. 'It's something I should have said a long time ago. I was just so...'

'Up yourself?'

'Okay, we'll call that the technical term.' They both laughed at that, then he stopped, abruptly, this wasn't funny, not really. 'I was wrong to do what I did. I mean, I know now, that I was terribly wrong, that I shouldn't have left you, not like that.'

'Okay,' Kate said, getting up to clear her coffee cup. 'Like I said, you were an arse.' She kept her attention on clearing invisible crumbs from the table.

'I'm sorry.' Todd reached up, touched her arm. Again, that captivating magic coursed between them. 'I'm sorry. That's all I wanted to say, for the way I treated you, I feel terrible about it. It was shabby and cruel and you deserved so much more.' He let her arm go; gently his hand fell onto his lap. He didn't need to say anymore. No matter what happened between them, an apology at least was long overdue. He watched as Kate walked towards the counter, dropped her cup slowly, her back still turned to him, her shoulders squared resolutely.

'Thank you, Todd.' She did not turn around to face him. She made no movement. He had a feeling that her clipped voice only just held back an avalanche of emotion. 'You should be going now, I have work to do.' He watched as she walked slowly to the back of the bathhouse.

The wind, low and cool on the morning waves seemed to breathe something that might have been forgiveness into his face. Todd cried with a candour that came from the very core of him. He walked back to the castle, his face wet with salty tears, but his conscience just a little lighter than it had felt in many years.

# 16

## Robert, 1957

In the weeks that followed, it took him over like a disease.
All Robert could think of was Iris. He had never felt
anything like this before. He had more women than any
other man in the county. It had been easy. Too easy, with
most of them. He had it off to a fine art, but now, somehow,
when pretty girls came into the bathhouse, it all seemed so
mundane. He still smiled at them – of course, he did, it was
good for business. Unexpectedly though, now, the will had
left him. Iris was there, at the back of his mind all day long.
When he went to bed at night, his dreams filled with her. He
realized, one morning as he was checking off a delivery, that
he would have to formulate a plan. Running the old ritual
with Iris was not going to work. He would have to play the
long game, but she was worth it. He had to gain her trust
first and he knew he would have his work cut out to do
that. He stayed away from the hotel for a few days, decided
to keep well out of her way. Then, as though providence
was looking out for him, he spotted her one day on the pier

chatting to Ellie Armstrong who had more children than the woman who lived in the shoe and not a lot more space than she did. On this particular day, she had an especially squally one with her and Robert picked up a sherbet dip with his newspaper before making his way over to them.

'There you go, son,' he said as he handed the little bugger the treat. 'It's a nice day for a walk on the pier, ladies,' he said and kept walking back towards the hotel. He could feel the two women watch him. It did not take a lot to have old biddies eating out of your hand. Ellie Armstrong wouldn't say a bad word against him anyway. He walked on towards the hotel, his step light; in the distance, a fishing boat was making its way towards shore, a halo of gulls proclaiming that they had a successful catch.

'Good morning, mother,' he said, kissing her lightly on the cheek when he reached the hotel. He sat at the large scrubbed table that filled the centre of his mother's kitchen, reached out to feel if there was any heat left in the teapot in the centre. He was out of luck. The pot was warm, but only because it wore a heavy cosy; the tea, he knew, would be black and heavy.

'Ah Robert, we haven't seen you all week, what have you been up to?'

'Not a lot, just keeping busy, you know, summer trade and deliveries.' It was true, the bathhouse was busy, busier than last year, and the seaweed business was really taking off. He and old Bill Lyons had big plans for the winter. Already they had a decent set-up for drying it out, but Bill was going to convert one of his sheds so they could continue the process over the winter months. 'I got a call from Cleary's haberdashery in Dublin, no less, to see if I can supply them with the Carrageen Moss.' He was delighted;

he could already hear the cash register chiming out the sales. Carrageen Moss was little more than seaweed, dried out and put in a fancy box, but the old wives said it held a cure. Robert would be hard-pressed to prove that it actually worked, but he trotted out the line that it helped with everything from asthma to amnesia if you boiled it in milk and ate it as a pudding twice a day.

'That's great news, Robert,' Archie said as he came into the kitchen; he was black with soot. 'Just doing the fireplaces, never know this time of year what the evening will bring.' It was true, even in the height of summer the hotel could be cold in the evenings. Robert would not be seen dead cleaning out the chimney in the bathhouse, though; he employed a local lad to do all the dirty work about the place.

'These are good,' Robert said, crumbling off the end of a fruit scone from beneath a tea cloth.

'Oh, yes, Iris was baking earlier. They're proving a real hit with the bridge crowd in the afternoons.' His mother gave him a side plate and some jam. There was no picking allowed in her kitchen. 'Iris served them up with cream and a button of strawberry jam and you'd swear it was the Ritz, the way they went down.'

'Well, it looks like you struck gold there,' Robert said, savouring the scone deliberately.

'For as long as we have her.' His mother gave a long sideward glance towards Archie. 'She has plans for one of the big hotels when the season is over. I've seen her scouring through the appointments page in the Dublin papers.' His mother sighed theatrically, as only a woman with forty years in a hotel could. 'Unless of course Archie was to propose to her.'

'That's not very subtle mother.' Robert laughed to hide his

discomfort. The danger with Archie was he could propose to the girl simply because his mother told him to. 'Perhaps Archie has his own ideas. You can't rush these things.'

'Sometimes rushing is the only way to get things done. We both know Archie has no ideas at all. It's half his problem, it's what the scarlet fever leaves a man with,' his mother whispered as Archie washed his hands in the outside sink oblivious to them. 'No, he won't do much better than Iris. She's a good girl.'

'Is she?' Robert said, smiling.

'Robert, you know she is. She would be perfect for Archie and he likes her, I've seen him putting flowers in her room. He treats her like she fell from heaven. She'd take the helm of the hotel someday and she'd make sure it remained a place to be proud of.'

'I'm sure she would, but maybe she has her eye on someone else. After all, her sister married an earl.'

'An earl's son,' his mother corrected him. It was true. Sir Clive probably would one day be the Earl of Mayo. His brother had returned from the war a shattered broken man with poor physical health and a nervous disposition that people tried not to mention. 'Robert would you have a word with him? You know, just mention that girls like Iris, well, they don't hang about, do they?' His mother turned towards Archie, her expression softening at the sight of him.

'I'm sure that Archie is capable of making his own way in the world when it comes to women.'

'Come on, let's put on the kettle and have a quick cup of tea, I can't remember when we all sat down together.' His mother was quick to change the subject.

'Speaking of which, where is father?' Robert asked.

'He wasn't feeling well this morning, so I told him to rest

for a while, he must have fallen asleep again.' His mother shook her head. Of course, what she would not say was that the old man was beginning to turn a little bit funny these last few weeks. Small, peculiar things he said at first, made Robert laugh, knowing that it was inappropriate didn't help of course, that was just Robert's sense of humour. He had come into the reception one day to find his father shining the old slate over the mantle with a pair of his mother's best bloomers. His mother hadn't been pleased. Still there had been no move made to take him for any kind of medical assessment. His father had just shook his head sadly. 'There's nothing to be done, son, old age, nothing to be done.'

'So then, Robert, what brings you to visit on this grand day?' Archie asked as he sat down opposite him.

'Just passing by and I thought I'd come in and sample some of these fruit scones the whole place is raving about.' He smiled across at his mother. Funny, but even now he wanted to please her. Knowing that she had her heart set on Iris for Archie put another obstacle in the way of having her and maybe it made Iris even more attractive for it.

'Has she been telling you about Iris and how she's desperately trying to matchmake us?'

'Sure, there's no harm in that, is there?' Mrs Hartley wanted more than anything for her sons to marry nice respectable girls. She wanted them happy and settled like every other woman her age in the village. 'Wanting the best for your boys, wanting things to go on as I've left them...'

'Now, mother, don't be putting pressure on poor Archie.' The last thing Robert wanted was a proposal out of this. They changed the subject to hotel matters. Robert sat a little on edge in the hope that Iris might arrive back and join them.

Before long there she was, standing at the end of the kitchen delicately taking off her light cashmere cardigan.

'Ah, my dear, you had a nice walk?'

'Yes, thank you Mrs Hartley. I've just been talking to Mrs Armstrong.' She looked over at Robert. 'You saw her Robert, you saw her little boy Oisín?'

'I didn't take much notice, to be honest,' but he made it sound as though he had somewhat lost his edge.

'He's very sick. The doctors say he'll hardly make it through the winter,' Iris was obviously upset.

'Oh, dear,' Mrs Hartley said. 'And there's nothing to be done?'

'There might be. If they had a spare couple of thousand to send him to London for treatment, but they don't have the money. Mrs Armstrong says it's hopeless.' Iris looked towards the clock. Robert sensed she was just passing time here, as though there was somewhere else she should be.

'Well that can't be right, can it?' Mrs Hartley said sadly. 'Surely, Robert, if everyone came together, something could be done.' Mrs Hartley looked across at Archie. 'Goodness knows, I remember what it was like to have a child at death's door. We should do something for them, Robert, will you see if there's anything we can do?'

'Mother, you know the Armstrongs are proud people, they won't want charity,' Archie knew the village people well, better than Robert or their mother. Robert had seen him often pay more than he should for fish or grain because he knew a family had hit hard times. Robert thought he was a fool for it, said it often enough and he darted a look at him now that silenced him immediately.

'There's always something to be done,' Robert said, sensing an opportunity to feather his own nest even more than some snivelling kid. He looked at Iris, she was swallowed up with concern for the child and he knew he had to grab this chance to move things forward. 'I'm going there right now, to do something about it; well, are you coming?' he said to Iris as he stalked out of the hotel.

\*

The Armstrongs lived in one of the small fishing cottages that lined up along the narrow pier road. The area suffered bruising wind in winter and abrasive sun in summer and still the overwhelming stench was of poverty. The houses, one as badly kept as the next, easily housed half the village population, with an average family size of around twelve children. Mrs Armstrong, for her part, had spent most of her married life pregnant. Her husband, a runt of a man, spent his either fishing or drunk, or presumably seeing to Mrs Armstrong. The child, Oisín, was sitting contentedly in his pram. His satisfied face covered in sherbet sugar and he had the swollen look of a child who might have been better changed an hour earlier rather than leave his nappy any longer. It certainly explained the squalling on the pier.

'Hello Oisín,' he said to the kid as he looked through the open front door of the Armstrong cottage. He could hear Iris's footsteps following in his wake. 'Mrs Armstrong, hello, Mrs Armstrong, are you there?' he called into the tiny cottage.

After a minute, Mrs Armstrong emerged from the far end, clothes pegs gripped firmly between her lips, an astonished look on her face.

'Oh, Mr Hartley, what can I do for you?' Her look said she wondered if perhaps he wanted the sherbet back.

'No, Mrs Armstrong, it's what we can do for you that we

wanted to talk about. Can we come in?' Robert's voice was like velvet. He watched as the old girl dropped the clothes pegs and smoothed her hair after she had hung her apron on a door hook.

'Of course, I'm afraid it's not as fancy here as you're used to, but you're welcome.' She pulled out a seat at the kitchen table; there was no offer of tea – that was a luxury, not offered quickly in poorer houses.

'It's just, Iris was telling me, about Oisín...' He looked across at Iris whose expression was unreadable to him.

'I hope it's all right, Mrs Armstrong, but I was so upset, he's such a lovely boy.' He was laying it on thick, but it seemed to him that most women couldn't tell the difference.

'He is that, and to look at him, you'd swear he's perfect, but it's the heart, you see, any bit of go at all and he's out of puff. There's no hope here, only a matter of time, I'm afraid. They won't chance a heart operation on a child in Ireland, that's what the doctor said.'

'That's what Iris told us, but she said that there might be help elsewhere?'

'Oh aye for the likes of...' She stopped for a moment, remembering who she was speaking to. 'A trip to London to some fancy hospital, well, it's not for the likes of us, I'm afraid. I'd have as much hope of my Willie bringing us there in his old fishing boat as I have of paying a fare to get across the Irish Sea.'

'Did the doctor mention how much it would cost?'

'He didn't have to, I know it'd be more than I can afford.' Mrs Armstrong bit her lip for a moment. The knowledge of the world she was brought up to know was not enough to cover things like hospitals in London. 'It'd be thousands, I'm sure.'

'Well, maybe we should find out?' Robert said gently.

'What would be the point? It would be like dangling a carrot before a rabbit and then whipping it away again. That's just plain cruel, that is.' She shook her head.

'There's every point,' Iris said the words quietly. 'Mrs Armstrong, what if we were to all join together and see if we couldn't raise the money to send Oisín for his operation.'

'But I couldn't ever hope to pay it back, you see, we'll never have that kind of money.' She gazed at the floor and, in that moment, Robert began to wonder if in fact she was even half as old as he would have guessed.

'You wouldn't be paying this back, it would be a...'

'Charity, the Armstrongs aren't charity cases. I'm sorry that you've...'

'I was going to say it'd be an honour to help.' Robert bent his head forward so it was close to Mrs Armstrong. 'It'd be an honour for me and it'd be the same for Iris. He is a lovely boy and he deserves the same chance as everyone else. It's not charity when everyone just wants to help a little.'

'So you'd get everyone to give a little?' Mrs Armstrong said, looking at him now.

'That's the idea. We could run a regatta or a few more tea dances or maybe a couple of big bingo games – I don't know, something that'd bring in money.'

'For a good cause?' Mrs Armstrong was shaking her head. 'My husband, I don't think he'll like this one bit,' she said.

'Mrs Armstrong, do you want some kind of decent future for the child or not?' Robert said.

'What kind of a question is that to ask? Of course I do, I am his mother amn't I? My heart is broken since the doctors told me, but what is there to do?'

'There's plenty.' Robert was getting up off the chair now,

his head just barely scraping the low ceiling. 'You leave Mr Armstrong to me, and we'll get moving on this straight away. The only thing you have to do is bring him back up to Dr Frayne and find out when he can get that operation done.'

'I don't know what to say, Mr Hartley,' the woman was smiling and crying all at once. A ray of hope had penetrated her miserable existence and she stuck her hand out solidly to Robert who shook it with the most warmth he could muster.

'Come on, Iris. We have work to do,' Robert said and they made their way out of the cottage. It seemed to Robert he appreciated fresh air more after the claustrophobic cottage. He wanted to take large gasping breaths to clear the stench of poverty from his lungs. It would be worth it, he had a feeling that Oisín Armstrong could be the key to having Iris exactly where he wanted her. The child brought something out in her and Robert had every intention of exploiting that to his own ends.

*

'Well, that was very impressive, Robert,' Iris said. 'One might almost imagine there's a bit of moral fibre lurking in there somewhere.'

'Look,' he rounded on her. 'I'm sorry.'

'Oh?' Her lips remained round for a second longer than it took the word to escape her and he knew he'd caught her by surprise.

'I should have apologized sooner for the way I behaved at the bathhouse. It was ungentlemanly and it was inexcusable.'

'Yes, Robert, it was.' She looked him square in the eye and he knew he had met his equal.

'I can blame the amount I had to drink or any number of other things, but I think we both know that I would be lying.'

'Please, don't.' Iris began to back away from him.

'Don't go, I haven't finished. I wanted to apologize; I wanted to go to the hotel and find you and say that I was truly sorry. I can see that my mother has her heart set on you for Archie and I wouldn't do anything to hurt either him or my mother.' No need to mention that Archie had his heart set on her too. He looked out to sea now, concentrating on something in the far distance. 'I suppose what I'm saying is that I wish you both well and I hope we can be friends.' It was a risk, but a calculated one. Robert thought Archie was so dry, Iris could dehydrate standing next to him, he was banking on her seeing that sooner rather than later. He turned to smile at her now, 'Otherwise family occasions will be very uncomfortable when you are married to my brother.'

'Robert, I...' He could see the confusion in her eyes, hoped he had managed to convey the hurt in his own. Then she placed a hand gently on his arm, 'Of course we can be friends. We'll start again?'

'For Archie,' he said and he took a step back from her. 'Now, you better get back to the hotel, they'll be sending out the search parties otherwise. I'll have a chat with Mr Armstrong on my own, if that's okay.' He knew as he walked away from her that she was watching him. Perhaps she did not quite believe the transformation, but it was early days and from now, it was game on.

# Iris, Present

Iris heard Kate's footsteps on the tiled corridor, knew that there was urgency in them before she could read her expression at the door.

'It's Archie; I think he's fallen on the stairs.' She was trying to keep her voice calmer than her eyes, but Iris knew. Fear propelled her faster than she had moved in many years. Archie, her precious darling Archie, meant the world to her. They rushed to where he was a crumpled replica of his normal self. There was a gash on his face and his leg held awkwardly behind him on the bottom steps.

'I'm not sure we should try to get him up,' Kate said, her finger on pursed lips. 'After all, we might just make it worse.' She pulled out her phone and called for an ambulance.

'Don't worry, Archie,' Iris said, but she knew her voice carried enough worry for them both.

'I can't remember what happened,' there were tears in Archie's vulnerable eyes. 'The last I remember is coming from the bathhouse, I had to take the letter and I...' He looked around him now, as though he hardly knew where he was.

'It doesn't matter, we'll find the letter later, when we get you sorted.' Kate soothed him and he seemed to take this in.

The ambulance men were kind and jovial. They were the right mix of gentle and strong and Iris knew they would take care of Archie for her. They put him on a stretcher, made light of the bodyboard supporting him and told Iris he would be dancing about the kitchen before she knew it.

They drove the thirty miles to the county hospital right behind the ambulance. Iris thought they would never get there, and still when they did, she couldn't remember the journey. The worst thing they could say was that something was broken, that he couldn't stay with her. She knew, they would not manage a week if he were confined to bed, never mind a season. Then again, with Archie sick, the business was the least of her worries, the truth was nothing mattered more to her than Archie.

The hospital was brisk and bright. Everyone, it seemed to Iris was in a terrible hurry. Nurses, doctors, and all sorts of people rushed about while they waited for news on Archie.

'We'll need to keep him in, just overnight, to keep an eye,' a doctor told them. She was young and foreign and Iris had to strain to hear her soft voice. 'There are no bones broken, but we are going to run some tests. Has he been forgetting things recently?'

'Well, it's our age, isn't it; we are both a little forgetful now.' Iris felt like she would be selling him out to say anything more.

'Do you think he forgets words, does he find it hard to get the word he needs sometimes?' The doctor was looking now at Kate. 'He has been telling us things and we think he's showing signs of dementia, has there been a diagnosis?'

'No.' Iris knew the word well; she saw his father in the end. She didn't want that for Archie. 'No, but if I'm honest he is a bit more forgetful and he mixes things up. He thinks he's back there,' she looked down at her wedding ring. Still it meant so much to her, more as the years had passed, 'Back there, when things were different. He mixes people up, sometimes; I think he confuses me with his mother.' She smiled, the first time it happened they had laughed about it. As it happened more frequently, now it did not seem so funny.

The hotel seemed huge that night, as though it had grown more rooms and shadows, noises and corners. It quickly occurred to Iris that without Archie here she could not remain alone. Even with Kate, or whatever guests might be staying, it would make no difference. With Archie she had a family, without him, she was adrift in a cluster of memories and there was no way home.

*

She would get used to it, Iris told herself this resolutely. Alzheimer's. She smiled, remembered when Archie had called it 'Old Timers'. She told them at the hospital, his father had it. It took him quickly in the end, but then Robert helped to finish him too.

'There are tablets; they help to slow down its progression.' The doctor, older this time, a man who had seen it all before, handed them a script. 'You'll have to go to your own GP who will explain how to take them, but there is no cure.' His eyes were gloomy; he gave this news too often. 'Take care of each other,' he said, getting up to continue on his rounds and Iris knew no one had time for the old. No one had time to be old and when you were, all you could do was take tablets.

*

The box of photographs came from a small drawer in Robert's bureau. He always kept it locked. With all the pulling apart, Kate had done on the place it was inevitable that old memories would surface among the cobwebs and dust. There were several of Robert taken at dances with various girls on his arm. He had been very handsome; a Cary Grant forever stuck in that time. The years had been kind to him. The pictures somehow brought him back to her. Iris could hear his voice if she listened closely; smooth but broad vowels lacquering charm on everyone he came across. He was not like the other men in the village. He wore linen suits and shoes made especially for him from imported leather. She remembered he smelled always of soap. Her memories of that time were so vivid it surprised her; it was all so long ago now. Iris looked at her reflection in the glass of the kitchen window. She was the right side of ninety, but she knew in her heart, the girl that she had been had all but disappeared now. She was beautiful then. Of course, it was only as she aged that she realized how beautiful she had been. Funny, it had not seemed important at the time, truly it was wasted on the young.

At the far end of the hotel, she heard the front door close. The weather forecast earlier promised gale force winds. She was glad that Kate popped in at odd hours; she kept the key to the front door and the back. 'Just in case,' Archie had said and he had found one of the old key rings with the Hartley name stamped proud into the brass. She was one of them now, no longer just a name never mentioned in correspondence from Pamela. Iris adored her. She was all Burns. There was none of Clive in this girl that Iris could see. Although there was so much they didn't know about her and she about them, Iris often wondered about Kate's mother – she had never met Adaline.

Once the hospital allowed Archie to come back to the hotel, Kate popped in for tea and home-made bread with them at the kitchen table and told them of her plans for the day. Archie had enjoyed watching the bathhouse being brought back to life. It was as though some deep part of him was resuscitated with it. Iris worried that seeing the place pulled apart might upset him. She couldn't have been more wrong. That first day, he came back invigorated, as though the ghosts were finally gone. Iris secretly dreaded going near the place.

Too often now, Iris found herself wandering back to that time in her mind. The last thing she wanted was to be standing there, where their lives, such as they were, had unfolded all those years earlier. Sometimes she caught herself up as she noticed Archie watching her. He knew she was still back there, every bit as much as he was. Neither of them could let it all go. Still, she was glad it was doing well; pleased Kate seemed happy, thankful she was near.

# 17

# Kate

Some might say it was a good thing that Todd walked into the bathhouse that day. It certainly got things out in the open. Of course, Kate believed, leaving London, that she was ready to leave him behind, that she was finally getting over him. Even then, the idea of having to face him would have thrown her. Now that she had done it, spoken to him face to face and actually held her nerve, well, she was free. More than free. She had a feeling that the ten years she spent dealing with her feelings for him had paid off, while he had just run away from that time and never stopped to take stock.

She looked out into the waves and thought about what he had said in the bathhouse, it had played on her mind for days. It had thrummed away while she drove to and from the hospital to visit Archie and it had been like a constant soundtrack in her mind when she lay exhausted in her bed at night. Could it be that he really was sorry. Could it be that he actually understood what he had done to her? She doubted that. Todd did not have the capacity to truly empathize, or at least the Todd she knew in London didn't.

What had made her fall in love with him all those years ago? She had asked herself that question many times since. She knew, straight off, he was selfish. Had she believed that he loved her enough to make an exception in the way he treated her? She fell for him hard, from the start, but her only consolation was she believed he felt the same way. They were together two years when he proposed. It was out of the blue, one of those crazy acts that he was good at and she loved him for. She was hardly blind to his faults. She had to admit that. She was too smart not to see beyond the shallow facade that he thought fooled the world. In the end, she knew what made her say yes was not his success, but rather his weakness. He needed her; she truly believed that. He needed her as no one had ever needed her before. He needed a home that was stable and safe. He needed people that were grounded and normal. He needed an adult in his life who was grown-up, and could keep him on an even keel. Mostly he needed to be loved for what he was, a vulnerable man in a world that was moving too fast around him not to have an anchor. That was another lifetime, she reminded herself, and people change. Perhaps Todd didn't need anyone anymore.

There was something else too, something that lurked between them. It sat, stubbornly and silently, between their words and the shy exchanges. There was still a connection there. It was something oblique and tenuous that time and pain had not managed to sever. Something – she wouldn't call it love, the wounds were too deep for that. But there was no denying that something unexplained was simmering under the surface for her and she could see it in Todd too, when she let herself admit it. That was stupid, wasn't it? Todd couldn't have feelings for her after all this time? Was it wishful thinking? He was dating a model and not just any model. He was dating Claudia Dey, the biggest name to come out of London in a decade. She was beautiful, cool, glamorous and famous.

Todd only ever wanted what he couldn't have and no conversion on the road to Damascus or in Atlantic City was going to change that. She learned the hard way what it was to fall head over heels for Todd Riggs. She could see how it could easily happen again if she wasn't careful. Kate Hunt was careful though. She was so careful, that she had not let herself fall for anyone since Todd, not anyone of her own time anyway. The first thing to come close to filling his place in her heart was Ballytokeep and the bathhouse that she had made her home.

She was still sitting in wonderful silence when Rita arrived. She had a large shopping bag filled with what looked like green metal-topped files, which she plonked on the counter with the brutality of someone who's taken the weight of it personally.

'You look like you've seen a ghost. Has Robert finally come back and asked you to marry him, or split the profits on this place?'

'No, nothing like that.' Kate laughed. 'So, come on, what's in the bag? Have you chopped up Duncan so we can make soup out of him?'

'No, he'd be far too gristly for soup,' Rita said and she tittered as though it might be worth entertaining the notion further. 'No, these, my dear, are for you.' Satisfaction coated her words. 'It's everything I could find that you asked me to. Deeds of the house, loans Duncan had for the business, it's all there.' They had drawn up a list of what she needed together.

'That was fast,' Kate moved towards them, eager to get started on the task ahead. Duncan Delaney was going to get his comeuppance sooner and starker than he expected. She looked into the bag. It was stuffed full of folders bulging with deeds and business documents. 'Hang on, does he know you have these?' Kate hadn't expected Rita to be so thorough, although she was glad for it.

'No, he's gone to a meeting in "Galway",' Rita wiggled her fingers in the air around his destination. 'In other words, he's taken his fancy piece off for a few days. Don't ask me where, but you don't need your passport to go to the next county.'

'Right, perfect. We'll have them back before he knows they're gone so.' Kate was going to enjoy this. Duncan Delaney was the kind of first-class cheating rat that made her want to exact the most excruciating payment and Kate wasn't talking about chewed shoes or allergies.

*

It was a day or two later that Kate heard news of Todd Riggs.

Colin arrived in to the bathhouse, his hair wet and sand tracing along his tanned arms. 'Seems there's trouble up in the Castle these days,' he said casually as they sat out on the rock sipping white wine he'd brought down from the cottage.

'Oh, why do you say that?' Kate tried hard not to seem interested.

'Well, it looks that way; Todd Riggs booked into the Hartleys Hotel this afternoon. He booked the room indefinitely.' Colin stole a sideward glance at Kate. 'Problems with some of the work, apparently. It seems a shame though, because he's only just moved in.'

'He's always lived in hotels. When I knew him, in London, all those years ago, he was living in a hotel. That's rock stars for you, I suppose.' She tried to sound nonchalant.

'There's another rumour doing the rounds too. It's in some of the papers; they're saying Claudia Dey has left him.' Colin sipped his drink. Kate suspected that the rumour wasn't new and the Ballytokeep gossip turbine was in overdrive.

'Well, you're asking the wrong one about that too. Todd Riggs's love life has nothing to do with me these days,' she smiled easily; it was, after all, true.

'Well, that's good news, isn't it?'

'Is it?'

'I know he hurt you, all those years ago, I'm just looking out for you.'

'I appreciate that, Colin, but like you said, it was a long time ago.'

'I wonder if he thinks so.' Colin was convinced Todd watched them some nights as they sat outside the bathhouse. Kate knew it was ridiculous; after all, from Rock Castle, the views across land and sea had to be awesome, he'd hardly be bothered watching them.

*

'Morning,' Todd was standing at the door of the bathhouse, early before any customers had even realized they were hungry. 'I don't ever remember you mentioning Archie and Iris?' He came to sit at the table across from her.

'I didn't.' She didn't actually know them back then, she

knew of them, but it was long before she met them. Then, they were just shadows in her grandmother's past.

'So you heard I've had to move out of the tower? And there I am staying in your aunt and uncle's hotel and I hadn't a clue. Honestly, I felt like a total fool. They're lovely, really lovely.' He smiled at her now. They were Todd's kind of people too, for all he lived the rock star life, he had always preferred ordinary and warm people like Denny and Meg.

'They are lovely, I'm very lucky. So, they're looking after you?'

'And then some. They're an amazing couple, Kate.'

'Did they tell you that they're sixty years married this year, and look at them, they're still madly in love.'

'No, but I got a feeling that she's not so keen on me, so maybe she wasn't up for telling me too much. I like them though, they're...'

'They're quite protective.' Kate smiled, 'Don't worry, I'm sure you'll charm Iris given half a chance. Coffee?'

'Okay,' he said smiling. He reached his hands out before the stove, as though to warm them, although it was not cold outside. 'These are great, aren't they? Another benefit to living where you can have a real chimney. Where do you buy your turf?'

'I don't buy it,' the thought had never occurred to Kate, did people actually buy and sell the stuff. 'Colin brought down a load of it when I started doing the place up.'

'Ah, Colin?' he said thoughtfully. 'How long have you two known each other?'

'Excuse me.' Kate placed a mug on the table before him, might have offered him a scone, but since she was already feeding Colin Lyons, she wasn't sure she wanted every hungry bachelor in the town on her doorstep.

'You and the sheep farmer? Did you know him before or...'

'You're asking me did I drop my life in London to move here for Colin.' She knew he was asking a lot more than that, but he nodded, so she played it cool. 'No, we met when I came to look at the bathhouse.' She placed a finger at the side of her nose. She was not going to satisfy his curiosity any more. After all, he had Claudia Dey still hanging off his arm, unless the papers had it right. 'What about you and Claudia?' She did not want too much information; just enough to stop the silence or maybe make sure that nothing passed between them that couldn't be taken back.

'Claudia and me?'

'Yes, did you meet in London or some far-flung exotic place?'

'She picked me up off the floor at a party in Mayfair, or so she says. I was smashed, of course. It was probably one of her minders who lifted me out of her way. What can I say, obviously, she was smitten.' They laughed, still sharing the same sense of humour at Todd's feigned bloated ego.

'Yes, I can see how she would be bowled over by a middle-aged, whiskey-drinking commitment-phobic!'

'Apparently,' Todd lowered his voice, 'I was quite the catch.'

'Well, you certainly make the celebrity couple.' Kate smiled, but her mouth was dry. She spent too many days trying to avoid Todd and Claudia on the pages of newspapers and magazines.

'It's not everything, is it?' Todd said and Kate wondered if he had seen her discomfort.

'I'm sure it helps, when you're selling records and modelling.'

'It does that,' Todd said sadly. 'You know, that whole scene, it's…' He sighed. 'Well, it's not all it's cracked up to be.'

'Anyway, you're here now.' Kate changed the subject.

'Speaking of which, you heard about the small hiccup in the tower?' Todd smiled. 'We have to put in a new top floor.'

'Oh, no. That's a big job.'

'Well, it is, but I suppose we were really lucky. I mean, there have been so many people in and out of the place, scaffolding and machinery and all sorts. We're lucky no one was hurt, the engineer said it could have come down at any moment.'

'When will it be finished?'

'This week, hopefully. I'll be moving back in on Friday, not that it'll be the Ritz or anything, but…'

'Better than the squat?'

'Only just, to be honest,' he smiled, perhaps thinking back to those early days. 'It'll just be a shell, with the basics, kitchen, bathroom, bed.' He smiled at her, 'You should come and see it, once I move in.'

'Oh, I…'

'Only fair, we're going to be neighbours.'

'When you're here.' She laughed at him, she could no more see Todd spending the rest of his days in Ballytokeep than she could imagine a Sunday in Ballytokeep with no mass.

'What's that supposed to mean?' He laughed.

'Well, you have commitments. In London? The band and Claudia, and Denny, too; I can't imagine you not having Denny and Meg close at hand.'

'You had commitments in London too.' His voice was low. He was leading her somewhere she did not want to go.

'That was different.'

'How was it different? I don't see too many divorce courts in Ballytokeep. You just up and got yourself a new life, I

don't see what's so unreasonable about me doing the same.'
It was a question, but it was one that Kate wasn't sure she
could answer.

'Well, maybe. I suppose.' She sipped her coffee. 'If it's what
you want.'

'That's the thing, Kate,' Todd sighed, his eyes filled with an
emotion she was not sure she could pin down. 'I'm not sure
what I want anymore, but I know that I've never felt more
content than I do now.'

'It must be a lot to take in,' her words were brittle. 'Having
a heart attack, you know, makes you see life differently, I'm
sure.'

'You know, no one else is getting that.' Todd rubbed his
eyes and Kate couldn't be sure if he wiped away tears. 'They
think that it's just a phase, that I can go back to how things
were, you know, with the band and living at the Embassy
Rooms and...'

'I'd say, for now, you need to take each day as it comes.
You're still getting back on your feet, Todd, and think of it,
when did you last take a holiday?

'Never,' he shook his head, 'not unless you count going
home for my mum's funeral.' He shrugged.

'No, we won't count that, Todd. You need to take it easy
for a while, get yourself sorted and listen to the waves.'

'Enjoy the view?' He smiled. 'Will you drop by and see the
castle? When it's done?' His eyes held the expectancy of a
child, light and blue and hopeful in that too familiar face; it
was impossible to say no.

'Of course I will. I might even bring you a present,' she
said, making a mental note to ask Colin about organizing a
couple of bags of turf for Todd.

# 18

# Todd

'So, you're happy with it? Like this?' The builder looked a little sceptical.

'More than happy, mate, this is like Buckingham Palace compared to some of the places I stayed when we were starting out. Don't worry; you've done a good job.'

'I could get someone to come and look at the place, you know, designer, or someone to…'

'Nah, you're all right. I'll get it sorted in a few weeks; the bareness suits me for now. Do you know what I do need though?' There were bills to be paid. The contractor had asked for half his payment in cash so he could sort out some of the men who had worked to clean and tidy up. He also had to close the account with the building suppliers – a cheque would do, but it needed to be settled up. 'I need a car to get to the bank and sort out what I owe you.' He looked down towards the bathhouse. He would ask Kate, any excuse to go back to the tearoom it seemed.

*

'Sure I'll bring you in the car. Remind me, are we buying a car today or are we just paying bills?' Kate laughed and Todd thought she was actually more beautiful now than she had been all those years ago. Age suited her; she would be thirty-six now; it sounded young compared to his forty two.

'Well, I'll need a car, that's for sure. I can't keep getting taxis or depending on the goodwill of neighbours.' He smiled, he was glad she was driving him. 'Nice car, by the way.' It was an old Peugeot. A woman's car. It was not what he would have imagined Kate buying in a million years back in London.

'It's Iris's. She hasn't driven it in ages, so she told me to take it and I can bring them about occasionally. They never want to go far, but still, it's nice to drive out into the country, she and Archie are excellent tour guides.' They drove on in silence for a minute. 'What about you? I don't remember you driving in London?'

'No, never needed to. I guess I'll have to get a licence and do the whole L plate thing, here.' He laughed when he thought about it. He drove years ago, but never legally. Then there came a time when there was no point, he preferred to hop on the tube even though the record label always had a limo waiting on his word.

'You might be grounded for a while so; I think getting a licence here is a bit of a headache, all that European legislation, it's all proper lessons and tough tests.'

'Maybe I'll content myself with a bicycle so?'

'With a basket, for your grocery shopping?' Kate shrieked with laughter at this.

They made their way into the next town and picked

up some groceries after he had been to the bank and the hardware merchants. 'Well, you have enough to get started, all the essentials, at least,' she said, 'and you know, I will be popping across again next Monday to the cash and carry, so if you want...'

'Thanks, Kate. I'd offer to buy you dinner, but I know you want to get back,' he tried to make his voice sound light, not a proposition, just a meal.

'Tell the truth, Todd – you just want to get back to that castle and get settled in!' She laughed again. 'Anyway, it's okay, you're off the hook. Colin is bringing down a nice merlot tonight and I fully intend to watch the sun set and devour a large slice of Rita's lasagne when I get back to the bathhouse.'

'Lasagne sounds better than anything we've passed along the way; you're probably getting the better bargain.'

'You know they say that rock stars are the tightest blokes going, so maybe I should make you buy me dinner.' She was just joking, but she stopped there. Todd knew she was afraid. There was an unspoken line and he had a feeling that Kate had no intention of crossing it. 'Anyway, we're almost home now,' she said the words softly. He knew that, like him, she was not used to feeling as if she'd quite come home yet and the novelty felt good as she said it.

'Ballytokeep is home, isn't it?'

'It is for me at any rate. I have Aunt Iris and Uncle Archie here, the tearooms and...'

'Colin?'

'Yeah, I've met some great people here, that's true.' She kept her eyes firmly on the road. 'But it's more than that. I feel complete here. A bit like you maybe, only I didn't have to have a heart attack to realize it.'

'Slow learner, that's always been my problem,' he made a face that was mock sad.

'Hm, you could have fooled me.'

He waited a moment in the silence of the car; neither of them had made a move to switch on the radio. 'What was London like for you? I mean, I know you were successful, but weren't you happy?'

'I don't know. I didn't think I was unhappy exactly, but then I came here and I realized that this place, the people here, well, it was like I found something I didn't know I was missing.'

'God that sounds a hell of a lot easier than having a heart attack.'

'It certainly is,' she said softly. 'Oh, it looks like you have a visitor,' Kate said as they made their way along the narrow road toward the tower. A large off-roader stood squat and ugly at the perimeter wall of the castle.

'So I have,' Todd said and he had a feeling it was Claudia, which should have made him even happier but when he saw her stony expression, he had a feeling that Kate was in for the better night.

*

Claudia greeted Kate with the sickly sweetness of conde-scension. It was as though she was trying to be mellow in the victory of not being the jilted one. Still, she draped herself about Todd as though he were a prop on a fashion shoot. Everyone was clear about exactly who belonged to whom. They were still a couple, even if they lived a thousand miles apart. Kate just smiled in that way she always had and left them to it. Todd could admit it to himself; Claudia had never been much of a judge of character.

'Well, well, well, wasn't that very cosy?' Claudia hissed as soon as Kate was out of earshot. 'Is this your new thing now, *Driving Miss Daisy?*'

'It's not like that, Claudia, and anyway Kate was just giving me a lift.'

'Oh, forget it, it's all the same. It's like retirement central, you pair driving her Noddy car to collect googleberries.' She flounced off up the stairs towards the kitchen, leaving Todd to trail in her wake with his two shopping bags. It was strange having her here, this place it was meant to be somewhere they could build a future, but somehow she just didn't seem to fit. Honestly, sometimes she made him feel like he was a pensioner. Although he should probably be thankful, she would convince herself that Kate was too old to be a threat – even if there was hardly five years between them.

Claudia hated the tower last time and if he thought its appeal would grow on her, he was mistaken. 'Look around you, Todd. This place, it's positively medieval and... I'm not sleeping here.'

'It was worse the first time you saw it, and then you said you loved it.'

'I didn't mean it though, did I? That was just for the press, babes, I am a London girl me. Give me Covent Garden any day.'

'So how long are you here for?' He had been looking forward to his first night in the castle, was tempted to let Claudia stay in the local hotel.

'Flying visit. I'm off to Italy next week, so I thought I'd catch up with you first and then it's non-stop for about a month.'

'Oh.' Todd knew, he should be delighted she was here. After all, there were plenty who'd love to have Claudia Dey drop in for a flying visit and, to be fair, he wasn't exactly inundated with people dropping by. 'It's good to see you, babe.' He meant it. 'This place will do you good, you look tired.'

'Yeah, well, I work, don't I? It's all well and good for you, Todd, to be able to sit back in your castle and count your money, but I'm still a career girl.' She stood at the sink, while he unloaded the shopping from Kate's car. 'So I thought maybe before I head off I could catch some extra sleep. And of course catch up with you,' she added.

'Sure, London quiet at the moment?'

'Like a dodo.' She exhaled then searched in her large bag for a bottle of her favourite designer water. 'Christ, my head hurts,' she said and she flopped into a chair to play with her social media accounts for a few hours.

# 19

## Iris, 1957

Iris was happy that Robert seemed to have fallen for a local girl. It was all very sudden, but Gemma was exactly the type of girl Iris could imagine Robert falling for. She was pretty, stylish and her family was well connected – the perfect hostess. Within two weeks it seemed like they had settled into something serious. 'Oh, once Robert sets his mind on something,' Mrs Hartley said one afternoon as they worked together in the hotel kitchen.

In some strange way, it took the danger out of him. When they met now she enjoyed his dry wit and they shared a common sense of humour, less polite than Archie approved of. Of course, she still had Archie and he treated her like a queen.

It was all very well Pamela being married to an Earl's son, but Iris thought there was nothing nicer than sitting on the veranda with Archie, knowing that a dozen girls in the village would give their best Sunday shoes to be where she was. He took her to the cinema, so really they were courting, although he never put a word on it. She adored Archie a little more with every passing day and sometimes she wondered if that would continue if they were still sitting here together into old age. He brought her the best roses from the garden and expensive perfume from the chemist, and occasionally he left gifts under her pillow. Silly things they'd been talking about during the day – a bar of chocolate or a magazine. She knew Archie would always try to make her life a little brighter.

On the other hand, she missed Robert's discreet devotion. Yes, she could admit it to herself; she actually missed the buried tension between them. She enjoyed feeling attractive to him. Damn it, she probably revelled in the illicit nature of it. She was still just a girl. If you couldn't crave a little danger when you were young, well, when would you ever really live? Then, at the back of all these thoughts was Mark. Her baby Mark, buried in Parisian soil, his grave now dry in the summer sun, and she wondered if Pamela would visit it as often as she might visit the grave of her own son, had he been the one they lost. She longed to write to Marianne, but what more could she say? And then she worried that her correspondence might get Marianne into trouble with Clive and Pamela. So, instead she tortured herself with thoughts of Mark buried among strangers far away.

'Oh, Gemma Routledge?' Mrs Hartley said and she sniffed approvingly when Iris mentioned Robert's new girlfriend. Gemma was from the kind of family Mrs Hartley approved of and fortunately for Robert she was easy on the eye and seemed to worship him.

'It won't last,' Archie said sadly. 'They never do. Robert has had more girls than...' and he stopped, he was too polite to delve deeply into the romantic affairs of his brother.

'Well, they seem to be very happy, he's bringing her to the county fair at the end of the summer,' Iris found herself defending Robert. She didn't stop to wonder how much of it was defence and how much was possessiveness. After all, he liked *her* first. Although she would not admit it to anyone, hardly even to herself, those first frissons of passion that stirred within her had never quite died. Now, she found herself watching him, wondering what it might have been like. Had they ended up together, how would it be? Abruptly, when she became aware of how her mind was wandering off course, she would pull herself back to the hotel and Oisín Armstrong and Mark. At all times Mark.

'Robert has always wanted what he can't have,' Archie said the words under his breath one evening as he watched his brother swagger through the hotel reception. 'Things lose their lustre for him once he's held them in his hand, or indeed in his…' Archie went off to check the back doors for the night. It was not a cold night, but Iris shivered all the same, wondered if Archie could read her mind sometimes.

Gemma Routledge was very pretty. A diminutive blonde who said all the right things and whose father owned a racehorse tipped to win the Irish Grand National no less. Robert brought her for Sunday picnics in his open-top car. They attended glamorous cocktail parties in large houses where Iris could not see past the front gates and long winding drives. Robert had mercilessly paraded Gemma about Ballytokeep and half the county. Even Mrs Hartley was expecting an announcement before the season was out.

'She wants him to propose,' Archie said one morning, raising his eyes to heaven as though nothing was less likely.

'He might.'

'Honestly, you're as bad as she is,' Archie said in a rare

moment of exasperation. 'He's using her, Iris, that's what he does. Can't you see it? God knows, you two spend enough time together these days, you're as thick as thieves,' there was something odd in his tone.

'Yes, but we don't actually talk to each other, not like that. We are just planning... you know, how to raise money for the trip to London and the operation.'

'God, what is it with Robert, he has you all fooled.' Archie stamped out the door angrily.

'It's a good cause,' Iris said, but she had a feeling he didn't hear and what did it matter anyway. She was not going to stop spending time with Robert just because Archie didn't approve.

The more Iris thought about the conversation later that day, the more the whole thing annoyed her. Who did Archie Hartley think he was anyway? He had not made her any solid proposal. He had kissed her on the lips, and true, it made her tingle in a way that was different to anything she felt before. When Archie kissed her, it didn't feel illicit, it felt right. Was that true love? She had never experienced anything like it before. An overwhelming sense that someone loved her, truly loved her, not in a taking kind of way. Rather, Archie made her feel that she was – what was the word, oh yes – respected.

Robert, on the other hand, with his dark good looks and his rakish smile – he made her feel like he could turn her inside out. She wasn't sure that this was a good thing either. He hadn't kissed her. But he had held her on that dance floor and she knew, deep down, she knew that if they kissed, she would have melted into him. Just like all those other girls before her.

'Archie,' she had to say something, she still didn't know

what, 'I'm not sure what I've done wrong. Is it helping Robert with the fundraising efforts? I really can't see that you have any right to be cross with me.'

'No, I suppose you wouldn't see, would you?' Archie sighed, a long deep gentle sound that made her think he had given up already.

'I shouldn't have to say anything to you,' she said, 'we've made no agreement, you've never put words on any intentions you might have.'

'No, but there wouldn't be any point, would there? Not if you feel what I think you feel for Robert?'

'That's a big presumption on your part. I'm not sure I should even answer.' Iris felt her heart sink uncontrollably down to the ground. There was much about Archie she admired; not in a silly, heart-fluttering sort of way, granted; but in a real and honest way. She knew from bitter experience that there were not that many men out there like him. He was handsome and funny and one day he would own this hotel. More than that, he was honourable and she knew the respect he had for her would never falter. The emotion she felt that night, when he kissed her hard on her lips, that was the kind of love she was sure would last a lifetime.

And Robert?

Whatever Robert Hartley felt for her in the past had faded already. You would have to be blind not to see that he and Gemma were made for each other. Robert Hartley had found his princess and good luck to them. She knew, in spite of all the chemicals in her body that drew her to Robert, she had the better brother here.

'It's you I love, Archie. You I love with all my heart,' she whispered the words and then she ran from him. Back at the hotel, she cried until she'd soaked not alone every tissue in her room, but the pillowcase as well. She knew then, if she settled for Archie, she was turning her back on more than just Robert. It meant she would not be returning to Paris and it meant that Pamela would be tending to Mark's grave instead of his own mother.

*

It did not take long to rally a group of do-gooders in the cause of Oisín Armstrong. Within a week they had a committee and by two they had news from the London specialist. Oisín would be placed on a waiting list, they had six weeks to gather his fees together. That evening they were gathering in the bathhouse for a meeting. In all, there were six of them and, between them, they had already organized a cake sale.

'Eight pounds,' said Mrs O'Hara who owned a little wool shop that carried out a great trade all year long.

'It's a start,' Ernie Petrie said stoically.

'Yes, Ernie is right. We have to start somewhere.' Robert took the centre of the room.

Gemma arrived and served tea to everyone. It was as though some tacit agreement had already been made between herself and Robert. Iris watched her; she was in her element, playing the hostess. She was quite beautiful with straw-coloured thick hair held back with glittering clips. She wore a full wide lilac taffeta skirt that owed much to the inspiration of the movies. It was topped off with a crisp white shirt, open at the neck to reveal a gold pendant that caught the evening light. To Iris's mind, she was the Ballytokeep equivalent of Grace Kelly. She couldn't help feeling a little pushed to the side in this girl's presence. They were from different social classes and Iris had a feeling, it wasn't something that Gemma was prepared to forget.

'Maybe, we should just try and do one huge thing, something that would put the village on the map at the same time...'

'I was thinking of doing a house to house collection, everyone would surely give something if we brought the little fella with us, so they could see him.' Mrs O'Hara sipped from the delicate china cup before her.

'Hmm. What if we could do something to collect money that would be fun and good for the village as well as for Oisín?'

'Have you any ideas, Robert?' Iris knew he had this well thought out. He struck her as a man who knew exactly what he was about.

'I have heard all about what they are doing down in Tralee. They started a festival, it's just a beauty contest really but...' he looked at Gemma now, smiled an acknowledgement as she placed more milk in the jug before them. 'They've brought huge numbers of visitors to the town, and not just the regular day-trippers, but they have busloads of Yanks and people coming back from England and all over. The town is wedged while this thing is on – and most of them don't even go to the beauty pageant.'

'So we invite back all the relations?' Ernie smiled. 'God knows, if every family got one son back from London or Boston for a day or two, we'd get a great crowd to the village.' Ballytokeep had been badly hit with emigration after the war – it seemed now, the older people felt it most.

'I don't know. Do we want a lot of foreigners running about the place corrupting the young?' Mrs O'Hara looked across at Iris.

'Oh, we wouldn't be getting just any types; we'd be looking to bring people on holiday that came from here years ago. People who've left and want to come back for a little break,' Gemma said and Iris knew that Robert had already told her his plan. She felt a stab of something go through her but caught it quickly before it turned to jealousy.

'And how would this benefit our Oisín, can you tell me?' Mr Armstrong had sat silently until this. He did not take any tea, maybe feeling that he was taking enough already.

'Well, once we get them here – they'll spend money. They'll have to stay somewhere, eat and drink and maybe even look for rides out on the fishing boats.'

'It's not bloody cruise ships we're running, you know that?'

'Yes, but I'll wager it's a lot easier to make a few bob carrying a boatload of people out to see dolphins than it is hauling in a net of mackerel,' Robert said, smiling.

'You might be right.' Mr Armstrong smiled too.

'We could finish up with a dance or a bit of a hoolie, rent out a marquee and charge everyone to come. Anything we make could go straight to Oisín. I'll wager we could make a good bit.'

'It's a lot of work,' Iris said, thinking that it was coming at the busiest time of year for all of them.

'I'd be happy to help,' Gemma said, standing behind Robert proprietorially. 'It's a good cause and it could be good for the village.'

Iris could feel a bubble of resentment rise within her. After all, she had started the ball rolling that day with Robert, now it felt like Gemma had slipped stealthily into her place and it rankled.

'Count me in,' Ernie said, winking at Gemma.

A show of hands and it was done. Gemma would be in charge of organizing it. Iris conceded grudgingly that she would be a very capable chairperson. Mr Armstrong and Ernie would rally the fishermen together and see if they could organize some kind of fishing competition in the boats and on the pier. Mrs O'Malley would keep a moral eye on all proceedings. They agreed to hold it on the last weekend in August, just as most people were winding down their summer.

'So, that just leaves our Gala Ball?' Robert said, smiling. 'Or perhaps just our village dance,' he was looking at Iris now who had not been voted into any role so far.

'Of course, I'll help with organizing that,' she said and she knew Archie would help.

'You can't take that on, all on your own.' Ernie was watching Robert now.

'I was thinking exactly the same thing,' Robert said. 'I'll give you a hand with it.'

'But...' Gemma said, and Iris thought for just a second that she saw something familiar flash across Gemma's face. Perhaps, Iris was not the only person in the room unsure of her footing.

'That's settled so. We'll meet again in, say two weeks?' Robert said, draining the last of the teapot before him into Mrs O'Malley's cup.

# Present

It took four days for the summer cold to clear. Iris sat, still and thoughtful for the afternoons, watching the waves crashing into the promenade. Sometimes, she felt like she had spent a lifetime looking out at the sea, lost in her thoughts. Often she wondered what might have been if her choices had been different. If she had not been so foolish to begin with. Then Archie, as though he could read her mind, would appear at her elbow, an understanding look in his eyes and she knew that things were as they should be.

She never asked him what had happened that night to Robert. They never spoke of that time, long ago. Maybe neither of them wanted to know the truth of how Robert spent his final hours. Some things were best left in the past. So why couldn't she just do that?

It was Kate, of course. It was Kate moving into the bathhouse, digging up the past with photographs and talking of times that Iris found hard enough to put from her mind.

'Isn't she beautiful?' she asked breathlessly as she sat in

the chair opposite Iris. She held a faded photograph out to Iris. Black and white, but the features remained strong, as though cast in a beautiful marble long ago.

'Yes, she certainly was.' Iris gathered her breath; it had become more laboured these last few days, she couldn't really blame it on the memories stirred up by the bathhouse, could she? It was the TB; they say it never fully clears from your lungs. Iris often wondered if it was something she passed on to Mark. The way she felt now, as though pushing each breath from her was an effort, was down to not getting fresh air as well as seeing this photo. Although, the layers of age that permeated her bones probably didn't help either.

'Who was she?' Kate asked as Archie came into the sitting room.

'Well now, Archie, look at what Kate has come across.' Iris held the photo out to Archie.

'She was Robert's fiancée.' The way he said the words, Iris knew it covered over many explanations.

'Well, his sweetheart at any rate,' Iris corrected him, but she could not catch his eye.

'One of many,' he handed the photograph back to Kate. 'My brother had plenty of girls after him, he was quite the catch.' Archie shook his head good-naturedly.

'Oh, Archie, you were handsome too.' Kate laughed and she took a second photo from her bag. 'I found this buried in the middle of a ledger, it's probably the last ledger he kept.' She handed it to Archie, a gift perhaps.

'It's from the tea dance,' Archie said sadly, 'the last photo we had taken together, all three of us.' He stood for a moment and Iris had a feeling that if he was alone he might have dropped a tear. He tucked the picture into his pocket and she wondered what would become of it. These days things seemed to disappear around Archie and then turn up in the most unusual places. On Tuesday, Iris found two fuses buried deep in the sugar bowl, as though Archie had hidden them there for safekeeping. Putting a name on it hadn't really helped. Archie didn't remember the doctor said he had Alzheimer's and it only served to make Iris dread what lay ahead even more than she had before. How could she watch her wonderful Archie suffer as his father had? She quickly pushed the thoughts from her and smiled at him; she adored him now even more than she had all those years ago.

She remembered the day of the tea dance well, the weather was warm and she was glad to get out of the hotel kitchen. It seemed for an afternoon that the world was an optimistic place. Ballytokeep had in it enough to keep her content for the rest of her days, or perhaps more than she felt she had any right to at least. She laughed with Archie, and Robert had danced with her. It was the start of everything, really. Had all that hope been captured in their eyes? Or would they look like strangers, people whose lives might not have touched each other at all, had it not been for one summer's day. Part of her would have liked to look at it; most of her knew she could not and perhaps Archie knew that too.

# 20

## Kate, 1992

'She'll have to stay in Ireland then.' Jeremy's voice was low, but not quite low enough. Kate could hear their conversation beyond her bedroom door. Her stepfather had even less to say to her than her own father did. Her mother concerned herself with entertaining his business acquaintances while Doris, the girl whose job it was to keep the house in shape, more often than not was left with Kate on her tail while she went about her business. 'Can't she stay with the Mornington-Hunts?'

'She certainly cannot.' Her mother's voice was shrill; Kate could imagine her coming down with a very bad headache as soon as Jeremy left for London. 'Over my dead body,' she said, too often now for the words to have the desired theatrical effect.

'Well, she can't stay here. I'm not paying that girl to spend her days and nights here while we are in the States. We could be there for months. She's twelve years old, for heaven's sake, it's time to get her a proper education, at her age I was away at boarding school and doing well.'

'Don't worry; I'll take care of it, darling. Just you don't miss your plane.' She was jaded. Life had done that to her. At twelve years of age, Kate suspected she had done that to her mother. The truth was Jeremy, keeping up the perfection, the life with absolutely no bumps, was wearing her mother down.

By the time Jeremy sat in his first-class seat to his important business meeting, Adaline had enrolled Kate in Rathmichael boarding school and Doris sorted her belongings by the week's end.

'You'll love it; it's a perfectly good school. The best there is to offer. And you're bright; the teachers are always saying so. They'll get you prepared for matriculation and in a few years' time you'll have your choice of the best colleges in Cambridge and Oxford.' Adaline told her as soon as it was settled.

The day before Kate left, the 'For Sale' sign went up outside St Kiernan's. Immediately, Kate was filled with the sensation that life as she knew it, empty and lonely and all as it was, was slipping away from her. She was saying goodbye to Dublin without being told she wouldn't be coming back. She had spent half of her life here. Her memories of her father were mainly tied up with this place and across the road, in the shared garden, she had buried Patch only last year.

'It will be a wonderful adventure for both of us,' Adaline said as she bundled her into the taxi and paid the driver. 'I would go, but I have to make a flight,' she said to Kate. They both knew the flight was the following day, but there were hairdressing appointments and the auctioneer to speak to. 'I will see you at Christmas, all right? We'll have a lovely holiday in New Hampshire, Jeremy has a charming clapboard house organized for us for the holidays.'

Actually, Kate did not see Adaline or Jeremy for almost three and a half years. There was always a business trip, always an emergency, always something more important than Kate. The Mornington-Hunts, the grandparents she never met, seemed like they were just pretend characters her mother had painted badly. Her father? He married again, in Montenegro according to the society pages, and again in London when she was fifteen. If he thought about her, it wasn't enough to get in contact. And then, one day, after four years in Rathmichael, she was called to the head mistress's office. Her mother, older, richer and more fragile than she remembered, her lips still painted red and turned down had come with news.

'Crispin is dead.' Adaline held a perfectly laundered white handkerchief at the ready. 'Your father is dead.' Perhaps they expected Kate would cry for him. 'He died in London. A car crash. They say he didn't feel a thing,' her mother – red-eyed, perfectly coiffured – said. For a moment, Kate wondered if Adaline had loved him, if she still loved him, in her own cold way. It never crossed her mind to wonder if she loved Kate. Some things were too painful to contemplate. Adaline's hands shook; everything about her looked thinner, daintier than Kate remembered.

'Well that's good,' Kate managed, but it didn't seem real. The man that was supposed to be her father was just a distant memory. He was a stranger who once brought home a puppy, kissed her and then got into a car, without so much as glancing back.

There was no funeral, just a memorial service. When she went in search of her father's grave, she learned that his wish to be cremated and scattered in an anonymous London park had been adhered to. It left her with a sense that it had all come to nothing. Moreover, the Mornington-Hunts seemed even further removed than ever.

It took until college before Kate understood how odd her family situation was. In that first year, she realized that Christmastime had to be marked in some meaningful way. 'It's what people do,' her roommate said as she bundled too many dirty clothes into a rucksack. She was 'heading home to middle-class madness, in the smallest town in England,' she told Kate. There was an anticipation about her that contradicted her attempt at urbanity. 'You should come, the more the merrier.'

Later, in that little house in Manningtree, with a family she did not know celebrating their holiday, Kate realized, that actually, yes, this is what people do, only Kate's mother had never seen fit to spend the time with her.

The following year, Kate made plans to stay with Adaline and Jeremy. They were living in Montreal at that stage. He was working his way steadily up the international corporate ladder. Her mother, for her contribution to society, was declining fast into a sea of gin. It became obvious, in one depressing holiday, what their lives were based on all along. They spent Christmas sitting uncomfortably around the dining table that was only used for entertaining strangers. It was apt, really, Kate thought, because that was essentially, what they all were. Strangers. It was all so different from the year before, where she spent those days with a family who were strange to her, and yet, they welcomed her as one of their own. In Montreal, they ate in silence. Each swallow was loud and uncomfortable. In Manningtree, there had been laughter, jokes, and jostling for the best seat and control of the TV remote. Before Kate sat on her return flight, she knew it was the last holiday she would willingly spend with Adaline and Jeremy.

So it was at twenty that life began again. Kate operated as though she was alone in the world; her psyche built a framework about her. You can't miss what you never had, right? Except at night. It was after that horrible holiday that the nightmare began. It started with being left at Rathmichael. Her mother dropped her off, left her on the steps with bags in hands and drove down the winding driveway. She was alone.

The dream stayed with her for years. It woke her at odd hours in the night. Nothing terrible happened in it, but it was the overwhelming sense of isolation that woke her with a heavy heart and too often sobbing into the silent darkness.

*

'Divorce is the kind of job that requires wine,' Kate said.

Although Rita was no drinker, she filled up her glass and gasped with every mouthful. It should have caused her sadness, but then maybe this was a relief. Thirty years was a long time to be married to someone you did not like much anymore.

'Why would he have most of his assets in your name, that's what I don't get,' Kate had copied every sheet on the small printer copier back at the hotel. 'The house, the business – on paper, you are a wealthy woman, Rita.'

'Bankrupt. He went bankrupt or near it. At the time, his accountants said, offload as much as he could. I was the lucky recipient,' Rita was po-faced. 'It means nothing, though, you know that. I'm not interested in his businesses or even in his money.'

'Not really the point, though, is it?' Duncan had played, unwittingly into their hands. According to his tax affairs, he might as well have been a well-paid employee. 'You could fire him, of course. Technically, he is working in your company, living in your house. You could have him out on his ear; stay married to him, for what that is worth. From what I've seen of life, his passion would soon cool then.' They laughed at that.

'The very idea, Kate, you shouldn't speak like that, don't you know I'm coming to an age where drink and my bladder aren't going to hold me together for too long.' She wiped her face with the back of her hand, dispelling the image of Duncan, homeless and jobless and dependent on her. 'No, I wouldn't want that. I've been thinking about it and, really, I don't want anything more than the house. I have my pension and my little job here. If I can stay in my home, hold on to that, then I will be happy enough.'

'Maintenance?'

'Not if it meant I'd have to see him or speak to him. Honestly, I'd just like to take a giant eraser and blot him out of my life for good.' She gulped back the wine. The bathhouse was closed for the night. Colin would not be calling this evening. They had a slice of pizza each, plenty of time to decide what Rita wanted before they showed their hand.

'Sure? You're entitled and you're in a really good position to hold him over a barrel.' Kate could feel the old adrenalin fill her up, this was how she felt when she had started out, before Todd Riggs came into her life and she allowed him to suck the joy from just about everything, maybe especially her career. 'You don't want to make him suffer just a little?'

'No, I just want it over, quickly and easily, and I want to hold onto my home.' That was it for Rita, it was her home, her chintz-filled, wallpapered home, with china figurines and dog scratches on the doors. It did not mean much to Duncan. It was just a piece of property he could offload, its only value monetary, or maybe soon an advantage with which to hurt her. 'No, just my home.'

'Sometimes, Rita, for some women, drawing out the process, it gives them... closure? You know, you are finishing a huge chapter of your life. Once it's over, I have a feeling, this really will be over.' Kate had to say it. Rita was her friend, and no matter what she thought of Duncan now, she could be sorry later. Many women chose to hang on in their marriages and for some it was the right thing to do.

'Oh, Kate. My marriage was over a long time ago. I'm not sure that there was ever enough to keep us together, but with this affair... Maybe I couldn't prove it, but I think I always knew. Even then, it was as much a relief as anything else. The only thing that has changed is me. Before, teaching, as much as I loved it, I was stuck, but working here, with you, meeting people every day and maybe just having Barry, I suppose I don't feel like I "need" Duncan anymore.' Rita closed her eyes for a moment. 'That's not right either. It's more that I feel happy and fulfilled. I suppose, I am ready to start a new life, one of my choosing. Duncan is the only thing actually making me unhappy in life and it's not this affair. It goes much deeper than that. I don't love him, and worse, I don't like him, haven't for a long time, why would I want to go on living with him when I feel like that?'

'Right, we'll use your ownership of the business to *encourage* him not to drag his heels and I'm asking for a payment to buy you out.' Kate put up her hands to stop Rita from protesting. 'It's just a tactic to stop him from trying to make things awkward; don't worry, you won't get stuck with his dirty money.' They both laughed at this.

'I could always give it to the dog pound?' Rita's eyes danced. 'That'd really get up his nose.'

'You could do whatever you wanted with it, I'll ask for enough to build a new pound and then you decide.' She leant over and clinked her glass against Rita's; it was a good night's work for their friendship.

# 21

# Todd

'So, how did you end up in Ballytokeep?' Todd said, they were walking on the beach and even if he looked ahead and tried to make it sound like small talk, they both knew that ending up here was just too freaky not to warrant a conversation.

'Much less romantic than you might imagine.' She laughed, she seemed to hold no grudges. 'It turned out to be a funny thing. After all those nightmares, all the family I ever needed was right here all along.' He hadn't thought about the nightmares in years, how she would wake, crying inconsolably and he would wrap himself around her until she fell into a stuttering quivering sleep again. How could he have forgotten that?

'So you came home?' he said, squinting ahead.

'Yes and no.' She smiled. 'I didn't really know it was home, actually, I'd hardly heard of Ballytokeep much less visited here. It was at Lady Pamela's – grandma's funeral, I met Iris there and we just rather clicked. Grandma died four years ago. Of course, my mother refused to go. They're in San Francisco now.' Todd did not ask about Adaline, what was the point in pretending that there had ever been a connection? 'There was a service, in Dublin and I just planned to go to that. You know, I hardly knew them...' she shrugged. 'Things never did get any better between the two sides.'

'I'm sorry. I know I complain about my family, but at least we all grew up together, got the chance to decide we didn't like each other,' Todd smiled.

'It's turned out well, I think.' She screwed up her nose a little. 'If not what I expected.'

'Not what I expected either,' Todd said; he was glad that somehow they had ended up here together.

They walked on in silence. Beneath them, the sea rushed in for a full tide in the darkness, the porpoises opposite were enjoying the fruits of the swell.

'And you don't miss London?' He knew she didn't. He would have to be blind not to see how content she was here.

'God no. I enjoyed it for a while, you know, the job, the city. It was good for the brain, just...' She thought for a moment, 'I suppose I came to the point where I wanted something that was actually good for the soul.'

'And that wasn't London,' he finished for her. 'I felt the very same,' he said, realizing he just never put it that way.

'Ah yes, but you are not finished with London yet,' she said, smiling.

'Why do you say that?'

'Claudia, of course. You may love it here, Todd, but I can't see Claudia settling in for a winter of gale force winds and wellingtons.'

'No?' She was right, but he had bought the castle for

Claudia, hadn't he? It seemed strange to think of that now, funny almost. Claudia would never settle here. This place, it just seemed to throw up the differences between them even more than before his heart attack. 'Can I tell you something?'

'Oh, Todd, at this stage you could probably tell me anything and I won't be shocked. I've spent over a decade as a divorce lawyer, I've probably dealt with the lowest humanity has to offer.' She smiled now, realizing the implication. 'Of course, I wouldn't put you in that category.'

'Maybe you should.' He smiled back at her, feeling suddenly light. 'Claudia doesn't want the papers to know that when I had my heart attack there was someone else there. A woman I met at the gig the night before. I couldn't remember anything about meeting her, but I'm sure...' It was worse saying it here, to Kate. 'I probably have her to thank for the fact that I'm alive today. She called the medics, she saved my life.' He shook his head. It was the first time it had occurred to him, he had not even said thanks.

'You don't need to tell me this, Todd.' The lightness had abandoned her voice.

'I need to tell someone. I need to get it straight in my head. Since I came here, it all seems so far away, London, the band, Claudia, and I'm not sure that I ever want to go back to any of it.'

'You've had a lot of... stress, first the tour, then your heart attack, even moving here, Todd. And your heart attack, that changes things, it has to remind you of your own mortality.'

'I have a sense that this place is helping to clear my mind. It's helping me to set things straight.'

'God, you've gone very deep and meaningful.' Kate was laughing at him again.

'I've been such a shit, all my life, not just to you. Isn't it about time I got *deep and meaningful?*' He stopped now, held her eyes for a moment. 'It is between us though, yeah. Claudia would skin me if she thought I said anything. Her worst fear is the press getting hold of the fact that I had a fling while we were technically meant to be madly in love.' Todd sighed, but at least he felt lighter, perhaps the mists were clearing now.

'But you weren't,' Kate inclined her head, 'madly in love?'

'Oh, Kate, I was very stupid. Like before, I suppose I didn't know what I had. I was ready to throw it all away. If it wasn't for my heart attack... Well, like I said, it's given me reason to think and count my blessings.' Todd squinted at the dying sun, he'd said far too much. The truth was, he wasn't sure what he felt for Claudia any more, but what he'd done to her in Atlantic City was unforgivable and even he knew she deserved more than that.

## 22

## Iris, 1957

The summer season seemed to make the weeks rush by and Iris felt like she spent much of the time in a tailspin between the hotel and the organizing committee for the summer ball. Most days she made time to drop in to see Oisín Armstrong. He seemed to be getting stronger before her eyes, but she had a feeling this was just wishful thinking on her behalf.

'It's awful good of ye,' Mrs Armstrong said over and again each time she called. Sometimes Iris brought something small, like an apple cake or a pint of cream leftovers after the dinner rush. Often, she just came as she was and took the child out for a walk along the pier in his huge pram. On those walks, she dared to imagine she was walking along some anonymous *rue* in Paris and the child with her was the one who dominated her thoughts and dreams.

'Nonsense, we're enjoying organizing it, and it'll be good for everyone in Ballytokeep. The hotel is booked solid and all the shops will get the benefit too.'

'My husband says that he'll hardly have time to go out fishing for the week with all the visitors he has booked on the boat for trips out to sea.'

'There you go.'

Iris was thoroughly enjoying the organizing of the festival. Already, they had sold far more tickets than they had hoped for. She met up with Robert a couple of times, down at the bathhouse. They had little to discuss at this stage, everything was agreed and Robert had gotten a second run of tickets for the night of the ball printed free of charge by the local printing company. More often than not, he poured her a large glass of sherry or Drambuie and they sat by the dying fire talking about whatever came into their heads. Sometimes she forgot the huge attraction she felt towards him, but then he would catch her eye, or make her laugh, or rub his hand too close to her and she would feel that urge shiver through her like electrical current. She was swimming out of her depth, but she knew, she couldn't go back to shore, not even if she wanted to. Guilt about how she felt for Archie or Gemma just seemed to fly out the window when she was alone with Robert.

'Are you happy, Iris?' Archie asked her one evening as they strolled along the pier.

'Of course.' She looked towards him, but the sun obscured his eyes from her. 'I mean, I know every day is really busy, but I'm enjoying working in the hotel and I love Ballytokeep.'

'I can see that.'

'So, why did you ask?' She rounded on him, stepping before him so she could look into his eyes. 'Are you happy?'

'Yes,' he hesitated slightly and she thought her heart might break.

'But?' She moved in nearer to him. He was always so

restrained, but when they stood this close, she could hear his breath, soft but ragged. Her own heart began to thrum faster in her chest, matching his connection, desire between them strong when he let her close.

'No, there are no buts. This is where I know I am going to live the rest of my days. I know that, I have always known that. I can see you're happy here. I suppose what you have to ask yourself is if you are happy in the hotel? Or if perhaps you wouldn't be happier in the bathhouse?'

'How do you mean, that you think I should work in the bathhouse instead of in the hotel?' Iris felt the air leave her lungs as though they were punctured, it was the last thing she expected. Archie still loved her, she was sure of that – but he was so damn honourable – she wanted him for once to sweep her off her feet, cast away her doubts and take her so there was no room left for Robert or Willie. Or Mark? No, she would never forget Mark.

'No, of course not.' He looked out to sea, his eyes seeming to cast towards something so far off into the distance they were lost to her for a moment. 'I love you Iris. I've loved you from the first moment we met, but I sense...'

'I've told you how I feel about you Archie. If this is about Robert again, I've told you that all we are doing is organizing the...'

'It's not about the Summer Ball, Iris. It's about feelings that I believe go much deeper than that for you.' The words were low, hung heavy with emotion. They hurt Iris far more than she had any right to feel, because they had a great deal of truth buried in them.

'Archie, if you have something to ask me, you need to say it, because I'm becoming very tired of this conversation.' She turned on her heels. It was true. Sometimes, when she watched Robert and Gemma together she felt so ridiculously jealous. Then sanity would return and she reminded herself that Robert was bad news for her. Robert was the kind of man who could take her world and turn it upside down, empty her out and then discard her as if she meant nothing. He was cut of the same cloth as William Keynes.

'You know there is something I want to ask you, but I'm not sure that you're ready for it.' He placed his arms about her and then held her at arm's length. 'I adore you, Iris, and I want to marry you, but I'm not sure that you feel the same for me.'

'Oh, Archie,' she had not expected him to propose now. Maybe, after the summer, when things were quieter, the fact that he did, only served to sweep her more totally along on the happy rush of young, true love. She reached her arms around his neck, fell into his arms, that simmering attraction obvious when she leant her body against his. He was the man for her there was no doubt in her mind about that. In these moments, alone with Archie, she knew that what she felt for Robert meant nothing. It was just attraction, not love, not really – it would pass whereas, what she felt for Archie seemed to grow deeper each day.

'No, listen to me.' He held her at arm's length, his eyes drilling into her face so there was no fudging their intentions. 'Robert will always be a part of our lives. He will always be there. If you feel anything for him, if there was anything between you, well...'

'It wouldn't be right. I understand that, Archie, but I have told you, nothing has happened.' She wanted him to believe her so badly; she wanted him to hold her, pull her close against him and put his arms around her again. She craved his lips upon hers and she heard the urgency in her own voice. Far out, the gulls cried, a lonely sound that wailed like a chorus to her desperation.

'I'm sure nothing has happened and even if it had, I don't think that would worry me so much as what could happen in the future, if you felt...'

'But Archie,' she searched for the words, honest words and then she found them. 'I've never felt for him what I do for you. I don't think I ever could. Don't you see? I have met men like Robert before. Men that are full of charm, but it's empty. They have nothing to offer, only what they can take.' That was the truth as she knew it in her heart, and surely she could overcome what was only physical attraction, no matter how strong the current of it.

'Darling Iris.' He pulled her close, his arms strong around her. 'Oh, Iris, I love you so much, I'm sorry for doubting you.' His body shuddered and she could hear his heart thumping hard and fast in his chest. The sound thrilled her, reminding her that he wanted her and the real passion that smouldered between them, when he let it. Eventually he stood back from her, just a little, looked down into her eyes. 'I just want everything to be right. Oh, God, Iris, I'd love to take you now, but I want to do things properly.' She could see tears, just sitting inside the rims of his eyes. 'Marry me?'

'Oh, Archie. Yes. I'll marry you.' It was her fairy tale ending. In that moment, standing in his arms, she put aside thoughts of her position just a year earlier. Perhaps it would make up to her mother for all the trouble she caused and she so wanted to marry Archie. She did, she wanted to be Mrs Archie Hartley, to one day be the mistress of the hotel and know she had a husband who would look after them both until they grew into old age. 'I'm so happy; we could announce it at the summer ball?' Iris said as they made their way towards the pier. She felt, as though everything was settled; she would marry Archie, and Robert would marry Gemma, and Paris was a very long way away from all of them. It was the right thing to do, wasn't it?

\*

'So, my brother has finally popped the question,' Robert said the next night they met at the bathhouse. They were sitting, either side of a small dying fire, sipping dry sherry, having agreed the final plans for the Summer Ball.

'Oh, he told you?'

'No, as it happens. Archie has never shared the details of his love life with me, riveting though I'm sure they are.' He laughed, a little cruelly, and then looked at her. 'Mama told me, but I'm happy for you.'

'Really, are you?' She felt a little of her happiness deflate. Had she expected Robert to fight for her? Perhaps, all these weeks, she'd been kidding only herself. He had Gemma now, what she felt was only one-sided. His tone gave nothing away, but Iris couldn't help but feel that she'd somehow missed something.

'Surprised? Of course, I am happy for you. Never actually believed old Archie had it in him. I thought maybe you'd both settle into lonely spinsterhood there for a while, at least while my parents were alive, or as long as you might have passions worth having.'

'That's mean,' Iris said, but she sipped her drink, not moving to leave.

'I didn't intend it to be. You know, that in the beginning, before...'

'Before you met Gemma?'

'Gemma? Oh, yes, before I met Gemma, well I thought you and I would make a smashing couple – we would have been the talk of the county of course, for all the right reasons.'

'Oh, Robert – you're incorrigible.' She laughed at him for a moment, but his eyes seemed to harden so she wasn't sure if he was joking any more.

'But then I saw you don't want that, you just want a quiet invisible life and you'll have that with Archie.'

'Robert, I think you're being really cruel about Archie and maybe about me too.'

'But Iris, there is nothing wrong with that. With the right woman, maybe that is what I would want too. Just to close my front door each evening and ravish you.' His eyes were drinking her in and she filled with tingling nerves that felt like they might own her. 'Of course, not you, not now you're going to marry my brother, but you know, someone…' He was almost embarrassed. Iris suspected it was more difficult than a slip of the tongue to embarrass Robert Hartley. 'Perhaps I should propose to Gemma now?' he said absently. 'Make a double day out of it? What do you think?'

'Robert, I'm sure you care little for what anyone thinks, and less for what I think.' She smiled as she sipped her sherry, happy that they had moved away from the brittle subject of her relationship with Archie.

'You don't mean that,' Robert said now, bending across to top up her glass of sherry. 'I care very much what you think of me, I have from the beginning, you know that.'

'Yes, but you have Gemma now, so…' She finished off her drink rather too quickly.

'Yes, I have Gemma and she is perfect.' The words cut a little into Iris's happiness, but she ignored that. She had made her choice and she was happy with it, wasn't she?

'So, there'll be a big announcement at the Summer Ball?' he said as he filled a glass of brandy for them both. 'That's only a week away now; old Archie will have to get you a ring organized fairly fast.'

'Oh, I'm sure he'll see to that in his own good time,' Iris said. Then she thought about her lovely engagement ring; she had a feeling Archie had already set about it. She picked something out for him, well, pointed him in the general direction of what she hoped he would buy.

'I'm sure he will,' Robert said. 'Well, bottoms up.' He held up his glass and clinked it with hers.

She had never drunk brandy before. The liquid was hot and fiery in her mouth, she felt a wave of sweat wash over her and watched as he topped up her glass again, but it was as though she was outside herself looking on.

By the time she stood to leave, she felt dizzy. Perhaps she was tipsy? He smiled as he held her coat out for her. The gesture seemed too personal, but Iris told herself not to be so churlish. She gathered it around her, aware of him still close to her, that familiar achy craving brushing through her once more.

'I should walk you back to the hotel?' he said.

'No, I'm fine.' She said and he didn't offer again. He was not as enthusiastic as usual and Iris wondered if, in the announcement of her engagement, she had lost some of her attractiveness. She shrugged it off; *see it as a blessing*, she told herself as she set off on the dark and lonely road back to the hotel that night. This was probably the last night she'd spend in Robert's company. After the summer ball, there would be no reason to carry on dropping down here. Everything would change once Archie announced their engagement. The thought suddenly filled her with something she could not place. It was an emotion that sat somewhere between fear and loneliness, perhaps it was the drinks, and now the fresh air seemed to magnify her panic.

She doubled back, quickly, before she changed her mind. She knocked loudly at the door of the little tearooms just as Robert was switching off the last of the lights. The hammering on the heavy door brought him running quickly. When he opened it, she was not sure who kissed who first, but she knew that she clung onto him as though her life depended on it. They kissed passionately before he pulled her inside, banging the door behind her. He carried her upstairs, his heavy breathing laboured with longing that felt like it might consume them both if it was not answered. When they made love, it was long and searching, urgent, painful and glorious. She had never experienced anything like it. She cried as she lay in his arms afterwards, but not for Archie, and that shamed her. She cried, because this would be all she would have with Robert and she feared that anything else would be second best by comparison.

# Present

Iris knew why Kate was so interested in the Hartley family history. It was not, as Archie suspected because of her love of the bathhouse. Although she did not correct him when he shared the opinion one evening as they sat outside the hotel, looking towards the dying sun. Rather, Kate wanted to know as much as she could about the family she was part of – if only through Iris's marriage.

It was good that she was spending time with Colin Lyons; Iris hoped that they'd make a go of things. Most nights, it seemed to Iris, Colin dropped in to visit Kate. Colin was quiet and loyal, nothing like Todd Riggs. Iris didn't want to like Todd, not once she knew what he had done to Kate, but she didn't get to choose whether she would like him or not. In the end, it had come down to Archie. 'He's a good bloke,' Archie said after Todd had found him wandering on the beach. 'Doesn't talk any nonsense, not like a lot of them round here, trying to pretend that everything is alright even when it's clearly not.' After that, Archie wouldn't hear a word against Todd and when he started to drop into Archie in his workshop, Iris began to see what he meant. He did indeed seem to be a 'good bloke.' All the same, Iris knew, Kate would be better off with Colin. They could make a match yet, they were young enough to have a family of their own – Iris would love to see that happen, more than anything for Kate.

'I never knew them, none of them really.'

'What about Pamela?' Iris asked. Oh, how she'd envied Pamela, first her child and then her grandchild. 'I always imagined that she'd want to take you away and never let you back to Adaline.' Iris had not met Adaline, but anyone who would abandon a child in a boarding school had to be very cold.

'No. I think because my father and grandmother were estranged, before he married, that was never on the cards. Maybe there was some attempt at reconciliation around the time I was born, but no, I'm not sure there was ever much of a bond there at all.' Kate smiled; it was all water under the bridge now. 'My mother says my dad – Crispin – was easy to fall in love with, but hard to live with.' She shook her head. 'In many ways they were well met, he was a gambler and she was a drinker. Jeremy has been the saving of her, I think; even if he hasn't made her happy, he's made her comfortable. I might not particularly have bonded with him, but he was good for her and, at this stage, I'm glad she has him.'

'It's a shame though.' Iris felt the familiar wave of regret that she'd let time and grief part her from her sister. It seemed the wise thing to do all those years ago. The thoughts of seeing Crispin every time they met, comparing him in her mind's eye to the child she lost, some things just didn't get any easier as she got older.

'It's really all a long time ago.'

'I'd have given anything to have you here, even if it was just for holidays.' It was the truth. The family she'd never had, for no good reason apart from karma, had made her life with Archie emptier. They told each other the void was down to the sadness of losing Robert, but they both knew a child would have made things better for them.

'And knowing that now means more to me than you will ever imagine.' Kate squeezed her hand affectionately. 'Anyway, that's enough about the recent past. Tell me more about what it was like growing up in St. Kiernan's.' Kate sat back, and even if she was only being polite, it was nice to think back to those times, before everything changed.

'You two girls still chatting?' Archie asked cheerfully as he came in for the evening. He loved to see Kate popping into the hotel. It would be hers one day, when they were gone. It was only right, after all, she was the closest now they had to a daughter – to any family really. Kate was the blessing they had waited for, even if they never realized it until she came. They had seen to it in the will; although she did not know it yet. Even now, although he could be forgetful, Archie was great for making sure that everything was just as it should be. They agreed they would not tell her yet. 'Better she's here because she wants to be, rather than because she feels she should be.' That's what Archie said, and of course, he was right. 'There you go.' He held out an envelope for Iris now. It was old, worn, and looked as though it might have spent weeks in his pocket. 'Came for you this morning, went clear out of my head. Now there was another letter...' and he ambled off towards the kitchen.

'How is he?' Kate asked softly as Iris looked at the post in her hand. It was an old electricity bill, out of date now, long paid.

'God alone knows where he found this?' Iris said, better to make light of her worries, perhaps it would stave off the worst for another while.

'Is everything okay?'

'Of course. He's taking the medication, he's fine.' Although she knew he could spend the next two days searching for a letter he thought he'd lost, which more than likely never existed to start with. 'He's fine. I just like to keep an eye on him, you know, so he doesn't do too much. He's always been so busy; I don't want him to wear himself out.' It was true. She saw his father. In the end, there was neither day nor night, rest or sleep, his whole world turned into a jumble. She did not want that for Archie. Feared the same end for him and she was not ready to let him go.

# Robert, 1957

Archie would marry her. Robert knew that, he knew it all along. Archie would marry her, but Robert would continue to love her. It had taken weeks, months – it had taken all his reserves not to bound in there and take her for himself and, of course, he could have. He could have produced an engagement ring that was twice the size of anything Archie could afford. He could have swept her off her feet. Of course, Mama would be furious. She wanted him to marry Gemma; she was everything Mama wanted for him. He would probably marry her, or one of her gang, eventually. But he did not love Gemma; and he was quite sure he wouldn't love any of her friends either. Oh, they were glamorous and smart and some of them were even quite witty, but there was no spark. He couldn't have Iris and so, he wanted her even more. He wanted her so much that it consumed almost his every thought. When they sat in the tearooms it felt like they could sit there forever and he would be content. It would pass, he told himself.

That night, the night she came to him, there were no words. Neither of them said a word, even when it was over, he wasn't sure if he could speak. He held her in his arms, both of them shaking, spent, they cried – in part, for what had gone before – he'd never experienced anything like it. He knew, even then, that he would never feel the same again. It changed some fundamental part of him and there would be no fixing it.

In the days that followed, Robert felt an impending sense of doom was devouring him slowly and systematically. He couldn't shake off the feeling any more than the tide could pause or the reefers still and suspend what lay ahead.

## 23

## Kate

Kate felt the night drawing in a little earlier, the winter chill rising from the sea on her doorstep, but she was looking forward to it. There would be no more sitting out on the rocks, watching the sun go down with Colin. Instead, this last week, he'd called down and they sat by the stove in the tearooms. They chatted while the moon peeped occasionally from behind thick clouds and danced silver rays upon the waves beyond the rock. She loved the idea of being here for the winter, with the gales blowing outside and only herself to please.

She had plans. The whole area at the back that she managed to ignore for the summer would be her winter focus. Sometimes, the ideas that skipped through her mind scared her. It would be a completely new business, one that would mean the bathhouse would be open all year round. She wasn't sure that was what she wanted, really, but, she had to give it a go. She needed to see what the potential was, maybe some of her ambition was returning. There were several double bathrooms. The copper baths now green with neglect, but not so bad you could not see how beautiful they could be.

The steam presses had come from a maker in Scotland. When she opened their doors, the fragrance of old wood, jasmine and eucalyptus still drifted before her.

A loud rap at the front door jerked her from her reverie and she made her way towards the tearooms quickly. 'Hang on,' she shouted at the insistent rapping.

''Bout time too.' Duncan Delaney pushed past her, bringing a cold sea breeze that swept icy into the room with him. 'You have some nerve, you know that...' He was speaking as though a conversation had started and he was in mid-flow.

'I'm presuming that you've heard from your solicitor, so.' Kate had dropped the divorce petition down to a pokey office hours earlier and knew without any doubt that the woman there was no match for her in terms of experience or talent in the divorce courts.

'Damn right I heard, and all I can say is you have a cheek. Coming over here, taking over this place,' he looked around the tearooms disdainfully. No doubt if he had got his hands on it he'd have flattened it and built a couple of apartments into the cliff face. 'Think you're something else, with your fancy accent and turning my wife's head. Well, I am not having it, you hear, I am not having it.'

'You have very little choice, Mr Delaney. I'm acting on your wife's behalf, carrying out her instructions.' She moved to his side, opened the front door of the bathhouse. She didn't want him here, there was nothing she had to say to him that she wouldn't say in a court of law.

'Rita doesn't know what she wants, that's the truth of it. Look at her with that blasted dog and this place. She thinks she's made up now she has a summer job and a pal with a fancy man in Rock Castle.' He spat the words and, in his eyes, Kate could see he had no respect for her, and even less for Rita.

'Mr Delaney, we will see about who knows what and fancy pieces when we go to court. You, with your girlfriend on the side and nothing in your name – you're in no position to talk about any of us. Rita could take the shirt off your back if she wanted, and let me tell you, that's exactly what I'll be encouraging her to do.' She held the door open wider for him, she was not afraid of him, she had lived life from a young age with no one to depend upon but herself and she knew she was more than a match for Duncan. 'Good night, Mr Delaney.'

'You don't know who you're dealing with. You ask people around here, I'm not just some old yokel who doesn't know blocks from bull. I'm a self-made man, and you'll be sorry you started this yet,' he said as he pushed past her. Kate could hear in his voice, he wasn't going to take any chances on losing anything more than he had to. She closed the door tight but softly behind him and knew that Rita had made the right decision. Duncan Delaney was no good and the sooner Rita had him out of her life the better for her.

*

'So, I see your friend is in the papers again,' Rita dropped a red top on the table in front of Kate. 'All I'll say is, leopards, spots, and I always had a bad feeling about him.'

'What's that?' Kate's stomach filled with the kind of dread that left no doubt; Rita was talking about Todd.

'Him up there, in his ivory bloomin' tower. I haven't read

it yet, mind, but sure we all know what it's going to be about, once a womanizer, always a womanizer.' She noisily opened the oven doors and carefully placed the baking trays she'd organized the night before. She had a 'system', or so she loudly reminded Kate regularly. It would not do for anyone to mess with her system, 'trays would not fit and then where would we be?'

Of course, in her own obtuse way, she was trying to be kind. To let Kate gather herself and read the article that dominated the front pages. Not that there was much reading, it was all headlines and dramatic black and white photographs. It didn't take long to the get the gist of things. The story that Todd had been concerned about had broken. Well, it was always going to happen, wasn't it? Kate had a feeling that Todd had been lucky for most of his career.

'I should call him, shouldn't I?'

'Why would you do that?' Rita banged closed the oven door. 'Why in God's name would you do that? You listen to me now, this is his mess. He has done enough damage to you already, broke your heart, well, once is enough. If you were my daughter, I wouldn't have let you outside the door with him. Walking along the beach indeed and Colin Lyons up there only gasping to bring you up to the Weaver's, any night of the week, I'll bet.'

'Oh, Rita. It's not like that at all.'

'No? Well, that's what it looks like from where I'm standing and I'll bet for most of Ballytokeep as well.' Rita plopped down into the seat opposite her. 'I can't see it myself, you know. He's shook looking, especially after that heart attack. What would you want with an auld crock like that when you have Colin, the finest catch in the county just across the fields?'

'You have it all wrong, Rita.' Kate started to laugh, couldn't help herself, even though she knew she shouldn't. After all, poor Claudia and Todd, a story like this could ruin their careers. 'I'm not interested in Todd Riggs. I haven't wanted him back, not since the day he left, well...' She knew that was not strictly true. 'Well, I certainly haven't wanted him since I left London, anyway.'

'Well, it is a bit odd, you buying this place, him buying the tower and then...'

'That's not in the papers?' She shuffled the tabloid, opened page four. 'Oh, no.' There they were, the same photos that had been dragged through the press years ago. Todd and Kate, caught in black and white coming from a club, late one night. In the dull image, she smiled, her bright eyes waiting for the future to roll out ahead of her, just as they had planned. He kept his head down, avoiding the glare of photographers, hiding his booze-filled eyes. Beneath the photograph, the caption, 'The girl he never forgot'. At the top of the page, a grainy image of them walking along the beach at Ballytokeep – she was serious, while he was gazing at her as he spoke. For a moment, it felt like the earth had turned in an unfamiliar direction. She stared at the image of Todd and herself, walking together; as though they were... she was not sure what, but together. It was too much. She felt that almost forgotten panic began to surge through her once more. She had felt it every day after he left her; it was too familiar not to place it. It was an emptiness that rose within her. It had no beginning and, for too long, she feared it had no end.

Todd and Kate, walking on the beach, together now, ten years after they had so publically split up. It suddenly hit her how ludicrous that was. Todd was her past. She never went looking for him. She had not tried to convince him or asked him to explain. She had simply gotten on with her empty life as well as she could. Until she came here, she had just gotten on with it. Maybe, before she came here, maybe walking along a beach with Todd Riggs might have seemed like the best possible outcome? But here, in her own tearooms, with the images before her, well the whole thing seemed preposterous.

Kate dropped the paper, felt her stomach flip sickeningly. She did not need to read the article to know instinctively where it was headed. 'Poor Claudia,' she said quietly. 'Poor Claudia.' She walked to the door of the bathhouse and looked across at the strand. It was windy; the tide was out, so the surfers were waiting in the comfort of camper vans, hidden from the breeze at this early hour.

They had gotten into the habit of walking the beach most evenings. That was all it took. The photograph conjured far more than what had passed between them.

# 24

## Iris, 1957

Iris knew she should tell Archie. Call the engagement off, it was only fair, after all. How could she marry him now? There were too many secrets to build a future on between them.

She walked hard into the wind, scarcely noticing that the sun was peeping up and over the town to the east. She let herself into the hotel, her heart hammering in her chest. Already the drapes were pulled back, fireplaces cleared for the day ahead. Archie had begun his day's work and she crept silently, guiltily, up the stairs, fearing that she might run into him.

In her small room, the light beat warm and dusty over the single bed. She took off her clothes, discarded them quickly and washed roughly in the cold water that stood on her nightstand. Then she sat on the side of her bed, she might have prayed but the nerve had left her. Instead, she waited for she did not know how long, lost in the ecstasy and guilt of the night spent with Robert. Tears streamed from her eyes, but deep in some part of her, a tension was rising, like she had never felt before and it frightened her. Robert Hartley had taken more than just her future with Archie from her last night. Now, this morning, with the harsh light streaming in on her tear-soaked face, Iris feared, she could not settle for that anymore. It would not be fair to any of them, especially not to Archie.

Archie – she still cared for him, the love she felt for him, though nothing like what was burning inside her for Robert, was true and genuine. She hated herself for the way she had treated him. She would have to leave here. She knew that. She couldn't stay, not feeling as she did for Robert. There was no future for them together. She had a sense that even if she could be so callous to Archie, Robert might not settle for her now. He would marry Gemma or someone like Gemma. He would marry someone who was well connected, sophisticated, and worldly. Iris was just a cook, a glorified pot scrubber, albeit trained in Paris. Although her sister was Lady Pamela, in every other way, her family were no different to any other working-class family. If she had grown up in Ballytokeep, Robert Hartley would not have looked at her twice.

Two light taps to her bedroom door brought Iris back to the present.

'Iris, are you awake?' Archie whispered close to the lock.

'Yes, I'm just coming.' She wiped her eyes and stood, straightening out her skirt and blouse and patting her hair before she opened the door.

'Are you all right?' Archie stood back from her a little, examining her reddened eyes. 'Have you been crying?'

'No, allergies, I've hardly slept, don't mind me.' She brushed past him. There would be plenty of time when the day was done for talking.

'Are you able for the breakfasts? I could manage, I really wouldn't mind.' He touched her arm and the connection almost made her jump.

'No, Archie, I'm fine.' She pulled away from him, could not take his kindness now. It really was too much after how she had treated him.

She set about getting the breakfasts ready without another word. If Mrs Hartley noticed anything amiss, she certainly did not make a comment. Instead, Iris worked silently, her mind a maelstrom of sensations and images of the previous night and guilt for the way she had behaved. As she carried out each task, a small voice whispered deep inside her that she would have to leave this place. She would have to leave Archie, Ballytokeep, and the life she thought stretched before her until she had made love to Robert Hartley.

It was the afternoon before he arrived.

'Go away,' she said and she made for the stairs, but he grabbed her arm so hard she knew that struggling was futile and would only leave a bruise. 'I don't want to talk to you, Robert. It was a mistake.' She looked about, thankfully, the reception was empty, the day was a scorcher and everyone had taken off to the beach as soon as breakfast was over.

'We both know that's not true.' He pulled her before him. 'Now, come on, either we talk here or we walk along the pier like everyone else today.'

'I'll get a hat.'

Iris ran upstairs to her room, grabbed a sun hat she kept on the back of the door and stopped for only a moment to pat her hair in place. Her face flushed indecently pink, inside she could feel a swell of butterflies rise within her, but she knew that it was wrong. She could not entertain Robert

Hartley, could not make things any worse than they already were.

He was leaning against the wall, smoking when she came out of the hotel. His languid pose almost fooled her into thinking that it was right that they go walking together. That in fact he felt for her what she felt for him. She stood beside him for a moment, looking out to the crashing waves far across the glassy blue sea. She loved this place, how could she leave it? She loved everything about it and it killed her to think it had come to this.

'It wasn't a mistake; you know that, don't you?' He said casually as they began to walk towards the pier. 'I mean, it wasn't a mistake for me at least and I'll bet it wasn't for you either. There was no mistaking that you ran into the arms of the wrong brother, or that...' He smiled at her, a crooked, sun-squinted smile that made her heart tumble in her chest.

'Well it wasn't right, either.' She looked at him now in spite of herself. She knew that if they were alone she would fall into his arms all over again. Perhaps if they were alone he would want that too. 'I have to leave here, Robert. I can't stay, not after this.'

'You can't leave.' He stopped short, spun towards her. 'You cannot leave me, not when we have just...'

'I'm not leaving you, I'm leaving Archie. After all, Robert, I'm engaged to Archie.'

'Nothing has been announced, you don't have to go through with it.'

'I made a promise. I can't keep it after last night, and I do care for him. I cannot humiliate him as well as break his heart. I've thought about it.' She had thought about hardly anything else.

'No, you haven't thought about it at all. Iris, you cannot

leave, not now. Break off your engagement with Archie but stay here. Surely, you can see that we... After last night...'

'I can't think, Robert, you have to stop.' It was true. The more he spoke, the more she couldn't decide what to do for the best. Of course, she knew the right thing to do was not to have slept with Archie's brother. When she looked across at Robert, she knew he was right; perhaps they did not have a choice. They were meant to be together, for better or worse. Surely, they were on a road to disaster. Even if she tried, she could not step onto the safety of the footpath and back to the life she had with Archie.

'Come to the bathhouse tonight, come and we will talk about things then.' He was begging her. 'Please, I promise, we won't do anything...' But they both knew that this wasn't true, the words meant nothing, they could no more keep away from each other now than the waves in the ocean beneath them could stop turning.

# Present

Iris spotted Archie heading purposefully, if slowly, out the front reception of the hotel with a large basket of turf. 'Where are you off to?' she enquired, but she knew when he turned to look at her he was lost for an answer. He left the basket at her feet, shook his head sadly.

'I was bringing this down to Robert, but that can't be right, can it?' he asked and the uncertainty in his voice made him seem very old and very young all at once. 'I thought he called earlier, looking for fuel for that old stove he keeps lit all the time, but...' Archie scratched his head, the words already fading into the room around them.

'Come on; let's set them up in here.' She patted his arm. By the time, they reached the drawing room he would forget all about going to the bathhouse.

The doctor had called in earlier that day. Dr Wall, she introduced herself as, whilst she peered into Archie's eyes, seemed to be looking into his soul, she was replacing Dr Jones. She prescribed more medication, 'for the Alzheimer's'.

She said the word like it was mumps. He would have to have more tests. Iris looked at the doctor. She was far too young to know what these things meant. If giving tablets out to halt the symptoms made her feel better, then she was naïve as well as fresh.

It was getting worse; maybe Archie knew that too, sometimes. It happened all the time now, Archie confusing himself, confusing her.

The first time Archie told her he had been walking with Robert along the back strand she nearly fell over. The words had tripped out as though he was talking about the weather. He knew immediately, maybe not exactly, but he knew that he had said something wrong.

It was why she could not show him the watch. It was why she didn't want him to see things that brought those times back. She didn't want him remembering things she hoped he had forgotten. All the same, she savoured the snatches of Robert that Kate brought to her, even if it was just a photograph or holding that watch. He wore it all the time that summer sixty years ago. Wore it when he worked and when he slept. She looked for it when they found his body, but he had not worn it then. After that, somehow she forgot about it until Kate brought it to her. It was right that Kate should have it. Kate had done so much to keep the bathhouse as it was, to keep his memory just as he would have liked it kept.

'I know it's silly, isn't it?' Kate said. They were sitting at the long kitchen table; two cups of half-drank tea before them. 'Sometimes, I wonder if it's morbid fascination – but then I suppose it's natural to be curious about Robert, he seemed to be a real playboy.'

'Oh, no, I can see how anyone could be enthralled with

Robert,' Iris said and then she stopped herself. 'Just be careful that you don't let life pass you by while you have your head stuck in his ledgers.'

'Oh, Iris, I'm just sorting through them; a bit like you and Archie, it's hard to let them go,' Kate said and then she explained. 'Anyway, they're probably better for me to read at the moment than most of the newspapers these last few days.' Todd Riggs had left Ballytokeep the morning the articles appeared in the paper. A noisy chopper had landed in the town square and he sauntered past the hotel as Iris was clearing away the dining room.

'Listen, there's more fish in the sea than Todd Riggs. You deserve someone better than any of them but time's not on your side, my dear.' She would love to see Kate settled with a family of her own.

'Oh, Iris, I have plenty of time, don't you worry.'

# Robert, 1957

Robert waited in the darkness for her to arrive. He stood in the window, the only light behind him the occasional trouncing blue flame of the turf fire he lit more for effect than for heat. In the distance, the occasional glint of Rossmoor lighthouse caught his eye. Iris was making her way down the small track, he could just about make out her silhouette in the light of the full silver moon over head. He had fallen for her, fallen for her more than he ever thought possible. If he were a man to care about the feelings of others, he would admit that the whole thing was a mess, instead, he convinced himself the passion between them would soon wear out. It was almost a week now. Each day she would tell him that she was leaving and yet, in the dark of night, he would wait until he heard the light tap on the bathhouse door. He sipped the dregs of his brandy glass. He would pour a drink for her when she arrived, make her forget all about Archie. He thought Archie was such a fool, always doing the right thing – he should be seizing life as Robert did, before it was too late and he was married off for better or for worse. Probably still a virgin, if he was a betting man, he knew he'd be safe putting the bathhouse on that. Robert was far too calculating for gambling.

A liberal tap on the heavy door beneath him pulled Robert from his thoughts. He opened it quickly, and for a moment his eyes were drawn back up the track where he saw a flash of something move. In that moment, he knew that someone had followed Iris along the path. The question was who? Gemma or Archie?

# 25

## Todd

He had been summoned – it was the only word – by Claudia and her publicist. When he arrived at her apartment, there was an army of people there. He could not blame her. It was everything she didn't want.

'What were you bloody thinking?' She fired the words at him as he walked through the door. 'What in the name of Prada were you doing with... *her*? God, you're all but spoon-feeding her strawberries and cream.' She was raging.

'Nothing happened.' He couldn't meet her eyes, to do so would only incur more anger from her. 'You know what the bloody papers are like, Claudia.'

'Of course it didn't.' Her words were loaded with the venom that comes from being sold out. 'It's just a coincidence, you buying that tower on her doorstep. Be honest at least, Todd. You planned this right from the word go.' She sighed; it was a sound too heavy for her delicate features. 'I'm not stupid, you should know that. We were done when you headed off on tour. I knew that. I knew about the tart in the room, I knew all that. And to be honest with you, Todd, I was good with it, because, if you hadn't had your heart attack, I was ready to move on too.' She shook her lovely silver-blonde hair. 'But that changed everything. I didn't expect you to marry me, but to at least show some respect, for the press, for my reputation.' The unsaid words were that she was the attractive one. She was the hip one, and if anyone should have been moving on first, it was she.

'The thing is, Claudia, you could come out of this very well.' He took a step towards her, then stopped, knew better. He'd been the wrong side of her temper before and for all her angelic looks he'd dodged one flying frying pan too many to get too close. 'Everyone knows I'm a shit. Everyone knows what I am like. I'm unreliable, jack the lad. You could come out of this like Mother Teresa, but obviously with better clothes.' He tried smiling, but she never got his jokes.

'You don't see it, do you? Todd, I don't want their pity and with this that's what I am going to get. I will be like Kate. A girl that's always pictured alongside you; yesterday's news. The one you walked out on. Well, I am nothing like her. I'm successful and younger and, for fuck's sake, women want to be me.'

'Well then, let's front it out. Let's tell them we are still together, that this was all just a mix-up. I can say I've been friends with Kate all these years, it's just platonic.' Todd had a feeling that Kate would not welcome this intrusion into her life now. He wasn't brave enough to say so to Claudia.

'Oh, yes, Kate. And tell me, Todd, who do you think leaked all of this to the press?'

'You think Kate would do this?' He shook his head and smiled, that was just madness. Kate had no interest in headlines. It was the last thing she would want. Wasn't it?

Todd dropped onto the oversized chaise long. An obscene purple lounger that would not look out of place in either a Barbie house or a brothel. Why would Kate tell the papers about him and Claudia?

'The penny beginning to drop now, is it?' Claudia sneered.

'No.' But his voice was uncertain. Kate was the only person he told about the girl in the hotel room. She was the only person he had talked to in the last few weeks. Even the fact that they got those pictures, he cringed when Claudia thrust them at him.

'Like a love-struck fucking teenager, that is what you are, Todd. A stupid kid who just got old but never grew up.' She was right; it was there, before him in black and white, from that pristine position so rarely afforded in life. Todd sat, shell-shocked, and looked at the photograph of himself and Kate walking the beach and, in those moments, he saw himself as a stranger, a man entranced and captivated by the woman at his side. This is what the world saw, and more importantly that was what Claudia believed.

'Well, what have you to say for yourself?' She was screaming at him, hysterical with rage and he could not blame her. He had been a complete fool and he had treated her almost as badly as he had treated Kate all those years ago.

'I'm sorry, Claudia, that's all I can say. I'm sorry for everything.' Then he got up from the chair that was too soft and walked quietly from her apartment and her world.

*

'Come over to ours,' Denny said. His voice was warm and familiar and since Todd had just wandered about London aimlessly for almost four hours he figured he should go somewhere. *Funny*, he thought, sitting in a black cab, *this city has never been home*. It was why he stayed in the Embassy Rooms. He never considered buying a place of his own. For all the years he'd been here, he'd stayed in a hotel, where the bar was his local and his friends were no more than passing through. Ballytokeep was different. He knew it was becoming his home. He longed to be there now. He longed to be home and he knew as he walked through Denny's familiar front door, that this was no longer the place he'd come to feel he belonged. It was someone else's home with unfamiliar smells of meals eaten earlier still lingering on the air, reminding him that life went on here with or without him.

'That's it then, it's all over with Claudia?' Denny led him into the faded kitchen that was packed with the vestiges of a busy family life.

'Yeah, I suppose it is.' Todd shook his head, hard to believe it in some ways.

'Ah, well, good while it lasted, and all that,' Denny was a man's man, he didn't 'do' cosy emotional sharing easily.

'Ah, Denny, can't you see, he's really hurting.' Meg reversed out of the larder, her arms laden with vegetables for their dinner. 'Don't you mind him, love, he hasn't the faintest.'

'No, Meg, it's all right, seriously, you know how things were, a couple of months ago I was ready to cut all ties. Just the last while, I've been a bit...' he thought for a moment, 'not myself.'

'As long as you can still sing and stand on a stage, you're going to be fine, mate.' Denny laughed.

'I'm fine already, Denny.' And he was, strangely, he felt lighter walking away from Claudia, he felt no guilt. Not this time. He'd have given it a go, maybe, not for the right reasons, but he'd have given their relationship a shot, if Claudia had been up for that. God, now he thought about it, he was relieved it was over.

'So, you're back in London?' Meg said as she handed him a mug of dark sweet tea as only Meg could make.

'Course he is, sure we always knew he was just going to relax for a bit,' Denny said and Todd found the cockiness in his voice annoyed him. 'No one really lives in them old castles; you'd go mad out there looking at the ocean every day.'

'Do you think?' Todd smiled at his old friend, knew that Denny could not survive a week without the sound of London's bells in his ears. 'I've really settled in, Denny, I thought you could see that when you came over.' He had seen it, and Todd knew it had surprised him. No one figured Todd for the settling type.

'So, you're going back, then are you?' Meg said. 'Is it that tower or is it Kate that's bringing you back?'

A crazy thought played about in his head all afternoon. If Kate had fed that article to the papers; did he really deserve anything better? The other thing that struck him was, even if he did not have the bathhouse to visit, he needed to be in Ballytokeep.

'Don't be daft, woman, what would he be going back to Kate for?'

'You saw them pictures just as well as the rest of the country did, Denny, don't be pretending that it isn't as obvious as the nose on your face exactly what we both thought when we saw them.'

'And what was that, exactly, Meg?' Todd smiled at her. She'd been too good to him over the years for them not to be honest with each other.

'Well you know, that you and she are back together?'

'No. I tore up the copybook there and I'm afraid there's no putting it back together again.'

'That's a shame,' Meg said sadly, she had been fond of Kate.

'Well, Claudia reckons that she probably tipped off the papers, so I'd say she's just getting her long overdue payback.' Todd was trying to convince himself of this at least.

'Much as I hate to say it, Todd, that's not really Kate's style.'

'No.' Todd shook his head sadly. He should be getting home. The only problem was that meant getting a plane organized and night was falling fast. The sensible thing would be to wait until tomorrow.

'Stay here, Todd.' Meg got up, turned on the small table light behind her. 'Stay here and things will look better tomorrow, they always do.'

'No, Meg, they'll look exactly the same as they do today. You forget, I'm not going to waken any more sober tomorrow than I did today.' He smiled at her. Meg was making her home-made cottage pie and he had to admit, he had missed that. 'Course, I'll stay, so long as you make Denny promise not to talk about the band.'

'We have to talk about it sometime. There are a lot of fans out there who've bought tickets and there's no sign of any concert coming their way.'

'Can't we give them their money back?' Todd had to face this sometime. He had left it long enough. There would never be a good time to talk about it.

'Not that easy, mate, we're only taking a small slice of the pie. There are venues to be paid, roadies, stage people, you name it, and they've all lost a lot of money thanks to your dodgy ticker.'

'And the rest of the band?' He hadn't talked to any of them, but then it was a two-way street.

'You know what they want. They want to do the dates, collect the cheque and then go home to their country piles and pretend to be gentleman farmers or whatever it is they do when they're off duty.'

'Insurance?' It was worth a try.

'I talked to them, Todd, but they're not exactly emptying the cash bags in front of us. They will cover some of the outlay, only cos they have to, but...'

'Thousands?'

'And then some, mate, and then some.'

'Well, at least we know where we are. I can't think about it yet, Denny. All I'm fit for now is dinner and sleep.'

'Fine.' Denny's voice was short and Todd knew that he was not sure any more how far he could push him. The truth was, he'd spent as many nights in Denny's spare room as he had at the Embassy Rooms. He'd been drunk most days, sliding chaotically through a life that held reason only for short periods, marked mostly by photographers snapping him and cups of tea with Meg and Denny. 'I'll hold them off for another while.'

'Ta, Denny, I appreciate it, mate.' Denny didn't meet his eyes. They both knew if the band went on the road again, they could sell every venue three times over. Todd's heart attack had prompted an outpouring of nostalgia and affection for the band. Todd could think of nothing worse than standing in front of a packed stadium, without so much as a fag for consolation. He had not been sober on stage in well over a decade, not that he would admit that to anyone else now.

# 26

## Kate

It was very confusing, Kate thought as she looked out into the frothing Atlantic waves. She woke earlier than usual, the odd sound of the wash against the wall beneath the bathhouse licking salt into the whitewash.

'Multiple swells,' Archie said when she saw him down on the rock beneath her window. 'Happens occasionally, don't worry, it won't come near your door.' Poor Archie, he looked sad all the time now.

'Fancy a cuppa with me, Archie?' she asked him and padded quickly downstairs to let him in. 'You have a key, you know, I wouldn't mind if you let yourself in, you could help yourself.'

'Funny, but this place…' He looked around and somehow, Kate realized, he would never be comfortable here without her. Perhaps the past held too much sadness; Archie liked the bathhouse in the here and now. 'I'm glad you're here, but you don't want an old codger like me giving you a heart attack in the morning.'

'Archie, you're my favourite old codger around,' she said, warming up a breakfast teapot and dropping in some loose leaves. She liked having Archie here, he felt a little like the grandfather she had missed out on. There were a couple of yesterday's malted scones on a tray, so she popped them in the microwave and brought them to the table with a slab of the home-made butter she bought each week at the local country market.

'You know he's up to his tricks again,' he said quietly after they had sat for a while eating the warm buttered scones and talking about the high tide. 'He can't be trusted, even now, you know that.' Archie's expression darkened.

'Oh, Archie, it makes no difference to me anyway,' she said and she thought she noticed the tower glint colder than usual at her in the sharp morning spray. Todd had hardly spoken to her since he returned to the tower a couple of days earlier. She spotted him, walking on the road behind the bathhouse, where before he would pass her door, usually around closing time so they could stroll along the beach together. The last few days, he moved quickly, his head lowered. He did not want to talk to anyone. So she backed away from the window, preferring not to be seen at all. It struck, oddly, that she missed their walks. She missed the banter that passed between them; uplifting and funny, as though the intervening years had been a glitch. A technical blip corrected now. She wondered, more than once if she was honest, if things between them physically would be the same. There was no doubt that there was still a connection between them on some level. Still, she'd learned an expensive lesson all those years ago and her heart would not be so easily broken again. She was determined that Todd Riggs would not get that opportunity.

'I'm saying, he'll break your heart again, dear.' Archie broke into her thoughts and when she looked at him, she recognized that faraway look in his eyes. 'All I'm saying is, you have your whole life to live and I think you could do better for yourself with someone who's a little more...' a small knot pulled in his long lined jaw, 'loyal.'

'Oh, Archie, you are so sweet.' She reached out and covered his rough hand with hers. She loved Archie's hands, they were big and manly and, it seemed to Kate, they carried as many tales as the depths of his eyes or the lines carved into his forehead.

'You don't believe me,' his eyes were sad, lost between two worlds; one he tried to keep a grip on, the other pulling him back to a time long ago. 'You don't believe me, but I've seen him. I've seen him walk along the road to this place in the evenings, and you think that he has only eyes for you, but...'

'Go on, Archie.' She was indulging him. Todd never had eyes just for her; she had convinced herself of that many years ago. Hadn't she only recently learned, he did not have eyes just for Claudia Dey either? If Claudia could not keep him from straying, well, Kate reckoned she had no chance.

'I've seen him, he brings them here at night-time,' he smiled a sad quiver of his lined mouth. 'Different women, all the time.' He shook his head sadly, 'None of them like you. Not one of them is a patch on you.' He set his knife down on the table, ignored the tea left in his cup. 'Maybe I shouldn't have said anything, but I know you've had your suffering in the past, before you came here, and I just... well, you know how I, how we feel about you,' a small tear was making its way down his cheek. 'Must be off, letters to pick up, you know.' He stood at the door a moment, pulling his jacket closer to his neck, looked back again sadly. Then his expression changed to one of confusion, as though the last few moments that had passed between them had somehow been sucked into the ocean outside. 'Don't be worrying about that swell, now Kate, it'll not come near your door.'

Kate sat for a long time after he was gone, thinking in the silence of the tearooms. It was not even seven o'clock. The visitors in the hotel would not be thinking of breakfast, the surfers would have to leave the waves for a few hours yet. Archie had unsettled her, with his talk of love and loyalty and whatever carry-on she had been blissfully unaware of.

*

'He says he's not having it, not any of it.' Rita was ashen, her eyes rimmed red and sunken deep in sockets that had aged overnight. 'Can he do that, really, can he? I can't be in the house with him for the next forty years; I just can't, not like this, Kate. It's awful.'

'Not at all, of course it's not up to him if you want to finish things.' Kate knew Duncan Delaney was a piece of work; she'd known it that night that he'd shoved his way into the bathhouse. 'He's just a bully, trying to push you around and he has to learn that it's not going to work.' It was nine o'clock in the morning. The beach was empty, bar a couple that were making their way from the Armada point, perhaps considering a cup of coffee and croissants for breakfast. 'Bugger that,' Kate said and grabbed her jacket. She pulled Rita with her and put the closed sign on the front door. The couple would have to get their morning coffee elsewhere today.

'Where are we going?' Rita said, dazed at the speed she

was being propelled along the narrow path towards the centre of Ballytokeep.

'We're going to show Duncan Delaney that he's not able to buff you about the place anymore.'

Kate's strides were long and determined. They reached Rita's house rapidly and she made her way to the kitchen. There, she found a roll of black refuse sacks and started ripping bags off one at a time.

'What are you doing?' Rita's voice was high-pitched with excitement.

'We are helping Duncan to pack, like any good wife does. I am surprised actually that you have not already helped him.' Kate shook her head in mock seriousness, 'Now where would he like to stay? Hotels are always good, but let's not inflict him on Iris and Archie, okay?' She handed the phone to Rita, 'Well, book him in somewhere; you don't want him actually homeless, do you?'

'No, I suppose I don't.' Rita put through a call to a hotel in the next town. It was near enough for work, but far enough away so she did not have to run into him every day. Between them, it took less than two hours to commit Duncan's life in the little house they shared to a half dozen refuse bags and load them into a taxi destined for the luxury hotel suite that Rita booked on Duncan's personal credit card.

'We haven't packed up everything, you know that.' They both eyed the underwear drawer full of Duncan's finest.

'No, we haven't, have we.' Rita laughed. She would love to be a fly on the wall as he searched through each bag to find clean boxers the following morning. 'I wonder, will he ring the cab company to see if they have them,' she said as she emptied the drawer into the kitchen bin and purposefully tied the top before dumping it in the rubbish outside.

'Well, that takes care of that, you have your home to yourself now,' Kate said, 'remind me not to cross you anytime soon.'

'You're quite safe, and thank you for helping me. I really didn't know what to do. But here we are, Duncan's gone and we're only giving him a taste of the misery he's dumped on me these last three decades.'

'And they say true love is forever.' Kate shook her head. As a divorce lawyer, she had seen much higher prices of revenge than a drawer full of underwear, but never with such satisfaction.

*

Iris told Kate not to mind him. Nevertheless, she looked uneasy. 'He's not always operating in the same decade as the rest of us first thing in the morning, dear,' she said and Kate could see the deep loneliness return to Iris's eyes. She was losing him, just a little every day, and Kate couldn't imagine what that must feel like for two people so devoted to each other. 'Sometimes, I feel as if it's not Archie anymore. I mean, he looks like my Archie and he speaks like him, but he doesn't have the same substance to him and I think when he looks at me he thinks the same. He can't remember me sometimes. Then I feel I'm losing him before my very eyes,' she told Kate as they sat in the warm dark kitchen of the hotel. Somewhere, children ran through corridors, excited and squawking in their unfamiliar surroundings and the sound reminded Kate of the holidays she never had as a child. 'Robert was lucky in that way, I suppose,' Iris said under her breath.

'How's that?' Kate asked.

'Well, he'll always be young and vibrant, won't he? Like your rock star, Todd Riggs? He'll always be what he was back then to you and maybe you'll be that to him too, who knows?'

'Oh, I don't know about that, I can see Todd's wrinkles and those flaws he had back then, I have a feeling that they've only deepened.' Kate realized the thought was slightly depressing. Perhaps she wanted him to be a better man after all this time. Oddly, his revelation that he'd been unfaithful to Claudia with a stranger had disappointed her. It was obviously true: some people don't change.

'Maybe,' Iris said and then she held Kate's eyes for a little too long, as though there was something she wanted to say, but she was undecided if she should.

'What is it, Iris?'

'Ah, don't mind me, I'm an old woman, what would I know?' She smiled sadly. 'Life passes by us very quickly, you only realize it when you're like Archie and me.'

'Oh?' Kate did not want to hear about Todd's antics again. She knew enough already and it unsettled her more than she cared to admit.

'I'm saying don't let something pass you by because you think you know the whole story. We're all the same, Kate, all trying to be the best people we can be and if we're not perfect, I think that as we get older we try to be better people. We're none of us what we were in our twenties.' She shook her head, that sad smile playing about her lips once more. 'Life has its way with all of us. It changes us whether we want it to or not. Could you ever have imagined Todd Riggs settling down in Ballytokeep in a draughty tower and never setting foot inside a pub from one end of the week to the next?'

'I suppose not,' Kate smiled, 'but then, I never imagined I'd settle for it either.'

'Exactly.' Although her voice was low and feeble, it held within it wisdom and truth far greater than any expert might ever manage.

# 27

## Iris, 1957

They were lying in his bed, high over the ocean waves below. At their heads, the open window blew in a gentle billowing gust that smelled faintly of bracken, but mostly fresh sea salt. Iris felt sure that she would remember this night forever, whatever the outcome of this time.

'So, this time tomorrow,' she began, hoping perhaps that he might say something to send the conversation where she so wished it could go.

'This time tomorrow,' he murmured and dragged long and contentedly on his cigarette. She loved the feel of his strong arms about her and now, in the moonlight, she watched the shadow of his outline above her, his hand angled elegantly when he held the glimmering cigarette to his lips. 'There'll be lots of dancing, that's for sure.'

'Will we make enough for Oisín? To send him to London, do you think?'

'I think we've already made enough, to be honest, what

with cake sales and collections, but we can't very well send them all back, so we may as well have our dance.'

'Have we?' Iris sat up in the bed, its familiar springing sound reminding her that she should move more gently or he would think she was a huge heifer of a woman. 'But it was over a thousand pounds, we couldn't have anywhere near that?'

'Gemma.' One word, it was meant to explain everything. 'Gemma and her country set friends. She's rounded up a fortune through personal donations.'

'That's...' She searched for the word. She didn't want to think about Gemma. She certainly did not want to talk about her. 'It's impressive,' she managed in the end.

'Yes, well, she's very well connected.' He mimicked Gemma's voice and they both laughed at that.

'Tomorrow night?'

'Yes.' He was getting bored; she could hear it in his voice.

'Archie and I? He's going to make that announcement, tell everyone that we're engaged.' She could feel the familiar cold sweat of denial and guilt draw through her. She loved Archie before this, but now what she felt for him had shrunk into something guilt-laden and pitiful. She still loved him, but it was nothing like what she felt for Robert. 'I can't...'

'Then tell him. For God's sake, it is simple, Iris: either you want to marry him or you don't. There are a million more men just like Archie out there for the picking.'

'So that's it? You don't care if I marry your brother. You have absolutely nothing to say about it.'

'What do you want me to say? At this stage, I'm sick of the whole thing.' He shook out another cigarette, examined it for a moment, set it to his lips. He was quiet for a few seconds and Iris thought the silence might eat her up. She wanted to scream, cry, thump something or at least stamp her foot crossly. She wanted to marry Robert, not Archie. It was as simple as that, but now she was not sure she could marry either of them. Robert turned towards her and placed the cigarette on the night table. 'Look, I know it's a mess, but seriously, we can still do this. We can still be together. Marry Archie, stay in Ballytokeep. You and I, we were meant to be here together, Iris, I have never met anyone like you.'

'And Gemma?'

'Gemma is different, it's not like this. She's not like you, she's...' He ran out of words, but he did not need to say anymore. He took Gemma to the local picture house, but he took Iris to his bed.

'She's the one you'll marry, whereas I'm just the one you'll sleep with?'

'Iris, we had fun, didn't we?' He was only saying what she knew all along, deep down. They were not meant for each other, no matter how she tried to reason it out.

'Oh, Robert.' She had been a fool. Once more, Iris knew, she had been a fool and to make things worse, she'd known it was wrong from the start. What was the matter with her? But she already knew the answer to that. This was not about Archie, nor about Robert – this was about Mark. She was trying to fill the void with something that would take over her body and soul. Robert and this mess distracted her from the longing that possessed her since she left Paris. There was nothing for it. This would be her lot, guilt and regret and longing for the rest of her days – it was as much as she deserved, she was convinced of that.

She gathered up her clothes and made her way out into the soft night. The road seemed brighter tonight than she'd ever seen it before. In the distance, a lighthouse seemed to call out his name. *Mark. Mark. Mark.*

When she arrived back at the hotel, Iris still had no idea what she would do about Archie. She pulled off her clothes as quickly as she could, hopped into the freshly made bed. When she turned the light off, she could have sworn she heard the thud of the front door. Later, as she tossed and turned for yet another sleepless night, she imagined footsteps in the hall, Archie's footsteps, and the soft hum of what sounded like someone crying. When she woke in the morning she forgot all of this, because that was the morning that everything changed.

# Present

'You know,' Archie said to her one morning over breakfast, 'it will be sixty years this Friday.' He shook his head sadly, as though it came as a surprise to him. 'Sixty years since the dance, and father's fall and of course Robert's...'

'I know. I had wondered if you'd remember it too.'

'How could I forget,' his voice had grown harsher in the last few days, as though there was something bubbling inside him trying hard to break free. 'He was my brother, after all is said and done.' He looked at her, and once more she wondered exactly what he knew about that night.

'We should do something, maybe visit the grave and bring some flowers, maybe some hydrangeas?' They were his favourite, odd for a man. Iris thought it was even odder still that they were the flower Kate had planted in large crates all around the bathhouse.

'There was a letter for you,' Archie said.

'When, Dear?' she said, mindful of bringing too many painful memories to the surface. They didn't need them now; it was all in the past, so long ago, wasn't it?

'I found it in the hall, on the desk. I put it somewhere, can't for the life of me think what I did with it.' He scratched the back of his hand, an old nervous habit, it had returned with the dementia.

'Who was it from Archie, can you remember?' Her voice was soft, but she had to be careful these days; sometimes, when she spoke like this it made him cross.

'I am not a fool, you know, never have been. No need to speak to me as though I'm stupid.' He topped his boiled egg and set about buttering his toast as though nothing had happened.

Iris watched him. She hated seeing him like this. She remembered old Mr Hartley; he went downhill very quickly in the end. Iris dreaded it could be the same for Archie. They said with his father that it was the shock of Robert dying so suddenly, so tragically. It started with Archie almost a year ago. She could remember it quite clearly. He was searching for a letter, and then it was a note. At first, it was from Robert and then someone he called Mary Ann, then he did not want the others to see it. She wondered sometimes if the sender changed. He told her on several occasions, he was certain she was meant to have it. A couple of months ago, he disappeared for several hours. He told her he had been in the bathhouse. It was good that Kate took the place over. Iris couldn't keep him safe when he was there. She worried that he would hit off down there some night when the sky was pitch and that would be the finish of him. She could not have borne that, just couldn't have endured it. Now, with Kate there, she could sleep easier at night. Surely, he would remember that Robert was not there, if he was constantly reminded that someone else was.

'I think it tells the truth, the truth of what went on.' Archie whispered conspiratorially across the table at her. 'Father said he would settle things, we shall have to wait until he comes back.' He was nodding agreeably and she wondered if he knew she was his wife, or if he even saw her there sometimes.

'Oh, Archie.' She reached across and wiped the butter from his chin.

'Don't worry, Mama, I hid the letter.' He looked a little anxiously at her, shaking his head sadly, 'If only I could remember where I left it.'

# Robert, 1957

He had done the right thing, Robert was quite sure of that. Quite sure. Yes, he was in love with Iris, but it would pass. After all, what was she at the end of the day? She wanted nothing more really than all the others. She wanted to tie him down and Robert wasn't sure he'd ever be ready for marriage. All the same, he had to admit, she did something to him.

He stood watching her make her way back to the hotel. Winning her had not been easy, but it had not been as difficult as he had expected. The prize was won now though, so what was he to do? Marry her? Did she really expect him to do that? In the beginning he really believed he was in love with her. It turned out she was like everything else in his life. Once he held her in his arms he began to want something else. Not yet, but he could feel that familiar twist inside him, like a bauble, she was gradually losing her sparkle for him. She was engaged to Archie. At the end of the day, he had to think of the bathhouse. The scandal would kill his parents, not to mention what it would do to the fine trade he was building up. No, he was not going to marry Iris. He was not going to marry Gemma either. He would bring her along to the dance the following evening, play the devoted consort. They could donate to that snotty child and be done with it. Either way, the whole thing was a great success. There was a throng of eager do-gooders just dying to organize the festival next year, so it was all good for Ballytokeep and all good for the bathhouse.

A loud banging sound on the door below shook him from his thoughts. He checked his watch, half past two in the morning, there must be something very wrong. Robert's first thought was an accident on the water, perhaps one of the fishing boats or kids playing about with little care to their own safety.

'Hang on, for goodness' sake.' He grabbed his smoking jacket from the side of the bed and flung it about his shoulders. 'Stop the racket, for the love of St Martha, you'll break the door down,' he shouted as he took the stairs two at a time. Robert pulled the door back as quickly as he could. In the instant that it swung towards him, he knew there had been no tragedy at sea.

# 28

# Todd

He set off early. He would not walk the beach now. He avoided the bathhouse and he did not want to run into Kate. In the beginning, when Claudia told him, he didn't believe her. How naïve; of course Kate had talked to the papers. There was no one else, apart from the blonde, and Todd knew she'd have contacted him first. She'd have tried to milk as much out of him and Claudia and then, inevitably, she'd have blabbed to the press. Todd wasn't sure how he felt about it all. Stunned was probably the best way to describe it. For the first few days, he'd been fuming. Angry with himself for being so stupid, irritated with the whole set-up and mostly annoyed that at the end of it all he had no right to be angry. So, each day he walked until he was tired, filling his head with melodies and words for songs that were taking shape in the early hours so when he fell into bed all he was fit for was sleep.

He moved like a zombie, not thinking, just empty emotions whirling about inside him. He'd fucked up. All his life, he'd been handed all of these opportunities and he'd gambled with them, as though they were worth nothing. Claudia, the band, the success, his family, even Kate. And it was Kate, at the final turn, who'd brought it home to him, how much he'd squandered. They could have been friends. He had believed that between them something was growing, something deeper than they'd ever had before. If there was a frisson of electricity between them, he had ignored it. He thought he was treating her with respect, hah – and she was playing him all along. As usual, Denny was right. His mother would have tutted, *There really is no fool like an old fool.*

\*

He was wakening earlier here than he'd done, probably since he was back in Belfast. His internal alarm clock set to rise with the sun, fall with the darkening sky. The castle had become his sanctuary. He tried not to look towards the bathhouse, and still he couldn't leave the place. Somehow, Ballytokeep had taken a hold of him and, for now at least, it was not letting go.

The year was trading towards the back end of summer, quickly trotting along towards short cold days, long windy nights. Todd was making the most of his time, hitting out into the sunshine before Kate had even pulled back her shutters. He made sandwiches, basic but sustaining, took a bottle of Coke from the cooler, and headed off towards Sleive Carr. The forecast promised a hot day.

It was a two-mile trek across bog before he got to the base of the mountain. It was hardly even a mountain, he decided when he was a quarter of the way up. The view from up here was silencing. Everything about the place made him aware of his own insignificance; it was vast, empty and isolated. In the distance, running up the side of a hill opposite, Todd could see an old graveyard. He wondered if it was still in use. There were worse places to be buried. It was remote, but not nearly as lonesome as the characterless graveyards of cities where graves haggled for space and there was little more than a grey slab to mark your time. Up ahead, a thick rhododendron forest fanned out across the mountain. It seemed to Todd that someone had stretched a florid cloth across acres on end. He probably should walk around it, but he figured that could take hours, when it was, to his eyes at least, a clear run through the thick vegetation. On a hot summer's day, he reasoned, what could be more pleasant than the aromatic shade of a forest of flowers. He set into it with vigour and, for a while, thoughts of Denny, London and the band slipped away from him. Maybe, he even managed to make peace with his feelings for Kate, for a while. It almost felt as though he was deep in the vegetation, but that was silly, he told himself. After all, if he turned back now, he'd be in daylight in a few short minutes. It was a little disappointing, he decided, that instead of the lovely fresh bouquet, beneath the heavy flowers, the air smelled of damp soil. It was a musty, chesty smell that made him feel like he might be sick. He checked his phone for time, there was no signal, but who'd be looking for him anyway? He figured it would take at least three quarters of an hour to get to the far side of the forest.

Two hours later, he was still under the heavy rhododendron cover. His legs, tired now, at least snatched his focus occasionally from the rising panic within him that he might never get out of the dense vegetation. He stumbled over a long knotted root and took it as a hint that perhaps he should sit for a while. Inside his bag, the sandwiches had grown soft and warm against the heat of his back. He opened them and ate, hungrily, if not enthusiastically. The sun was at full blast above his head. It was hard to imagine light of any strength drying through the damp of vegetation. He lay back on the root. Just for a moment, let his mind wander. It would calm him as much as anything and he thought of Kate.

When he woke he knew with certainty that he was lost. He checked his phone, but here there was no signal, no data, no way of contacting help. Not that he was sure he would anyway. After all, the last thing he needed now was for the whole world to know he was a complete dunce. He could see the headlines, 'Rock Star Lost in Flower Patch'. Far above him, in the skies overhead, he heard the rumble of a jumbo jet, perhaps heading across the Atlantic. The echoing sound haunted the empty landscape around him. It reminded him that he was solitary here. His life was lived in chosen isolation, the fences about him built from arrogance and self-absorption. He did not see the dip, not until he felt the ground beneath him dissolve. He was in mid-air; a humping bumping caricature, plunging into darkness he never knew existed. He landed with a thud, a bone-cracking sickening bounce that left him breathless. For a long time he lay, contemplating all that was wrong with his life and maybe what he would do to change it, if he had another chance.

# 29

## Kate

Kate watched as Todd set off across the bogs. In some ways, here in this Celtic ghost-filled, magical place, she was as much in awe of him now as she was when they first met. It had been at a charity fundraiser, something organized by the music set. She could hardly remember how she had ended up there. It was the week she won the biggest settlement ever in a British court. The press had labelled her the hottest divorce lawyer in London. There was music and champagne and life seemed to be stretching out before her full of promise and opportunity. When she bumped into Todd, the electricity between them had caught them both by surprise. Even then, Kate was cautious. It took Todd months to woo her, but when he did, it was at once torrid and sublime. Even now, a decade later, she shivered when she remembered the chemistry that sparked between them. Hard to believe it, she thought as she watched him make his way into the giant purple forest that clung to the mountainside in the distance. She set down the brass spyglass, laid it carefully on the desk before her.

'You should get out of here for a few hours,' Rita said to her. She could feel the nervous energy bounce off Rita today, perhaps she needed the space of being alone to bake and think.

'It's getting quieter, isn't it?' Kate could see it in the till takings.

'Aye, we'll soon have all the time in the world for walking the beach, me and Barry.' Rita sighed.

'It's been a good season, we won't close up shop completely, you know.'

'You don't know what January is like here.' Rita shook her head. 'Although, maybe you do, sure isn't that when you came at first?'

'It was, but I'm thinking we'll run some stuff, open a few days a week and take time to get ourselves ready for next season.'

'That sounds good to me,' Rita said and she threw a mound of pastry onto the marble slab before her. 'Off you go now.'

*

Kate felt like she was mitching off school as she headed towards the hotel. The afternoon sun was blasting its full heat down on Ballytokeep and the smell of hot tar and fresh salty breakers were a heady combination, bringing waves of nostalgia for the childhood Kate had hoped to give her own children someday.

'There's nothing nicer than this, is there?' she said as she sat down at the front of the hotel with Iris. 'Where's Archie?'

They had settled in the shade of the veranda that ran for some way along the west-facing side of the hotel.

'Oh, he's getting ready for Todd. Actually, he's running really late, they should have started already.' Iris checked her watch.

'Started what?'

'Todd offered to help with two loose slates at the back of the hotel. I'm grateful really, because you know what Archie is like when he gets something into his head. He could be up there on a ladder before I know it; no point reminding him he's in his eighties now.' Iris shook her head good-naturedly.

'Is he back then?' Kate tried to keep her voice neutral. She hadn't mentioned that she and Todd hadn't spoken since the press suggested they were an item. He'd been avoiding her. She wasn't sure why; after all, she'd never made any suggestion that she wanted anything from him. If there had been any spark between them, she'd been determined that she would not be falling for Todd Riggs again.

'Back, dear?'

'From his walk? He headed off early this morning, last I saw he was going into the rhododendron forest up Slieve Carr.' She sipped her tea.

'He went this morning?' Iris looked at her, as though checking that she'd heard right. 'Into the fairy forest?'

'Well, yes, I saw him from the bathhouse, I'm sure it was him,' Kate tried not to sound defensive, wasn't that why people bought field glasses – to enjoy the scenery in the distance. Robert Hartley's had provided her with endless hours of entertainment watching the sea birds and whales, playing in the bay on balmy summer evenings. 'I wasn't spying on him,' she said, dropping her voice.

'No, dear. It's not that, you don't understand, most people

when they come here, they don't realize…' She pulled herself forward in her seat. 'The fairy forest, as we call it here, it's not a safe place to walk. Tourists have gotten lost in there for days on end – and Todd Riggs, well, let's face it, he's not exactly an experienced hill walker, is he?'

'No, but…'

'Maybe he came back and there's nothing to worry about.' Iris tried to smile, but her eyes gave away her worry.

'And if he is in there? Still?'

'Colin Lyons will know what to do.' Iris nodded. 'Colin will know.' She nodded towards the table where Kate's phone rested. Kate tried ringing Todd's mobile first, but it rang out as though he was out of coverage. Then she tried Colin. She managed to get through to him on her second attempt.

'Hi Colin, we're in a bit of a tizzy about Todd Riggs.'

'Why?' He always sounded tense these days when she mentioned Todd.

'He hasn't come back from his walk,' she said lightly. 'I saw him head off up Slieve Carr earlier, he went through that big rhododendron forest.' Kate watched Iris's expression as she spoke to Colin; there was no mistaking the worry in her eyes. 'But that was hours ago, he should be back by now.' Todd told her once he had taken to going for longer and longer walks in London, but this was not London. There was no tube station to shoot into if he got tired halfway up a mountain. And, to begin with, mountains were no place for a man recovering from a heart attack.

'Is he off his head? No one goes into that place. You could be weeks in there before you find your way out.' Colin blew out a sigh long and hard. 'We'll have to make sure he's not in the castle first, then…'

'What, what then?' She tried to keep the worry from her

voice, couldn't help but pick up the note of panic in Colin's words. What if Todd died? Funny how that might not have bothered her so much when he had his heart attack, but somehow things were different now.

'We'll have to get a search party organized.' Colin was moving now. She could hear him, banging doors, could imagine him pulling on walking boots. 'You check the tower, I'll see if I can't round up a few of the men locally.'

'I want to help,' she sounded much stronger than she felt.

'No offence, Kate, but you don't know the place either; last thing we want is to have two people missing.'

'I'll stick near you. Please,' she was pleading, not sure what she could actually do, but she knew she didn't want to stay here and wait helplessly for news – that was never her style.

\*

There was no sign of Todd around the castle. He had locked up before he left, but still, Kate could almost feel the emptiness of the place. It only added to the nagging worry that was gnawing at her more viciously with every passing minute. Kate grabbed her coat as she rushed back from the tower. The nights were getting chillier and if they had to stay out all night to find him, there was no point getting pneumonia. She met Colin at the shortcut up towards the farm. They ran along the narrow track, Colin helping her to cross into one of his ditches so they could make their way towards his jeep faster. The Defender roared to life and hurtled across the dried out land, knocking bushes and hillocks as they were bumped about inside.

'Ring the Hartleys; tell them if he contacts them, they need to let us know. The search and rescue people don't like coming out unless they have to.' Colin shook his head. The chopper was already on a call-out to find a missing fishing boat – *tourists*,' Colin said, as though they were an unwanted species. By comparison, to a mission at sea, Todd was taking second place on the priority list. 'I don't know; there are bloody signposts all over the place. Last time this happened, it took two days to find the buggers who got lost here. And, then there's Brogan's Drop.'

'What's Brogan's Drop?' Kate knew he was not talking to her, just muttering to himself, but it sounded ominous, she needed to know.

'Sorry, Kate. It's just that vegetation, it's so wild and thick, about three quarters of the way up, there's a dip in the hill, only you come on it very suddenly, so it's almost like a cliff face, it's not far off twenty foot down.'

'Christ. So if he's in there, how do we get him out?'

'Chances are if you saw him going in, he's still there. He could walk about that place for days and never come to the end of it. The rescue boys have heat sensor equipment, they'll find him easily enough when they arrive, but that could be quite a while.' Colin looked in his rear-view mirror. The sun was orange on the sea beneath them. Over the last few evenings, darkness had been settling a little earlier. 'I reckon we have about two good hours of light.' In the distance, Kate heard the chopping sound of helicopter blades cut through the evening sky. Colin pulled the jeep up to the edge of the forest. Already, some of the other locals were there waiting with flashlights and rescue gear.

'Groups of two?' Colin asked one of the older men.

'Aye, twos, but no more than a couple of yards distance between us.' He looked towards a youngster tying blue rope around one of the larger trees. 'We don't have much time before it's dark, so the faster we get moving, the more chance we have of finding him.'

'That's our central line,' Colin looked at her. 'We keep that in our sights, otherwise, we could end up getting lost too. You stick with me, yeah?' he said, pulling a heavy jacket on. Kate had no intention of moving too far away from him.

As they set into the forest, the sun was turning mellow orange reddening the late evening sky. 'We have a couple of hours before it's actually dark, but in here, it's dark anyway, with night, it'll be pitch.'

They seemed to walk for ages in silence. Occasionally, she would hear one of the men call out, but there was no sign of Todd. Far from the picturesque landscape she'd imagined, the forest was a spongy undergrowth that felt like it might swallow anything up in its hollow belly.

'So, that's it between you and Todd Riggs, eh?' Colin said. He'd been busy the last few weeks, so it felt like there was a cooling off in their friendship – he put it down to fencing and getting his farm set up for the winter months, but now she wondered.

'How do you mean?'

'Oh, come on, Kate, he's still in love with you, you must see that.' Colin did not look at her, instead he stared determinedly ahead, moving slowly and purposefully.

'I certainly don't see that at all. I had hoped we'd be friends, but maybe I was wrong about that.'

'Like you and me?' He looked at her now, the fizzing current that had passed between them in the beginning had softened into what she hoped would be a true and long friendship.

'Yes, like you and I.'

'Hmph. I'm not sure your Todd Riggs has the same idea.'

'He's not *my* Todd Riggs.'

'Well, he's certainly not Claudia Dey's anymore.'

'Colin, not that it's any of your business, but...' She saw something in the distance, an outline, something that moved, only slightly, and then it was gone again. They were moving in what appeared to be a straight line, if it was a badger he would have time to get away. If it was Todd? She hoped it would be Todd. God if anything happened to him, the thought struck her from nowhere. She pushed it quickly from her mind. Looked at Colin, she wasn't sure what she wanted to say, but she knew she sounded a lot crosser than she should. 'It's nobody's business but Todd's.'

'How would you feel if he doesn't come out of this okay?'

'I'm not having this conversation.' But, there was a heavy feeling cutting into her, a foreboding sense of incompleteness.

'Good.' Colin went silent and between them Kate could feel a rising air of something much stronger than discontent, maybe it was the sound of their friendship crumbling.

'What does it matter, anyway?' She looked at him now, caught her breath; he looked so wretched. She was not so sure herself how she felt about Todd. Not now, not standing here on the edge of a mountain, where he could be dead or alive with Colin Lyons beside her.

Then she saw the movement again, like a quiver, but of course, it must be so much more because it was a distance away. She moved forward, began to run, her heart thumping in her chest with fear as much as hope.

'Come back, Kate.' Colin's voice roared behind her. But she kept moving, towards that indistinct shape. She could sense the panic rise as Colin called her back again, but she ran on, not out of sight, not so far she would get lost.

She stopped within a couple of feet of the shape. Somehow,

up close, it looked lifeless now, and she realized that what she'd seen was his rucksack, snagged and hanging, bending branches ever so slightly, so it moved rhythmically on the stale air. She wanted to cry, she had feared the worst when she saw its swinging shape in the darkness.

'Todd. Todd are you here?' she called out, moved forward and felt the forest floor move slightly beneath her feet. Brogan's Drop – she looked down, it was dark and deep. 'Todd, are you down there?' She looked behind, could make out the luminous glow of the men's jackets moving towards her. She listened hard, just for a few seconds, then she heard him. Low and short of breath.

'Kate? Is that you? Kate?'

'I'm here. Todd, I'm right here, there's a whole search party here, looking for you, hold tight.' Her voice sounded strange here in the darkness, a mixture of fear and relief and that uneasy realization that maybe she was worrying about someone who didn't really exist. After all, what was there between them anymore, she had no claim on him and no right to feel so worried that he was safe.

'My leg, Kate. I think...'

'Is it broken?' She bit her lip, thinking how on earth they'd get him out of here if he'd broken his leg.

'I... I don't know.'

'He's over here. Colin!' Kate shouted back at the advancing jackets, the men otherwise invisible apart from the waving flashlights before them. 'It's okay, Todd. You're going to be okay now.' When she turned to Colin she couldn't keep the worry from her voice. 'He may have a broken leg.'

'Christ,' Colin said as he stood on the edge of the drop beside her. 'He really couldn't have picked a better spot.' He was being sarcastic and Kate thought it didn't suit him. 'Your leg, mate, do you think you can walk on it?' he shouted down, but cast his eyes to heaven.

'I... I'm not sure. I'll try.' Todd groaned, and Kate suspected that he was trying to stand.

'We can assume climbing is out of the question, so?' Colin looked at one of the other men. 'He sounds like he can hardly stand on it. Jimmy,' Colin looked at a youngster that Kate had only ever seen in the Weavers, 'have you brought your gear?

'Take it easy, Todd, you'll be out of there in a few minutes.' Kate sounded more confident than she felt.

'We have an experienced climber here, Todd. We should be able to get you out of there quickly. Can you stand on that leg?'

'Yeah, yeah, I'm standing now, I have a feeling it was...' He muttered something. 'I'm fine.'

'Cramps,' one of the older men guffawed and stopped abruptly when Kate threw him a dirty look.

'I'm fine, if I knew where I was going, I could probably climb out of here.' Todd's voice was echoic, as though he was looking upwards and about him.

'Okay, mate. We're throwing down a rope.' Jimmy moved to the edge of the drop. 'I've secured it here, so it's quite safe, but once you start to climb, we'll put a bit of tension on it our end. Kate here will be our eyes and ears, so she's going to be the one you're talking to. All right?' He threw down a thick rope, spangled with small flashing red lights spaced out along its length. 'If you think you're not up for the climb don't even try it. We can think of something else.' He turned to Kate, and said, quietly, 'Mightn't be as dignified, but we'd bring him up in the commode chair.' He pointed over to where the men had carried a fold-out chair.

'No, I'm good to climb. I have the rope and I'm tying it round my waist.' Todd's voice sounded stronger now.

'It's not a long climb, more like a really steep hill walk and only a short one at that,' Colin said as he grabbed the rope to help the men apply a little pulling power to it. 'From down there, to him though, it probably seems like climbing Kilimanjaro.'

'You okay, Todd?' she shouted down towards the bottom of the drop. Then she saw the tension on the rope and knew he had started to climb before she heard him fall back down again. 'It's okay, take your time.' She winced every time she heard his body thump against the hard rocks and wet roots, his occasional groan giving affirmation that he was in pain and that made her wince all the more.

His climb up seemed to take forever, but at least it was straightforward. The men pulled him over the last mound when he reached the top, tired, dishevelled, his clothes ripped. Kate hardly noticed. She was too relieved; he was okay and suddenly she realized just how important that was to her.

Spontaneously, Kate threw her arms around him and, for a flash, it felt normal, as though she should be in his arms because they were... what? She realized too late and pulled herself awkwardly back.

'I...' he started to say and she saw her own confusion mirrored in his eyes. 'It's... thank you,' he said in a blanket of silence, where Kate could hear nothing beyond the two of them. Then he moved a little away from her, embarrassed at their sudden intimacy and perhaps at finding himself in need of rescue at all, particularly by Colin and Kate. 'Thanks to all of you, I think the drinks are going to be on me for a very long time. I'm glad to be out of that,' he looked beyond the slope he had just climbed up with their help.

'You can thank Kate there that you're out of here tonight,' one of the older men said. 'She was the one who raised the alarm and she was the one who saw your rucksack.'

'So, this time it's thank you,' he said quietly to her and she could see in his eyes that there were a million things that could be said, but the time for saying them was over. He shook her hand instead. It sealed the awkward silence between them.

The walk back to the edge of the forest seemed much shorter than the walk in. Perhaps it was the fact that Kate was no longer afraid that they were too late. She walked between Todd and Colin and the silence was heavy, but she was still flooded with relief.

Colin left them off at the castle and waited until Todd went inside.

'So, where to now?' Kate needed a strong drink and to sit for an hour making small talk to create some sense of what had just occurred.

'Well, I'm going home.' Colin started up the engine. 'You need to ring the hotel, let the Hartleys know he's all right and decide if you want to sit at his bedside for the foreseeable.'

'I really don't see why you're so angry, Colin,' Kate muttered as she rang Iris to tell her that they'd found Todd.

'No, I don't suppose you do, Kate.' He jumped into the jeep and thundered back towards his cottage, leaving her standing alone in the evening darkness.

*

The divorce petition was probably the fastest ever moved through the Irish legal system.

'I can't believe he's agreeing to everything,' Rita said when

Kate explained some of the jargon to her. She was thrilled that it had arrived. She could keep the house and sign whatever needed to be signed to extricate her from Duncan's dodgy business deals. She did not know where he was staying. One too many nasty phone calls after she threw him out of the house and she took the phone off the hook after she warned him that if he came near the house she'd set Barry on him. Every time she came across a forgotten sock or a memento from their lives together she happily consigned them to the rubbish or recycling heap.

'Well, not everything, but yes, he's being more generous than I expected and he's agreed to say that you've been separated for three years; if he didn't do that you were stuck with him for the foreseeable.'

'He's afraid of you,' Rita said as she looked down through the document that had arrived with the post before she left for the bathhouse. 'He thinks you're going to clean him out in fees if he doesn't get it over with quickly,' she smiled.

'And the house isn't too quiet without him?' Kate thought Rita looked happier than she had ever since the first time they met. Although that did not mean she wasn't lonely, or grieving for the death of her marriage.

'Lonely? For Duncan? You must be joking. Barry and I are happy as pigs in muck. I can cook, eat, clean what I like, and when I like. If I wake in the middle of the night, I can turn on the light and read until morning if I fancy it and eat biscuits in bed, too, what's to miss?'

'Sure, you're not *protesting too much*, it's a long time to share a home with someone not to miss them?' Kate had seen enough marriages break up to know that there was always some grieving afterwards.

'You know what they say; I'd miss an earache if it suddenly

disappeared after years too. I'm sure, you probably think I'm a cold fish, but I've done my crying for almost a decade. Seeing him leaving, for that last time, taking his horrible car out the driveway, it was like a weight being lifted, as though I could breathe properly for the first time in years.' She signed the pages with a flourish and blew out a sigh of relief. 'We should probably have champagne?'

'Not yet, I believe in waiting until all the ink is dry and the last "T" is crossed.' Kate folded the documents into three. They could go in the return post, once she read over them one more time. 'Anyway, I thought you preferred tea?'

'Oh, I'm a new woman now,' Rita laughed, 'when Duncan is paying, it's champagne all the way. Wait until I get that cheque over to the dogs' home, then we'll be hitting the strawberry cheesecake with gusto.'

# 30

## Robert, 1957

'Busy spot you have here, son,' Ernest Hartley said as he walked towards the stove and held his hands out before the soft dying heat. 'I could have sworn I saw Iris making her way along this path earlier?'

'You're out late, father?' Robert said calmly, he knew that with the way his father spoke these days, the goings-on from tonight would fade from his memory very fast. 'Shall I make some tea for us?'

'No, that won't be necessary.' Ernest Hartley took down the bottle of brandy from the shelf beside the stove where Robert had left it earlier. He poured a measure silently, the only noise an angry thump when he heavily left the bottle back on the shelf. Ernest Hartley was not to be trifled with when he was like this. Robert had noticed it for a few months now, perhaps even a year. There were times when his father seemed like a different man, as though someone had rewired him so his patience narrowed. His temper rose quickly over things that wouldn't have bothered him before. 'Robert, you have let us down. Your mother expects more from you than this.'

'And you, father, what do you expect?' Robert watched as one tear made its way silently from his father's faded eyes.

'I know what you're like, Robert. Always have,' he shook his head sadly. 'I suppose, I wanted more for Archie, he deserves better than leftovers.' He held out a letter and placed it on the table between them. Robert went to take it up, but his father put his hand across it. 'Archie loves that girl, Robert, you knew that. Archie loves her, and God knows, we didn't think he'd ever meet anyone with a bit of pluck to them and there you go, he's met the girl of his dreams and you managed to whip her out from under his nose.' He nodded towards the envelope and Robert noticed it had a French stamp and was postmarked Paris.

'From her sister?' Robert asked.

'No, I should think that's the last person she'd want to hear from. I'm in two minds what to do about this,' he rubbed his temple with those long tapered hands, as though he might rub away some of the worry that creased his forehead. 'Look, all I will say is, that letter tells you more about the girl than even you have managed to learn and let me tell you, she's made of hard stuff. Maybe even tougher than she realizes herself. Perhaps we should just get rid of this tonight and let that be an end to the whole business.' Ernest swallowed the contents of his glass and Robert thought sometimes he trembled on the edge of complete madness, and then other times he surprised him with his astonishing logic. He looked about the bathhouse. 'You're happy here, aren't you? Happy with how we've set you up?'

'I am very grateful for the bathhouse, Father, you know that, and I'm making a good go of it too.' Robert knew that the place would be his officially in a matter of months. His parents agreed that on his next birthday he would become the legal owner. It had always been a mere formality, but tonight, the glint that lit his father's eye made it seem suddenly less of a certainty.

'Well then,' his father said, taking down the bottle once more, 'I think we can agree that if you want to continue here, you know what's the right thing to do by your brother.'

'I promise, Father, I won't see Iris again.' There was no point lying to his father, they both knew, he was the only one who had always been able to see right through Robert's lies.

'Not just that.' The brandy rattled a violent gasp from his father's chest and he put the glass down with a final messy thud. 'Robert, you'll marry Gemma. You'll announce it tomorrow.' He held up his hand to still any protests from Robert. 'You'll announce your engagement to Gemma tomorrow and that will be the end of this sordid nonsense. Now, get me a cup of tea to settle my stomach after that brandy.'

As Robert went back towards the kitchen, he saw his father lift the letter from the table. He would give anything to read it. What secret did Iris have that made her stronger than any of them realized? It was a secret in Paris, he was sure of that. He placed the kettle on the gas stove, he would make a pot of tea for both of them, perhaps by the time it was drank, his father would have forgotten all about what had just happened. But Robert was shaken by it. The most important thing to him was the bathhouse; he had worked very hard to establish the business. He did not intend to lose it over a couple of nights of illicit passion. As for marrying Gemma – well, his father could forget about that too.

'Would you like something to eat father?' It was the

middle of the night, but his father did not eat regular meals anymore. It seemed to Robert; sometimes he did not eat at all. He had become almost gaunt over the summer weeks. He looked out into the tearooms, but there was no sign of his father.

The bathhouse door swung open as he approached it, the glimmering light cast a weak yellow shadow across the rock but could not last the distance to the sea. He called out to his father. Perhaps he had set off for the hotel again. He was in funny humour these days, unpredictable, more than just losing his memory. It was as though sometimes Robert could see a darker character emerge from beneath the familiar generous man he'd known all his life. He reached in his pocket for his lighter, tapped out a cigarette from the box. He set it alight and watched as the blue smoke wafted before him into the black night. He thought about that letter and its delicious mysteries taunted his dancing thoughts. Such a shame his father remembered to take it with him, he would give anything to know its secrets.

# Iris, Present

The clock told her it was almost four in the morning, but the moon outside was luminous and the sea reflected an even brighter light into her bedroom. Iris waited for a minute or two for Archie to come back to bed. She lay thinking about the morning breakfasts and the porridge that sat in the large bowl her mother-in-law once used for Christmas cakes. The quantities were smaller now than years ago, still she added Baileys, cream and nutmeg and would not tell a soul for love or money what gave it flavour. All these little secrets – she always thought they would die with her. Now they were Kate's – she was passing them on and it contented her as though in the passing there would be something left of her to endure when she was gone.

At ten past four, there was still no sign of Archie. She raised herself in the warm bed, placed a hand where Archie slept; it was too cold. A foreboding understanding rippled through her. She gathered up the clothes she had worn during the day, dressed as quickly as she could. She had a feeling he would

not be in the hotel now. It was a full six decades today since
that terrible night and Archie had been on edge all week.
His grasp on the present was slipping quickly, like a sheet
of gossamer gripped by a force both obscure and abysmal.
They could not win this battle. She turned on extra lights as
she checked each of the landings throughout the hotel. If she
feared the worst, she would not let her mind go any further
than perhaps the sheds at the back of the hotel, where he
pottered about each day, mending, fixing, and gathering turf
for fires that burned bright in the grates.

Perhaps he would be in the kitchen. Years ago, if he could
not sleep he would sit at the kitchen table. She arrived down
to prepare breakfast once and he was still sitting there, a
thimble of brandy in a glass, poured out hours earlier and
never touched. This time, the kitchen was warm from the
heat of the day, but Archie was not there, sitting alone with
his jumbled thoughts. She would have to go down to the
bathhouse, she knew with crushing certainty that was where
he'd gone. She moved slower now than she had all those
years ago; slower, but with far greater urgency.

In the darkness, with the waves on her left and the night
sky star-filled above her, she could be back there now. She
could remember so clearly making her way down here that
night; the flickering light in the window and the shadow of
Robert watching her as she made her way along the track.
The curling ribbon of cigarette smoke, catching occasionally
in the moonlight, and now, if she closed her eyes, she could
almost smell it on the waves. She picked her way carefully
along the neat track. Everything took so much longer
these days. She had to rest twice to catch her breath;
determination and fear made her carry on. She leaned
heavily on the thick wall that kept the sea at bay. She could

feel her heart fluttering at odd beats in her chest, but Archie was more important now. She called his name, hoped he would hear it on the wind. The last thing she wanted was for anyone to know he was missing. After all, she could bring him home; she could take care of him, couldn't she? They could live out their lives together in the hotel, surely that was not too much to ask.

'Archie, are you there? Can you hear me?'

When she had walked back, that final night, she wondered if someone was watching her. It came to her with ferocious clarity later, the enormity of that possibility. She had been a young silly girl, not even twenty years of age. She knew that now, more clearly than she had known it ever in her life. She had so much to lose back then, so much more than she ever realized. She shivered when she thought how things might have turned out, still counted her blessings even if they were mixed with guilt now for how she'd treated Archie long ago.

'Archie?' She could hear the desperation in her own voice. She was almost at the bathhouse now. She had only been here once since Kate took it over. They had cut the ribbon together, her, Kate, and Archie, but it was all too much for her. She could not face it. There was too much nostalgia icing over the poignancy of the place. Robert was still here. She could feel him, but his presence was darker now than she had ever realized. How could she not have seen that before? How could she not have known it all those years while she had Archie in her bed?

Archie. She called him again. If the doctors knew they were down here at four o'clock in the morning, they would both be carted off; she had no doubt about that.

'Iris, is that you?'

'Kate, I'm so sorry. I've woken you too? I'm looking for

Archie; he wasn't at the hotel, so I thought I'd try here.' There was no point in fibbing; perhaps he was sitting, at this very moment, drinking hot chocolate in the tearooms.

'I heard a commotion earlier, thought it was youngsters on the beach.' Kate switched on the powerful lights that she had dotted about the bathhouse. 'That's what woke me, to be honest, and I haven't slept since.' She pulled closer a heavy cardigan that looked like something Robert had worn years ago. 'Come inside, I'll put on proper shoes and help you look.' She pointed down to her bare feet. The night was warm, the rock beneath them holding onto some of the heat of the day. The ocean breeze was only keeping it temperate for the morning.

'There's no need for shoes,' Iris said as she gripped Kate's arm. 'He won't be far.' In an instant, Iris knew exactly where Archie was, he was looking for Robert, of course he was, sixty years too late.

*

They found him at the foot of the bathhouse, far beneath the bedroom window that looked out towards the western horizon.

'Archie,' Iris barely whispered his name when she saw his crumpled body lying on the rock. Yards from his white hair, waves fought their way back and forth, in a symphony that for now, thank god, was pulling the tide away from him. 'Archie, can you hear me?' She realized he had not spoken.

'Hang on, I'll get a pillow, some blankets. I had better call the...' Kate raced inside for her phone.

Iris bent her body as close as she could to him. Archie's breathing was ragged, there were no words and, for an awful minute, Iris thought they were going to lose him, right there on the rock.

'Iris,' it was a croaky whisper on the waves. 'Is that you, my love?'

'Archie, I'm here. I'm right here with you.' She reached her hand down, stroked his cold forehead, there was a filmy sweat just settled there, as though he'd been running and he'd just sat down to rest. But he was still here, he was still breathing and Iris knew that was all she could hold onto for now.

'Iris, I have to tell you.' His breath was jagged; she wanted to tell him to be still. 'I have to tell you that I'm sorry, I'm so sorry.'

'It's not your fault, and when we get some help, we'll get you out of here and we'll be back at the hotel and...'

'No. No. Not about this.' He shook his head and in the moonlight she caught desperation in his eyes. 'No, Iris. I'm sorry about Robert.'

'Oh, Archie. It was all such a long time ago now. We just have to get you back to the hotel and everything will be fine.'

'I know he loved you, Iris.'

'I...' Iris did not know what to say. Perhaps it was best to say nothing. 'Shush, now Archie, everything is going to be fine.'

'No, Iris. No. It is not going to be fine. Don't you see, it can't be fine?' He shot a glance at Kate.

'The ambulance is on the way, Archie; they're convinced you've been on the beer...' Kate tried to joke, but her voice fell flat when she saw his expression; she fell to her knees at his side and glanced at Iris.

'You should know this too,' he said and then he looked away, his head angled oddly against his long bony frame. He looked as though he might have slipped. Iris had a feeling he was probably backing away from the window high above them. She shuddered when she realized how close he'd come to falling into the sea. 'It's about Robert, my brother. He died here, this night, exactly sixty years ago, did you know that?'

'Yes, I've been reading his papers,' Kate said. 'I knew he died on this night. He died here?' She was only confirming with them.

'This is where they found him, but...' Archie looked at Iris. 'He wasn't who you thought he was.' Archie began to cry.

'I married the best man for me, Archie, I have always known that much,' Iris conceded, perhaps she had wondered about other things over the years, but she knew she had married the best of the brothers.

'No. I'm not sure you'll think that when I've told you what really happened.'

'Archie,' Iris leaned in closer to him, 'it was all so long ago, and it doesn't matter anymore.' And it didn't, because if this was all she had left with Archie she wanted it to be happy for him, not lost in memories.

'Oh, Iris, of course it matters. It matters now more than ever. Can't you see, there isn't time to pretend anymore and it affects Kate too?'

'I never thought more of him than you.' Iris felt the air fall from her lungs, as though pierced by something much fiercer than an arrow. Maybe she had spent her marriage thinking of someone else, but mostly it was Mark. Certainly, he still filled so much of her heart.

'No. No. You never meant me to know that, but how could I not. It was my fault, you see. I kept that letter.'

'The letter?' Iris shook her head. The letter Archie had

spent recent months looking for and she was never sure that one had even existed.

'Father brought it from the bathhouse, that night, the night Robert died. I heard you coming in, your footsteps so soft on the stairs, so delicate in picking out each step, as though your foot were whispering to each board. So different to the day, when you would race from room to room and march about the kitchen content and confident in arranging everything for everyone. I'd heard that step before, a few weeks earlier, and when I called you the next day, I knew that something was not right.' He smiled then, a sad twisting of his narrowed lips. 'Father handed it to me, of course he did.' He looked at her now, saw she did not understand. 'It was everything my happiness was built upon and I was afraid if you read it, I would lose you.'

'Oh, Archie, don't say these things. You don't know what you're saying.' Iris leant her head down and into his chest, felt his shaking strong hand caress her head. 'Oh, Archie, everything will be fine.' With that, she saw the glimmer of blue lights high above them.

Kate rushed to the end of the rock to guide the paramedics to them.

'Iris, I have to tell you before it's too late.' Archie's voice was soft and frail, 'I loved you so much, everything I did was for you.' He raised his hand, groaned as he did so and there, crumpled, was faded paper undelivered for so long.

Iris recognized immediately Marianne's faded script.

# 31

## Todd

A t least he could be grateful that the press had not been alerted to his foolishness. He was relieved to be safely tucked up in the castle. There were hours when he had given up all hope of rescue. He must have lost consciousness or more likely fallen asleep for a while. His leg was fine, just dead from the damp ground and cramps from lying awkwardly. They found him long after he had tumbled down into what felt like the belly of the mountain. He was no mountain climber, not like Colin Lyons. He was a joke, he could hardly look Kate in the eye. Oh, how she could laugh at him now. She could add this to his list of foolish antics. And still, he knew, he couldn't leave this place. Even with Kate Hunt on his doorstep, probably hating his guts. He couldn't leave Ballytokeep, because here, something was keeping him calm. Something – he wasn't sure what – was nurturing his empty spirit and he needed to be here if he wasn't going to end up back in another cardiac hospital bed.

Colin Lyons. The name reverberated about his brain. He

was the one Kate loved now. Todd stole a decade from her, probably her best decade. Claudia convinced him that Kate leaked those photographs to the press. And why wouldn't she? She had plenty to be sore about. After all, did he really think that a smart woman like Kate would just forgive and forget? She was used to winning. She enjoyed it, thrived on it; she did it for a living, one case after the other. He had been naïve to think that she would not want to make him pay. Even if she had been the one to lead his rescue, somehow it felt to Todd now that it only added to the debt he owed her. No, she had moved on and that's what he would have to do too. That was the thing about being famous; you learned that everyone wanted something from you. Even Denny.

Sure, they were friends, but Denny wanted him back on that stage. The band, and by extension Denny, would make far more if they toured than if they sat at home and waited for the album to sell. 'Doesn't work like that anymore, mate,' Denny told him. 'It's all about stadiums now, all about the numbers, packing them in and then giving them a night to remember.' Yeah, Todd thought as he drifted off into a sleepy haze, everybody wants something.

He blamed the sun and heat of the day for the dreams when he woke halfway through the night. He never took sleeping tablets; didn't need them if he drank enough whiskey. They made his mind foggy, bleary and sometimes, when it got like that, well, it brought out his Belfast prickliness. He dreamed of Kate, not as she had been back then. Not, as he imagined she would have looked on their wedding day. He dreamed of her bending over her flowerpots, tending them with the kind of love other women bestow on husbands and children. When he woke he cried, because somehow, he knew, he had done her out of all that. Worse, maybe he had missed something better too. Of course, he knew, it was too late for all that now, so he lay there, in his too warm bed, and let the tears flow silently down his cheeks.

When he woke, he knew what he had to do. He rang Denny immediately.

'Made my day, mate,' Denny was delighted. 'Made me bloody day!'

# 32

## Robert, 1957

Robert Hartley heard Archie before he even touched the front door of the bathhouse. Robert was sitting on the flat roof, considering his options. His father was becoming so absent-minded now that the events of this evening could be forgotten by the morning. All the same, it bothered him that his brother should be marrying Iris, for all his coolness with her earlier, he knew that they were not finished, maybe they would never be quite finished. The letter, whatever it contained, intrigued him. He had no doubt that it held a secret far greater than the one Iris shared with him and it made him want to know even more, maybe even possess her just one more time.

Archie's mannerly rap on the door was almost a relief. If he expected anything of his brother at this hour, it would be that their silly fool of a father had taken a fall on his way back to the hotel.

'Come in. I'm on the roof,' Robert called down to Archie. He heard the heavy thud and rattle of the iron staircase as it shook with the weighty step of his brother. He was moving faster, heavier than usual.

'You bastard,' Archie said, his voice was thick with tears and emotion and Robert knew if there were more light than just the watery moon his brother's face would be blotched and tear-soaked. 'How could you?'

'Listen here, Archie mate…'

'Don't bloody mate me. You know how I felt about Iris, we were engaged.'

'You're still engaged, I think.' Robert knew that his smooth manner wouldn't wash with Archie. Not this time, but old habits were hard to ignore. He could not become someone he wasn't just to calm his brother.

Archie shook his head, stifled what he could of a sob. 'How long?'

'How long what?'

'How long have you been sleeping with her?'

'Who said I was sleeping with her?' Robert tried to sound affronted, but he knew every word that he uttered now could haunt him for the rest of his days. Perhaps, if they both stuck to their guns, cried innocent, he could still come out of this without his mother pulling his inheritance from beneath him. 'It's a mistake, Archie. There is nothing in it. I am marrying Gemma, we decided weeks ago. She didn't want to announce it at the same time as you and Iris. You know Gemma…' He tried to sound offhand, swigged the dregs of the brandy bottle. The early hours were no time for fancy glasses, Robert's mood had been dark coming up here, now with Archie, it was as black as it could get.

'I don't believe you, Robert. You must think I paddled over here on a banana skin if you think I'd take your word on anything.'

'Believe what you want, but ask Gemma, why don't you?'

'You've always been a selfish prig, Robert, but I really never knew you could stoop so low. I had a feeling something was going on for weeks now. But tonight just before we announce our engagement? What kind of brother does that?' Archie was turning away, but there was something in his voice. It was something Robert couldn't put words on if he tried, but it was there in the air between them. Robert knew that if he didn't sort out Archie now, he would spend the rest of his days with his brother looking down his nose at him.

'You think you're so much better than me, don't you?' Robert hardly heard the words escape his own mouth. They came from some deep part of him. They had a resonance and honesty that did not require volume. 'You always have. Mother's favourite. Well, do you really want to know the truth of it, Archie?'

'Robert, you wouldn't know what truth was if it hit you between the eyes.' Archie turned towards the stairs; he was not a fighter. Anger had propelled him to this point. Now he would go home, lick his wounds and consider what was best for everyone.

'I know a whore when I see one and if you marry Iris, that's exactly what you'll have. A whore.'

'You...' Archie stopped, stood tapping his foot slowly, deliberately. He stood for what seemed like eternity with his back to Robert. When he turned, his movement was sharp and violent. 'I hate you, Robert; I hate you now more than ever before.' He lunged at him, but Robert managed to swipe to the side, holding the brandy bottle aloft. He thought of the bottle falling and the effort of having to go down to the tearooms to get the dustpan and brush. It was all too much work, so he swung about, saved the bottle, but somehow, he ended up far closer to the castellated wall than he expected. In the movement, he lost his balance, it was an odd feeling for one normally so graceful. His body bent a little too far, his step a little too frantic and before he knew it, he was falling, falling into the darkness.

When he hit the rock below he shouted back up towards Archie. 'Not so perfect after all Archie, well, now we know, don't we?' He heard Archie scamper down the stairs. He did not come back around the bathhouse; instead, he made his way towards the hotel. *Good bloody riddance*, Robert thought. Suddenly he felt giddy and light-headed all at once, as though the turbulence of the evening and the brandy and stress of the long day caught up with him in chorus. He was falling into a deep sleep, maybe that was all he needed, he thought, to fall asleep and everything would look so much better in the morning. The combination of brandy and fresh air, it could knock him out faster than any anaesthetic. He forgot the tide was coming in quickly and the promised swell would be lapping up against his body within thirty minutes. Robert died just half an hour later, drunk, oblivious, alone and bequeathing a lifetime of guilt and remorse on more people than he had any right to.

# 33

## Kate

'He's got a point,' Rita said. She bent down to rinse out the oven she had spent the last half hour scouring. 'I mean, there you are, entertaining him every night of the week, drinking his wine and looking out to sea. Next thing, he sees you splashed across the newspapers, all in all with Todd Riggs.'

'There's nothing in it,' Kate threw her hands up in the air. It was exhausting, explaining herself again. She knew she sounded surer than she felt.

'Well, if there is nothing in it, are you sure that he knows that?'

'Who?' Kate was cleaning one of the huge flycatchers that were living up to their name after the long summer weeks.

'Exactly, if you need to ask, then...' Rita made a huffing sound that Kate knew demonstrated her own righteousness more than any discomfort as she polished the glass oven door.

'I am not...' Kate nearly lost her balance. Rita could be truly infuriating.

'Look, I'm not judging you, Kate. Honestly, I would say you're a mile better off without any man, but that is just in my experience. I think we both know that you are going to have to get your head straight. Men like Colin don't wait around forever and men like Todd...'

'Men like Todd?'

'Well, you know better than anyone that Todd isn't going to wait around either.' Rita liked Todd, but it did not mean she couldn't see right through him.

*

It was true, that evening, when Colin did not visit, the bathhouse seemed too empty to stay in it. Kate walked along the beach alone. She really did not think she'd be much company for anyone now anyway. So she walked for miles along the beach, returning as the light no longer picked out the familiar shapes that normally overhung her home. The tower was in darkness, and Kate wondered what it would be like if it wasn't there. She realized, that this place, Ballytokeep, would not be the same without it, just as her life would not be the same without Todd.

Were they meant for each other? MFEO, as the youngsters carved in impermanent letters in the sand. She sighed and made her way onto the rock, sitting in one of the heavy chairs that soon would be stored inside. It was pointless trying to figure out how she felt. After all, she really didn't know how Todd felt now. He had not come near the bathhouse since the article had appeared in the papers, she hadn't seen him since the night on Slieve Carr. Who knew how he felt after that experience, it had certainly thrown Kate. For all she knew, he may have raced back to London, first chance he got and proposed to Claudia. It was possible; after all, technically, they were still together. It dawned on her then, that unless she read it in the papers now, she actually did not know if they were together anymore.

*He has not come back to you.* It was a stark realization and, in that cold wind, she felt hot tears roll down her face. And tonight, as she looked up at the tower, she had a feeling he wasn't there anymore. Kate cried as hard as she had cried all those years ago and she realized, that perhaps yes, she had started to fall in love with him all over again.

\*

The next day dawned cold but bright and Kate woke from her troubled sleep with a resolve that she would not let Todd Riggs take another minute of her future. Whatever happened, she had a good life here and she was going to make the very best of it. She marched down to the tearooms just as Rita was putting her key in the front door.

'Sleepyhead,' Rita said but there was a lilt to her voice and a twinkle in her eye.

'Rough night, but not for you, by the looks of you,' she said and switched on the kettle for breakfast.

'I met the postman on my way, didn't I?' She held up a letter, opened and slightly crumpled from the top of her bag. 'The dog pound.' She fluttered it in the air and then took out the letter, handing it to Kate. 'They've said that they're going to use the money for a new dogs' home. They're so thankful to Duncan!' She could not keep the laughter from her voice.

'Did you tell them that the hundred thousand was from him?'

'Well, in the end, I took your advice. I donated fifty

thousand and the rest I am keeping as a nest egg. But, yes, I told them it was a gift from Duncan and he'd very much like a plaque put up to say he'd given it.' She threw her head back and laughed, 'And I get to choose where the plaque goes. Priceless, isn't it? I'm giving them a lamp post, and putting his name on top.'

'You're not,' Kate said, but looking at Rita's face, she really could not be sure. Rita was a changed woman, these days she was moving to the beat of a drum only she chose the rhythm to. Duncan Delaney should watch out. Rita was no longer his downtrodden wife with a love of cake and a face lined with worry.

'Watch this space, isn't that what they say?' Rita smiled and, indeed, Kate had a feeling that this was just the beginning for her friend.

*

When Colin did not call, Kate knew there was nothing else for it. She tramped across his fields at a time when most civilized people were taking the train to work. His cottage was tidy about it but grim. It lacked any decoration beyond what was necessary. The path to the front door was laid with stone, but it was functional. At the windows, heavy curtains snarled shut, no ornaments stood on the windowsills, no roses about the door, no creeper ivy along the trellis. It lacked a woman's touch. The thought came to her unbidden, but once it settled in her mind she could not shake it.

'Colin,' she called as she rattled the old knocker on his door, 'are you there?'

'Are you trying to wake the dead?' He opened the front door to her, still bleary-eyed with sleep.

'You haven't been down to the bathhouse and I was worried, I...'

'No.' He walked back into the tiny porch and she followed him quickly, didn't wait for an invitation. 'I was up all night with a sick ewe.' His voice was gruff and she noticed his eyes looked red and tired.

'Oh. I just thought...'

'The world doesn't just revolve around you, you know,' he said and he flicked on the kettle, took down two mugs. 'I fancied catching up on some sleep so... Anyway, you don't need me now. You're going to be closing up soon for the winter.'

'I suppose, it's just I enjoy your...' His expression made her cut off her sentence. 'Look, are you angry with me? Have I done something wrong?'

'Why would I be cross with you,' he mimicked her English accent just a little.

'Well, you haven't come near the bathhouse since...' When she thought about it, it was longer than since they had to rescue Todd. It was perhaps since the newspaper article had appeared with pictures of Todd and her walking on the beach. 'I thought maybe I had done something or said something to offend you.' She watched as he sat at the table. He raked his hands through his hair, making it stand even more on end than before.

'No, I haven't been to visit lately, have I?' He shook his head, but somehow he seemed different.

'Have I done something wrong?' Kate was sure she hadn't. They had talked about their friendship once, laid it all out. Perhaps, there was a lingering attraction between them, but they had both agreed, it was not enough to risk what could be a good friendship.

'I think I told you, I'm not great husband material.' He smiled at her, trying to overcome his embarrassment.

'I think you did, and I was fine with that, I still am.'

'I get jealous, you see. It's why, well, it's why I'm on my own.' He shook his head. 'I'm better off like this,' he spread his arms out. 'I have flings, but not relationships. Can't handle them. Not at all.' He shook his head, more emphatically than before.

'But we're not... I mean, that's not what we have, Colin. We're friends, right?'

'Yeah, I suppose we are, but these last few months, I've become very fond of you...'

'I can cope with fond.' She dropped to the seat opposite him, reached out to take his hand in hers and gasped when he pulled his hand away roughly.

'No. It's more than that.' He sighed. 'I've fallen for you, Kate. Hook, line and proverbial sinker and I just don't want to be in a relationship with anyone, not even you.' He held her eyes now and she knew he was speaking the truth.

'I don't understand.'

'The last night, out at Slieve Carr? I could feel it then, that awful black feeling that I had before. It's like it swallowed me whole the last time round and...' He thought for a moment. 'I can't help it, you know.'

'But you can see it; surely that in itself is something?'

'Maybe. It frightened me when I realized that maybe you still had feelings for Todd Riggs. I saw you both, walking on the beach. I thought that maybe if the papers knew, well... Maybe he would go back to London and that would be the end of it. But he didn't, did he? He came back.'

'Did you tell the papers he was here?'

'I...' Colin shook his head, too embarrassed to meet Kate's

eyes. 'I'm ashamed to say it, but I did.' He sighed, long and hard and Kate realized that this place, this house suited him. Its remoteness and emptiness, in some ways, they mirrored that part of him he would always keep separate from her and from the rest of the village. 'I'm sorry. But it's better if you go.'

'Can we still be friends?'

'It would be better for now if we're just neighbours.'

'I'm sorry, Colin,' Kate said as she made her way out the door and she was. She wasn't sure she understood, but she was certainly sorry.

# 34

## The Letter, 1957

Archie put Robert from his mind. Running from the roof, he hated him. Roberts' words rang out in his ears as he arrived out on the rock. He did not want to see him again, so he raced towards the track to avoid Robert coming from the back of the bathhouse. His brother was still jeering at him as he made his way back. Archie ran back to the hotel, frantic with grief, with rage and with an emptiness that spelled the end of his dream that he would live happily ever after, running the hotel with Iris and living here in Ballytokeep until they both became very old. He could not marry her now. Not knowing what he knew. If they left this place, went far away from Robert, then maybe. No, he knew, he couldn't leave Ballytokeep. Could he live with Robert's gloating face at every turn? Could he endure what had happened between them? Never fully trusting either of them again? His father was waiting at the hotel for him.

'You've had it out with Robert?' he said to him and Archie could smell brandy on his father's breath.

'You knew?'

'Of course I knew, I'm not completely senile yet.' His voice was gruff. He handed him a folded page. 'It's a letter, to Iris. It is up to you now, what happens to it. I think you'd be better off finding a nice girl in the village, but love's a funny thing and I'm no expert.' His father, old and weakened, stood by his side, an ally in this daunting place where everything rested upon the decision he made next.

'I love her father,' he felt the words escape his lips in a gasp that was filled with tears as much as anger or grief. 'I love her and, to be honest, even if she married Robert tomorrow I'd still love her and only want to be breathing the same air as her. I've loved her from the moment I laid eyes on her.'

'Then, she's yours to take; your brother will not cause you any more trouble.' Ernest outlined the threat he had earlier spelled out for Robert. The bathhouse would not be Robert's if he did not marry Gemma and stay true to her. 'I'm telling you this, because I know my mind is fading fast and I want to commit it to a good memory before it's too late. Maybe we can't make it legal, but you know now how much it means to Robert.'

'And the letter?' Archie held it in his hands, feared what it might contain, surely nothing as bad as what had happened with Robert.

'That's for you to decide. But I'll say this to you, if she reads that letter, I'd say she'll be on the next train out of Ballytokeep, that's a chance you'll have to take. It'd be a brave man that would hand it to her, but I'll not judge you either way.' He placed a firm hand on Archie's shoulder. 'You know, we may never speak of this again?' He shook his head. They both knew that by the time the breakfast was in the dining room, Ernest Hartley would have forgotten all about it. It would be Archie's secret to live with or to share.

'Maybe, it's for the best, father, eh. Maybe it's for the best.' Archie put the letter into his jacket pocket. He could not think about anything else now. He knew too much already. Whatever the letter contained, it wasn't going to change how much he loved her.

# Iris, Present

Iris's hands trembled. Even in the moonlight, she had recognized the faded script, the carefully rounded letters on Hermès notepaper. It was her sister's favourite, but the words were Marianne's'. She had kept the letter close, still afraid to open it while Archie lay on the cold rock. She couldn't think about it now, nothing was more important than Archie. All the same she was aware as she worried for Archie that it sat in her pocket. Occasionally, she reached her hand in, rubbed its smooth surface between her worn thumb and fingers. This letter had survived sixty years. Iris did not know if Archie had kept it from her, or if he'd found it in the last few months. Part of her assumed it turned up in the bathhouse, but Kate was adamant, she had never come across it when she was clearing through Robert Hartley's things.

This was, of course, more important than Robert. Iris knew that instinctively. The letter had come from Paris. It had come from Paris, addressed to her and the few letters from that time, Iris kept locked in her memory, not daring to keep them. When Mark was still alive, they made her feel like she could still be a part of him, she knew them off by heart. Then suddenly they stopped. The telegram that tore her world down had also signalled the end of the little notes from Marianne. This letter, unread, in her hand was different, written, no doubt when the rest of the house was fast asleep. It was written quietly, covertly, lovingly. Marianne loved Mark too. Iris knew it. They all knew it. Mark was the firstborn, only by a few weeks, but it was long enough to secure the lion's share of love from everyone in that apartment and then he was gone.

'Are you going to read it?' Kate asked. She was sitting opposite her; there was nothing they could do for Archie now. They had finally left him sleeping soundly in the hospital. The nurses insisted he needed his rest and so did Iris. She wasn't sure what she was meant to do now she was back at the hotel, but Kate poured them each a measure of brandy and Iris sat for a long time willing Archie better. The doctors told them time would heel his fractured leg and changing his medication once more might halt the march of his memories so they didn't devour him whole. For now, he was staying in the hospital – but soon she would be able to take him home again. The tides had not been so kind to Robert when he fell on the rocks by the bath house sixty years earlier.

'I'm sixty years late getting it.' What did another day or two matter? Iris dropped back in her chair to gather the best of the light from a small reading lamp behind her. She squinted a little, in spite of her glasses; the writing was old and faded. She felt a familiar swell of emotion within her, thinking of Mark still brought her back there. When she closed her eyes, she could still remember what it was like to hold him in her arms and nestle him close beneath her chin. 'Would you read it for me?' She passed the letter to Kate.

Kate moved across and sat next to Iris. It was almost breakfast time now and Archie should be bustling about the kitchen, the hotel was so empty without him. 'Okay,' she cleared her throat. 'It is dated July 1957, there's no day, but there might have been, except where it was been folded is a little damaged.' Kate spoke clearly, as though she was reading the six o'clock news. This was an out-of-date bulletin, but no less the precious for it. She did not want to mix anything up.

*Paris.*
*July 1957,*

*Ma chérie, Iris.*

*I count you my dearest friend still and that is why I write to you tonight. In so doing, I am putting my work with Sir Clive at risk, but I feel that my friendship to you requires one final act of loyalty. Perhaps I am creating trouble for you, I do not mind it so much for myself, but I could not live with myself unless I told you the truth of things here.*

*The child we buried was not Mark. The child we buried in a small wooden coffin was the child that Pamela gave birth to. Crispin was a feeble child from the start, an unhappy and unsettled child. I had my fears for him from the day he came into the apartment. His colour was unnaturally white and he cried more than he slept or ate or smiled. In the end, he died in the middle of some kind of fit.*

*I do not know what they told you around the circumstances of his death, but I know that when I visited the grave today and saw Mark's name on the cross above the child, I had to tell you the truth. Your child is still alive and I am taking care of him for you. Perhaps it is easier, to think that he has left this world and maybe it was Sir Clive's intention to give you a happy release, but Iris, I know how much you love the child and so this gift is yours. He will grow into a strong and handsome man and I will watch over him while you cannot.*

*Mon amie, I fear your sadness more than my upsetting you with this news. I am here to tell you all you ever wish to know about your son, you need only ask, but I understand it may all be too painful. Lady Pamela tells me your life is moving on, so I will not write again, unless it is your wish.*

*My love always and best wishes in your happy future in Ballytokeep,*

*Marianne, xx*

Kate's voice began to wobble, she looked down at Iris, knew already from the way her body trembled beside her that grief or shock had overtaken her. Iris would have found it hard to identify which emotion was running over her, but tears streamed from her and they were tears of joy.

Kate sighed, a deep and understanding well of oxygen. Kate shook her head. Of course Iris never saw the letter, so Marianne had no way of knowing that she very much wanted to hear all about Mark.

'Oh, Kate.' It took Iris a long time to regain her composure while she pieced together her and Archie's lives and what this letter meant to both of them.

'Have you thought what this means now, Iris?' Kate asked her when her tears had subsided just a little. 'Have you realized what it means for us?'

'It means you are my granddaughter?' Iris began to cry again. She had missed out on a lifetime with her son. The son she thought had died sixty years ago had lived until his mid-thirties. He had a child. 'It means you are my granddaughter and I have probably been more loved in my life than even I realized.' Iris knew that Archie loved her, but if she had found this letter decades ago, she wasn't sure she'd have been so forgiving. It was funny how a lifetime of love and almost losing Archie put everything into an altered perspective. He had loved her, in spite of what he knew of herself and Robert, in spite of the fact that she had been as they called it back then a 'fallen woman'. He had loved her so much, he hid the truth from everyone in case he might lose her or she might be hurt even more. In the end, she had told him the truth, she had married the right man all those years ago.

# Iris, 1957

Iris packed her bags. Her ring, shining and safe, sat in its box on the bedside table. It was simple. She would walk out of the hotel, walk to Riley's corner, take the first bus back to Dublin and forget about this place. She would settle into the guesthouse again with her mother and make the best of life as she could. Perhaps, in time, she would find some peace of mind. She placed her jacket across her shoulders, smoothed down her hair before she took those stairs for the final time.

It was just after eight o'clock. Archie had not even called her this morning, perhaps he knew already. She would take the pain out of it for him; she would just go. There had been no official announcement, if she left now they were just losing a cook. There was no scandal or shame in losing a cook. A fiancé was quite a different thing.

'Where are you off to at this hour of the morning, Missy Iris?' Ernest Hartley startled her. Honestly, she was never sure where he would spring from next or which direction he was headed.

'I'm leaving, Mr Hartley.' Iris said the words simply. She was not sure he'd ever liked her that much anyway, not like Mrs Hartley, not like Archie.

'Well, it's a fine day you've picked to leave us. Have you not heard our awful news?'

'No.' Ernest Hartley looked as though he had just walked out of an electric shock chamber. Who knew what went on in the poor man's mind. 'No, Mr Hartley, has something happened.'

'Oh aye. Down at the bathhouse, they're not rightly sure about what happened, but the finish up is our Robert is dead and that's all there is about it.' He had the look of a man emptied of emotion. Iris knew that his grasp on reality was not as strong as it might be.

'Robert? There must be some mistake, he was...' Words deserted her and she wasn't sure how long she stood under the watchful gaze of Ernest Hartley. She couldn't trust her own words not to say too much. It felt as though the blood was travelling fast from her head to her feet and she might fall over. Shock. It was shock, she realized.

'Aye, I know very well exactly what he was and where he was and where you was too, Missy Iris. The fact remains, he's down there on the Giant's Plate and we're only lucky he hasn't been pulled out in the morning tide.'

'Oh, my god,' she heard the words skip from her lips, sounds uttered; they meant nothing. She had to gather herself. 'I'm so sorry, Mr Hartley.' Iris dropped her bags, rooted to the hallway. She was not sure whether to go back or forwards. She watched, silently, as Mr Hartley picked up her bag and carried it back into her room.

'Aye, I know you're sorry. But if you truly want to support us now, you'll stand by my Archie and give him your support, if that's what he says he wants.'

'I...' There was so much to say, but Iris wasn't sure where to start.

'I know you think I'm for the birds, Iris, but let me tell you this, Archie adores you. It may be that it's misplaced. For my money, he'd be better off with a plain and simple girl from down the village, but it's you he wants. He will not care that Robert had his fun with you before. He'll live with all of that, if you will.'

Ernest turned away from her and began to sing some song he had learned many years before.

With each step of the stairs, Iris gave up a prayer; her thoughts were a collision of thanks and sorrow, guilt and shame and, of course, hope. Perhaps, she could make up for what she had done. Perhaps it could work out for her and Archie.

# 35

## Kate

Iris and Archie had made up their minds about the hotel, weeks ago apparently, if the paperwork was anything to go by. 'It's yours, if you'll have it,' Iris said and her eyes danced with anticipation and excitement. 'It's time we took it easy.' She looked devotedly at Archie now. The last few days had only made them stronger.

'We're going to settle into a couple of the ground floor rooms. If you don't want the place, it'll just fall in around us.' He smiled at her. The doctor said his leg was healing surprisingly well and so far it looked like the change in his medication had halted the progress of his Alzheimer's. 'It's the rest too and knowing that I don't have to worry so much.' It was true, handing over that letter seemed to have taken a weight off his shoulders – maybe off Iris's too. She could talk about Mark now and they could celebrate having a granddaughter.

'Are you sure about this, both of you?' Kate was flabbergasted. 'I mean the hotel, it's been your whole lives...' She couldn't believe it. They were handing her their life's work to do with as she wished. They had already written their wills and she was their only beneficiary. 'I don't know what to say, I really don't.' It wasn't about the money – this went much deeper than that. This was about belonging, it was about family and it was mostly about coming home. If they knew the truth, she could probably buy a couple of hotels right along the coast.

'We want you to have it. We wanted you to have it before I knew you were Mark's daughter.' Iris's eyes were filled with emotion, but it wasn't sadness at letting things go, rather it was joy at having someone to share with. 'And, now, well there's even more reason to see you there.' It had taken a few weeks, but finally everything seemed to be slipping into place. They'd talked for hours, all three of them about the lifetimes that had hinged on gossamer threads so fine they'd been obscured before by keeping secrets that should have been told long ago. Somehow it all made sense now. Crispin or rather, Mark, was just like his father. He was like Willie Keynes and perhaps that was why Pamela and Clive had severed their ties. God knows, Willie had already brought enough misery on the Mornington Hunts over the years. It was why they kept their distance from Kate and of course, from Iris. As luck would have it, Kate was nothing like her father and nothing like her grandfather. Kate, it turned out was a Burns, apart from those eyes, really, Iris thought, she should have known when she'd looked into those striking eyes that were handed down directly from Willie Keynes.

'I really am so...' Kate threw her arms around Archie's neck, she was just glad he was getting better; anything more was a bonus.

'Oh, Kate, you've done a wonderful job on the bathhouse,

the hotel is going to be a piece of cake for you and I know you'll enjoy pulling it all together and running it properly,' Iris said. Kate knew that seeing the place fade with the passing years had saddened Iris, maybe she'd be doing them a bigger favour than any of them realized by getting stuck in there.

'Just say thank you and let that be that,' Archie said and he smiled at Iris, he didn't want her thanks, he just wanted everyone to be happy.

*

Kate determined that she would keep the bathhouse open until the end of September. Although tourists were rare, it gave her a chance to cater to the locals. On her last day, she held a coffee morning for the local dog pound. She hoped Todd would show up and the disappointment when he didn't surprised her a lot more than she expected.

'Ah, well, it looks like you might have to walk up there yourself,' Rita said as they tidied up after everyone had left. 'You've never actually called to see the place, have you?' That was true.

'No, but...'

'Let there be no buts about it. He's going to be heading off on that world tour one of these days and then you'll have all the time in the world to be minding your pride. You can't expect him to do all the running; after all, he spent the whole summer hanging around your front door just to walk the beach with you.'

'You're bloody impossible, Rita Delaney, do you know that?'

'Not for much longer, I'm not.'

'Oh, excuse me, Rita soon to be ex-Delaney and now Kenny!' They both laughed at this. 'So, what are you going to call yourself when the suppliers are looking for payment? Or when the good food guides are putting up the plaques outside?'

'How do you mean?' Rita looked up from the table she was clearing.

'Well, when you take over this place next summer?'

'You mean I can run this place?' Rita's smile beamed broader than Kate had ever seen it before. She had told her about the hotel and her plans to revamp the place for next year's trade. She was going to put Hartley's back on the map. Make it into the most beautiful boutique hotel in the country.

'Well, who else is going to do it?' Kate laughed. It was the right decision. Rita needed something of her own, something more than just Barry to dote on, and she'd make a great job of keeping the bathhouse on the straight and narrow. 'Actually, Oisín Armstrong said he'd help out, bringing up the seaweed for the baths or doing any of the little jobs you need to do that are...'

'Stop it, Kate.' Rita blushed. She did that every time Oisín Armstrong's name was mentioned these days. Well, she was a free agent and so was he – widowed for almost a decade, he'd make a lovely partner and he had a soft spot for Rita. 'Anyway, I'm too old for all that malarkey.'

'Oh, Rita, we both know you're never too old for love.' Kate looked up towards Rock Castle, these last few weeks, not seeing Todd around; it seemed to her that it had become sterner in its domination of the skyline. She sighed. 'Everyone deserves a second chance, don't they?'

*

As soon as the day was behind her, she grabbed the package that she'd carefully wrapped weeks before. It wasn't much, it wasn't big, but it meant something to her and she hoped it would mean as much to Todd.

She walked slowly towards the tower, her steps as intrepid as her mood. She knocked loudly on the heavy door, wondered if he would hear her high up in the spirals above. Then she felt, more than heard, his paces jogging down the stone steps, taking them two at a time. He opened the door with the curiosity of one who does not often have visitors.

'Oh,' he said by way of welcome. He looked well, relaxed. She'd read in the papers that the band were going to finish the tour. Of course, Rita could tell her that the doctor had given him the thumbs up – but that was the blessing of living in Ballytokeep. It was hard to keep secrets in a small town.

'Hi.' She wasn't sure what else to say. She thought of that night, when he'd been battered and bruised by his fall in the rhododendron forest and she'd thrown her arms around him. The image brought with it a flood of emotion and not just embarrassment. Since then, she had thought about how it felt to be in his arms and she knew that what she felt was more than just relief that he was safe. That connection was still there between them, and it set off her nerve endings every bit as much as it had done all those years ago.

'Well, you'd better come in, I suppose.' He led her up towards the next floor. The stairs were scrubbed flagstones, the walls clean stone, naked except in places where he had retained a handrail or ship's lanterns cast ambient light upon his many gold and platinum discs. He spotted her looking at them, 'I can thank Meg for them, she kept them all and got them hung as soon as my back was turned.' He couldn't be angry with Meg for interfering with his interior décor, he was far too fond of her.

'I just thought...' But so many thoughts had swirled around her mind these last few weeks, she stopped there. 'I like what you've done with the place,' she smiled. It was where he lived, she realized; this room was where he spent all his time.

He showed her into his kitchen. Against one curved wall a giant fridge stood robust and glossy red. His kitchen stretched in a free-standing semicircle taking up half the floor space, it was huge – four times bigger than her commercial kitchen, although she knew it got a very small portion of the use. Red gloss cabinets, metro tiles at the rear and pristine white marble so any speck or crumb could be brushed away instantly completed a retro rock star look. A captain's table ran halfway across the room, and Kate wondered if Todd would ever have the required eighteen guests to fill each seat. An acoustic guitar leant lazily against one of the chairs, before it a scatter of pages, pencils and a neglected cup of tea. It looked like he was writing songs here and perhaps that explained why she hadn't seen him walking the beach recently. Against the other wall was a day bed and music system. It played a low jamming base guitar that seemed to hum in resonance with the heavy wood and unnerved Kate as it made her heart crash harder in her chest to its endless thrumming. Dominating the room, a long narrow window looked down upon the bathhouse.

'Yeah, I know, it's pretty... obvious?' he said and smiled. 'But its home.'

'Even now?' When he arrived she'd have wagered he'd be in Monte Carlo or Ibiza by September – maybe leopards can change their spots

'Most especially, now.' He moved closer to her, held his

hand out for her jacket. 'I'm glad you've come,' he said, making a bit of a deal of taking her coat and hanging it across the back of a heavy carver. When he turned to her, he held her gaze for what seemed like an eternity but was probably seconds. 'I don't blame you for the photographs.' His words were soft and some part of Kate felt herself react to them.

'I didn't... that wasn't me.' She blushed, but she knew she was the most obvious person to suspect. For all he knew, she might have been just waiting to take her revenge upon him, and had it been a couple of years ago, well, he might be right.

'Sure now?' His voice was playful. He did not mind even if she had. Perhaps life had brought them to the same place in terms of more than just Ballytokeep.

'I'm sure. I know who did, but I only found out a week ago. I'm sorry, if they caused you any upset, they weren't about you.' She tried to find the right words. 'Well, maybe they were, but they were about me too.' She knew she was not making any sense. She had spent time thinking about things. Maybe someday Colin could be her friend again and he did not need people to know what she knew. 'Anyway,' she said, handing Todd the gift she brought him, 'this is for moving in, if you're staying that is. I never actually gave you a moving-in present, so...'

She waited for him to open the wrapping paper, watched his face as his eyes crinkled up in surprise. She chose it specially, the frame that held Robert Hartley's image for so long, but it was time to let him go. Instead, she replaced it with a picture of the tower, with the bathhouse obscured in the foreground, knew that it was the right thing to do now. She had seen him, most nights, sitting there, looking down at the bathhouse, watching over her.

'I have so much I want to say,' he said and he moved closer to her, but this time, it felt good.

'"Thanks" will do just fine.'

'No, I mean, about before, about everything.'

'Todd, I have a feeling there's plenty of time to say all you need to.' She smiled at him. 'Friends?' she said.

'For now,' he pulled her close, so she could feel the heat of him against her. For a moment, his lips lingered over hers; she caught her breath and felt him do the same. Life was good again, Kate knew. Life was good again.

# Epilogue

Todd moved quickly once the band touched down in London. Heathrow was jammed with weary people making their way home and, for once, Todd was one of them. Unlike many of the jaded people he saw, he felt elated, as though he was starting something new. Across the city, he had a plane chartered to take him back to Ballytokeep – he couldn't wait to get home.

'You sure you're not interested in staying for a while, mate?' Denny asked, only because he always said it when they got back from a tour.

'No, will you tell Meg, I'll miss her sausage and mash.'

'Back to Ireland?' Denny said with the resignation of one who knows he has lost. 'Kate would be welcome to come over too, you know, Meg always had a soft spot for her. She always thought you were a bit of a klutz for dumping her.'

'I know that, Denny.' Meg had said it often enough over the years. 'Looks like she was right all along.' They both laughed at that – they knew she usually was, even if Denny didn't like to admit it all the time. 'Listen, mate, just because the tour is done, well, it doesn't mean that we're finished.' They'd always be friends, but Todd was in a different place now. He'd started to write songs – he hadn't done that properly in years. His own songs, and already they were creating a buzz. Without the whiskey, his mind was clearer and his conscience weighed lighter, or maybe it was just love, but he was filled with inspiration. Maybe that was what he'd do in Ballytokeep – if Kate didn't put him to work in the hotel!

'Seriously, you saw the lads, they're as sick of it all as you are. Tell the truth, if you had to do one more night you'd probably hate it.' Denny was smiling now.

'It's been a great run though, hasn't it? I mean, we've gotten twenty five years out of it.'

'Yeah, it's been a good run all right.' Denny shook his head. 'I'm kinda glad we're done if you want to know the truth.' He smiled now, defeated, or perhaps caught out. 'These last few years, I've been pushing you because I thought it was the right thing, not because I was enjoying it. I hated leaving Meg at home, staying in hotels, and all that foreign food was killing me.'

'That's funny.' Todd smiled.

'What?'

'I knew you hated it, I suppose; I didn't think you knew it though.' Todd knew it from day one. Denny had organized them all, held their hands, but he hated touring. 'We're all getting to the stage where we've had enough of touring.'

'Yeah, well, whatever about that, I'm glad to be taking things down a bit.'

'Retirement?' Todd thought the word suited Denny.

'Maybe, mind, I don't think I'll be growing marrows any time soon.'

'No.' Todd shook his head. In his breast pocket, he could feel the ring he'd bought in Amsterdam. He'd picked it out alone, a simple band with a sprinkling of diamonds around a centre stone. The shape, when he saw it first, reminded him of a bird over the ocean, but in his hand, it seemed dainty and feminine. He hoped that Kate would like it. 'Maybe soon you and Meg will come over, just for a weekend?'

'Maybe.' Denny didn't sound too enthusiastic, like everyone else, he just wanted to get home and have a decent cup of tea and relax.

*

Knock Airport was as busy as he'd ever seen it when he landed later that day in Ireland. Kate was waiting for him and when he saw her something inside him flipped, as though he'd come home in a way he'd never understood possible before.

'Hi stranger,' she said, but he just held her close, he never wanted to let her go again. When he kissed her, it was as though the world around them melted away and everything at once seemed right and settled in his life.

The little car that had once been Iris's bounced along the country roads while Todd and Kate chatted happily. There was no catching up, not as there might have been in the past. Somehow, over the course of the tour, they'd become like Denny and Meg. Todd spoke to Kate several times each day. She kept him up to date on Archie's progress back to health and her plans for the hotel. He heard all about the work at the bathhouse, the tides and the news from the village, although he hardly knew anyone there.

The castle was cosy when they got back to it later that evening; Kate had moved in while the plumbers were sorting out the baths and replacing the old radiators at the bathhouse. Todd hoped to persuade her to stay in Rock Castle with him. These last few weeks, he started to think it would be a magical place to have a family. Outside, the winds howled loud and insistent, rain sheeted against the long narrow windows and he held Kate close so they both knew they'd never be lonely again.

Later, he lay awake, listening to Kate's light breath beside him. In the distance, he heard the sound of church bells in the village, ringing in a new day. Tomorrow, they would have dinner together, with Iris, Archie and Rita and he would ask Kate to be his wife.

This time, he intended to turn up; after all, not everyone gets a second chance at happy ever after.

# Author's Note

The village of Ballytokeep does not exist, however, just a
few miles from my home is the lovely town of Enniscrone
in Co. Sligo. It is a small summer town that fills with tourists
when the sun shines. Many years ago, it had two bathhouses
catering to visitors who wished to experience the health
benefits of seaweed. Still today one operates, Kilcullens, where
you can avail yourself of baths and various other treatments
and finish up with afternoon tea.

The Cliff Baths, a small white castellated building is no
longer in use, and although it is still white, it is greatly
enhanced by my imagination. It was built on an outcrop of
rock in 1850 by the Orme family. There are, to my mind at
least, few things to surpass walking along Enniscrone beach
on a dry and crisp winter's day, the sun glinting on the water
and the bathhouse in the distance, and who knows, maybe
someone will resurrect it too, one day!

http://www.enniscrone.ie/cliff_baths

# Acknowledgements

Once more, it has been an absolute joy to work with Caroline, Sarah, Nia, Yasemin, Heike, Jade and Blake – the Aria Ladies – you make everything so easy. Truly, a dream team, thank you.

Thank you to Judith Murdoch, my wise agent who I still can't quite believe is at my side – I am indeed very lucky.

Thank you to the only person I would trust with a first draft – Bernadine Cafferkey, no matter how much I'm doubting she manages to be gentle and critical all at once.

Thank you to Christine Cafferkey – for so much more than I could ever write here.

Thanks also to Seán, Roisín, Tomás and Cristín – you just have to be yourselves to make everything perfect!

I've dedicated this book to my personal PR team, almost pro-golfer and avid plane watcher – James Hogan, I couldn't have done it without you.

Finally, I would like to thank you – the reader who picked this book and chose to spend some time with the people in it. I've spent almost a year with them, Kate and Iris, Archie and Todd – wandering about in my imagination. If you enjoy them as much as I did, I'd love to hear about it.

Till then,

Faith x